D1378808

3 3501 00006 2933

A SUMMER AGO

George Scarbrough

State Library of Ohio

SEO Library Center
40780 SR 821 * Caldwell, OH 43724

St. Luke's Press·Memphis

Library of Congress Cataloging-In-Publication Data

Scarbrough, George, 1915
    A Summer Ago

    Summary: One summer in a boy's life stands as a landmark on his
passage into adulthood.
    1. Title.
    PS3537.C18S78   1986   813'.54 [Fic]   86-6758
    ISBN   0-918518-46-6

Book and jacket design by Susan Watters

Excerpts from "North" from POEMS 1965-1975. Copyright © 1966, 1969,
1972, 1980 by Seamus Heaney. Reprinted by permission of Farrar, Straus
and Giroux, Inc.

ISBN   0-918518-46-6

Copyright © 1986 George Scarbrough. All rights reserved. No part of this
book may be used or reproduced in any manner whatsoever without written permission except in the case of brief quotations embodied in critical
articles and reviews. For information address: St. Luke's Press, Suite 401
Mid Memphis Tower, 1407 Union Avenue, Memphis, TN 38104.

ST. LUKE'S PRESS
Memphis, Tennessee

86-36597

56-36597

Keep the eye clear
as the bleb of the icicle,
trust the feel of what nubbed treasure
your hands have known.

Seamus Heaney
from "North"

This Book Is Dedicated

To the memory of my father, William Oscar
Scarbrough (who because of a deep-seated
distrust of all learning would not have
understood it at all)

My mother, Louise Anabel McDowell Scarbrough
(Who would have understood and loved it because
of a reverence for learning, and who could,
with a little encouragement, have written it,
or one like it, herself)

My oldest brother, Robert Lee Scarbrough
(who appears in its pages but who would have
scoffed at it all the more for that reason)

and for

My youngest brother, Joseph Kenneth Scarbrough
(who appears also in the book and who, though
he may not always have understood the brother
who wrote it, has nonetheless been supportive,
himself an artist of another kind, in his own right)

and for

All the other Scarbrough siblings, Edith Emmeline,
Charles Spencer, William Athol, and Blaine Pleasant
(who have found me, I think, more of a confusion
than a clarification)

in short

For the whole family, whether they appear here
or not, I have written this book.

Prologue

SCHOOL was out, and the long green summer days fastened themselves on the hills of Walden Valley and browsed, slowly and gently as cows graze, throughout the low swales between the hills. Days impartially and equally wide in point of time and sun. Or so it seemed to the boy. And the broad, earth-lapping dye of the season fled in leaping, jade-colored flame straight up to the sky and took possession of the heart of the sky, so that it also looked green.

It was on one of these days in early June that the boy and his brother went for the boy's first time to see the twin rails of the railroad track shimmering in the sun of Dead Man's Cove. Away and away down the cove beside Muddy Bottom Creek, emptying from the valley, the rails ran, seeming to become one before they hid themselves behind a shoulder of the mountain. Afterwards, when they climbed the ridge, the brothers could see the tracks, like silver ribbons in the haze, falling in gentle swoops to the flatwoods beyond.

Standing beside the track, waiting for the train to appear, the boy felt a knowledge of what he had never seen running in his blood. His mouth was stone-dry, and he could hear his tongue rasping across his hot lips. Wonder, like some swift-blooming flower, opened in his flesh. Something from out there was coming in. The smell of tar and creosote bedded in his nostrils, and he felt his heart to see whether it beat the way it seemed.

To the north of him, at the turning of Muddy Bottom Creek, the train whistled, the wild metal notes falling like a shower of stones over him. The stunted trees on the hills, the rich timber of the valleys, even the ferns laced in the strong green grass of the cove, shook with the sound. The spring-fed valley was receiving the train.

The boy gripped the station platform with desperate, white-knuckled hands, as the train gained on the downgrade. He was sick with fright, wanting for some terrible reason to run forward shouting and fling himself under the swift-pistoning wheels of the train, to beat upon the great black engine with his hands. The huge walk and stride of the train compelled him. Perhaps he could turn it over with one strong, upsurging heave of his shoulders.

Shuddering, he turned his eyes against the gray planks of the shack that served as station, sick with a fear that he might obey his impulse, white and weak with a fear that beat its dusty wings over his trembling body and told him not to be afraid.

His brother said, with a pleased grin watching the last car round the mouth of the cove, "She sure makes the noise, don't she?" The yellow caboose glinted in the sun, and he added to impress his brother, "That last one is the toilet."

The boy tried to smile and felt the tightness of his lips trembling across his teeth.

That night he woke screaming from his sleep, cowering down in his bed, hiding under the quilts. No one had any notion why he kept repeating, "The train! The train! The train!"

1

THE new bull calf was the only animal on the farm that Alan owned, all by himself and with that comforting sense of being unchallenged in his possession. The animal had been his since its birth and his mother had said that she was tired of fooling with bulls.

"They aren't worth the raising," she said. "Only the milk-givers are worth the time and trouble to pull them through. You may have the bull calf if you will teach him to take his milk from a bucket, and later on to eat, when he grows large enough to be fed with the other cattle in the long shed beside the barn." She added, studying ways to interest Alan in accepting the responsibility of caring for the calf, "You can sell him before school time and pay for your schoolbooks this fall."

Had there been no other reasons, having all his books for one time in his life would have been sufficient for Alan; besides, he wanted a pet, something alive that he could call his own. The calf filled his desire exactly. The thought of his books, however, kept also fresh in his head. No longer would he have to study with someone else, or go without. He had grown exasperated at having to ask anybody in sight for the loan of a book in order to get his lesson.

So he became the owner of the new calf, which he called Buckeye because of its rich redddish-black color. He watered and fed the young bull and led him about the farm until the calf seemed to Alan to be the finest calf in the whole country. One day, when Buckeye was about two months old, Alan noticed that shiny nubs of horns had begun to grow in the tufts of stiff hair above the calf's ears and eyes. The surprising appearance of the soft, rubbery knots he discovered one morning under his hand while rubbing Buckeye's head.

"Dad," he said, "I do believe Buckeye's getting horns."

"Chickens have feathers, don't they?" Alan's father, Oscar McDowell,

9

said, without turning from shelling corn into a dishpan. It was milling day. "Get along with your work, boy, and stop wasting time with that calf. You've got to take this corn to the mill. Finish feeding the cows and saddle up Old Ranger."

Alan gave Buckeye a final pat on the nose and moved away to the long manger that ran the length of the feeding shed. He pulled down hay from the loft and stuffed it between the cross pieces for the cows. Then he came back into the barnyard and stood with his hand on Buckeye's head, feeling the spongy lumps that already seemed to have grown larger under the short red hair. He tried to imagine how Buckeye would look with horns. He would be a very handsome calf, so handsome, in fact, that even Oscar, who showed a certain hostility towards Buckeye, would take an interest in the calf's appearance and boast to the neighbors about the fine animal he had growing on his farm. Alan's dream decked his calf out in the fine, heavy splendor of full growth, forgetting for the moment the small space of summer ownership, and the sale of Buckeye in the fall. Oscar had said that he would not winter Buckeye for what he was worth. For the time, however, Alan's pride and happiness in Buckeye were complete.

He gave the calf's cold, wet nose a stroke with his finger and went into the entry of the barn.

There, he saddled Old Ranger, an aged gray horse with eyes like oily pools with trees growing in them, dark and almost hidden below the surface. Alan liked to place his eyes as close as possible to one of Old Ranger's and stare down into the depths of the horse's strange gaze as he might have tried to see the bottom of an unclear puddle, in whose depths a webby fern might be drowning. Old Ranger always blinked just when the boy seemed about to dredge up the shape of the submerged plant, and turned his head away. Human eyes made him nervous . . . Alan knew this, but the horse's great eyes were a mystery to him, and he liked to probe the depth of the beloved old animal's vision.

As he threw the saddle across Old Ranger's back, he heard his father tell Lee to load the corn. Straightening the blanket under the saddle, Alan tightened the girth, and Old Ranger was ready for the trip to the mill. Leading the horse to the front of the barn, he mounted. Lee heaved at the sack on the ground, shouldered it, and with one quick, upsurging motion of his body flung the heavy sack across Alan's lap, dividing the grain equally in the middle so it would not become unbalanced and fall off into the roadway. Alan was always afraid of losing the corn before he reached the mill. Accidents of any sort, whether to himself or to others, always made his father angry.

"Things happen, Oscar," Alan's mother was always saying. "They just do. They happen to everybody."

"Yes, I know, Belle," Oscar would answer. "I know they happen to everybody. But they seem to happen to me first."

Beyond the gate, Alan turned and waved to Buckeye, who was standing with his head thrust through the planks of the board fence. The calf wanted, as always, to follow. "Be back soon," Alan called. "Behave yourself."

Buckeye heard and bawled and tried to squeeze his shoulders through, managing by turning to his side to step one leg between the boards, so that he hung in the fence, struggling and bawling.

Oscar, who had been listening, came to the rescue. "Talks to this critter like he was human," he said aloud. Then to Buckeye, "Dad-blamed nuisance. The sooner you're big enough to beef, the better off we'll all be." He lifted Buckeye backward out of the fence.

The calf stood by the gate, following Alan with his eyes until the boy and the horse were lost in the distance down the roadway.

2

ALAN liked the cavernous old barn in which the wheels turned underfloor and above-stairs the fine, warm meal itself showered down the wooden trough into the bin, from which Mr. Wyatt, the miller, scooped it into the white cotton bag the corn had come in. Alan's mother always sent the bag to the mill freshly washed, and between them, he and Old Ranger, not to mention the miller himself, who treated the precious sack with a fine carelessness, always managed to return it to her smudged and greased-spotted, a sad commentary on its former immaculate self.

"Couldn't you be just a mite more careful?" Belle always asked, seeing the dirty sack entering the house on Alan's shoulder. Her sense of cleanliness was outraged. "I do believe you wipe your feet on that sack." Sometimes, she scolded him soundly, inquiring whether he knew it was bread he carried in such a mess on his shoulder.

For the life of him Alan couldn't see how the bread was hurt. To clear himself of her charge, he would explain, "Mom, I hold the sack on my lap. The saddle's dirty. And so's Old Ranger. He always wallows in the biggest dust pile he can find. You've seen him. He just loves dirt."

"And I don't," she would say. "Next time see if you can't be a little more careful where you put your feet."

While Mr. Wyatt attended the grinding, Alan wandered about in the cool, dusky light of the big building, seeing, high up, the small-paned, cobwebby windows through which the daylight came softened, almost drained of the sun blazing outside. Brown beams, ancient and shaped by the wielder of some long since dulled axe, were strung above him, showing the strength of mortice and tenon and here and there the square heads of the iron nails used to hold the building together. There was the smell of cornshucks and cobs everywhere he went in the dim interior, as well as the faint ammoniac odor of urine. He recognized rats, seeing their gnawed holes everywhere in the planking of the floor and the lower walls. A few of the larger holes had been boarded up with tin bucket lids; others, smaller, had pieces of tough corncobs stuck into them, like so many corked, flat-topped jugs, stoppered and containing the furtive, whiskered lives of the animals trapped behind the panels.

Outside, its marshy brink resounding with a chorus of spring peepers that seemed to Alan like a long whistled note, was the millpond itself, with its dam and flume line for the water that flowed under the mill to the great horizontal wheels that furnished the mill its power. A few worn millstones lay about the yard, grooved and broken. A rusty hayrake with its curved, uneven teeth rested beside a fence. The place seemed like a graveyard. Suddenly, Alan wondered whether Mr. Wyatt really kept coffins in the attic of the mill. He had heard it whispered that the loft was filled with coffins; old ones, of course, but still coffins, held over from a day when the miller had also been the community undertaker. If he remembered, he would ask Mr. Wyatt before he started home. In the meantime, he had the great waterwheel to claim his attention.

His search for the small, nearly invisible frogs whose thin chant he had heard brought him below the waterwheel. Green with moss, dripping with a steady trickle of water, the wheel had not been used for years. No one of his acquaintance seemed to remember when it had been in use, and before the flood came, no one was even sure that it would turn any more. Alan remembered the great blowing dawn that followed the cloudburst in the mountain, and how, after years of silence, the wheel began to turn. The children heard it from their beds, above the sound of the wind in the trees, and below the smaller sound of wind in the keyholes, and rose to see. No one told them "The mill!" There was no need to. They ran from all points in the neighborhood, some in their nightshirts still, as though a promise to them were being fulfilled. Voices could not have stopped them. Even the voices of the children's parents, the round tones that shaped them a round world, could not have brought the children back to breakfast or to bed. They fled engaging gyves into the millyard, where the emerald great wheel rolled drunkenly under the immense encouragement of the flume, which yesterday had carried only a summer trickle from an upland meadow of flowers—a trickle suddenly transformed at morning into deluge, thunder, and power. It had been such a morning, with such a great going in the treetops as well!

When Alan, running with Lee, reached the mill, the sound that split the morning light had, in its shivering grind and beat and flap and roar, something that charmed him like wooden wings attached to flying houses.

Alan climbed up the slippery framework that supported the wheel and rested for a moment in the cool, water-smelling shade of the great circle. He noticed that the blades were covered with colonies of periwinkles, shaped

13

like the horns of unicorns he had seen in a book Miss Woodson, his fifth grade teacher, had lent him at school. Last year he had become interested in mythology, especially Greek, and his teacher had become interested in him. Lee teased him about his relationship with Miss Woodson. But Alan cared little for his brother's teasing. Like all the other larger boys, Lee, he supposed, had to have something to torment the smaller boys about. That was the way the game was played.

He was trying to turn the wheel with his hands when Mr. Wyatt called to him that the meal was ready. Clambering down, Alan returned inside to the dim, sweetly-odored interior of the mill, where the white sack, minus Mr. Wyatt's generous toll, lay folded slightly upon itself, warm and damp to the touch as though some of the water and some of the fire as well were contained in it. The sack and its contents felt almost alive. Alan buried his nose in the sweetness. The odor of bread made his mouth water.

"The staff of life, son," Mr. Wyatt said, watching him. "Man's history is a long breadline."

The words sounded famous and fine. Alan suspected the miller's talk came mostly from the Bible because his mother was always telling him that man did not live by bread alone, making her comment especially strong when he was wolfish with hunger.

He remembered he had a question to ask Mr. Wyatt, though he really didn't know how, the subject seeming too ghoulish to be brought up in the middle of a bright summer day. He gazed at the planking laid loosely above the beams; his eyes slid to the top of the ladder that entered the attic and then, rung by rung, descended again to the millhouse floor. Still he could not find the right words to use in asking about the coffins. The whole story may be the product of somebody's imagination; at the moment it sounded too far-fetched to be anything but silly.

Mr. Wyatt read his thoughts. He chuckled. "Yep, they're up there," he said. "Want to climb up and see?"

Alan swallowed nervously. He wanted to see the coffins, but he felt cold at the thought of climbing up into the brown, dusty shadows of the attic all alone. He was about to refuse, when Mr. Wyatt said, "I'll go with you, of course, son. Couldn't trust your footing on all those loose planks." He chuckled again. "You wouldn't have caught me up there alone at your age, either."

Alan felt grateful. He followed the miller to the ladder, where the man stood back with a twinkle in his eye. Alan halted, looking at the ladder as if it were a crawling thing. "You go first, please, Mr. Wyatt" he said.

"It's easy to remember your manners at certain times, isn't it boy?" the miller said, smiling, beginning to climb, slowly and stiffly, ahead. "Careful of your footing," he called down as the boy began to ascend the ladder after him.

There was no door to the attic, only an opening in the half-floor over the big lower room of the mill. The ladder came straight up off the main floor into the midst of the coffins. Alan gasped. They had been there all this time, right over his head every time he came to have corn ground! His eyes adjusted to the shadow, and he could see that most of the plain, unpainted boxes were rectangular; but there were two shaped ones, in the general form of a human body, leaning against the wall. Alan half-expected to see wrapped figures in them. He shivered.

Mr. Wyatt was saying, "We don't make them any more. Too much high-priced competition nowadays. You can get one of these ten-dollar jobs in town now for $150." Seeing Alan's eyes caught by the box no larger than a rabbit trap, Mr. Wyatt added, "That one was made for a baby we thought was going to die of pneumonia. He fooled us though, and came out of the fever. Grew up to be a strong man and moved to the wheat farms in the West. Came back though a few years ago for a visit, and I showed him what would have been his coffin."

The miller's matter-of-fact attitude calmed Alan. Coffins, after all, were only pieces of pine wood nailed together. The attic became a friendlier place. About eveything was the honeysmell of old pine boards, so familiar to Alan's nostrils; and over everything was the eternal white sift of the meal like a light drifted snow. The one window visible in the loft was dim with the dust and sagging webs, themselves white and ghostly as fluttering old lace. There was still something in the air of the upper chamber of the mill that set Alan a little on edge. The miller rubbed a corner of his sack apron over the panes. The warm sunlight poured through.

"You see, boy," the old man said. "Things are mostly what you make them. Light is a marvelous thing for cleaning up the corners of a dark room, or of a man's mind, for that matter."

Alan peered through the window. Below him, the familiar daytime world of milldam, waterwheel, and flume was visible. Now three white ducks had come to sail slowly over the green water of the pond. The peepers, still chanting, seemed from the height to be singing in response, like two sections of the choir in church. Somewhere, a bobwhite called in notes so clear the sound was like mountain-water purling over stones. Somewhere in the willows that fringed the blue-green pond, the bird was hidden, making his music to others of his kind especially, but generally to the world. Suddenly anxious to be outside again in the world of summer, he preceded Mr. Wyatt down the ladder.

Back on the floor, he looked up at the attic once again. Already an atmosphere of cold mystery was beginning to settle there. The old dread fostered by the stories he had heard returned; his mind, shorn of its intimacy with the pine boxes, found in them what it had found before: something gruesome and sad and clammy, as alive as an old glove filled with wet sawdust.

I wonder if things are what I make them or if I am what things make me, he thought, surprised at the direction Mr. Wyatt's words gave to his thinking.

"Thank you," he called, after he had mounted Old Ranger and the miller had placed the sackful of ground meal, again evenly divided, across his lap. "I'll see you in two weeks."

"Come again any time, boy," Mr. Wyatt said, as Alan headed Old Ranger towards home and dinner and Buckeye.

"Well," Oscar remarked, "you certainly took long enough to plant the corn, grow, harvest, *and* mill it. What was old man Wyatt doing, beating the water out of the bullfrogs to make the millpond rise?"

Alan grinned at his father's joke. "There weren't any bullfrogs," he said. "Only little old peepers, about a million of them."

"He's been counting them," Lee put in. "No wonder he took all morning."

"Who rattled your chain, boy?" Oscar said to his older son. Lee frowned.

"You couldn't count them," Alan explained. "They couldn't even be seen."

"You never did say why it took you so long," Oscar said.

"Mr. Wyatt showed me the coffins," Alan explained. "They're really there. One, made for a baby that didn't die, looked like a rabbit-box." He poked at the food on his plate, not interested in eating any more. "We climbed up a ladder as tall as a tree," he added. "Me and him."

"Who went first?" Lee asked slyly, wiping buttermilk off his underlip with the tip of his tongue. "You did, of course."

Alan was sorely tempted. He wanted to say, "I went up first by myself and looked all around, and when Mr. Wyatt finished the grinding, he came up too, and told me all about them." He shied, even in his mind, from the use of the word "coffin," trying to lock the dread image outside his thinking. Yet he wanted to appear brave, to tell a lie about the morning's adventure. But his mother's eyes were on him, their gaze sticking to his face like two fat summer flies that were impossible to brush away. He couldn't lie.

"He went first," he said sullenly, angry with Lee for having pushed him on. "It was his mill."

"Ain't you the polite one?" Lee teased. "The guests are supposed to go first. Any other time you'd have trampled anybody to death who happened to get in your way."

"I remember," Oscar was saying, "when Fatty Poston died. Nearly three hundred fifty pounds he weighed, and no taller than me. Some man I can tell you. They made his box short and stout—so stout they had to take out a double window to get the coffin in and Fatty out of the house. I was one of the pallbearers. I thought my back would break carrying Fatty between the churchhouse and the burying ground." He helped himself to apple pie. "It's been a long time now since anybody's used one of them boxes. Even if they wanted one, Mr. Wyatt's too old and too busy with the mill to make it, now that his boys are gone."

"His boys?" Lee asked. "I didn't know he had any boys."

"You wouldn't," Oscar answered. "They were both older than me. Both of them in Detroit now, I believe, working in the automobile factory."

"It's a fine subject for the dinner table," Belle said. "Enough to turn a body's stomach. Hush now, and eat your dinner." To Alan she said, "I see you did it again. That mealsack looks like it has been dragged through a mudhole."

Alan started to explain.

"No use wasting your breath," Belle said. "I've heard it all before."

They finished the meal, and Belle began to clear away the dishes. Alan helped, placing the half-full bowls of left-over food in the warming-closet of the stove for supper. Lee brought a fresh pail of water from the spring.

"Get some rest," Oscar said, leaving for the barn. "I've got a little job for you two this afternoon."

The noon train blew as Alan stretched himself out on the bare boards of the front porch. Had he been in the field, hoeing or plowing, he would have looked down at his noonday shadow to see whether he could step on his head. If he succeeded, it was time to leave off work and go home to dinner. He knew, from having heard his mother blow the great conch shell to summon them home, that the blast of the train whistle, his own short shadow bunching under his feet, and the sound of the horn blowing came within minutes of each other. All morning he would have been watching his tall shadow grow shorter from the head down, coming towards him from the edge of the west wood, where its head had seemed to rest as the sun rose. At mid-morning, he would have begun stretching a leg to see whether he was able to step into the middle of the dark round shape of his face that now came so tantalizingly near, but withdrew when he leaned out to step. When he tried leaning backward, his shadow-face came nearer, but his step was shortened. When he did finally manage to stand on his head in the reversed world of shadows, he knew the time was approaching high noon. All morning, he would, of course, have kept an eye out for Oscar, who had little patience with his son's eagerness to get through the first half of the day.

Afterwards, when dinner was over and he had slept his allotted thirty minutes on the front porch, he watched his shadow go away, this time to the east, lengthening with each hour until, at sundown, when he was allowed to stop his field work, he was impossibly tall, monstrous as a giant with his head resting in the edge of the other wood.

Sometimes his father caught him loitering, inspecting his shadow with a doctor's critical interest in the well-being of a patient. "Get a move on there!" Oscar would yell. "This is not time to be catching gnats. You can catch gnats at Christmas."

Was catching gnats, Alan wondered, something you did when you had all the time in the world on your hands? That would take more time than counting peepers. Gnats were so small. And what did you do with them after you caught them? Skin them? His mother was always saying about some of her acquaintances that they were so stingy they would ruin a good knife to skin a gnat for its tallow. Maybe you swallowed them. Apparently some people did, for his mother said his own father would strain at a gnat and swallow a camel. Was a camel easier to swallow than a gnat? His mother was a funny person.

He was beginning to drowse, timelessly, on the edge of sleep. The planks of the porch seemed to dissolve under him.

He dreamed. The meadow was full of rich grasses, gray and green-tipped and feathered with the dust of bloom. There was the darker green of the leaves of violets and the lighter green of dandelion leaves, and all the unknown blades and tassels, blue, shadowed, light with the pallor of lavender, egg shell, and gold. Alan himself stood knee-deep in the starry vegetation while the dark, ungilded train came, not gliding but rocking, blowing trumpets, ringing bells, coiling the sound of chains over the gold and blue flowers, whose petals he thumbed while the dark train shook his entrails. It was no toy train that rocketed out of the north—the toymakers of trains were all dead, and all the gay pictures of make-believe engines painted by names in a book were set laughing: I think I can, I think I can, I think I can!

On came the train, past the lead-colored box of the station. "All aboard!" shouted the man with his head stuck through a window. "If you can't get a board, get a plank!" Sounding like his father. There was the noise of hammering and sawing, peculiar in a train. Alan wondered what they might be making.

The train was coming nearer now, rocking out of the depths of the meadow, rearing and plunging like a rockinghorse, while the various ragged heads of meadow flowers stood at attention by the press of their crowd, inflexibly civil, sternly upright, and over them the train passed without image, twinkling no bloom.

To his surprise, Alan saw that the cars were all pine boxes, plainly rectangular, all but the front two, the double engines, which were shaped like a human body, head and shoulders first. "Hellohellohello!" said the train, slowing down beside him. A door opened in the side of one of the cars, and someone put down a rabbit-box. The man with his head stuck through the window snickered. And suddenly all the blue and gold flowers in the meadow exploded in Alan's face. He woke with a gigantic sneeze.

3

SNAKES were plentiful that summer, appearing abundantly at the very first of the warm weather. On the banks of Muddy Bottom Creek Alan had seen the watersnakes in the spring, sunning themselves on the bare earth, knotted and twisted in clumps; he had heard them falling from the low limbs into the water, splash after splash, until the willows seemed to be shedding snakes as easily and naturally as they dropped their brittle twigs in the high spring wind. The meadows were crossed and criss-crossed by the slender blue racers, their heads suddenly periscoping above the grass. Corn snakes hunted in the crib and grain bins. Small, harmless garter snakes ran for cover under the hollyhocks and cosmos plants. Clockwork, the rooster, went around for a whole morning carrying in his beak a limp brown ring-necked snake, which he put down occasionally, gobbling deep in his throat and dropping his wings in a fighting gesture, before he picked it up and continued his progress about the yard. Only the dangerous varieties, the rattlers, water moccasins, and copperheads, were not so much in evidence. Oscar had killed a copperhead behind the hogpen, and a moccasin near the watering-place below the barn. And a neighbor had reported that some hikers from town had come upon a rattlesnake den on Walden Ridge, a deep well in the rocks, at the bottom of which dozens of the snakes had congregated. When a heavy stone had been dropped into the well, the neighbor said, a sickening, frightful odor had arisen from the disturbed reptiles. The whole of Walden Valley had become very snake-conscious.

And so Oscar warned Lee and Alan about their work of the afternoon. "You boys," he said, "need to clean the lovevine off the lespedeza in the corner of the pasture field. I'm afraid it will spread and get into the hay. Be careful about snakes though. They're everywhere this year."

Just the day before, he had called Alan to see the brilliant cornsnake hanging between the slats of the corncrib like a gay ribbon puzzlingly knotted in the middle without making the bow customarily associated with ribbons. "Got him a rat," Oscar said, "or an egg."

"He won't eat for a day or two now," Lee explained, coming in from the garden where he had been pulling ragweeds for the hogs. "He'll lay around until he digests whatever it is, then he'll go hunting again."

Sometimes Lee annoyed Alan by giving him detailed information which he already knew. Just because Lee was older, he imagined himself to be some kind of walking encyclopedia. Mr. Know-It-All, Alan thought. Lee the Lion-Hearted, who, even now on their way to the pasture, made him walk behind to protect him from the snakes. Didn't his brother know about the sneak snake, the copperhead, that always struck the second person in a row? Some protection he was getting from Lee!

They threaded their way through the high weeds by the hogpen, Lee in front dividing the weeds, making a path for Alan to follow. Here was a veritable paradise for snakes, if paradise was what they wanted, Alan thought. After all, snakes had been in paradise; the Bible said so. The devil himself had been a snake, at least for a while. So snakes must be here, in these rank smelly weeds by the smelly hogpen. But nothing struck swiftly from the dense growth; there was no sound of anything gliding away. You never could tell when you were threatened. Snakes, like the devil, got you unexpectedly.

A hen, cackling, scuttled away from them through the weeds. Lee stopped. "Long-tailed Annie," he said, "has stolen her nest. Mom said so." He began carefully to part the weeds in the direction of the fleeing hen. Alan joined in the search, but the boys found nothing. "It's like looking for a needle in a haystack," Lee said. "If it was in the barn loft now, I bet I'd find it." The boys competed all year long in the finding of the treasure troves the hens hid in the loose hay in the barn. Nothing gave quite the same pleasure as finding the round hat-shaped nests in which the white eggs gleamed in the semi-dusk of the haymow, particularly at Easter time, when extra servings of eggs were on every plate and the kitchen smelled of the rich egg custards which Belle baked so well. The pleasure of the holiday depended on the number of eggs in the kitchen basket, and the anticipation of that pleasure gave an added interest to the constant egg-hunt that went on about the farm.

As they climbed the cross-fence between the orchard and the pasture, Alan asked, "What's the best way to find a needle in a haystack, Lee?"

"Use a sifter," Lee answered, "and sift every straw. Or get a lodestone and draw it out."

"No," Alan said. "You just slide down the haystack. If the needle's there, you'll find it in the seat of your pants."

"That's a jolly one," Lee said. "I can tell you made it up by the way it stinks." He held his nose. "Smells like a rotten egg."

The sun was throwing great golden staves of light out of the west, marking the sky there with radiating gold like the ribs of half an umbrella, when the boys reached the corner of the pasture where the dodder had begun to grow, flinging its yellow parasitic web in a stranglehold over the lespedeza.

"You know," Lee said, wading into the brilliant mess, "if you put a piece of lovevine on a fencepost and it grows, your girl loves you. It's better than mullein for truth. Mullein's got too much chance to grow."

He was speaking, Alan knew, of breaking a mullein head in the direction of the house of the girl you loved. If it didn't die, but straightened up and lived in spite of its bruises, and still pointed in her direction, it was sure proof of her devotion.

The boys began to strip the shining vine away from its victim, putting the hairy gold strings into a two-gallon bucket which they had brought for that purpose. It was easy to gather the mature vines, but the small, strangling knots made where the vines encircled stems of the lespedeza were more difficult to pull away. Here, too, were the buds, forming a pale berry-like mass, from which the seeds fell to the ground to begin the cycle all over again: first with a true root and then, maturing, taking to the host plant and living with only a secondary connection with the earth. The boys were careful to remove the buds, no matter how much they resisted, breaking, if necessary, the crippled stem of the host and transferring it whole to the bucket.

Soon, with only a fraction of the patch cleared, the bucket was full, and Lee carried it to a sandbar in the creek and dumped the glowing tangle into the sun, where it would wilt quickly. "It will burn before sundown if this heat keeps up," he said.

A second bucketful had to be emptied, and a third. Gathering the fourth and last batch of the beautiful, crippling parasite, the boys were startled by a small breathing sound that grew up in the cooling nightfall air—a thin, insistent whistle like steam escaping from under a kettle lid. Between them, a small, upsurging motion was evident against the sun-colored stems of the dodder. Looking closely, they saw a bright garter snake throwing itself in violence towards them, blindly trying to escape the tangle of the pasture growth. Lee kicked savagely at the suddenly running thing, watching the grass part and divide farther on. "Just a big put on," he said. "Wouldn't bite a flea, no more than a spread-adder. Not half as dangerous as Suzy Overholt's garter."

Here he goes again, Alan thought. I've heard Suzy Overholt until I'm sick and tired of him and her both. He closed his mind to what Lee was saying. The snake had awakened a memory of himself and his mother on a blackberry hunt several miles away from home. They had teased a spreading adder to see it widen its head until it was almost flat, and watched it sway back and forth, hissing, in what it hoped would be a frightening display of its powers. Since they would not go away, the snake had rolled over and played dead.

"He's sulled," Belle said, "like a possum. He won't move as long as we watch him."

Later in the day, they had come upon a man hopping up and down in the roadway, his arms outflung like a shield to protect his wife and child who were huddling behind him. In the sun at the center of the road sprawled an enormous rattlesnake.

"Kill it! Kill it!" the man cried, dancing like a puppet on a string.

And Alan had killed it, whipping it to death with a cane he had picked up in the grass at the edge of the roadway, while the man and his family looked on triumphantly. The snake had displayed no fight; it had merely tried to run away towards the safety of the weeds and the ditch. Alan had been sorry to see the beautiful spoon-shaped head bleeding in the dust, and the cold, dispassionate, broken eye.

"Why," he asked his mother, as they walked away from the small group still huddling in the sun as if for warmth, "were they so excited about a snake?"

"Their whole lives," she had answered him, "are bound up in the serpent principle."

It was an annoyingly secret thing for her to say, and he wanted to ask her what she meant. But he was afraid she would begin to make him a sermon. Some days she took to texts like—he fumbled for a thought—like snakes to blackberry patches. Anyway, he knew vaguely that she referred to the situation in the Garden of Eden. So he called her attention to the century plant's shaft of rich white bloom rising like a tower in the hot blue air. His mother loved all flowers and herbs, and knew them intimately.

"Yet for all its beauty, it stinks," she said. "Now here's a beauty as well as a good heart medicine." She offered Alan a leaf of the wild ginger she had found during their tramp through the fields. Crushed or chewed, it was spicy and good for the circulation, his mother claimed. Heartleaf had kept her alive for twenty years, she said; ever since she had her first heart trouble and her father had taught her what the plant was and where to find it in its native places. At the root of one of the plants she had pulled up whole was a tiny brown vegetable cup, shaped like a dainty lipped pitcher, and covered with pretty purplish dots. "Its spores are down in here," she told him. "That's how the young plants are born."

But the thought of the snake in the roadway and the man's excited reaction haunted Alan still. Obviously there was a great deal more to snakes than just the snakes themselves. He tried to fit the pieces of the snake puzzle together. There was what he had seen in town, for instance. On the courthouse square was a mob of people. Seeing them that day, Lee had begun to run down the street, shouting for him to follow. Pushing their way into the tense crowd, they had listened to the preacher mounted on a platform under a tree. He was a ragged, wild-eyed man, who made Alan think of a picture of John Brown he had seen in a textbook at school, with one electric arm flung out over the heads of the chained men he meant to free, while in his other hand he held a closed black book.

The preacher had held a book, too. But what fascinated Alan was the rattlesnake wound about his extended arm. Behind him, on the platform floor, was an open box, over whose side another snake, a copperhead, was sliding down to the boards. The place looked like a snake den in a zoo.

As the preacher exhorted the crowd, the snake moved with the motion of his arm, licking out its tongue above the heads of the crowd, whose faces were turned upward shining with an exuberant, glorious horror, mingled with dread and fear. On them all was the look of a terrible happiness. Alan had felt disgusted and coldly sick at the pit of his stomach. And when the woman rushed up the steps of the platform and tried to kiss the snake in the preacher's hand, he suddenly wished the man would drop the rattlesnake into the upturned faces. The spectacle, a churchless meeting he was told, had left him shaken and resentful, but against whom he could not have said.

"The snake is still the symbol of man's lost glory," Belle had replied in answer to his question about the meeting. "So he is taken up as an act of faith. For by faith, evil may be embraced without harm."

Her answer had not clarified anything for him. It was much too one-sided. Wondering why all the important things in life carefully showed one face, and kept the other, the face that really mattered, darkly concealed, he was reminded of the hymn he had heard at church: "Farther Along We'll Know More About It," and fervently hoped he could wait for the revelations. Waiting wasn't going to be easy though.

"Come on," Lee said. "Snap out of it. Any jackass can go to sleep standing up. It's going to be dark before we get this danged dodder done." He grinned. "How's that for poetry, son?" He often teased Alan because Miss Woodson had praised a poem Alan had made.

"Not too bad," Alan said. "But I like this one better." He began to chant:

> There was a young fellow named Lee
> Who sipped honeydew like a bee;
> He made a dead ringer
> Except that no stinger
> In the proper position had he.

Lee looked surprised. "Where did you learn that?" he asked.

24

"I didn't learn it, I made it," Alan said, proud of his rhyming ability.

"And my grandmother," said Lee, "was queen of England." He picked up the bucket. "Let's go to the creek and burn that stuff," he suggested. "It's getting too late to stay out here, pulling this wretched vine."

He took a bottle of kerosene from his pocket and saturated the heap of dodder and lespedeza on the sandbar; then he scratched a match against his thigh. The rough cloth of his trousers sang under the savage swipe of the match. The smell of sulphur mingled with the strong odor of the kerosene as a blue flame arose and gave birth to a golden fire, which seethed and flamed over the oil-soaked mess. Long after the plants were consumed, the sand burned on; then it smoked sullenly for a longer time. The boys watched. It takes a fire a long time to die, particularly a summer fire. And the weather had been too dry for carelessness. At last, Lee flipped handfuls of water over the hot sand.

The sunset was like an orange pool with purple fish in it as the boys started home. Small slivers of cloud changed from blue to purple and then to black while the sky behind the clouds metamorphosed from orange to green to silver in a constant kaleidoscopic shift of tint and color. The night would not be long in coming.

Pretty Boy, the black pup, met them at the gate, wagging his short, fat body from end to end. He was only six weeks old and looked, from a distance, oddly like a black bumble bee with his stinger out. Not being allowed out of the yard yet, and feeling lonely, Pretty Boy waggled himself so hard he fell over when Alan spoke to him. Taking the pup in his arms, Alan carried him to the porch and left him there. "Keep out of the way," he scolded. "I don't want anything to happen to you."

The first dog he and Lee had owned had been caught in a steel trap in Four Mile Swamp and had starved to death. They had found his body, a skinful of bones, weeks later while hunting the cows after the cows themselves had been lost for half a week. In the deep woods beyond the farm, and particularly in the swamp, to be out of sight was almost like being exiled in a strange, lonely world of rocks and moss and trees. Alan himself was especially affected by the sycamores, whose great pale limbs, scabbed with brown and gray, looked like the lifted arms of a leper, or so his mother had described them when he spoke to her of the mottled trees flaring and gleaming one afternoon following a rain storm. Their color was amazing, and when the sun came out, drying the wet face of the faint cliff beyond the sycamore grove, there was such glitter among the weathered and broken stones where the quartz was embedded that Alan felt as though he looked at some magically worked picture whose painter had managed, through a kind of depth paintings did not ordinarily possess, to infuse a sense of a real door through which the spectator might walk naturally in among the great trees to the foot of the cliff itself. Sometimes he ached to see the color of the land. Sometimes tears unaccountably stung his eyes.

Alan turned at the woodpile and looked back at Pretty Boy. He certainly didn't want anything to happen to this dog, or to his calf either. Loving Pretty Boy as much as he did, he loved the calf still more. Buckeye was the most precious thing he owned, because he owned him entirely and did not have to share him, not even with Lee. But joint ownership had its compensations. Half-owning was better than not owning at all. And the dog had his own ways of making himself loved.

The smell of the cedar poles he was chopping for the kitchen stove was pleasant and set his teeth on edge, with just enough of pain throbbing in his jaws to make his senses acute. When he split one of the thicker pieces, the inside colors, copper and purple and light green, seemed so much a part of the strong, piercing odor of the wood that he was unable to say which sense, smell or sight, was being more activated. His nose ran, his eyes ached, his teeth pulsed in his jaws. Feeling immensely alive, he chopped two armloads of the cedar wood before he stopped. Ordinarily, his father did not burn such valuable wood for fuel, but used it instead to sell to the sawmillers in the neighborhood, or as fence posts because it endured so long in all weathers, being, along with black locust, the one wood that did not have to be replaced every two years in the soft, wet earth of the bottomlands. But these slim poles were from the pasture where the dark cedars grew plentifully and starved the thin hill-grass under them. His father never allowed them to grow to any great size, but chopped them off even with the earth when they were large enough to furnish the short round sticks for the kitchen stove. "Only a king could afford to bake his bread with cedar fire," his father said. And there was in the kitchen when the stove was lit a kingly smell, a mingling of the brown crust with the wood burning like incense. It was a joy to sit down in the kitchen to the sweet white milk and the brown bread. Alan felt that a king had nothing he could envy, whatever a king had.

He carried the wood into the house and dropped it noisily into the box behind the stove. Now for the kindling. From the smokehouse he took a handful of another rich substance, heart-pine, and carried it to the chopping block. With the poleaxe he split the pungent, almost crystallized wood into thin slivers. The resin was caked and glassy, like sugar inside his glass when he oversweetened his lemonade. Pine made his teeth ache, too, but mostly because he remembered Lee's persuading him to chew some of the resin and the vile taste it left in his mouth for days afterwards when he tried to eat hot bread. The resin simply would not wash off his teeth; nor would the white rags he chewed do more than stick to the crowns of his teeth, so that he ended up with a mouthful of fiber that felt like chicken feathers. He was angry with Lee as usual. But he could not learn to distrust his brother, especially when Lee chewed resin with no dire consequence.

Perhaps it was because Lee also chewed tobacco. In any event, Lee's cud of resin rolled away from his teeth like chewing gum. Alan complained to his mother. "If you can't chew pine resin, you can't chew pine resin," she said. "Every tub sits on its own bottom. Besides, the stuff will rot your teeth. Leave it alone."

"It will rot Lee's teeth, too," he said.

"I've told him," his mother said impatiently. "If he insists, he'll have to take the consequences. A little time with these," she added, taking her false teeth out and laying them on the table, "will make him remember. Only it'll be too late then. I used to chew pine resin, too." Her voice was ominous.

Alan gathered the fat-feeling pine sticks in his hands and placed them carefully on the kitchen floor beside the woodbox. Breakfast was prepared for, anyway.

Down by the barn, Lee was milking. Alan could hear the soft squirt of the milk in the pail. Oscar was feeding the hogs, whose grunting and squealing rose higher than any other sound and dominated the barnyard. "Get your feet out of the trough, you hog!" his father yelled. Alan grinned because he knew his father was grinning, too. Oscar loved the useful, ugly animals, from the time they were born, wet and ratlike in the raw spring weather, to the time he slaughtered them in the fall. Something about their unabashed hunger and their utter indifference to cleanliness and to each other amused him. Alan had no patience with the larger hogs. He loved only the little ones that had to be wiped dry at birth with an old sack to keep them from freezing to death in the spring cold. Later, when fat and pink and engaging as only a young ugly animal can be, and ill-tempered as a March wind, they fought viciously among themselves, tugging and pulling and falling in the mud of the barnyard, Alan liked to watch their endless struggles, their little sharp cries reminding him of the squeak of a rusty hayrake.

And they would bite, too, when he caught them, turning swiftly in his hands like a short, fat worm doubling back on itself, to pinch sharply whatever flesh they could lay hold of. Careful to grasp them just back of the forelegs, as he would have grabbed a crayfish directly behind its pincers, Alan made a game of creeping up on the young animals and catching them unaware; that is, as long as the sow was not in the vicinity. If he saw that old she cyclone anywhere about, he let her offspring alone. He had learned, in his mother's sermonizing words, that an ounce of prevention is worth a pound of cure, particularly where a mama pig was concerned.

His work finished, he went back to the pup on the front porch. Pretty Boy was asleep against the clapboard under the window, snoring gently. Sphinx moths were hovering over his mother's hollyhocks and petunias. These softly colored, hawk-like insects seemed to prefer the petunias, which for some reason known only to the maker of flowers began to send out waves of cloying perfume as soon as darkness fell. In the daytime they smelled hardly at all. Alan followed the moths about the yard. While they seemed most numerous over the petunias, they were feeding on the hollyhocks as well; occasionally, he noticed, they visited the jimson weed, the rankest weed in the yard, beautiful of flower, but coarse and sticky and poisonous. A good remedy for piles, his mother said. Alan was fascinated by the green burrs just forming on the plant; seed cases, he knew, but looking like green land mines, or the spiny marine explosives the sailors dropped over the side of their boat to catch an enemy. Touched, the spines, were flexible and resilient. They would harden toward fall, and finally split, flinging their hard lacquered seed over the adjoining earth for another crop the following season. Alan had never been able to explain satisfactorily to himself the presence of the spines. Now, if they were cockleburrs and came loose on some animal's hair, he could understand. But the jimson weed burrs never came loose. They could be found in mid-winter still on their stalks, cold-whitened and stiff to the touch, still capable of wounding. Unless the armed case was intended to ward off potential eaters of the seeds, he decided, there was no apparent reason for its being armed at all. He knew that with the plant's offensive odor, it would take a strong stomach or a very hungry one to dare a taste. Yet, he knew also that there was a reason for things, hidden though it might be. The puzzle was too much for him. Above all things, he yearned for certainty. And his mother told him, short of faith in God, there was none. Any answer found in a book, she told him, was only another man's opinion. And since Alan knew man was fallible, he was left adrift in a sea of questions.

He wandered to the corner of the yard where a moonflower's buds were tightly twisted like a rolled umbrella. In a short time, touched by some mysterious force, the flowers would begin to unroll their white petals and become pale and shell-like in the gloom, really like moons caught in a green galaxy of vine. The folds in a blossom began to move as he watched, as though a bee were inside, pushing; another crease in the damp, waxy petal loosened. Soon, with a working motion that did not again altogether cease until the flowering was accomplished, the moonflower opened with a faint breath of perfumed rot released on the night air. A sphinx moth came, and then another. Alan had the feeling of being present at some ritual.

"Hey, moon-calf!" Lee yelled from the backyard. "Supper's ready."

Alan washed his hands and face at the water bench on the backporch, where Lee was already scrubbing himself dry with a towel. There was a faint smell of cows left on the towel when Lee finished drying. Alan frowned, thrusting his face into the towel. It did look like Lee could wash his hands clean.

28

4

WHEN he entered the bedroom, he found his mother had already turned down the covers at the head of the bed. In the half-darkness, the white sheets glimmered, and he could see the white lump of the pillow on Lee's side of the bed. But there was no pillow for him. Belle refused to let him have one. "A pillow puts a crook in a young back," she said. "Sleep straightened out, and you'll walk straight."

"But Lee has a pillow," he complained.

"Lee has headaches, too," she answered. "But he's like Collins' ram. He's got a head of his own."

Naturally, thought Alan. Otherwise, how could his head ache? His mother, fortunately, had not begun to retell the story of Collins' ram, the headstrong animal that, managing somehow to climb into the barn loft, slipped through the loose planks and hanged himself by the horns. The entire McDowell family knew the story and its implication.

As for the pillow, Alan didn't really want one. He hadn't slept on a pillow as long as he could remember. You had to have something first before you could miss it. He had started the argument only to get his mother to talk. Sometimes conversation with her became very lively and exciting, depending, of course, on her mood and humor.

The bed he loved, even if Lee did snore. It was sometimes a kind of ship to him, a ship with wooden sails at the head and the foot; again, it was a nest and he a bird snuggled in it; or sometimes it might be a magic carpet on which he took impossible journeys over flat wooded country to strange towns beyond the blue mountain. He loved to go to bed because the sheets and the quilts smelled so sweet and clean he felt bathed all over in a kind of sun and soap fragrance that relieved him of all tiredness and set his mind conjecturing about all sorts of exciting things: the book he was reading, a song he knew, something he owned, a ghost tale he had heard. The bed was his place for getting his back against a wall, behind which the world and its shifting circumstance could not go; it was his cave, from the darkness of which he would gauge the happenings of the light hours, placing all of them in front of him, to be measured, relived, transformed to suit his will. Behind him rose impregnably the thought of his safety, like the walls of Troy, to be breached only by the horse of daylight, the gift he could not nor would not refuse.

He burrowed down under the light quilt, thinking of Buckeye. In his half-dreaming state, the calf became a library, a new geography book with covers on it, a clean speller written in by no one but him, bearing no one else's name; a reader with only the stories he had never read. It was a fine armload of books he carried. But they were far too heavy for their size. He put them down, all but the reader, which he opened. Buckeye's blue eyes looked out from the pages, accusingly. He dropped the reader and took up the speller, whose back felt warm and hairy, like Buckeye's sides. He laid the speller down and walked away. He would not open the geography, knowing somehow that the country it contained would be the country Buckeye knew, the barnyard, the pasture, the hill field where he had grazed during the spring's dry weather.

Starting awake, Alan turned over, his mind edged with a new knowledge that frightened him and at the same time made him glad. Books or no books, he did not want to sell the calf. He would rather borrow or go ignorant instead. He would tell his mother tomorrow. Feeling immensely happy with his decision, drowsing on the edge of sleep, he ran with the calf through meadows filled with sunshine and flowers, by springs dripping with cold bright water, to the top of a high hill, only somewhat lower than a mountain. There, he and Buckeye settled down in the long grass, safe and happy, listening to the sounds in the earth about them, the long conversations in the grass, the squeaks, the squeals of the insect world under the waving blades and tassels of the mountain growth; they heard the wind come by and fan through the young pines with the dry sound of corn being poured into a hopper. The earth was filled with a water sound, dry as splashed water seething on a warm stone. The whisper of water at the schoolhouse pump moved in the leaves and twigs beyond them, over the lip of the small plateau where they lay and sunned themselves free of all ambitions and questions. Only their comradeship was left, something real and natural and outside the pages of books; something, because it was not written and never would be, that could only be known by themselves; something experienced in their own inner feelings, which were the wall behind which the world and its circumstance could not possibly go.

But as he neared true sleep, Alan's semi-dream evaporated as water evaporates; the dry noise of plants he heard became the flipping of the pages of a book; the wind became the shaking out of a gigantic sheet of paper. A pulse began, rhythmic and repeated, like four sounds beaten on a gong, four syllables accented loud soft loud soft into a running account of a progress across space and time into the velvet darkness of sleep.

Again Alan dreamed of the train. But this time, strangely enough, his dream was a winter dream, a Christmas dream. From the window he listened, under eaves softly impounded with new snow and the first nubs of ice.

As though a divisive wind divided wheels from whistle, and bell from both, off in the fields of that country of no bells a bell was ringing softly as apples knocked together or a child beating round red globes of gorgeous glass together through a crib of silk. Was it really a train muted by snow, its rumble glazed along the ground, and only the bell melted into the air?

Brother Lee favored the train, approving the freeze as he would have approved the sun or shower. But, Alan knew, climate does not alter trains so. Summers, he knew, a sound of doom came with them onto the fields: horns, and hollow floors being thumped with anvils, and chains folding in miles of length, and drowned in steam, the bell. Winters, the steam rose more fiercely, hissing under the hard run of the train, there still with its sound of doom, but winter-tightened as the skin, foreshortened on the landscape, and the bell chilled in its cup to clang of iron and hammer, hardly sounding. Oh the shrill protest and the spitting fury in the open air!

Climate, Alan dreamed, makes the kind of difference between open and shut, but does not alter trains. He felt a slow anger at being taken for a dunce, forgetting to be grateful then for being taken at all. Lee usually overlooked him, in both presence and opinion. But in the dream Alan could hold his own.

A death, a holocaust, a wedding would have sufficed. But it was not time for any of these in the calendar. Only a birth was possible, and he could not imagine who owned the baby, who the bell. Even the bell had lost its plangent connection with the train. A sense of redness brimmed at his ears. The world was white, white, and only white, under the first nubs of ice, and yet the bell was apples, globes of apple glass beaten through silk, and scarlet berries streaming across the snow. It was, he thought in the dream, the blood of love pounding the listener's ears. But first of all, it was only the bell, no more, no less, than the rocking bell. He had always resented Lee's easy explanations.

Easily his dream shifted as a shadow on a windowpane. It was his time to have a train for Christmas, and also he was being given away. "Come to meet us at the bridge," his father had written. And the days between were deep with snow as if an order issued somewhere had been filled to the last flake for their journey on that day. The snow fell as company to the wonder waiting in the next county whose sound dropped like a stone into his wooded world.

All summer he had heard the train running there behind the woodland, in distance unimaginable. The autumn sounds grew louder, enlarged upon the landscape until it seemed the leaves fell at a whistle. Then the gray trees leaned nakedly against a blue that heaved remarkably at train-time. And his father wrote the letter, and the snows came.

Then on the morning of the day when all children are born, some with a star, some with apples, and the lucky one with a train, Alan and his father traveled endlessly in the same snow, by the same bowed cedars, as if, their tracks knocked out behind them, they moved in a circle, until they came to the iron bridge in an immensely white place looming briefly on the road ahead. Then, traveling more narrowly still, dimly fenced by the black bars vague as the marks on an ancient game board, they crossed the hissing green water where the flakes fell. Suddenly, louder than wheels on the loose boards, sweeter than angels it seemed to Alan, dreaming, they heard him singing. Through the flurry of the snow his dark figure emerged on the great circle of the road, shouting: "Good morning, Oscar! Good morning, Boy!"

"Christmas gift!" his father said, halting the team. "Christmas gift, Brother John!"

Alan did not know Brother John. He was only the gift exchanged between his father and the stranger. Brother John took his hand, and the men parted in the whiteness, nodding their heads. No words followed his father into the flying snow, going swiftly back over the bridge; but the muffled thunder ran in Alan's ears like trains approaching blindly in the snow, and he was afraid. But walking quickly now, Brother John was smiling.

They came later to the slate-blue station: the old quaint architecture in the snow. And Alan felt somehow as if he gazed in a warm room upon an icy painting of past time. The tracks stretched endlessly both ways, black but fading, and a flare burned orange and red emptily under the snow. Brother John looked at his watch. "Five minutes," he said. "Let us go in."

Inside the store that made a lean-to to the station the sights and sounds of Christmas warmed Alan through: candy as big as fence-posts wound with ribbons, and nuts larger than plumgrannies. Looking, he forgot the train. But Brother John remembered and put him outside when the whistle began to blow, the look of him saying he gave Alan a fine sight, an inestimable gift for the holiday.

Alan would have given back the gift unseen. But something there was coming in. He felt it in his body shaking, in the wall he leaned against shaking, as the train began to rush by. It came like a storm from the north and shot southward, heaving with thunder, its whistle shattering the last refuge on earth. "Brother John!" Alan screamed in the swift circle of the nightmare, "The train! The train!"

Inside the store the laughter and the talk of Christmas ceased as Brother John, huddling the boy in the greatcoat he was wearing, pressing him against his thin man's body, sang for him a Christmas song, to which all the other men in the store answered: "Alleluia! Alleluia!"

5

AND so the dream changed, and remained always the same dream, until the mind wore it out, and the country of the mind which the train filled grew exhausted with its thunderous burden and put it down, not as a memory but as part and parcel of the heart-tissue, the blood and bone of the dreamer. Once awake, in bed with his brother, seeing through the window the early morning-glories on the garden fence, he forgot the great journeys of his sleep and remembered that his mother was pregnant and that before the end of summer he would be sent away from home for the arrival of the new baby, as if there were no room in the house for both of them together. Arrangements had already been made for him and Lee to spend the birth-time with the Wades, their neighbors on the other side of Muddy Bottom Creek.

He could hear his mother singing as she went about preparing breakfast. It was a song that had made him cry when he was smaller because of the death of the bird and the way all the other animals went about helping their dead friend to be properly buried. All but the sparrow, who was Robin's murderer.

> *Who killed Master Tommy Robin?*
> *Who killed Master Tommy Robin?*
> *"I," said the sparrow*
> *"With my little bow and arrow:*
> *It was I. Oh, it was I!"*
>
> *Who saw him die?*
> *Who saw him die?*
> *"I," said the fly,*
> *"With my little bitty eye:*

It was I. Oh, it was I!"

Who caught his blood?
Who caught his blood?
"I, " said the fish,
"With my little silver dish:
It was I. Oh, it was I!"

sang Belle from the kitchen, from which now came the odor of boiling coffee and the smell of sidemeat frying. Mingled, the sad little song and the glad, almost speaking joy of the food filled him with an odd elation, surging and quiet at the same time: the kind of feeling he sometimes got from reading a book that took him outside himself and swept him away into another world that was superimposed upon the framework of the earth he knew like a sunrise transforming dark trees into the light and golden shadow of living green. He loved his mother's singing, remembering it as far back as his memory went. Belle's singing was different from his Uncle Granville's. The dried-up little man, with the thin monkeyhands, sang a different kind of song, placing one brown palm against the side of his singing jaw to keep the tune.

Alan smiled to himself, recalling the first time he had ever heard the ballad about the billygoat that swallowed the red flannel shirt and then, when punished for his crime by being tied to the railroad track, coughed up that fiery garment and flagged the train. Uncle Granville had sung it, remarking that a red flannel shirt was enough to give the goat a heartburn. Then he had sung a ballad about Kaiser Bill, and how the devil planned to give his job to the ambitious German when he got him down in hell.

Alan liked to see his uncle coming along the valley road to make a visit, for his mother never sang such songs as were in his uncle's repertory— songs that bordered sometimes on the bawdy and vulgar. Secretly, these songs delighted Alan, making him feel warm and mischievous on the inside, grown-up and daring, though at the same time leaving him feeling insecure, as though in danger himself from the dark powers hinted at by some of the words. The closest his mother ever came to singing an off-color tune was the ditty about the old man who lived by himself. As he remembered it, it went:

There was an old woman named Barbara Blue,
Barbara Blue, Barbara Blue;
There was an old woman named Barbara Blue,
Bar-Bar-Barbara Blue-Blue-Blue.

If you want me to sing it, I'll sing it to you,
Sing it to you, sing it to you;
If you want me to sing it, I'll sing it to you,
Sing-sing-sing it to you-you-you.

There was an old man who lived by himself
Lived by himself, lived by himself;
There was an old man who lived by himself
Lived-lived-lived by himself-self-self.

The old man died and was laid in his grave,
Laid in his grave, laid in his grave;
The old man died and was laid in his grave,
Laid-laid-laid in his grave-grave-grave.

There grew an apple tree over his head,
Over his head, over his head;
There grew an apple tree over his head,
Ov-ov-over his head-head-head.

The apples got ripe and were ready to pull,
Ready to pull, ready to pull;
The apples got ripe and were ready to pull,
Read-read-ready to pull-pull-pull.

There came an old woman to gather them off,
Gather them off, gather them off;
There came an old woman to gather them off,
Gath-gath-gather them off-off-off.

The old man rose up and gave her a thump
Gave her a thump, gave her a thump;
The old man rose up and gave her a thump,
Gave-gave-gave her a thump-thump-thump.

The old woman ran off with a flippity-flop,
Flippity-flop, flippity-flop;
The old woman ran off with a flippity-flop,
Flip-flip-flippity-flop-flop-flop.

The bridle and saddle hang under the shelf,
Under the shelf, under the shelf;
The bridle and saddle hang under the shelf,

Und-und-under the shelf-shelf-shelf.

If you want any more, you can sing it yourself,
Sing it yourself, sing it yourself.
If you want any more, you can sing it yourself
Sing-sing-sing it yourself-self-self.

This ballad had its own humor, Alan conceded, but lacked the pure animal fun of the goat vomiting the shirt, possibly a sleeve at a time. Goats were hilarious animals, anyway. The only one, a kid, that he had ever owned trimmed all of his mother's rosebushes to canes despite the thorns, could walk a fence like an acrobat, and once, unaccountably, had climbed to the top of a conical haystack in the barnyard and seemed to be standing there, leaning out, as Alan told his mother, "on thin air."

Belle had muttered something about being thinner than air the next time she caught Can-Can at her rosebushes, a threat which, unfortunately, had not reached the goat's ears. For, in addition to tin cans, from which he had been named because of a strong preference for them, probably for the salty taste they contained, he liked more than any other plant on the farm the sour-sweet, almost apple-ish taste of the rosebushes. So the disaster could not have been avoided. The rosebushes suffered, and so did Can-Can. Alan could remember still the smell of the goat-meat cooking in the big iron pot on the kitchen stove. Thinking of his pet, he stayed away from the table. But not so, Lee, who had his own grievance against the young billy.

Lee had mightily enjoyed teasing Can-Can, who, like all members of his tribe, liked trying the strength and sturdiness of things with his head.

"That goat butts coming and going, hind part and fore, and wrong side out," Oscar had said one morning, after seeing Can-Can rush Clockwork, striking the big red rooster from the rear and sending him, startled and screeching, high in the air. Coming down with a whortle deep in his throat, Clockwork had turned to fight, only to see Can-Can, head lowered, coming at him again. The rooster fled.

Angry because he claimed Clockwork as his own, Lee had enticed Can-Can to the low rock wall that separated the yard from the apple orchard above the house. Because of the slanting ground, Can-Can, in Lee's estimation, would not be able to clear the wall and so would give himself a headache he would not soon forget.

Getting down on his knees, his back to the stones, Lee called, "Can-Can, Can-Can. You old son-of-a-gun, come here!"

Hearing his enemy's voice, the goat stopped picking grass and turned toward the sound. Seeing Lee on his knees, his hands waggling, his tongue out making a bleating sound, Can-Can charged. Lee ducked, throwing himself flat on the grass. The goat, surprised, skidded to a stop and backed away. Lee got to his knees again and made more sounds, hopping about and waving his hands. Can-Can charged again. Lee dropped to the ground, but caught his bare arm on top of a bull nettle, and surged upwards again, just in time to offer a shoulder to the rushing goat. Can-Can caught him full tilt and sent him sprawling. Then, leaping to the wall as though he had been a feather wafted there by the wind, the animal skipped with a dry laughing sound into the orchard and disappeared.

Lee lay slightly addled in the grass for several minutes, and then, hoping that the small battle had been unobserved, slunk away by the wall. But Oscar had been watching. And at noon, to Lee's chagrin and embarrassment, Oscar told the family.

Alan felt quite justified in the pleasure he experienced at seeing Lee get his come-uppance. For once, when he had been crossing the barnyard, Clockwork, without warning, had spurred him deeply in the thigh, leaving a hole so painful and narrow his mother had great difficulty in getting turpentine to the bottom of it. He had limped for days, while a blue ugly bruise spread around the wound. His father had talked of taking him to town for a lockjaw shot. But nothing had ever come of it. In Belle's opinion, no sick person about the McDowell place ever was attended to, unless it was Oscar himself. "Then, he gets a move on," she said.

Lee had only laughed at the incident. "Don't ever turn your butt on Clockwork," he said. "He's always looking for a target."

In the small, fierce wars with his brother, Alan usually came out second. But with Can-Can's help, he had finally scored. So he felt little pity for the morning-glory color that spread throughout the fleshy part of Lee's left shoulder, though the blow, placed a bit more to the center of the body, might have resulted in a broken collarbone. He was glad, however, that it had been Lee's left shoulder instead of his right, for that meant Lee would still be able to milk Old Cherry, a job which Alan hated. Straining at the cow's teats while she tried to protect herself from the flies by switching her tail and tramping about left him nervous and sweating.

And washing her udder in preparation for milking sometimes became a mammoth task, and one beyond his power either to perform or contemplate with any balance of mind.

Now, lying on his back, smelling the delicious odors from the kitchen, he grinned at Lee, who was still sleeping, his mouth open, and with the sound of a trapped bumble bee in his nose.

"Sing 'The Preacher and the Bear!'" he shouted to his mother.

Lee woke with a start, clamping his mouth shut and sitting up in bed. "What are you bellowing about?" he demanded crossly.

"The house is on fire!" Alan yelled, sputtering with laughter, remembering the boy his mother told about—the boy who could not speak but who could sing. He had been left, Belle said, to guard the house while his family went to work in the field. In the middle of the morning, the boy had come running to them in great excitement and uttering a mass of confused, wordless sound. The boy's mother had said to him, "If you can't tell it, sing it, son. Sing it!" The boy sang, "The house is on fire, pye cod! pye cod!"

Lee grinned. "You're as crazy as a loon, or Enoch Wall," he said.

"Get out of there," Oscar called, "or something else will be on fire. Your breakfast's ready."

Picking up his trousers from the floor where he had stepped out of them the night before, Lee inspected them carefully. "Speaking of fire," he said. He began to recite:

> "*Poor Richard McGuire*
> *Ran through town with his trousers on fire;*
> *He ran to the doctor and fainted with fright,*
> *For the doctor told him his end was in sight!*

I don't need any doctor to tell me my end's in sight. If I had a mirror, I could see it myself."

The verse was another of Belle's contributions to the rich lore of the household, a lore so interwoven and wide that it penetrated existence, filling it with such a wealth of old story and humor that at times Alan felt as though he lived inside the pages of some fantastic country legend, composed of all the colors and sights and sounds possible in the seasonal turns of his wooded world. Occasionally, contemplating the richness of the things he heard, and the strong color of all he saw, he became a little ecstatic, a little wild in his head, perhaps. Maybe Lee was right. Maybe he was brother to the loon, that laughing northern bird he knew only by hearsay. Maybe he had just barely escaped having feathers instead of skin. Come to think of it, he'd like to see a loon. They lived in the North, he knew; and were something like a duck. Though the mallards and teals that Lee sometimes shot at as they winged, high and arrow-shaped, over the farm, had no suggestion of craziness in them. A loon must be really insane to have his reputation creep so far south of him. As for Enoch Wall, everybody knew he was crazy. In Walden Valley, that went almost without saying. Alan didn't really mind any more being told that he was as weird as Enoch. The comparison had lost its power to sting.

He poured clean water from the bucket into the washpan, and lathering his hands and face, stooped over and washed himself free of the clean-smelling soap. Emptying the pan into the zinnia bed by the backsteps, he hung it carefully over a nail through a hole in the rim, and dried himself. The towel, damp and limp from use, he left hanging on a nail driven into the post that supported the other end of the washbench. Smelling his clean fingers, he went in to breakfast.

His mother was standing by the stove, pouring coffee, her body almost spherical under her cotton dress. Alan wondered whether the new baby would be a girl. Lee didn't exactly dispose him toward wanting another brother, but, all told, what fun would there be in a stay-at-home girl? Girls were a mother's delight, he supposed, knowing Belle wanted a girl. As for him, though he loved his mother and preferred her in almost all matters to his father, more exciting things, he realized, belonged to his father's world of barnyard, fields, swamp, and mountain. No, he decided suddenly and firmly, he wanted a brother, a brother he could feel friendlier toward than he had ever felt toward Lee. Maybe they would become best buddies, the best there ever was. If they could become that, it would be worth giving up his place in the family circle to the new baby. Amen, he said to his silent wish, and sat down to eat.

6

THE morning was high and windless and blue, just losing an eastern border of greenish silver and rose as Alan, Lee, and Oscar came out into the yard. From the north flew a straggling row of crows out of the pinewood where at nearly all seasons they nested by the hundreds. Up where they flew, there seemed to be a wind, for occasionally a wing tilted crazily and the bird skewed sidewise until it righted itself; or a sudden slide was evident without the motion of a feather, denoting a passage down some hidden hill of the air. Undoubtedly the birds were wind-buffeted. Lee watched them with a huntsman's eye, knowing that with the sentries they posted and their raucous warning cries, he would have trouble ever coming close enough to kill one, for all his silentness in the vicinity of the roosting place. Only twice in his life as a hunter had he managed to shoot a crow, and one of those he shot from the top of a fencepost by the wheatfield. The ebony of the bird against the ripe wheat, so like a drop of tar on a yellow cloth, had afforded too much accuracy of sight for him to miss. The other, which seemed to be the only one in the woodlot where he was hunting, he had shot from the top of an oak tree. This had been pure luck, for apparently there was a nest close by; some minutes after he had tossed the dead crow into the underbrush, there had come to him the sound of young crows calling. Which fact made his success all the stranger. For, as he knew, in nesting time crows rarely relaxed their vigilance. The bird, he had decided, had got a bait of crow poison and was far too ill to fly.

Lee took great pride in his ability to handle a gun, feeling his marksmanship to be somehow a measure of his fourteen-year-old manhood. And Oscar watched him with pride. About Alan, the father was puzzled. His younger son seemed not to care about guns at all. In fact, guns frightened him. He always carried his rifle awkwardly as though it were an extra limb his body had no use for, and when he shot, usually into the air, he flinched at the sound. Well, Oscar told himself, if it takes all kinds to make this world, I've got two of them.

"Ock, Ock, Ock!" screamed a crow.

"They've seen you, Dad," Lee said, meaning the crow was calling his father's nickname. He put up his arms as if he were holding a gun and shouted: "Pow! Pow! Pow!"

"Missed again as usual," Alan said. "You couldn't hit a fat bull's behind with a frying pan."

"Look who's talking now," Oscar said. "Remember the snake in the spring, boy?"

Alan remembered all right. The snake's spoon-shaped head periscoping across the small pool had made a perfect target. But the pistol in his hand kept leaping and jumping so after each shot that he had almost missed the spring entirely. But it didn't matter. He hadn't really wanted to shoot anyway. He was just tired of hearing Lee always boasting about his own prowess with a gun. Secretly, though, he had a greater respect for his brother following the sad marksmanship at the spring. Apparently a man did not just pick up a gun and start shooting accurately right away. Skill was involved. And Lee could shoot. He had to admit that.

"About knocked the spring dry," Oscar told John Wade, the neighbor from across the creek. "If the snake died, I suspect he starved for water."

Alan had reddened under his father's laughter. He felt better towards Oscar, however, when he added, "That boy can read though. I never saw a boy so crazy about a book. Expect I'll make a lawyer out of him yet."

"Let him be," John Wade said. "We ain't got any real need for long hunters any more. Squirrels are poor pickings when it comes to shooting for a living."

The talk had turned to other topics, and Alan, still feeling resentful towards Oscar, moved from the sunny roadway into the shade of a giant hackberry tree shaped like an enormous emerald umbrella. The shade was bitterly odorous, green and stinging, a smell peculiar to the hackberry, and so familiar to Alan that he could identify one of the spreading trees with his eyes shut. They seemed always to grow at the ends of bottoms, where the cornrows terminated, furnishing with their iron-gray trunks and skinny leaves a welcome haven from the sun and a cool spot of soil to dig a hole for the burlap-wrapped water-jug. He dawdled in the coolness while Oscar finished his conversation with John Wade. He heard his father say, "I believe I'm going to have to have his tansils tooken out." The new speech forms Oscar had adopted from his sons sometimes came out in a reversed pattern. Ordinarily, Alan would have felt sorry for his father. But the memory of Oscar's betrayal in the matter of the snake in the spring made him glad that his father had made a verbal fool of himself. He smothered his laughter. Out in the road the men were laughing, too.

"I got my tangue tongled up," Oscar said.

"You can't teach an old dog new tricks, Ock," John Wade said. "We bark the way we were raised to bark."

"And I was raised out here in these whiteoak acres, and never knowed much until I was a man," Oscar said.

"Same as me," said John Wade. "If a kid don't get an education now, it's nobody's fault but his own, what with nine months of school out of a year. When I was a little shaver, there was only three months, and the weather so bad that I couldn't get to and from."

Alan's laughter dried on his face. He felt ashamed. Crawling quietly from under the tree, he had gone quickly off in the direction of home, a new knowledge in his brainpan, an odd pity for the grown-up world that he had never felt before stirring in his consciousness.

7

AT the barn, much to Alan's surprise and grief, there was no Buckeye.
The calf had disappeared during the night, with only a broken slab in the
fence to denote his passage from the enclosure into the wider world of fields
and mountains. No footprints were visible in the stony road.

"Well, boys," Oscar said, "he might come home and again he might
not. We'll let the cane go and hoe it tomorrow. Today, we'll find Buckeye.
I'll take the swamp and you boys look in the meadow at the foot of Walden
Ridge. Better put a sandwich in your pocket."

Belle placed slices of left-over bacon between chunks of bread, making
three portions of lunch. "Watch out for snakes," she warned. "And stay
away from Enoch Wall's place. The man might harm you."

Lee and Alan walked toward Walden Ridge, stretching from north to
south in the distance, greenish-blue in the clear morning air. Already
pushing up from behind the ridge was a white, steaming horse's head of
cloud, promising rain before the day ended. Near the base of the ridge,
visible among the trees, was the rampart of rock on whose summit Enoch
Wall had placed his runnered house, to be free of the neighbors who teased
the half-witted man by hitching a team to the great sled on which the house
was built and pulling it about the country in Enoch's absence. Often he
had come home to his yard only to find his house half-a-mile away in
another area. Since he had moved, it was rumored, he was rarely away
from his house except for short journeys to the store for supplies; it was
also said that he slept on the flat roof of the cabin, and that he now kept
a gun. Pistol fire from that direction could be heard frequently, and the
boys had been told that Enoch lay on his bed and fired through an open
window at the sky. Exaggerated tales, Alan imagined. But since the day
he had seen Enoch in town buying the six dazzling cake plates, he was
not sure.

The hardware owner had pocketed the money with a grin. "Had a good day telling fortunes, Enoch?" he asked. Enoch had only grunted and stomped out of the store in his high-heeled cowboy boots. Alan had stared as he always stared at the bright yellow bandanna Enoch wore about his neck, the red shirt, and the broad-brimmed black sombrero. With his leathery brown face, Enoch was a composition in strong earth colors. Later in the day, Alan had heard Enoch preaching from the platform in the courthouse yard, the bundle containing the plates lying on a bench near him. People had gathered to hear the sermon, but not in any reverent mood. "Pray for the crops, Brother Wall," someone shouted.

And Enoch stood still and prayed: "O Lord, bless ye the sorghum cane, and make it a living sacrifice. Give to it good heads and make its stalks large and tender, so that the juice will pour out at the grinding, and the sweet syrup pour from the fire." He walked towards his audience, who retreated a little before him, still praying: "Give to the tree acorns and nuts, mast for the squirrels, persimmons for the possums. Make every tree a living sacrifice, and bless us all. Amen."

"Thank you, Brother," a man called as the crowd moved away to other amusements, leaving Enoch with his hands outstretched. "A living sacrifice," he repeated.

It seemed to Alan that he had been hearing a book read, so direct and Biblical were Enoch's words. Perhaps it was only the tone in which the man had prayed. Alan could not quite lose the impression that there had been something slightly heathenish in the prayer, sounding as it did like a plea to the Vegetable King, the god of leaves and branches, the goddess of fruits and flowers. Maybe Enoch wasn't crazy after all, just different in his ideas. Perhaps it was only his difference that people called crazy, themselves being normal and ordinary because they were alike.

Now, looking for Buckeye, Alan stared at the white cliff, which was beginning to withdraw into shadow in the light of the rising sun, and tried to imagine something real about the life of the man who lived on its summit. All that he had seen and heard thus far had the ring of a fairy tale, was infused with such improbability that, even in a book, it would have to be marked down as fiction. Some day, he decided, he would go see for himself. For some reason he could not quite put into words, it had become necessary for him to discover what kind of man spoke words Alan's own minister would not have spoken, and bought plates for his table that only a spendthrift woman would have chosen.

By the time the brothers reached the mountain meadow the sun had crossed a quarter of the sky. Nowhere had they seen any sign of Buckeye, though here and there the crushed meadow grass told of deer having slept there the night before. Once, crossing the meadow near nightfall, after an afternoon's hunt for hickory nuts, they had seen, grazing as peacefully as cows in a pasture lot, a small herd of the slender, tawny animals, beautiful, Alan thought, as a picture in a book. "Oh, if I had my gun!" Lee had breathed, rapturously, thinking of the hero he would be, bringing home enough sweet meat to last the family for days. Alan had been grateful Lee didn't have a gun, knowing his brother was thoughtless enough to shoot despite the game laws. Only after he had been caught in the act would Lee have regretted the action, not the sin particularly but the discovering being his concern. Lee had shouted suddenly, and the herd began to run, lightly, barely keeping touch with the earth; at the edge of the meadow, almost under the first trees was a rail rence, which the animals cleared like blown milkweed seeds. Such effortless motion made even Lee stare in wonder.

Here and there the boys could see where the deer had bedded down in the grass. Rich in various vegetations, the meadow was split with a watering stream, on whose banks grew masses of blue-eyed grass and mountain daisies, which, Miss Woodson said, the Anglo-Saxons had named the day's eye, from the sun, whose warm, life-giving rays they worshipped. There was one flower, with leaves delicate and lacy as fern, but not a fern at all, which he wished his teacher was there to identify. Back home, in a row by the garden, grown from a package of seed she had given him, were the young asters that would soon be in bloom. For a moment, but for a moment only, the summer seemed long, as he wondered what books Miss Woodson would have in the little glass case with the locked door when he returned to school in the autumn. These were her prizes, from among which the better students, as a reward for work well done, were allowed to choose for their free reading. He was glad he would have Miss Woodson another year. After that, he would move into Mr. Llewellyn's room for his seventh and eighth grade classes. He was not anxious to leave Miss Woodson for the man, especially since Lee said the teacher was a hotheaded wielder of the yardstick. He had punished Alan lightly one day with his hand after the boy had mashed Myrtle Moore's nose with a corncob because she was teasing him about Elsie Cronan, an untidy girl with loose, stringy hair and a red face. Alan had not been sorry, however, to see the blood on Myrtle's face. But he had been terrified of the towering man who picked him up and spanked him soundly. Mr. Llewellyn's knee gouged into the boy's stomach. The boys and girls in the schoolyard tittered. Alan was furious. The Cronans were as good as the Moores, and Myrtle had no business making fun of them. But when he saw Elsie Cronan smiling at him, he was angry with her, too, and wished for another cob to mash her nose.

But this morning in the meadow, searching for Buckeye, he let all memory of school go. He was worried about his calf, although having something lost was nothing new to the McDowells. If it wasn't a calf or a cow, it was a pig or a mule. Something was always being misplaced or misplacing itself. Even Lee had been lost once for a day in strange trees on the west side of Walden Ridge. If it hadn't been for the sound of wood-choppers in the distance, he might have stayed lost even longer. Alan had no doubt that Buckeye would be found. Nevertheless, the calf was only a few weeks old, and there were half-wild dogs in the neighborhood, fully capable of killing him.

The boys stopped by a spring trickling out of a mossy bank to quench their thirst. Someone had placed an iron pipe between crevices in the rock, and the water poured in a thin, jerking stream into the boys' mouths as they twisted their heads and looked skyward to catch the cold liquid, so cold it hurt to drink it. Something deeply hidden under the limestone seemed to be pumping the water. A light wind stirred the trees, and from the creek came the scent of sun-warmed branchmint and cedar, both of which strongly-odored plants responded to the sun as the petunias in the yard at home responded to nightfall. The air was racy with perfumes.

Lee had begun to call: "Buckeye, Buuuckeye! Sook, Buckeye!"

The boys entered the shade at the upper end of the meadow and fol-lowed the stream, which entered the mountain field there, a distance back into the immense trees that stood in the narrow valley formed by centuries of running water. It was dusky under the low branches, and still. Only the sound of water murmuring and falling from higher up the cove could be heard. "Sook, Buckeye!" Lee called in the silence. Then he too grew silent, oppressed by the cold quietness of the wood, half expecting something, he didn't know what, to come walking toward them from the trees. "I bet there's a still up there," he whispered. It was common knowledge that moonshiners worked in the coves that split away from Walden Ridge.

The wind hissed a little in the branches. And then, piping clear from somewhere above them, the direction undiscoverable in the grey gloom, an insect fluted the word: "Pharaoh; Pharaoh!" The thin sound chilled the boys, not with fear, but with a foreboding sense of the mystery of things past and present, and both unexplainable. Their mother had told them that the locust, the insect of the plague, cried the name of the Egyptian ruler in remembrance of Moses and the Hebrews in bondage in Egypt.

"Let's get out of here," Lee said.

Alan's arms were knotty with gooseflesh.

The brothers turned and, crossing the stream, followed the opposite bank back down into the meadow. At the edge of the wood, Lee called again, his voice tremulous: "Buckeyeeye! Here, Buckeyeeye!"

Alan appreciated his brother at times like this. Lee had more courage than he had, he admitted to himself. Something like love crept over him at the sight of the thin, nervous body in front of him.

As they passed under a sweetgum tree, whose branches grew almost to the water's edge, a green treesnake, like a necklace dripping through a girl's fingers, looped almost across Lee's face. He struck at the snake furiously. "Bite a man right in the jaw!" he yelled, threshing the leaves. But the snake escaped, twisting from twig to twig as bodilessly as a beam of green light. The tree snake was not dangerous, merely frightening. The grape arbor at home was a favorite hunting place for the thin, leaf-colored reptiles, that often came writhing across their line of vision as the boys gathered the ripe grapes for their mother. It was the suddenness that dismayed, and the fact that a snake was a snake, whatever his kind, with a snake's history. Lee and Alan were well acquainted with what had happened in Eden.

"Old bastard!" Lee said, scrubbing his face with a shirtsleeve.

Nowhere could the boys see any evidence that Buckeye had ever been near the meadow. When they called and listened, there was only a humming sound around them in the sun-dried grasses, where the bees, now that the dew had burned off, were busily gathering nectar, their thighs thick and heavy with pollen.

"Let's split," Lee suggested. "You go toward the swamp where Dad is, and I'll head for the quarry pit. Buckeye might have fallen in there."

South along the ridge, over a mile away, the boys could see the quarry pit gleaming in the sun. Bits of quartz flashed from the broken walls where the county mined stone for the highways.

Alan was a bit reluctant to be separated from his brother, the events of the morning having left him feeling none too confident. But he imagined he could find his father by calling when he approached the swamp. "All right," he said. "I'll see you later on at the house."

He watched Lee walk away into the trees, whistling. Anger seemed to have steadied his brother's nerves. Alan had had no such correction. For a moment, he wished he were going with Lee, but stifled a desire to call "Wait!" because he knew his brother would tease him for being a coward. Then calling became too late. For Lee had crossed the creek.

Alan set out alone toward the swamp. As he moved along in the sunshine, away from the shady trees, his spirit grew warm in his warm body. It was near noon now, and he sat down on a rock to eat the sandwich, which had grown moist and soft from the heat of his body. Nevertheless, the bread and the bacon tasted good, making him think, suddenly, of his mother's small brown hands cooking and wrapping the meat and bread for him to eat. He sometimes thought of her as Ceres, goddess of the gardens and the fields, whose hands held in their small grasp all the true goodness of the world.

Rising from a cold drink which he took directly from the stream, he veered to the right in the direction of the swamp, leaving the meadow behind. Half a mile farther on the creek bent almost at right angles to itself and, because of the slope of the land, flowed northwest for another half mile before ending in the swamp. But before it lost itself in the acre of willows and matted grass, the creek formed a deep marshy pool at the foot of a ledge of limestone. Here, the boys went swimming when they were allowed, and occasionally, when the opportunity presented, without the consent of their parents. Alan was tempted. He stripped and splashed about in the shallow edges of the pool and then lay with his head pillowed on a heap of warm sand, his body stretched out into the water. From this position, the world became one of clouds and sky, fringed with the tops of cattails and green willow trees. Directly above him, the sky was blue and deep. As he gazed, the blue seemed to become granular like a powder he could see through, beyond the outer grains to the inner and on and on to depths he had not realized the sky possessed. The distance he was peering into had nothing to do with space and rocketships. This was an immediate unscientific distance, something that had to do more with color than with miles. The clouds grew up around the blue well of powdery sky, ragged, mountainous clouds, turning from steaming white to brown and occasionally being touched with pink at a faint pulse of lightning. Somewhere a low rumble of thunder filled the air.

Alan dressed and, alarmed now for his calf, went quickly among the willows, calling "Buckeye, Buckeye!" stopping to listen after each call. He felt guilty for pausing at the pool, as though, by forgetting the calf momentarily, he had betrayed him,. His cries, however, brought no response from the dank place, which seemed to lie in a vast, wet stink without beginning or end now that he was surrounded by the stunted, half-drowned growth. "Dad!" he yelled. "Daaaad!" his voice high and piercing. Hearing him, a hawk answered with a scream not unlike his own. Under his feet the earth shook and moved whenever he stepped. He came to and passed by the patch of calamus where he and his mother had once dug calamus roots for his mother's kidney trouble. He called again and again. Thunder rumbled closer now, and Alan saw, to the west above Walden Ridge, dark thunderheads thrusting ominously into the air. Laced around them was a flickering orange edge of lightning. He began to run still calling, "Buckeye! Here, Buckeye!"

The swamp grew still and gloomy as twilight. The water about Alan's feet seemed lighted with circles of color, oily and spreading. He leaped from one hummock to another and, as his feet struck landing, from the water under him a swirling sphere of light began to mount. He screamed in spite of himself at the jack-o-lantern that began to roll and spin away among the bushes. "They belong to haunted places, " his mother had explained to him. He ran heedlessly now, splashing in pools up to his knees, forgetting the water moccasins that might be there.

Nearing the trees on the south side of the swamp, he saw Buckeye huddling against the lee side of a limestone outcrop. Rain was falling heavily as he reached the calf and pulled him into the shelter of the overhanging rock. It made almost a cave. Buckeye pushed against the boy and bawled. Hugging the warm body of the calf, Alan watched the storm bring the swamp to its knees, pounding and whipping the willows to shivering shreds. The whole world seemed to be trying to blow away. Near their sheltering place, somewhere above them in the rocks, lightning struck five times in succession, like so many cannon shots. Never tell me, the boy thought, that lightning doesn't strike twice in the same place. He'd never believe that old plum again.

The storm passed almost as quickly as it had come. The sun came out. Raindrops glistened among the torn green leaves as Alan and Buckeye made their way, damp but warming in the low afternoon sun, towards home. His mother was waiting on the porch, sharp and worried.

"Where have you been?" she demanded.

"Looking for Buckeye," he said, surprised that she should have forgotten. "Where are Dad and Lee?"

At the barn, shucking corn," she said. "They came in hours ago. Lee'll think twice," she added darkly, "before he runs off and leaves you again. I'll take the shirt off his back."

Alan was about to explain that Lee hadn't really run off, that their parting was an agreement. But he knew that Lee, being the older, would always carry the blame. And he knew, suddenly, that he would carry the blame for whatever misdemeanor his younger brother, when and if he arrived, managed to get himself into. That was the way it was. No use to argue about it. He went on toward the barn, leaving his mother scolding on the porch, talking furiously to herself.

8

OSCAR McDowell was a dark man, of whom his sons were afraid, not with the lost fear that comes, even in daylight, from strange trees to grip a child's heart, though it did arise from something of the same source, but with a lively, warm fear that stemmed, first of all, from the vivid coloring of the man. There was something about him of the bitten red of sumac, the bitter black of haws, in the winged ebony hair and the ruddy face that turned deep crimson, almost blue, under the impact of the winter wind. Or when he was deeply stirred with anger. Given to swift, mercurial turns of temper, he could not be trusted to go steadily from hour to hour as Belle, his wife, under ordinary circumstances might be trusted to do. His coloring seemed to change with his mood, not only visibly in the deeply dyed hues of his face, but subtly in his way of speaking, in the altered rhythm of his walk, in the movements of the large, rough hands. So that his sons sensed his temperament as though by electrical discharges from their father's body, though they watched his face as they might have watched a thermometer to tell the weather.

Not that his sons were able to define this sense of supercoloration to themselves, as they would have recognized a red flag as a sign of danger, conventionally established and respected. They only knew that on some mornings, so far as their father was concerned, the wind blew wrong, and they were able to detect, as of some rainy sense in a breeze from the west, the altered nature of the man, and to keep themselves well oriented during the day as to which quarter of their world he stood in.

The name "McDowell," their mother had told them, meant "son of the dark stranger." Her maiden name, "Abernathy," very old and Scotch-Irish like their father's, was the name of a sept of the Scottish Leslie clan. A sept was a family who pledged their allegiance and service to the chief of a clan in return for his protection and the privilege of wearing the clan tartan. If she remembered correctly, she added, the Abernathys had come from an island north of the Irish Sea. When Alan had wondered how she knew these things, she answered, sadly he thought, that she had read them somewhere long ago.

"The name, you might be interested in knowing," she told him, "means 'over the brook.' Just why, I'm not sure. Some fact of ancient family history, I suppose." She remembered, too, that once her father had described the Leslie coat-of-arms as having winged lions and a crown at the crest, and as bearing the motto: "Grip Fast."

"What is a coat-of-arms?" Lee asked.

"A family symbol," Belle answered, "as well-known and recognizable as the family name. Sometimes a man had a coat-of-arms before he had a name even, and he painted the symbol on his shield or had it embroidered on his banner, so he would be known wherever he went."

Such bits of information, scattered and tantalizing as they were, filled Alan with a desire to know more about everything. It seemed to him that even names left their imprint on personality, and now that he knew the meaning of Oscar's name, and his own as well, he could make more of a sensible pattern from his father's moods and the events they precipitated. Young as he was, he was beginning to understand that people are more than the bodies they walk around in. Such a thought filled him with a vague uneasiness, as though he stood in the presence of those airy beings called ghosts, in which he could not bring himself openly to believe but whose evidence seemed at times about to materialize before his eyes. He had an inkling, also, that men came before names, were previous to any personal tag of identification they might be given. For he had been fearful of his father from his first memory of him.

Perhaps it was that he had always been envious of his father. He remembered the great roan animal which Oscar had led to water at the cress-filled stream in the pasture. Alan had been, perhaps, two-and-a-half years old, and at the time had been only loudly afraid, wailing to see the stout-horned bull that was somehow the symbol of the strength and wildness of the world being mastered by the small man, who played out his wild charge on the rope as fate might play with us all, now giving, now withdrawing, but always master, the sense of freedom and of slack notwithstanding. Alan's bawling had brought his mother into the yard to rescue him from his first memorable experience. Later, at the barn while his father milked, he remembered creeping away and peering through the slats on the shed door into the darkness where the bull stood, massive, almost blue in color, his heavy head swinging near the ground at his feet. But it was the eyes he recalled most vividly, expressionless animal eyes that shone like oil in the darkness. From that time, he had loved and feared the great animals, and always in association with them, leading them as

Alan himself, had he possessed one, might have pulled a toy, was his father.

Somehow the memory of that hour in the pasture never left Alan and formed a real barrier between him and the man. Even on the night when his father came home, bringing with him his son's first gifts, outside that of life on this earth, a gay red bucket and a child's spade, the accessories of a rich man's son down beside the shining sea, Alan accepted them fearfully, the dark, vivid look of his father burning down upon him and outweighing the bright figures that danced around the painted sides of the pail. It was the first thing the boy had ever owned. Later, he learned that the lady who had sent these things to him was soon to die giving birth to her second son, born by Caesarean operation, after two previous children, a boy and a girl, had been carried stillborn from her tortured presence. Out of love for a child that was never hers, she had given the colored gifts to him. It was from the spade and pail, whose color burned scarlet into his memory, that his love for all things deeply hued might be said to stem: the color of hollyhocks, cosmos, and morning-glories, and the deep, precious hue of blood that filled him always with an unreasoning exaltation and at the same time, a respectful fear, as if the secret of life itself were in the deep tonalities of the red. And always with the sense of blood came the impression of the white lady in the white bed, whose sheets glimmered coldly like snow, in an immensity of colorlessness. Even the head and foot of the bed had been enamelled white. So that the picture Alan could now draw was one of impeccable pallors, stared through, delineated by, the brilliant ruddy face of his father, as though his mind through piecemeal memory prepared from selected pieces a fabulous collage of his earliest consciousness. Dominating the remembered scenes, however, was the presence of his father, whose face and figure burned straight into the texture of the rough walls against which the memory was laid. Alan imagined he could see him yet in the yellow smother of lamplight, and seeing him, was made afraid, inchoately desperate, as if he realized that danger was always inherent in the scarlet flowers and dark, dynamic characters of this earth. To be safe, the boy had long ago decided, was to be mousy and afraid, to retire willingly even into the colorlessness of the dying woman on the bed.

But with his growing knowledge, safety was not easy. Born to the color as he was of two who had changed the earth for him because they were more than ordinarily in it, how could he be mousy and afraid, even if he practiced the self-withdrawal he now began to seek in his own mind and in the silent seclusion of the schoolroom. For him, the world was too vital and alive to be so lightly chucked away. Yet he was afraid of the world, the fantastically set stage on which his mother, even she, had made an unexplained entrance.

His first remembrance of Belle, for example, showed him a slight young woman walking in an unknown wood, lifting her hands to the leaves, as if she were going through some wondrous, adult ritual which he could never understand. He followed her in childish amazement, only half-sure she was his mother. He remembered they went on and on in trees to where a stream began in a grove of sycamores and willows. And there the sun entered a little field and some old trees were blinding white against the hot blue sky. Kneeling, his mother lifted water to her face and wet her hair. It was as if some consummation had occurred, some stage and spectacular moment had arrived. It was, he could realize now, his first theater, the first play he had ever seen; and it was the reason, no doubt, he loved plays at school. For despite his mother's love of what she did, and without any question as to the authenticity of her action, it had served to instill in her son a love of the ritualistic that would go beyond reason, so that, if he should ever get into heaven at all, it would be by ritual and not by any hard cognizance of the baptismal fact.

But, then, squatting in the grass, looking his first upon the cedar waters of that country, he saw her pale hands gleam softly in the cold, blue spring and was made afraid by the astounding color of his new world. And for no more reason, he began to cry. His mother never spoke to him, but took him by the hand and led him home to his father waiting in an orange-red sundown beside the barn, milk buckets gleaming like silver in his hands. But because his mother was gentle with him, he had developed no fear of her. Only at times, when she was sharp and worried, he could sense a bitterness in her, a hollowness, as of something unfulfilled, a wish gone wrong, that made him afraid, not of her but for her and for himself as if there were not only battles among the actors in the drama life was, but sometimes also a real set-to between the players and the scenery.

The difference between his father and his mother, Alan felt, was the difference of words, the fact, for instance, that his mother found words to describe the miracle of the bucket and spade. He trusted in words. He began to live for words then, for the first time, when his mother described his gift in terms of names and colors; for previously he could not remember any speech at all. He believed he loved his mother because of her words and that he did not understand his father because his father had none, or did not use any that he could really comprehend beyond the daily patterns. But Oscar's very silence made him the center of another kind of love and respect altogether; in his wordlessness he was strong. Alan's mother might with words make color drip and cry; his father could with words make, not only color, but the forces of darkness and evil as well, appear and disappear in a chameleon world like a magician practicing a sleight of hands.

That these forces were in and of his father's own nature, Alan seemed to recognize; the world, for him as for most of us, centered in the light and darkness of the human beings that surrounded him. Let the universe not care, let it not be concerned with human life any more than with the life of the worm; that is the prerogative of the universe. And its shortcoming; for in its failure to care lies its translation into the myth that has been powerfully told by man of the mother nature in things, the imposition, as it were, of man's frail sex upon the mechanical government of the stars. Under them a son is given, who, in turn, gives to them the significance of an added, an extra, existence: that of a benign or malicious influence upon the fortunes of a gratuitous child. Confused, irrational: any boy, upon second thought, would grant that. But we deliberately, in the rich mesh of consciousness, which throws out feelers to the utmost limits of our dominion, which is all, grant to ourselves eternally the opulent centrality of our desire. And our first desires are lodged, warmly and incestuously, in the bodies of our parents who, like the eagles in a more golden thread of the tapestry, give their blood for our feasting. The boy finds in his father his beginning and periphery, and in his mother his center and circumference; and these dimensions from point to outpost, are the universe. And so become, through the personal characteristics of those who furnish them, the universal attitude towards the living mote named the human mind. The universe, as such, does not and will never count. Only sons and daughters, and their sons and daughters, furnish the sky with any place to fall.

And Alan, in his creation of the universe, was about to witness to the one flaw in his composition, was about to go from stars to barn to messenger on the road; from love and fear to great love, final love, and the fear that has no name, but of which death is the fearless manifestation.

"Belle," Oscar was calling softly from the doorway. "Belle, Reuben is dead."

"Oh, Lord! Poor Kate!" Belle began to cry, thinking of Reuben's mother. "When did he die?"

"This morning," Oscar said, "about five o'clock. Lance just came to tell us. He's down at the barn now."

Alan raced to the barn. His Uncle Lance was leaning against a gatepost, staring at the ground. Lee was shelling corn, automatically, as though he could not stop. The bin under the sheller's spout was too full already. It began to run over. The corn was wasting. The soft sliding noise of the grains falling upon themselves brought the grinder out of his trance. His lips quivered.

"Is . . . is . . . ?" Alan began to ask the useless question.

Lee nodded mutely, pointing towards the uncle by the fence.

Alan knelt and began to pick up the corn, very carefully, blowing it clean with his breath.

"Boys," Oscar said, coming into the entry, "your mother wants you."

He walked to his brother and touched him on the shoulder. "Lance," he said, "we'll be there this afternoon."

At the house, Belle told the boys to wash themselves clean. She seemed to insist on cleanliness with an emphasis she had never used before. "From head to foot," she said. "Scrub, and no pretending." Her eyes were red from weeping.

Curiously, Alan experienced none of the grief his mother was obviously feeling. Neither was he upset without grief as Lee was. He seemed only to be detached from events, a cold observer bothered with a cold tune in his head, a counting-out game which he had played with Reuben the last afternoon they were together.

> *Wire, brier, limber-lock,*
> *Three geese in a flock:*
> *One flew east, one flew west,*
> *and one flew over the cuckoo's nest.*
> *O-u-t, out goes he.*

His cousin had become angry because he was always counted out. "You don't play fair," he had told Alan. "I couldn't be It everytime."

"I'm not cheating," Alan said. "That's the way it comes out."

But Reuben had refused to play. Now the ring-song would not stop repeating itself in Alan's mind. Over and over it went, singsong, like a needle stuck on a phonograph record. "Three geese in a flock. One flew east . . . O-u-t, out goes he." "I won't play, I couldn't be It everytime."

He tried to imagine his cousin lying still on a bed, all the anger drained out of him, his face white and dropped under its living expression. But there was too much energy in him. "Cheater!" Reuben screamed. "You don't play fair! I know you don't play fair!"

"Lie still," Alan told him, a horror beginning to grow up in his mind. "You're dead. D-e-a-d! You're out. O-u-t!"

"I won't be dead," yelled Reuben. "I couldn't be it everytime!"

Was death, Alan wondered, like being buried in cotton? Lee had buried him once under the soft dusty stuff and when he tried to breathe, it had clung to his nose like a fluffy stopper. He had come up, flailing his fists at his brother's chest, choking with dust and anger. Lee had run, awed at his unusually mild brother's assault. Death could be like that.

In the single-seated buggy, behind Old Ranger, the family made a load too heavy for one animal to pull. But the mules were in the pasture, and Oscar was in a hurry. There was no time to drive them in and hitch up the wagon. By taking his time, the horse could make it. "We'll drive slow," he said. "The boys and me will walk up the hills." Not once, however, did Ranger falter, plodding straightaway into the afternoon as steadily as time itself, topping the last rise before they reached the house with a hard breath, but not faltering. From the hilltop, encircled by a white cloud mass that seemed another kind of woodland, acreless and snowy, they could see, at the end of the downgrade, the house and a small knot of people gathered in the roadway.

Alan had begun to panic. His hands, cold in his lap, were clammy with sweat. his mouth felt dry, his lips thick. He noticed that Lee was standing straight, even importantly, a set, grown-up look on his face that seemed at odds with the young features. Miserably, he glanced at his mother. She was straining forward, as though her eyes were already inside the room where the dead boy lay. He knew that she had forgotten him.

It was his father who pushed him inside the house, saying, without any apparent reference, "This is him." Whether he meant to show the dead boy to Alan or Alan to the dead boy, no one could tell. In the cold dither of the room, stumbling on cricket boards where the honeysmell of sunrotted old pine mixed with the scent of camphor, Alan saw Reuben, lying on the bed, without energy, uncomplaining, two silver coins on his eyes. A neighbor dipped a cloth in a dish of soda water and bathed the dead boy's face. Belle stood with her arms around her sister-in-law, both women weeping industriously.

"This is him," his father said again, nobody acknowledging the introduction.

In the room, full of the sounds of summer flies and bad colds, shouldered by clutches of ornamental grasses come from God knows where, Alan viewed his cousin, the small, pale master, opulent-eyed, who seemed with his silver stare to be assaying the live boy, looking him up and down, until Alan could no longer bear it. He looked away, through the window, into the bare yard, where a tuft of grass helped him to stature in this new community. The dime in his pocket scalded his thigh.

Then the train, bending radiantly through the mountains, spoke, mangling magnificence of summer with unseasonal reason concerning the planetary perturbation on the bed, the child with moons, convener of solo journeys: "Under the coin is the other side only, under the coin is the other side only, underthecoin, underthecoin, underthecoin!" Alan began to weep as his father pushed him on into the next room.

In his dream it was morning, and in the dream he looked into a mirror to see whether his face was grave or shone with the night's tremendous barge of dreams, always hooting him sleepward; but he saw only his face, smooth and well-formed, suggesting merely a child with chocolate eyes and a half-caught frown, intently staring. But not at himself. He saw himself only in passing, an image of an image, seeing behind his eyes other eyes that looked out from behind eyes farther on. "What was he looking for?" he asked himself. "A dream?" If so, he found only a child's face with head

57

enough to fathom it was not a face at all but a mask for faces revealing other faces through an infinity of seeming endlessly back to the door of what he sought.

And that door was silver on black, water and isinglass and white ice, behind which spotted parrots and red-gilled monkeys and mice—ah, the beautiful mice!—in gray muffs of corn shouted in the darkness: "Come in! Come in! It's snowing, it's snowing, it's snowing!" But not loud enough for him to hear. Only a wavy light from the beveled edges of the mirror shook the shadow of faces, as silver eyes peered out in multiple rings from silver eyes farther on, as self discovered self discovered self in the maze of his neverlasting dreams, always hooting him dayward, as he found in the shape of his head the ultimate of dreaming repeated backward, always backward, into the heart of darkness.

He turned on his side and slept again, deeply but briefly, and then as from a printed page he read an old copy of another dream, he entered the next phase of the night's business, repeating himself, telling himself even while dreaming that he had dreamed this dream before, only that before the dream had not been prepared for, only stimulated by, encouraged by an old man with dust in his eyes, who had shown him his treasures in a high brown room. He recognized the mill before he entered the meadow.

The meadow was full of lush grasses, clutched from God knows where outside the county, for none of their like grew normally here. Richly ornamental, opulently leafy, green, gray, green-tipped, feathered with the gray dust of bloom like the dust of ground corn, they waved their branches in the sun of the meadow like miniature forests of some tropical nature, odorous as the thyme and sage in his mother's garden, smelling faintly too like the taste of baking soda. There was the darker green of the leaves of outlandish violets, and the lighter green of dandelion leaves, and all the unknown blades and tassels, blue, silver, shadowed, light with the pallor of lavender, egg shell, and gold.

He stood again knee-deep in the starry vegetation while the dark ungilded train came, not gliding but rocking, blowing trumpets, ringing bells, uncoiling the sound of chains, as for the letting down of some heavy object, over the gold and blue flowers, whose petals he thumbed while the dark train thumbed his entrails. "Who let him down? Who let him down? I said the crane with my little silver chain, O it was I!"

On came the train, past the lead-colored box of the station that, he noticed now, wore a spire like a high hat, and its own bell pealing. "All aboard!" shouted the man with his head stuck through a window, only the window now was the window of the church. He heard the sound of hammering and sawing in the church, and wondered what they might be making.

The train was almost upon him now, rocking out of the depth of the meadow, rearing and plunging like a rockinghorse that looked very much like Old Ranger, while the various heads of the rich tapestry that was the meadow stood at attention, not speaking, from the press of the crowd, inflexibly, expectantly civil, stiffly upright, while over them the train passed without image, wrinkling no bloom.

In his surprise, Alan saw that the cars were all pine boxes, plainly rectangular, all but the front two, the double engines, which were shaped like a human body, head and shoulders approaching first. "Hellohellohello!" said the smart train, slowing down beside him. A door opened in the side of one of the cars, and someone put down a rabbit-box. The man with his head stuck through the church window snickered. And suddenly all the blue and gold flowers in the meadow exploded as the sky began to fall. He wore with the same gigantic sneeze and lay still in the warm groove his body had made in the bed, the strange feeling of having been playing just recently in a familiar place with Reuben heavy upon him.

9

THE road approached the graveyard through a depth of trees. On all sides of the clearing the trees stood equally deep, so that the church and its grounds seemed a summer pocket to those who arrived there from the close shade. Rambler roses, with their gone-to-seed color and perfume, suggesting a family too long concerned with marrying its own cousins, ran the sagging fence; here and there a woodbine added a more pedigreed hue. Among the stones in the older half of the cemetery grew several ancient cedars, their ribbed trunks the color of a paperwasp's nest, the ground beneath them covered with tracery of myrtle still bearing, in midsummer, a sporadic lilac bloom. The stones here were almost uniform in shape, and more slablike in design than otherwise; weathered to grayness, they leaned like ruined teeth in a rake across the green carpet of the myrtle. Above them, the cedars were almost blue by contrast, the green changed by the frosty cedarberries to a sullen color that contrasted lightly but stubbornly with the mid-July sun that tried to illuminate it. That was the word most apt for the church and its surroundings: it seemed illuminated, from the white clapboards to the last rose in the farthest corner of the half-acre. There was, too, a honeysmell of old pineboards mixed with the more stringent odor of cedar, as though together they made an oil which had mummified the premises into a kind of set picture, secluded, womblike, unlikely to change. Above the front door of the church was a board bearing the words: Founded 1826.

The McDowells were buried in the new part of the graveyard, except for one great grandfather whose dates showed him to be the first member of the family ever to be interred in the grounds of Friendship Church. Perhaps by the time of his death, the older section had grown too full of graves and his was the last possible to be crowded in. Around his thin, worn stone, dated 1801-1889, there were others still more worn and bearing more ancient dates. The oldest among them read: Isaac Reed, 1794-1856. Inspecting the stone, as he had done many times before, Alan knew Isaac Reed had come to Walden Valley before Tennessee had been admitted to statehood. The old section of the graveyard fascinated him, giving him a greater sense of history than he could manage to get from history books. Here lay the perished hands of those who had felled the trees and guided the plows in the beginning of the valley. Here were those who had borne the sons and daughters, sung the ancient hymns, laughed and wept their lives out in the vague, suspect past before he was born. Here were the children, too, their status denoted by the size of their stones among the other graves, who, like Reuben, had died before they had lived.

From the church he heard the congregation singing "In the Sweet Bye and Bye," and moved farther away, down the old section and across the center road into the new. Here, he could still hear the singing, but only faintly. Around him lay the McDowells, fully a dozen of them: grandparents, uncles, aunts, cousins. He stared at a pile of raw clay heaped up at the end of an angling row of graves. Here was Reuben's. He walked to the edge and stared down into the red earth; a bit of water had seeped into the bottom of the grave, an opening crowded between the graves of two adult McDowells, small and almost unobservable except for the pile of clay. On the grass nearby lay a forgotten gravedigger's tool. For some reason he could not explain, Alan took the mattock and hid it behind a large gravestone in another plot.

The song at the church had changed to "God Be With You 'Til We Meet Again." Afterwards, he could hear quite clearly the preacher's words borne on the summer air: "Man born of woman is of few days and full of trouble . . . Let not your hearts be troubled; ye believe in God, believe also in me . . . The Lord giveth and the Lord taketh away."

Then the preacher forgot texts. He spoke to them of the boy. "Rejoice," he said, "that he has gone away in his childhood, before life touched him with the real sickness of men, the loss of faith, not in God, but in the beauty and goodness of living." Men could lose their faith in living, he said, and retain their faith in God. But they were already dead souls, waiting only for their earthly parts to be buried to come into their rewards, which, the Lord knew, would be small. "Heaven," he pointed out to the mourning congregation, "is only the remembered best of earth. The treasures we lay at the feet of God are compounded of the excellent things we have, through God's grace, managed to find about us in His created world. Even the colors, the tastes, the scents of this earth," he said, "will there be only magnified; so that we build our heaven or lose it as we go along." His voice dropped into silence.

Inside the church there was a low, scuffing sound which Alan knew meant the congregation was moving past the open coffin. This was the part he could not have stood. The more he had thought of looking again at Reuben's dead face, the more he had rebelled. His mother, shocked, had argued with him, to no avail. He simply could not, he would not do it; not if he were disgraced forever, as she said he would be.

Now he heard weeping and knew the coffin was being carried in his direction. He moved farther away and stood against the fence, watching. For some reason the receiving box had been left on open ground. The men carrying the narrow white coffin placed it carefully in the larger yellow box, which, Alan thought, was a little too faded to be new. Wondering whether it had come from Mr. Wyatt's pine store over the mill, he saw them lower the body of his cousin into the gaping red hole prepared for it.

Reuben's mother wept loudly, accompanied by Belle and the other women. The men, stern and self-contained, gazed away from each other, out over the cemetery to the woods beyond. The preacher prayed: "O Lord, receive this boy into thy care. His stay on earth was short, but his sojourn in heaven will be only the longer for his having left us, his grieving parents and friends so soon. Make his heaven bright, Lord, inasmuch as the earth he left was bright for him. This we ask in Jesus' name. Amen."

The women led Reuben's mother away. The men began to fill in the grave with quick, heavy shovelfuls of the red clay. Two young girls, cousins of the dead boy, waited with bunches of flowers in their hands.

Alan turned away from the grave, feeling as though all about him was a presence he would like to strike with his fists if only he could tell what and where it was. Returning to the buggy, he waited for the long condolences to be over.

10

THE room Alan and Lee slept in was the second large room in the house, there being, besides the lean-to kitchen which served for cooking and eating, only the front, or sitting room, left in the building. For the reason that Belle had lived in her childhood in a house whose kitchen was a smaller outhouse in the corner of the yard, she referred to her front room as the "big house," and from her Alan had learned to say when he had finished sweeping all the floors that he had "swept all the houses." In school he had learned that rich houses in early America practiced the separation of kitchen from main building, possibly, Miss Woodson had said, to keep the living quarters free from the smell of the preparation and cooking of food.

The McDowell house was more like a frontier cabin, in which, Alan knew from his reading and the pictures he had seen in history books, one room was all rooms combined. He already knew the difference between the tidelands and the mountains, with the long, socially graduated piedmont between.

Sometimes Alan felt like celebrating the house in which he had been born, not because it had witnessed the entrance of a prodigy into the world, nor because it had sheltered the birth of a monster. But because, like other houses, it was the backdrop of a human advent into the kaleidoscopic world, of a child possessed of his senses in a degree of normalcy the world, despite its gradations, has always praised. An ordinary child in an ordinary house, with the praise of life for both.

But the house had laid varying impressions upon his child mind.

First of all, it had cheap windows. Magic in a cheap window that refracted the world he looked out upon, as if enchantment were reduced in price for the son of a dirt farmer, who could ill afford magic at that, if the window was ever broken. His attachment to the romantic schools of life was as assuredly gained through that window that gave on the bare backyard of his house as it would have been had he been permitted to gaze first upon the world through the splendid rose glass of some glazed and unique old mansion.

The window made long, wavy motions in the earth; it transformed the space between the side walls and the chicken yard into a somber ocean that ran off with long swells into the stunted trees. And when he changed positions, the waves changed. Without knowing anything about tides, at three years, by a swift changing of his stand at the window, he could make them come and go, without reference to the moon, which body, then as it would continue to do as he grew into boyhood, had filled him with a hollow sense of ghostliness and fear.

He would stand for long intervals staring, through the window, until his head swam, and he could stare no more.

Then the chimney intrigued him, especially in winter, for then in the cold, he could see from a distance the rising smoke which told him his mother was there, waiting, tending the fire. Often he began to run when he sighted the chimney.

It was a curious construction, built half-way up with clay and rocks from the fields and boasting on top a shining half of corrugated drainpipe from the county road, a glorious crown made of the proper stuff of a culvert. It was this crown that made their chimney different from all other chimneys in the neighborhood, and made him always turn his eyes in that direction whenever, as a young child, he was allowed outside the yard to play in the sloping pasture. The chimney made the McDowells different, and Alan, for one, took proper pride in thinking that what they had was in no wise similar to that of the neighbors.

In summer a great rosevine blossomed on the front porch, climbing the posts and spreading over the roof. His father wanted to cut it down because the growing tendrils pushed between the boards and caused the porch to leak. But Alan and his mother opposed Oscar, successfully, but only to the extent of the porch; any vine seen reaching towards the main roof had to be chopped off immediately. And Alan, in early summer, was often on the rooftop checking the green growth. From there, he could look down into the yard, overgrown with flowers, where hollyhock, cosmos, old maids, four-o-clocks, and a profusion of other blooms turned the small enclosure into a garden. Since the demise of Can-Can, with the exception of the chickens that flew over the paling fence to scratch in the shade of the flowers, no intruder played havoc with Belle's plants. From the roof Alan could see the dairy, an underground room in which his mother kept milk and foodstuffs, in a corner of the yard, its red-clay covering grown over with cosmos and pepper plants. His mother always planted pepper there, and in autumn, with the peppers turned red and the cosmos mixing its colors with the stringy scarlet pods, the dairy was a sight to behold. Outside the fence, Alan could see the spring where, in the hottest weather, Belle kept the milk in great stone crocks tied up with cloths and weighted with plates on which she placed clean stones.

Alan loved it all and would not have traded it for anything he knew.

His room itself was heavily insulated against the summer heat and the winter cold by a thick overlay of old newspapers pasted to the walls. He called the room his library. Here, he had been born, opening his eyes first of all to the plain hieroglyphics of the English tongue, perhaps the least ornate alphabet in the world. And here, as he grew able to read, he found the accounts of battles ringing with French names; and under them the little heroisms of San Juan Hill and the bluff, sullen chronicles of Shiloh and Atlanta. Here, he would spend rainy hours, reading, deciphering the shields and bosses of his native speech; and here, on a crude shelf he himself had tacked to the wall were the few books he had been able to bring together: an old copy of *Pilgrim's Progress*, his mother's copy of *The History of Tennessee*, medical books that had belonged to his Grandfather Abernathy, *The Titanic*, a coverless Bible stories, Lee's old geography, *A Dog of Flanders*, and copies of *Comfort Magazine, The Key to Happiness in a Million Farm Homes*, which he had saved because of the Cubby Bear stories.

Over the shelf was a picture, the only one in the room, which Belle had found somewhere. It was a copy of the Madonna of the Chair, the mother stooping, tightly circumferenced over her child and the child's visitor. Alan had wondered whether the other child was a brother until he read the story of the painting in a book Miss Woodson gave him at school, discovering in the process why the painting was round. The artist had sketched it on a barrelhead.

Around the painting, in lieu of a frame, his mother had sewn an edging of black velvet from a bundle of remnants she had bought for quilting. Finished, inside their ebony borders, the pure blue and the rich scarlet seemed as if a sky fell and a poppy bloomed. But most of all the clear flesh colors of the hands and faces were incredible.

A picture of his Grandfather had once hung on the wall at the foot of the bed, but he had balked at the stern eyes, and his mother had taken the picture away into the front room, where it now stared darkly at him as he entered the door. Perhaps his mother's stories about his grandfather had been partly responsible, for in them he appeared a strangely contradictory person, learned himself, but careless about the education of his children, for one thing. Belle loved his memory but was bitter about her lack of schooling, which she attributed to this indifference in her father. She hinted darkly, too, that women had pursued him and that he had not been averse to their pursuit. Being a doctor had exposed him, Belle said, to the worst in women.

This darkly handsome man had also been a preacher and a teacher, the latter profession being one of the major impediments to Belle's understanding of why her father had neglected to send his own children to school. Among the family's possessions were his grandfather's books and, in a worn leather case whose edges were beginning to show the wood of the framework beneath, there was his stethoscope, coiled stiffly now in its place in the box, unable to be unwound. The velvet with which the box was lined was a blue velvet color slowly turning crimson with time. Owned, too, was the scruple with which, on a long vanished balance, he had weighed his drugs; the family had as well his Odd Fellow lapel button and a finger-ring.

It was the account of his grandfather's preaching that Alan liked most of all. He must have been a malicious man, Belle said, for he deliberately preached big words to his mountain congregation to confuse them, and smiled about it afterwards. He would mention unheard-of-places from his reading; the Hellespont, for example; possibly because his own name was Joseph Leander. And perhaps, Belle said, because he considered himself a ridge-running hero. His congregation considered him a show-off. Alan always laughed to imagine him coming with his medicines, physical, mental, or spiritual in his mountain poke, glad to be there, happy in his polysyllabic assistance, feeling assured and superior among his patients, patrons, and parishioners. "He was," Belle admitted, "a big fish in a little pond." Alan was of the opinion that this grandfather of his would have been a big fish anywhere.

"He was so different from my poor mother," Belle explained. "He never cared about the material things of life. Whether he collected a fee for his doctoring did not matter to him. He would go time after time to doctor people who never gave him more than a half bushel of dried peas or a gallon of molasses in payment." In growing bitterness, she added: "People ate us out of house and home. They would come from miles around to get their pills and plasters, or to be married, and then stay all day. And mother would have to kill the last chicken in the yard to prepare dinner for them. That's what I had to put up with."

Alan knew from his mother's chronicles that she had been one of thirteen children, and that his grandmother had been largely responsible for the welfare of the six among them she had been able to nurture to maturity. "The last thing I heard at night," Belle said, "and the first thing in the morning was the sound of my mother's spinning wheel, or her hammer as she half-soled our brogan shoes. Without her, we would have starved and frozen to death. Much as I loved him, he was not a good husband and father." She had returned, as she always did, to the larger, more magnificent memory of her father.

These stories, no doubt, had influenced Alan in his reaction to his grandfather's picture. Now that the picture had been removed, however, and he was not forced to wake to it each morning, he found himself at times standing before the crayon portrait and studying it. Only his grandfather's face. The proud, calm face of his grandmother, beautiful but set and determined as stone, did not interest him. Slightly behind her husband's shoulder, she stared, axe-clean, against the probabilities of the future, completely unafraid, while his grandfather's eyes were already daunted, full of high hopes and fears even at the time of his marriage. He was always seeing ghosts, Belle had told Alan. He was a hag-ridden man. Whether she meant by her last remark, ghosts, witches, or his hypochondriac flock of women patients, Belle refused to say.

About his father's people, except for the uncles and their families, Alan knew nothing, for Oscar's mother had died when Oscar was eight and his father had been killed when the boy was in his thirteenth year. He had heard Oscar say that Grandmother McDowell had died of tuberculosis, and that his grandfather had been killed while tending a threshing machine. Someone taking fish illegally from the river had hidden dynamite in a shock of wheat. Grandfather McDowell had been feeding the thresher when the explosive entered the machinery and blew a threshing tooth through the man's breast. Oscar did not talk much about such things. Alan had learned, so far as his paternity was concerned, to put bits of information together into a coherent pattern. He did know from his mother, however, that there was no stone in Clear Springs Cemetery to mark the spot where the McDowells were buried. "It is a shame," Belle said, "that those boys have spent enough money to erect a monument to the memory of their parents. And now they don't even know where they lie."

Nevertheless, the little that Alan knew about the McDowells was also alive in the house; moreover, because he knew little, his imagination enlarged the bare facts of his father's people, so that in his mind's eye they loomed larger in many ways than the millers and farmers he knew them to have been. Mr. Wyatt had told him once that his great-grandfather, Milburn McDowell, had been one of the best mill-wrights in the country. Mr. Wyatt's own father had told his son so. "I thought you might like to know, Alan," the miller had said. "For later on."

So the room was also a library of people, a gallery of real, pictured, and imaginary faces; such a room might, with proper provocation from the outside, enlarge the horizons of a county-bound boy and become a link between the past and future through the alchemy of the present. Alan felt this, though he could not have set his thoughts down in words. At going on twelve, the world was mostly feeling, shapeless and mercurial almost as changing cloud patterns that were, one moment, a castle; the next, a fish; the next, a horse's head; the next, a rising, tossing wave of some never-glimpsed ocean.

11

THE sun rose as usual, Alan noticed, after the day of the funeral. Lying beside Lee, quietly accepting the fact that no one is indispensable to the machinery of the great clockwork of the sun, Alan heard the clock strike seven. Odd that Oscar should have allowed them to stay so long in bed. About the house there was the air of an extended holiday. After it finished striking, the clock sounded again as if a spring had slipped.

Through the door leading into the front room, Alan could see the clock on the table under the window. It was a marbleized affair, the one gorgeous possession, he thought, the McDowells owned; though he did wonder whether there really was a stone that was gold in color and veined with a rich rusty vein that was almost black. Built like a fine house, the clock had two Corinthian columns on each side of its face that made him think of the classic front supports he had seen on buildings in pictures of the civilization of ancient Greece. The clock was fly-specked, its color flaking away as it might actually have done if the clock had been a real building exposed to the erosions of the weather.

Alan knew the history of the clock, as he knew the history of everything in the house that had a recountable history. Bought secondhand in a jeweler's shop in Cleveland, the clock had cost his father four dollars, money he could ill afford even for time. But it was money that could not have been spent more esthetically so far as Alan was concerned, for in the plain house the clock became the one object of beauty that became a cult with him and his mother, who washed and polished its gilt surface endlessly and complained of the flies that came through the torn screens at the windows and gradually dimmed its luster by years of acidulous specking.

But its sound was as good as ever. Alan liked to think of its round face as a door opening into morning, noon, and night. He listened in wakefulness at night to hear its bell-like strokes counting the hours by.

Or paused to count the strokes whenever the clock struck in his hearing. This morning he wondered whether the clock was indeed giving out, as Belle said it was. Everything, she was constantly reminding him, wears out. "We start wearing out the day we are born," she said.

It was not a happy thought, and one that Alan tried to dismiss.

From the barn came the sound of a rooster crowing. Cows lowed, hogs grunted. It is late, Alan thought, shaking Lee awake.

His brother yawned sleepily, then lay quiet. "What did Reuben die of?" he asked.

It suddenly occurred to Alan that, not only did he not know what had killed their cousin, he had never even thought to inquire. The thought puzzled him. Was death a fact that rendered useless anything that went before it? Certainly Reuben's death has disassociated him momentarily from much of his own living. He had not yet accepted the fact of the boy with the coins on his eyes, not altogether; but he had not thought to connect the death of his cousin with any previous state or condition.

"I don't know," Alan said. "Maybe mother does."

The brothers lay staring at the ceiling until their father, coming in from the barn, called, "Time to hit the floor, boys."

"Why didn't you call us to help?" Lee asked, seeing the full milk pail on the table. Being allowed to sleep while the chores were done was a luxury he was not accustomed to.

"Sleeping late one day in the year won't hurt you," his father said. "Get washed for breakfast."

There was genuine kindness in Oscar's tone, a disabling gentleness, to which neither the father nor the sons could well adjust. The boys would be glad when the holiday air disappeared from the house, and life could resume its old way of aggression and defense. With his awkward new posture, Oscar was not recognizable. He felt his own awkwardness and became irritated. "Godamighty!" he said. "Do I have to tell you a dozen times?"

At the table, Lee asked, "Mom, what did Reuben die of?"

"Summer dysentery," his mother replied. "He wasted to death through his bowels."

Oscar, still uncomfortable, said, "I told you boys about those green apples. Now maybe you'll listen to me."

After breakfast, Oscar started back to the barn. In the yard, he saw John Wade's big bronze rooster that daily crossed the creek from the adjoining farm and tolled the McDowell hens into his own yard, where they dropped their eggs in nests inaccessible even to Alan's gift of discovery. Oscar was furious. Eggs were a hard, materialistic fact in a hard, almost immaterial time. He picked up a hoe and with the handle struck across the red-gold feathers of the rooster's neck, hushing his invitation. Alan, watching from beyond the hollyhocks, saw his father pick up the dead bird, nervously, and then fling it down again.

"Lee!" Oscar called. "Come here. I've got a job for you."

Lee came, and at his father's direction, took the bright, crumpled bird in his hands and disappeared uphill with him, beyond the fringe of trees, into the wheatfield that crowned the farm.

Since the rooster was gone, and the hens herded at home, Alan found the number of eggs at night appreciably increased. His father looked less apoplectic when he counted them, and even his mother smiled.

But two days later, while the McDowells were at breakfast, there came a crazy, gobbling sound from the direction of the wheatfield. It was not a rooster's normal alarm, but a thick broken cry that left the diners thoroughly startled. Oscar looked at Belle, and then both of them looked at Lee, whose mouth, arrested in the motion of chewing, gave him an odd, senseless look.

"That's Old Shag, or Old Shag's ghost," Oscar said. "Did you bury him?"

"I just threw him in the wheat," Lee said. "He was good and dead."

"He never was good, and he ain't dead," his father said, flatly. "After breakfast, you go attend to him, and properly this time. I don't want him back down here. Wade's already beginning to wonder what happened to his precious rooster."

"Did he say anything when you saw him?" Belle asked.

"Only that he thought a coon had been getting his eggs lately," Oscar said, grinning at her. "Alan, you go with Lee this time, and help him."

Back up the hill Lee went, accompanied by his brother. They found the rooster huddling in the wheat, blind from the blow Oscar had laid across his bright, nervous neck. The bird started up sightlessly, hearing them, a dark and red and gold fumbling in the forest of straws. His head pivoted to all points of the compass; his feet stretched awkwardly to touch the hidden ground. Gobbling in defiance, he struck a fighting attitude.

But Lee did not hesitate, being the child of his father. He crashed into the rooster with his young hands, fighting the thresh and beat of the bird until he found the feet, and then, sitting almost on the golden spread of the wing, like a gnome squatting on a golden pallet, with a field stone he beat the head into silence and blood.

Alan, his mother's child, fled downhill, seeing around him in the trees and over and under him in the sky and in the grass, a terrible mosaic of flaring neck feathers and a crooked, bleeding beak. Never again, he felt would he feel exactly related to his obedient brother.

12

IN late June the thresher had come and stood spouting wheatstraw in the barnyard like a rickety old dinosaur spitting twigs from between its teeth. The faded red body of the machine with its long galvanized neck dominated the mind and movement of the farm for half a day before it moved on to another barnyard and another harvest.

From a spout in the side of the thresher poured a small stream of shiny golden seeds, bread-tasted and chewy in the mouths of the workers; seeds that would eventually find their way to Mr. Wyatt's mill and return as white flour to furnish the McDowells with their winter's bread. A choice remnant would, of course, be saved for the next planting. With the wheat as with the corn, the best was always saved to start the new generation. And without knowing it, Oscar was helping the process of evolution in a time and place which would have rejected the thought as blasphemy. For among the older people in Walden Valley, and here they were still in full control, the idea of an evolving creation was heathenish and ungodly. Only the young were beginning to entertain the idea that they, themselves, might take a small hand in completing God's world, as hairraising as the idea sometimes seemed even to them.

The wheat had been sacked and stored in the barn on trestles made from loose planks laid on sawhorses whose legs wore shields of tin fluted downward to discourage the rats. The seed wheat had been placed in the sun to dry thoroughly to prevent a vegetable heat, and then Oscar had sacked it carefully in several cloth sacks and hung these by wires from the beams in the barn. His seed corn he would, in time, store likewise.

The straw, for most part, had been left in the stack it made in the barnyard. But a small portion of it, the shiniest and best, was carried to an empty stall to be used later, when Belle was ready, to stuff the ticks for the beds. The McDowells had never owned a mattress, a comfort which in Alan's mind was equated with wealth and affluence.

Lee and Alan always welcomed the thresher, not only because it was a major social event in the life of the farm, always accompanied by a big dinner, but also because it was, from Lee's standpoint, a chance for him to work alongside of men who treated him like a man. As for Alan, the general excitement of the threshing, the blowing straw and chaff, and the way he felt about the grain itself, a feeling compounded of his mother's almost pagan worship of wheat and of his own reading about the part grains of all sorts had played in the history of the world, stirred him deeply. Along with corn and apples and milk, he felt, wheat was one of the basics, one of the fundamentals of human existence. That he was in his thinking also quoting Miss Woodson he was not aware; he existed individually, as it were, between the individualities of two strong women. And like a compound, which is different from any of the elements that have gone into its composition, he existed separately from them. His other associates were merely like the weather to which an element might be exposed, to be dulled and worn away, perhaps, but never normally to be drastically changed. His feelings, however, remained inchoate and elementary. Outwardly, he only rejoiced in the day and the dinner.

Belle's table that day had fairly groaned with blessing. On the clean white cloth were chicken, fried and boiled sweet-corn, potatoes, blackberry cobbler, sliced tomatoes and onion, and radishes in a dish all to themselves, late lettuce smothered in hot fat and sauced with appled vinegar, boiled cabbage, a dish of wild plum marmalade, and a jar of honey. Stacks of bread and pitchers of milk, sweet and butter, completed the spread.

It was to the McDowell boys as good as an all-day meeting with dinner on the ground, as festal as a summer Christmas, minus only the snow and the gifts, of course. Alan almost forgot to eat, watching Lee dispose of the food. He ate gargantuanly, like a man, passing his plate even for a third helping of the things he liked. His mother let him be. He had worked hard, and so she could dispense with any regard for manners.

"Maybe," Oscar said slyly, seeing Alan staring at his brother, "if you had worked harder, son, you would have felt like eating."

Alan felt anger rise against his father. Oscar was always picking on him, especially in company. It wasn't fair. Nobody had asked him to do anything except to keep Buckeye out of the strawpile, which he hadn't exactly done; for he liked to see the calf, bucking and blowing in excitement, charge the straw and fling it headstrong into the wind. Once, Oscar had threatened to tan Alan's hide. Eventually Buckeye had to be taken into the barn and fastened in a stall, where he bawled steadily throughout the morning.

"That dratted calf," said Oscar. "A man can't hear himself think."

A thought would have to be mighty loud, Alan imagined, to be heard

72

over the noise of the threshing machine, under whose rattle and roar Buckeye's plaintive bellow was like the sound of a cricket hidden under the rush of an autumn wind.

Nevertheless, the dinner had been splendid, an event that would make the boys look forward to another year. Even Oscar and Belle enjoyed the work-weary but festive occasion. As for the threshing crew, summer was the fat season for them; they lived quite literally off the fat of the land, finding on every farm the fulfillment of the Biblical promise of milk and honey.

The great machine, looking like a prehistoric monster being dragged away by some fiercer, smaller being, as an ant might drag a grasshopper, left the barnyard immediately after noon, there being nothing more for the men to do but dismantle a few parts for traveling. The boys and their father watched the tractor belch away with its oversized load, leaving the barnlot snowed over by thin drifts of straw. The air was heavy with a sweet, musty odor, generative and fulfilling, an odor that Alan would remember long after with a new knowledge, and to which he would affix a meaning greater yet smaller than the sudden ecstasy of a boy.

Between the threshing of the wheat and the day on which Belle would renew her beds, the McDowells made soap.

In the corner of the yard was a wooden barrel, with a spout in the bottom, into which Lee and Alan dumped the ashes which, all winter, had been removed from the fireplace and stored in the dry shed behind the smokehouse. They were gray oak ashes, saved especially for their strong alkali content, which was the best the farm afforded for the smelly, dirt-cutting lye soap Belle used to keep her wash a snowy pleasure. She coveted white sheets as other women coveted new clothes or a piece of furniture for the farmhouse parlor.

Into a depression scooped out in the center of the barrel, the boys began to pour water carried from the spring, careful to direct the flow into the heart of the hole to lessen the number of gallons needed. After awhile, they could see a liquid, barely tinged with color, showing slowly in the runnel of the spout. Alan had once supposed this odorous stuff to be the same as tannic acid, but Miss Woodson had explained to him the difference between the solution leached from the dry, crushed bark of the oak tree and that now running like a thin, brown wine from the spout of the barrel. "It is only a matter of chemistry," she explained. "But that can make all the difference in the world."

Already the lard can set under the drip was accumulating a dirty-looking fluid, and around the perimeter of the liquid Alan could see that something was happening to the can. A strong discoloration was spreading on the tin. Another of Miss Woodson's chemical changes, he thought. For she had impressed him with her account of these changes, saying about the properties of the oak tree that the change worked in the burning made drastic and useful difference between an acid and an alkali. The one could be used, for instance, in the tanning of leather, building up compounds that resisted decomposition in the shiny saddle he rode to and from the mill; the other broke down the acids in fats into a cleansing agent. Her explanation had been clear enough so far as words went, but the chemical change of understanding had not worked well for him. He was still rather baffled by the undercover world of chemistry, and feeling that he had more to unlearn than learn, he stooped and thrust a finger into the lye, running richer now that the ashes were becoming saturated in the lower half of the barrel. His finger burned. Whatever it was, the power of the stuff was not to be doubted.

The lard can was standing at half-full.

Banging his bucket against the side of the hopper, Lee heaved a dramatic sigh. "Where is it all going to?" he demanded. "The dratted thing would drink Jordan dry."

To Lee, the Jordan River was the symbol of things everlasting.

But now the small trickle was becoming a rich, stringent red that burned the nostrils as well as the skin. The odor went all over the yard. The can began to fill rapidly. Above the liquid, a feathery, grayish-black design, like tendrils of dead moss, etched the tin.

"Don't use anything made of metal to catch it in," Belle had warned. "I don't want any of my buckets ruined. Use a crock instead."

But Oscar had brought the lard can for the boys to use.

"It's no good anyway," he said. "Not fit to hold lard or molasses. We'll use it for a slop-bucket. Lye is good for hogs. Keeps them from being wormy."

When the fat in the big wash kettle, under which a hot fire was smouldering, had melted to a bubbling consistency, Belle poured in enough lye to eat up the grease, adding the liquid carefully, a little at a time, to control the quality of her soap. She stirred the mass constantly, wearing out any lumps it might yet contain. Gradually the heaving in the kettle calmed, and she left it to cool, returning later, when the soap had hardened, to cut it out in squares with a butcherknife. These she stored in the smokehouse, hoping that she had used sufficient lye to keep the maggots from infesting the bars. If not, any day, she knew, she might expect to find the soap working with the young of green flies.

13

IT was towards the last of July that the day came when Belle decided she would "change" her beds. In the morning, Oscar and the boys had carried the strawticks to a sidehill in the pasture and emptied out the old straw, making three trips, for the extra bed in the boys' room, the guestbed, must also be renewed. Then, after the boys had filled the washkettle with water from the spring, and Oscar had built a roaring fire, Belle shaved two whole bars of the new soap into the boiling water, so that a sparkling, foamy head sprang up, in whose pyramiding, summiting bubbles Alan could see his face repeated over and over. He was reminded of a dream he had once had, of a mirror in which he could see his head in a mirror in which he could see his head in a mirror. Watching the bubbles grow and burn with a crazy chain color of red and blue and burst, finally, with a faint hiss, was fascinating.

Belle brought her washing. Shaking out the ticks to free them of clinging straw, and carefully avoiding the flame, she dropped them into the foaming kettle. "Keep stirring," she told Alan. "And don't let up for a minute. I want these bedclothes to be real clean. Watch out for the fire," she added, as Alan began to turn the soapy ticks enthusiastically, circling water above the kettle's rim. "Don't put it out, for heaven's sake. And don't catch on fire yourself."

"Do, do, do; don't, don't don't," Alan said to himself. "To hear her, you'd think I had crippled brains." He stirred more enthusiastically than ever. The fire hissed and sputtered but did not go out. The blaze seemed to thrive on soap.

Boiled and rinsed and smelling as only clean cloths can smell, the bedticks dried quickly on the clothesline at the side of the yard. Belle left them there until the middle of the afternoon. She had planned to fill the ticks with new straw after sundown, in the cool of the day, but a cloud arose,

75

and her plans were changed.

In the barn lot, clean straw was spread over the ground. On top of this, the ticks were stretched out, their split centers opening upward; and Belle began the hard work of stuffing them. She knelt clumsily over the swollen middle of her body, leaning, as if the motion pained her, toward the center of each tick. She could not kneel on the tick itself and fill it at the same time.

"Help her there," said Oscar, who was carrying armloads of straw from the barn.

"Just let them shake the straw clean and hand it to me," she said. "I'll do the filling. Anybody else would be more of a hindrance than a help."

"Well, work as you can stand it," Oscar said. "You shouldn't be down here in the first place."

"If not me, who?" asked Belle. "I'd hate to sleep on a bed you three would fill."

Her beds were the objects almost of devotion. They must be evenly packed in the beginning, and carefully, evenly re-arranged each morning of the year. It was also her proud belief that she kept the cleanest beds in the valley. To that end, between the washing of the ticks and the filling, the wooden bedsteads had been scalded with a strong solution of the lye water, and stood now drying in the sun against the side of the house. They had had this yearly bath so often, in Belle's battle against chinches, which she would not call by the more hair-raising title of "bed-bugs," that they were now paintless, bleached gray, with here and there a darker streak where the grain of the wood showed. They actually looked better with the varnish gone; but beauty had not been Belle's aim.

After the ticks were stuffed and standing out like white whales, Belle put down the broomhandle with which she had strutted the farthest corners, and said, "While I rest a bit, you go put up the beds."

She sat still, red and sweating, in the midst of the straw, her hair blowing across her face. Yet, she was beautiful somehow, like a symbol-filled picture. The men of her family were startled. About her the thin golden straw had begun to toss in the wind.

"Hurry," she said. "We must get these in before it rains."

Oscar and the boys quickly set up the beds, placing a lid from one of Belle's fruit jars, filled with kerosene, under each caster. This was another of her precautions against the hated chinches. Then they worried the bedticks to the house, warned by the mother not to drop the clean beds on the ground. They worked quickly, for already the stormcloud had crept up toward the center of the sky.

As they brought the last slippery burden into the house, a sprinkle of rain had begun to fall, a light patter that increased momently into a steady downpour. A sense of triumph filled the rooms. The weather, always a potential opponent, had been bested again. Through the wavy window the sideyard looked filled with gulches in which torrents ran, gulches that changed their direction as the eyes moved. Lightning turned the interiors of the house into a pumpkin yellow. Thunder, like hard bolts being shot in locks, shook the house. Rain fell in sheets.

Oscar began to watch the barn lot anxiously. In a small pen on the creek side of the barn, he could see Buckeye taking the storm. The calf had been fastened there to keep him out of the way while the strawticks were being filled. The sense of triumph in having beaten the rain in one matter was beginning to fade disastrously in another. The creek had begun to rise swiftly, the water already washing around the feet of the penned animal. Buckeye bawled complainingly.

"Boys," Oscar said, "Buckeye is likely to drown."

Lee and Alan dashed after their father to the barn. The creek was rolling high now from the partial cloudburst. The water had reached Buckeye's belly, sweeping over half the barn lot, and in one low place already waist-deep between the boy and the calf.

"Alan," Oscar shouted, as the boy fought his way through the muddy flood, "for God's sake come back here." He flung himself after the boy, Lee following his father.

By the time Alan got the gate open, water was under his arms. Buckeye, with his head thrown back and his eyes rolling, struggled toward him. The water caught them both with added force, and both went under. As they came up, Oscar clasped the boy and the calf in his arms, and half upright, half submerged, dragged them to higher ground. Lee splashed after them. Belle was at the gate now, in the drenching rain, her face white with anxiety.

"Go home, Belle," Oscar said. "Get out of the rain. The boy's all right." He stared at the muddy tide now creeping into the edge of the tobacco patch, the crop that meant the only spending money the family would have. "If it ain't one thing," he said aloud to whatever listeners the elements afforded, "it's another. Looks like a man can't win."

But occasionally men do win, for the rain slackened and the creek, after a few minutes of turbulent increase, began to fall back into its course, leaving only two rows of the tobacco slightly damaged in the lower leaves. As if to cinch the matter, a splendid rainbow appeared against the eastward-moving cloud, brilliant and perfect against the blackness of the storm. Covenant, a bridge between heaven and earth for the feet of a goddess, or merely the curved, heavenly arrow pointing to a pot of gold, the bow was a shimmering, almost unbelievable thing over Walden Valley.

Lying high on the new bed, in the smell of clean linen and fresh straw, Alan drifted towards sleep and dreams. In the edges of half-sleep, he felt water tugging at his body, a creek that became a river, a river that widened into a sea, a sea that broadened into an ocean. It was also a winter dream. Leaning buoys called storm, and birds scream-skimmed waves' lather fathoms down shore, sounding gravely under deck, sounding somber-ascendant in the storm's stir. And the great waves' wind answered the snowbow on the heads of Atlantic hills, under the steel-eaved, gusty pit of Atlantic morning, fish-webbed and fierce with pale battling blue marking the world-line.

Day died on a star lower than windward. Clearly from secret leaping seacaps, islands of whispering substance as snows fell into the winter's aguish ocean, the polar bow belted the midriff sea to homesick carnival of impromptu autumns: leaf-light, red gold blue in a chatter of wind, a dingle of haze dying.

A seal bawled, gray and lonely, in mid sea, a calf with eyed face luminous as twin moons, opalescent and stony. And birds cried in the luminous lasting light for moments only, cried the sea-turns, and tides eddying not home under the bow swept black and throats darkened in the dells of small music, echoing furtively the fled force, the sea's aptitude for stopped motion.

From the cold rich blue of bird whitened in flight's echeloned heave in winter seeking warm in rise, snows fell, winds wavered. Voyaging accumulated without distance. Black fins moved corrupt water, swerving islands under.

"Look to windward now, Voyager," sang the stopping sea.

Fins turned under the hillocky blue heave and heavy snows. Birds screamed as the snowbow, clipped, flowed backward flag-like in bleak wind. The moaning of a foghorn, the sounding of a bell, and his bed changed from a high-prowed ship fronted with a calf's head, to a bed in a room which he recognized as his own, where he lay listening to a train whistle and waiting for his brother to come home from prayer meeting. Again he could not remember his dream, as he never wholly could. Left with him was only a faint impression as of a fleeting glance at some compelling portrayal of the strange power of the sea; nevertheless, he sensed that he had come home from an alien passage, feeling in his mind the leftovers of tremendous journeys, fragments of space and time. He was cold in the secret, scented straw as though he had been standing in the year's first snowfall under the blue pines at the orchard's edge.

The lighting of the lamp made him aware of Lee's coming home. Undressing in the yellow circle of lamplight, hanging his Sunday clothes carefully over the back of a chair, Lee was trying to tell him something about Suzy Overholt. "I took her home," his brother said, "right out from under the nose of Ira Wade. Boy, he was madder than a sore-tailed cat."

Lee crawled into bed, his knobby knees jabbing into Alan's stomach.

"Heck," he said, "I forgot to blow out the lamp." Back across his brother he went, knees pumping into Alan's defenseless middle. The wash of yellow light dried up in a brown puddle of shadow. When Lee climbed back into bed again, Alan flipped over on his stomach and was gouged in the kidneys, for all his trouble. His dream was fled.

Lee snuggled down beside him. "Boy, she's a honey," he said. He began to snore happily.

The night turned in its middle. And the household slept.

14

ABOVE the sandy pool the creek made before entering the swamp, a low ledge of limestone was fringed with wild plum bushes, low, thorny shrubs that in early summer were laden with the fruit from which Belle and John Wade's wife, Hannah, made marmalade, but which were, for the rest of the year, gouging, arresting trees for all those, man or animal, who entered them. While swimming the boys of the neighborhood used them as handy hangers for their clothes, spreading them out man-fashion on the short branches. From a distance, clothes spread there resembled a suspended species of humans, footless, handless, and headless, with the wind moving inside the shirts so that they seemed to breathe. Once, when Alan and Lee approached the pool, they had seen Ira Wade's trousers hanging on the plums, the fly partially buttoned, so that a long trumpet vine could find an anchor and dangle there. Ira himself lay floating like a white stick on the surface of the pool, his summer-red face in odd contrast to his pale body.

"The tree of life, buddy!" he shouted to Lee, who was already stripping off his clothes in preparation for swimming. "The real, living vine!"

Ira had been a point in Alan's education, a pivot on which his summer world had turned, the larger boy furnishing some items in particular thinking for which Alan was not yet completely ready. Ira himself was a comprehensive lecture in the subject he was most physically demonstrative of. So Alan, engulfed in shame, ran with the body he was criminal with, being no nakeder than he thought, shielding himself with territorial hands when a finger would have done, against Ira's soaring laughter. The allusions to his body were intolerable to Alan.

As a result, he tried to persuade Lee to go with him to the pool at hours when he hoped Ira would not be there. But each time they had gone, Ira *was* there, embalmed in blue and certified in coolness, for then and forever, it seemed. Since Alan loved the clear cold water on his summer-warm body, he would not be deterred by the laughter of this enemy who, seeing him reluctant to remove his clothes shouted, "Oh, shuck 'em off, sonny!" And when the young boy crept hesitatingly towards the water, half-way deciding to return to his clothes, Ira called, "Leave 'em alone now. You can't fly, birdy, with your feathers down!"

"He's a bastard, anyway," Lee had told Alan privately. "Not a real one though," his brother added wisely. "Only a self-made one."

Once he was in the water, shielded from Ira's mocking gaze, the ordeal lessened. Alan could almost persuade himself that nothing unpleasant had happened, watching Ira's white muscular body shoot and twist in the deeper green water in the middle of the pool like some expert, finless fish, sliding and turning with an ease that seemed miraculous to the young boy immersed in his own clumsy motions. Learning to float was Alan's concern, and he stayed in the shallow reaches of the pool, away from Ira and Lee, who catching him on his back, shoved him mercilessly under. He always came up gasping and strangling from the ducking.

Ira and Lee had invented a game. Diving from the cliff, they carried a leaf to the bottom of the pond where they released it, and then with eyes open, hunted it back to the surface. The leaves moved in zigzag fashions through the water, Lee said, and you never knew where they were going or how long it was going to take for them to surface.

"You should see down there," he said to Alan. "Believe it or not, the sun shines through the water. And it's not green either. The water is yellow at the bottom, not muddy yellow, sun yellow. You try it once."

Ira jumped with a whoop from the rock, feet downward, his legs lifted and spread, so that he looked like a white-painted frog spreadeagling to the water. He slapped the surface with his buttocks, grabbing his nose as he went under. When he came up his behind looked raw and spanked. "Boy, that one shook my grandma." He somersaulted in the water. "Watch the moon rise," he said.

Lee chuckled. "If I'd had a plumgranny," he said, "the moon would have gone down and in a hurry."

Alan waded toward the deep water and squatted, forcing himself against the buoyance of the water to the bottom, where, holding his nose, he sat and opened his eyes. Lee was right. The water is yellow, he thought, like cane juice running out of the grinder. Strained through it were bits of drifting light like motes in a sunbeam. Towards the shallow edges of the pond, the color lessened, so that he seemed to be sitting in a yellow bowl whose rim was ringed with bands of paler color. Suddenly out of the yellow a huge white form came sailing. Ira swooped by like a seal, turning as he went and seeming to spiral upward. Alan followed him, popping to the surface like a pulled cork. His eyes stung in the sunlight, his chest heaved.

"How was it?" Lee asked.

"Like you said, only it's a great deal colder down there," Alan told him.

"There's a spring in the middle of the pond," Ira said, swimming by, on his back, his body, except for his hands, stiff and motionless. He seemed to be propelled through the water by some mysterious force. At times like this, Alan admired John Wade's eldest son. "When I dive in the deepest part, I can see the sand boiling where the stream enters."

Lee dived, trying to find the spring. But he could never force his light body to the bottom. In the deepest part of the pool, the water was nearly ten feet deep, where the current had caught about the base of the ledge and by its circular motion had cupped out the depth.

"Get a big rock," Ira suggested. "It'll take you down."

Lee found a large limestone, and holding it in front of him, attempted to dive. But the weight of the rock threw him off balance. He fell into the water on his side with a tremendous splash, and disappeared.

Almost immediately he was on the surface again, gasping and sputtering. "I found it all right," he said, displaying a skinned elbow which had dug into the sand. "Believe me, it's down there."

Ira flipped over on his back and lay still, laughing. As he laughed, he sank, all the air in his lungs expelled. "Go under the water, Alan," he said when he re-surfaced, "and say 'rotten eggs' when you come up."

Alan dived. "Rotten eggs," he said, coming up.

Lee and Ira howled.

"What's so funny?" Alan asked.

"I said 'What did you have for breakfast?' and you said, 'Rotten eggs,'" Ira explained. "Only you didn't hear me."

Alan was not surprised that he hadn't heard. The water was always like pointed, sharp stoppers in his ears.

The three boys swam and cavorted for half the afternoon.

"I suppose I'd better be getting home," Ira said. "The old man needs me to help him wash his Willys-Knight."

Lee and Alan knew Ira referred to his father's old surrey which John Wade had affectionately named Sweet Chariot.

"I'm getting damned tired of the old man's driving that shebang to town," Ira said. "You should see her," he added, a note of admiration in his voice for his father's achievement. "He's got her polished till she glows like a chestnut. If she had a motor, I wouldn't mind driving her myself. How'd you like to take Suzy home in that, Lee?"

"No, thanks," Lee said. "I'll take walking. After all," he added slyly, "the longest way home is the sweetest."

Ira flushed. "Hell," he said. "I wouldn't have Suzy off a Christmas tree." He climbed out of the water. Dressing, he tossed the trumpet vine into the water's edge. "It'll be a long time before you have one like that, Alan," he called, and disappeared beyond the plum trees, going home.

"What's he got to be so proud of?" Alan asked his brother, who was now sunning himself on the ledge.

"What do you mean?" Lee grinned. "What's the subject, the surrey or the trumpet vine?"

Alan flushed. This must be an instance of Miss Woodson's "lack of proper reference." "The surry," he explained. "Why is he so ashamed of having his father drive the surrey to town?"

"He's in high school, you know," Lee said. "He runs with the town gang. I guess he's afraid they'll find out the surrey belongs to his old man. If they did, he'd be disgraced, particularly with the girls."

"I don't see why," said Alan, who rather enjoyed riding with John Wade in Sweet Chariot.

"When you're older, son, you'll understand several things you don't understand now," his brother said, condescendingly.

Alan became angry. "I make better grades than you do," he said. "I can't see that there's anything I don't understand."

Because Lee was three years older was no reason he should play like God.

"This," Lee said softly, secretly, as if remembering some wondrous happening for which words were wholly inadequate, "has nothing to do with grades." He stood up and dived.

"I don't blame Ira," he said, coming up. "You don't see me riding in the buggy to town with Dad, do you?"

It occurred to Alan that lately Lee *had* begun to walk into town on Saturdays, even when the family was going. Last Saturday, he remembered, when his father had taken Belle to the doctor's office for an examination, he had refused to ride home, saying he'd rather walk than crowd his mother in the buggy. So that was it. Lee was ashamed of the buggy and Old Ranger. Maybe ashamed of the family, too. His own father and mother! Alan burned with rage against Lee. If this was what growing up amounted to, then he didn't want it.

He lay on his back in the cup the pool made and stared at the sky, blue and bending towards him at the edges like a folded leaf. Again he was struck to see the blue become powdery before his eyes, melt into a kind of dust that opened inward as snowflakes seemed to merge into various depths when seen between him and a light. From this prone position he saw a changed world of pool and cattail, rock and plum tree and willow, and farther on, beyond the low side of the pool, the calamus stand and a brown bird, probably a hawk, touched with an unusual sunglow. He remembered lying on his back in the yard at home and watching a hen run by. How silly she had looked, seen from her bottom side, the yellow legs skipping below the gray feathers. Hens were silly anyway, about as senseless as a hog. His mind wandered. A hog would charge back and forth all morning right past the hole where he had got out, and never think of returning to the pen. "A hog," said Oscar, "doesn't have the sense of a last year's bird's nest."

Just what is the I.Q. of a last year's bird's nest? Alan wondered. Or a this year's bird's nest? They were only heaps of mud and straw, so easily torn apart the wind sometimes blew them, young and all, to the ground. He remembered one nest that had been so thin he could see the gray underfeathers of the sitting bird.

He stopped paddling at Lee's call. Dressed already, his brother was waiting for him on the ledge.

"Come on," Lee ordered. "Get your clothes on." Before Alan had shaken himself dry, his brother added, "Stop standing there naked as a jaybird, and hop to it. Boy, you're slower than the seven-year itch." Lee pronounced it "eech."

Small, round clouds, remnants of a mackerel sky, floated in the west above the sycamores as the boys started home. The trees themselves were like giant white stalks on which the small clouds bloomed, or like stiff strings attached to colored balloons. Two of the clouds, more elongated than the others, resembled fish, one pink, one apple green, diving in a mottled pool. An evening wind blew from the west, from beyond the purple rim of Walden Ridge where it turned southwestward. Insects scattered in the grass before the boys' feet. It had been a good afternoon for both of them. For Alan, the pleasant aspects of the swim had outweighed Ira's jibes and jocularities. By himself, Ira Wade was not so detestable; it was only when Lee was around that he outdid himself to be grown-up and vulgar.

Halfway home the boys were met by a familiar sound, a steady drone that filled the air as if some hunter put his lips to a gun barrel and signaled home his hounds. They had stayed too late at the pool. Belle was blowing the sea conch, the great shell which had belonged to Oscar's grandmother, to tell them of their lateness. The shell had been cut at the closed end, and so a passage made into the beginning whorl was converted into an excellent horn. When Belle blew the conch, and she was the only member of the family who could, she placed her fingers in the great crevice, or lip, of the shell and, throwing her head back, sent out a stream of alarm to call her menfolks home. The Wades used a big bell which stood in their back yard on a high frame. Hannah Wade made the countryside resound with booms when she needed her husband or her son. Belle summoned her family with the shell. Alan had spent many hours listening to the sound to the sea in the shell's chambers, imagining the dry rustling of the air as it curved through the spiral to be the actual sound of the mysterious place from which the shell had come.

Now the sound echoed and re-echoed through the hills, demanding, questioning, scolding, and comforting at the same time. "We'll catch it when we get there, I reckon," Lee said.

As they came into the barnyard, Oscar, with his face several shades deeper than its usual hue, so that it looked almost purple, was limping about, doing the chores.

"What happened?" Lee asked.

"That infernal calf," Oscar said, "hooked me in the leg. As soon as I'm able those horns are coming off there."

Oscar's leg was blue where Buckeye's young horns had bruised the flesh without breaking it. The calf now stood peacefully chewing a shuck, looking mild, and about as dangerous as a pigeon, Alan thought. He went up to his pet. Buckeye dropped the shuck and touched the boy with a wet nose.

"Watch him," Oscar said. "He did me that way, and when I turned, he let me have it. He's getting to be worse than a goat for butting."

But in the one action all hostility had been drained from the calf. He followed Alan into the pen, and bawled plaintively when the boy fastened the door and left him. Alan hated to see Buckeye's horns go. With them, his calf was different, beginning even to be actually handsome, he thought. But hooking was hooking; and knowing Oscar's capacity for holding a grudge, Alan doubted that his father would let the outrage go.

He helped to finish the chores. Lee had gone to the house to chop stovewood.

At supper, Belle said, "You boys certainly took your time swimming. You could have been helping me here." She looked worn and tired, almost breathless. Her body, swollen with the unborn child, sagged with a great weariness as she moved between the stove and the table. "Blowing that horn took my breath," she said.

"What was the attraction?" asked Oscar of his sons. "I thought you only wanted to wash off a little. It looks like a mite of dirt went a long way." He groaned, moving his leg.

"Ira Wade was there," Lee said, "shooting off his mouth about this, that, and the other. Mostly about John and Sweet Chariot."

"I've told you," his mother said sharply, "to call him Mr. Wade."

"Still wanting a car, huh?" said Oscar. "Ira's just a mite too big for his breeches. He doesn't know *A* yet."

Oscar always used the first letter of the alphabet in his constant demonstration of boyish ignorance. To him, *A* represented the first slight acquaintance with the real, the first inkling of what things are really about.

"He's got a lot to learn," he said. "Like you boys."

Lee and Alan squirmed uncomfortably. Their father never let an opportunity go by to give them a sermon, no matter who the sinner was.

"Since he's been going to high school," Belle put in, "he's learning different things. I can see his point, though. The surrey *is* old fashioned and out-of-date. Like our own buggy. But it's the best we can do. And the Wades can't do any better either," she added. "You have to crawl before you can walk."

At times like this, proverbs usually went the round; texts flew; treasured bits of wisdom were dragged out for an airing.

"This is what we mean," thought Lee. "Ira, me, all the young folks in this valley. But they can't see that. They're like John Wade, thinking what was good enough for them is good enough for us. They don't know times have changed."

Oscar was saying, "He's even getting too big to be seen in town with his own pa and ma."

"It's not them, Oscar" Belle said. "I told you it was the surrey. Ira's afraid the high school crowd will find out it belongs to John. That's why he runs. Hannah Wade told me so."

"He's afraid he'll lose his girl friend," said Lee.

"Girl friend!" snorted Oscar. "Why he's not dry behind the ears yet. Hardly out of diapers."

Lee flushed. This always made him burn.

"It's that high school," said Oscar. "If I thought sending a boy of mine to high school would make him ashamed of me, I'd keep him at home till the moss grew over his back."

"Ira is young," Belle said. "And so are Alan and Lee. Youth will be served." This was one of her best expressions.

"And I'll help serve them," Oscar said grimly, "if ever I hear of my boys making such dad-blamed fools of themselves." He looked puzzled and hurt, as though he could no longer remember the impossible time when he himself had been their age. Or perhaps he remembered too well. In any case, the puzzlement would have been as deep and genuine, the hurt as incomprehensible.

Alan looked at his brother. Lee never raised his eyes from his plate.

15

LATER in the week, Lee and Alan went in the afternoon to bring home the big gray crock Hannah Wade had borrowed for pickling beans. The weather was dry, had been dry for days now, and the boys found Ira carrying water from the creek in the barn lot to wet Sweet Chariot's wheels. "To swell the rims to hold the tires on," he told them. The tires were thin metal bands on the wooden felloes, which had shrunk so appreciably in the dryness, Ira could with a finger slip the metal back and forth. "He wants to drive her to meeting on Sunday."

Lee offered to help. Ira gave him a bucket, and the work went on. Alan wandered over to Sweet Chariot. The surrey had been backed into the barn lot to make the task of carrying the water easier. Behind the vehicle, but nearer the creek and blocking the runway to the water, was a temporary plank enclosure.

"Quicksand," John Wade told Alan in reply to his question. "It shifted during the last big rain. The planks are to keep the cattle from getting in there. Once they're in, there's no getting them out alive."

"You could hide a house in that hole," Ira told Lee, stamping the ground near the creek. Under the boys the ground shook slightly, as if it floated on a substance only heavier than water.

"Hurry up!" John Wade shouted, seeing Ira and Lee together heaving a large rock into the quicksand. "We've got other things to do."

"Always sittin' on somebody's tail," Ira grumbled. "Or his own," he added, watching his father sitting high and proud on the front seat of the surrey. "One of these days, the town council's going to give him a bucket and a broom. He's going to have to make a clean sweep one way or another."

"Sounder than a dollar," John Wade told Alan, who had climbed up beside him. "It'll outlast any of us by a dollar and a half."

"My back aches," Ira complained to Lee. "We'll never get this done. "Why don't we roll the surrey down here?" he shouted to his father. "Closer to the water?"

"Suits me all right," his father said. "Come up here and help me and the boy roll her down."

The boys held back on the tongue to check the speed of Sweet Chariot as she rolled backward down the slope towards the creek. Ira's father steadied the surrey in its progress by holding onto the back gate. The rolling was easy, almost too easy. "If it wasn't for him out front," Ira thought, "we'd let her go. Once in that quicksand, it'd be good-bye Betsy Brown."

Just above the plank barrier they stopped Sweet Chariot, and Ira scotched a hind wheel with a large stone.

"Well," his father said, "there she is. Water her up. And when you're done, call me and I'll help you roll her back."

Ira and Lee sloshed up and down the runway, reaching and dipping their buckets in the quaking water just beyond the bottom plank of the enclosure. They poured gallons of water over each wheel, repeating the wetting each time the surrey began to look dry. Up, down, up, down, they went, until their legs felt as if they had been left sticking in the tight sand each trip they made.

"This old crate would drink Jordan dry," Lee said, beginning to be dissatisfied. His own back had begun to ache.

"Wash me and I'll be whiter than snow," sang John Wade from the barn, where he and Alan were shucking corn.

"Wash her and she'll be ready to go, ready to go, ready to go!" Ira said, beating his bucket like a drum. "And I know where she can go."

"I think you've gone already," Lee said.

Ira only laughed. Slipping up and down in the soft, sandy mud of the creek bank, he was thinking: If Dad would only go to the house for a minute and give me a chance, I'd show Lee something. He looked furtively over his shoulder to where Alan and John Wade were carrying armloads of shucks to the milking pen. His father's back was toward him. One little toe caught under that scotch would send Sweet Chariot running in to the quicksand. What a beautiful accident it would be! She couldn't be got out by Sunday. Maybe, O blissful thought, she couldn't be got out at all.

"Stand back and watch out," Ira whispered to Lee as he passed him.

Lee looked at Ira, and then stood back, watching him, wondering what he had on his mind. Lee was tired of carrying water, anyway.

On his next trip from the creek, Ira could see his father's back still turned toward him. He would have to work fast before John faced around. He stooped quickly and pulled the scotch almost out from under the wheel, leaving it hanging only by an edge. The stage was set. He walked nonchalantly towards the creek again trying to whistle, but his mouth was too dry. Licking his lips, he could hear the dry sound his tongue made in motion. This had to work. It was now or never.

Two trips later, he found his father's back turned again. John had begun to sharpen a hoe in preparation for cutting weeds for the hogs. Now was the time. Stepping back, Ira took a swift kick at the stone. It dislodged, snapped outward by the weight of the wheel suddenly applied, and Sweet Chariot started to rumble and roll toward the creek and the quicksand. The temporary fence would never hold her, Ira knew. He began to yell, heaving himself at the hindgate of the surrey as she left, as though with his own body he might halt the surrey's progress. Literally pushed aside by Sweet Chariot, Ira grabbed at a rear axle and was thrown face-down into the mud of the cattle run. He scrambled to his feet, shouting.

Sweet Chariot hit the fence, splintering it as so much matchwood as she fled. Bucking and romping like a young heifer, she plunged over the bank, giving her front end one tremendous flirt as she went. In a fury of momentum, she carried far out into the creek, where she rode on her polished bed, still clean and shiny above the water line, in the sand. She creaked, settling unequally in her quarters. At last she came to permanent rest, as thoroughly caught as if she had been set in a huge vise.

Lee could see Ira grinning through the mud on his face.

"Godamighty!" shouted John, running down the knoll.

Ira was down on his knees, nursing his hand, blowing and kissing at the mud dripping from it. "Almost broke my hand," he whined, "when she jumped her scotch."

"Fetch the team," his father said, "and be quick about it."

Ira and Lee ran to the barn to harness the mules. Ira prayed as he went that the young mules would never be able to pull Sweet Chariot out of the sand. They mustn't, he thought. They mustn't. But how they could fail, he couldn't imagine. The young mules could almost pull a mountain.

Alan and John Wade were searching in the shed for more planks, those at the creek having been demolished far beyond use in the course of the charging surrey. By the time Lee and Ira had geared the team, Alan and John Wade had built a causeway out to the dash of Sweet Chariot and were placing a fencepost in the soft sand under the front axle. The creek boiled furiously about the workers, and several of the planks disappeared in the sand as fast as they could be laid. The commotion had caused the surrey to settle even farther into the muck of the creek bottom, and hope welled up brightly in Ira's heart.

"They'll never do it!" he told himself exultantly as he brought the team to the runway. "They'll neve break the hold of that sand. O glory! Glory!"

Ira and Lee stood on the bank and watched John fasten the heavy logchain to the front of the surrey. Looping it around an axle, John, on his knees, looked the distance up the causeway to where the boys stood, silently watching.

"Okay," he said, getting up and coming away from the island Sweet Chariot made in the creek. "You got it in. Now let's see you get it out." He stood back, arms folded.

Ira went to the team's head and held their bridles. The mules flung backward from him, snorting and blowing. "All right now," he said. "Settle down." Run, he was saying inside himself, jump, seesaw, do anything in God's world but pull.

He led the team forward. The mules leaned against the weight they pulled, frantically. There was a rush of water, the hard sound of gravity giving up where the bed of the surrey lost the suction-hold of the sand. The surrey rose, her bright red thimbles, washed clean by the surge of the water, coming into sight; and Sweet Chariot almost had her wheels on the firm roadway of the planks anchored under the water. But the ground where the mules pulled was soft, and they lost their stance and came falling back, dragging Ira as they came. Sweet Chariot settled again, deeper now than ever in the roiling honey-colored water.

John Wade's breath was a rattled sigh on the air.

"Try again," he said.

Thinking to help, Lee suddenly gouged a stick into the flank of the mule nearest him. Snorting, the animal flung itself sideways and then ahead, forcing its mate with it, and nearly trampling Ira in its fury. Both mules were plunging now, seesawing, surging at the dead weight lying behind them. Little by little, Ira worked their heads down and they began to pull, marching irresistibly forward. There was a ripping sound and a great struggle at the center of the creek where, suddenly released, planks floated free, and Sweet Chariot, heaved upon intolerably, parted nearly in her middle. Her front wheels carrying the high seat from which the top had been completely torn away, came rolling on dry land like the remains of a wrecked Roman chariot. Pieces of weathered plank, black lacquer shining wet and golden-specked with sand, wavered gently in the water and then floated off downstream.

John Wade turned and walked away from the boys and the creek, toward the house, a look of grief on his face. "Why doesn't he say something, like Dad?" Alan wondered. For a moment he had thought John Wade was going to cry. But the man neither wept nor spoke; he only stared straight ahead, as if he did not dare to look in the direction of his son. Behind him, by the creek, Ira was laughing. "Well," he said to Lee, "he can't drive half of it, and that's for sure."

The crock was heavy and hard to hold. Several times it almost slipped from the boys' grasp into the roadway, being glazed and slick as a piece of china. One of Belle's most prized possessions, she had not wanted to lend it to Hannah Wade. "But a friend in need is a friend indeed," she said, sending the jar on its way in the sled Ira had brought to haul it to the Wade farm. In the making of kraut, a body had to work when the signs were right, she added.

Now her own late cabbage was ready, and the crock had to be brought home.

Alan and Lee walked a while, and rested, changing ends of the jar frequently because the open end was easier to grasp than the bottom, and when the hand sweated from effort, it was more likely to slip if it had nothing to hold to but the polished gray end of a six-gallon jar. Lee had tried carrying it alone, clasped in his arms, but soon found himself breathless from the pressure he exerted on his lungs by hugging the vessel to his body.

When they entered the yard, struggling with their burden, Pretty Boy began to bark, not recognizing his masters, who made a curious pair of Siamese twins joined by a gray ligature. He was growing fast, almost big enough now to follow the boys around the countryside; but he had lost in his growth the puppy charm which had caused Belle to name him Pretty Boy. Now he was neither pup nor dog, neither pretty nor ugly. "Just a dog," Oscar had said, when Ira Wade asked what kind he was. And in the middle period of his development that was enough said. He was, from overeating, too fat in his middle, so that his ends, front and hind, looked somewhat like the points of a double top, with spinners both ways. His hair was intermediate between pup slick and dog pelt. All in all, Alan decided, Pretty Boy was a mess.

But Pretty Boy had grown big enough by now to challenge Clockwork, sometimes pulling a mouthful of feathers from the rooster's tail. For half the summer that red and gold and black magnificence of a bird had strutted among the hollyhocks, mastering his world, the golden circle of feathers around his neck standing out like a ruff when he felt himself challenged by man or beast. Several times he had given Pretty Boy a severe flogging, sending the pup yelping under the floor of the front porch, from which hiding place Pretty Boy refused to emerge for half a day. Once when Alan went to the pup's rescue, Clockwork turned on the boy and would have spurred him; but a stick of stovewood sent the rooster clattering in the other direction.

"You'll kill my rooster, if you're not careful," Belle said. "Then what would we do?"

"What difference would it make?" Alan asked. "He doesn't lay eggs."

"Don't you know anything?" his mother asked, preferring not to explain. Seeing the puzzled look still on his face, she added, "The eggs wouldn't hatch. There has to be one good rooster in every flock to fertilize the eggs."

It was a male and female world, Alan knew. Rooster and hen, bull and cow, horse and mare, man and woman. He had learned this much from the baby calves and pigs, and pups and chickens and kittens. His own mother was going to have a baby brother, he hoped. But there were still a good many things he didn't understand. So far as Lee and Ira Wade were concerned, what they said in his presence only confused and shamed him, they made their talk so secretive and dark and forbidden. If sex was so wrong, he wondered, why were his own parents involved?

So he did as he was told, shooing Clockwork instead of belaboring him with a stick when the rooster showed fight. But still he wondered. The question of the new baby had grown so large in his mind that he found it difficult to be interested in the growth of Pretty Boy or, at times, in the care of Buckeye. For the moment, the birth of a new human creature into the world dwarfed all other concerns, even a calf whose sale in the fall meant that he would have all his books at school for the first time in his life. Something immense and filled with great possibilities, it seemed to Alan, centered around a boy's birth, there being no question at all in his mind as to the kind of baby the McDowells should be getting. Lincoln had been born, and Edison, and Coolidge. Animals were all right, he decided, in their place. Miss Woodson had told him that men were animals, too; but, if so, he felt they were special animals, and deserved special consideration.

Take Pretty Boy for instance. When the pup had been bitten by a snake early in the summer, and had swollen until his head looked like a half-gallon bucket, Alan had known the dog might die. But if Pretty Boy did die, it would be an inferior kind of death, and not like Reuben's at all. The dog would not even have a funeral, might not even be buried. Oscar would have Lee toss Pretty Boy's body into a lonely wood somewhere and leave it there for the buzzards to pick clean. The dead mule he and Lee had come upon near Walden Ridge had proved that. The grotesquely swollen body lay, its ribs beginning to be exposed above its belly, filled with the rattling of a million bugs like castanets. A turkey buzzard had flapped heavily away from the mule's neck when the boys had disturbed him at his dinner. Alan, from some sense of loyalty to the dead animal, had flung a rock at the bird, and Lee had laughed.

"How would you like," Lee asked, "to have someone rock you away from the table?"

Remembering, Alan felt angry and sick. There was no dignity for anything in death except men, he felt; and he was beginning to suspect that men dignified death only because they were afraid. Maybe it was better to be tossed out into the wind and sun. The Indians had sometimes done that with their dead.

"What on earth are you standing there, mooning about?" Belle asked. "There's work to be done at the barn."

"Tomorrow," Oscar said to him in the barn lot, "after you boys help ma with the kraut-making, and I get some rub-blocks made, we're going to dehorn Buckeye before he hurts somebody bad. He took another swipe at me a minute ago when I drove him into his pen. He barely missed. Same leg."

Funny, he never tries to hook me, thought Alan. Maybe he knows I'm his friend.

He shelled corn for the chickens, Pretty Boy stepping into the pan and scattering the grain in his efforts to lick Alan's face. "You're a nuisance, son," he told the dog sternly. Nevertheless, he set the pup carefully on the ground beside him. Pretty Boy yapped, sounding for all the world like a dog whose voice was changing.

At supper, Lee said casually, "I don't guess Mr. Wade will be driving the surrey anymore. Not soon anyway."

"Why?" asked Oscar, suddenly interested. "Has he broken down and bought that shavetail of his an automobile? I always thought he couldn't stand the pressure that boy was putting on him."

"No," Lee said, "there was an accident. This afternoon, while me and Ira were watering the wheels to swell the tires for Sunday, she jumped her scotch and landed in the quicksand at the watering-place. The mules pulled her in two when trying to get her out. Her hindend is still in the quicksand."

"He'll never get her out then," Oscar said. "I know that quicksand. There's no bottom to it."

"Well, accidents will happen," Lee said, parroting his mother. His voice was guarded. He kept his eyes on his plate.

"We'll have to let them have the buggy," Belle said. "I can't go to meeting Sunday anyway. There's no reason for Hannah to miss the sermon."

Alan remembered the low voices of Lee and Ira as they took the team to the barn, voices in which something was secret and hidden, guarded as though they were saying things not for his ears. He remembered John Wade, too, sitting on the front porch, staring into the distance. He had not spoken, even when the boys were leaving, to thank them for lending the jar. Something about the accident was unsettled, some phase of it incompletely understood in the minds of at least two of the participants. Or had they been merely witnesses? The thought almost formulated itself in his mind as Alan dropped to sleep that night, hearing Ira's voice bouncing from the center of the swimming place: "I'm getting damned tired of the old man's driving that shebang to town."

But the thought was lost as a memory of sun fades from darkened water.

16

LEE was bitter. He had wanted to go to Quinn's Spring for the Fourth of July celebration, but Oscar had said no. There was too much work to be done. The boys might have their choice though: chop the weeds from the bottom cornfield or go blackberry picking. "Some choice," Lee grumbled, "between work and work." He had unpleasant visions of Ira Wade's buying Suzy Overholt a mutton sandwich at the affair, and of the two sitting in the shade by the river, talking, about him more than likely. "Picking blackberries on the Fourth of July," he said disgustedly, for he had already made up his mind that the weeds could grow in the corn, at least for another day.

Alan was disappointed, too, but said nothing. He rather liked picking blackberries as it gave him a chance to roam the countryside, searching for whatever he could find, arrowheads, fossils, strange flowers and plants, even old birds' nests. In his collection of natural odds and ends from the valley and its surrounding ridges, he had a fern beautifully imprinted on stone, a petrified shell (which Miss Woodson told him meant the land in the valley had once been a part of a great sea's bottom), several arrowheads, an Indian axe, and two huge paperwasps' nests, which gray globes he kept hanging on the walls of his bedroom. He especially prized the "squirrel arrowheads" he had found, the very small ones, balanced, beautifully toothed, which Miss Woodson said had often not been used to shoot small animals and birds at all, but had been used as money. Shells, she had told him, were not the only medium of exchange. Barter, too, had been practiced widely among the Indian tribes. Alan had been particularly fascinated by her account of how even an unfriendly tribe had tied its merchandise to a limb of a tree and retired into the woods to wait for the "buyers" to come and leave their goods in exchange. In that way, the traders never came face to face.

The jaunts about the countryside helped to reinforce Alan's school knowledge of what the valley had been like in other days. Actually, it seemed to him that learning more about the valley might be just as important as sitting under a tree at the celebration, drinking lemonade and eating the mutton sandwiches which had been so thoroughly publicized by the committee from town. Nevertheless, he felt a small pang at missing the picnic, despite Oscar's declaration that it was being put on by a bunch of penny politicians from Woodside. Lee, however, was privately profane. Picking blackberries meant only tramping around in the blistering sun all day, getting chiggers, and spraining his back stooping and reaching for the elusive berries. He knew the Woodside High School band would be at the picnic. There would be flags and, in the early evening, firecrackers. And there would be Suzy. And Ira. He swore under his breath.

"Wait until the dew's off," Oscar told them, when the boys informed him of their decision, "and work towards the ridge. There ought to be some fine berries on the edge of the meadow above the swamp."

It was there that Alan and his mother had picked in other summers, finding great handfuls of berries, wet and shining, like blobs of pure juice coagulated on the ends of the stems. And it was there that over the sunny wood that rose up from the edge of the meadow to the foot of the ridge, they heard the mixed sounds of the summer insects, wind, and water. It was a sound, warm and leafy, that made him imagine gods were hidden in the trees, waiting to step down into the meadow when his back was turned. It was also here one day that his mother told him the story of the hoopsnake, with the poisonous dart in the end of its tail. It rolled, she said, with its tail in its mouth, letting go when it wanted and flinging the deadly sting into its victim. Even trees died from the effect, she said. Miss Woodson had said there was no such thing as a hoopsnake. It was all a fable. But Alan half hoped to see one of the rolling serpents come circling out of the trees and plunge its arrow into some target, as long as the target was at some distance from himself. He wanted to believe. At the same time, he was trying to repudiate many of the fanciful accounts of beings and events in which he had once so strongly delighted. The matter-of-fact tone of some of the books he read had destroyed a part of the real joy he had previously felt in living. That was possibly what Miss Woodson had meant when she told him that learning was mostly a process of unlearning. To discover that some fascinating account was only a fable, even when he did not wish to believe in it because of its utter unreason, left him feeling a little naked, stripped of something he felt unwilling to lose. He was too young to know how to let go and to hold on to a belief at the same time. Preacher Musgrove had thundered that belief was belief, and nothing else, solid, unshakable, eternal. Miss Woodson had said in her discussion of Greek gods that the substance of belief remained fairly constant, that only the form of belief changed. He hadn't really understood either one of them. The darkness he stood in, in his mind, was broken only now and then by a glimmer of light like sunlight penetrating through leaves.

But the day was beautiful, high, blue, and promising great heat near noontime. It was really no time to wonder about the dark undercurrent of things. It was a day to roam, bucket in hand, through the fields and over the hills, breathing, feeling the pure summer warmth, looking for the fruit of thorny stands of blackberry briars. Alan put on his worn last winter's shoes. This was the only thing he didn't like about blackberry picking. But to tramp through the patches was impossible without shoes, and he resigned himself to having his feet pinched and bruised by the stiffened leather of the castoff brogans.

Across the alfalfa field, the boys went. Here and there about them in the rich green of the new growth of hay were the deep yellow hearts of daisies surrounded by the snowy petals which had given the flower its name. The day's eye, Miss Woodson had pointed out; called so by the Anglo-Saxons. How his teacher knew so much, Alan could not understand.

Lee picked one of the flowers and began to pluck off its petals, repeating "She loves me, she loves me not," as he pulled the yellow heart naked. He came out with "She loves me" and brightened for a moment. Then he slumped again. Even if she did, what chance did he have here, with a bucket in his hand going blackberry picking, and Ira there, buying her a mutton sandwich? He scowled darkly, kicking at the lovevine that had begun again to cover small areas of the alfalfa with its golden entanglement. Some people had all the luck, he decided. And some couldn't win with a mile's headstart.

"Look," said Alan. "Dad's going to have us in here before long, pulling this dodder. It's spreading like wildfire."

"Let it spread," Lee growled. "If there gets to be too much of it, pulling it won't be worth the effort. We'll just pull out the alfalfa and let the dodder grow." Rebellion was like a sour taste in his mouth.

"I know," Alan said, "what we can do. Let's see who finds an arrowhead first." Lee said nothing. "Or let's name the wild animals the early settlers found in Walden Valley. Mr. Wade said practically every kind of game animal once lived here; not just a few either. They were all over the place."

"Mr. Wade," Lee said with mocking emphasis, "is always saying something." But he was interested. "You name one first," he said.

"Opossums," Alan said.

"Raccoons," Lee said.

"Rabbits and squirrels," Alan added.

"Turkeys, groundhogs, and quails," Lee said.

"Bears, deer, muskrats, ducks, and geese," Alan counted.

Lee thought a moment. Then he said. "Fish, all kinds, frogs, turtles, mussels, pigeons, doves, grouse, woodcocks, and skunks."

"But you can't eat skunks," Alan protested.

"Who said anything about eating?" Lee said.

"I did," Alan said.

"You did not," Lee said. "You said 'game animals.' And that don't necessarily mean animals you can eat."

"It does so, too," Alan declared.

"Who said so?" Lee asked. "Miss Woodson?"

"I said so," Alan shouted. Lee's quoting his authority before he did angered him.

"You're crazy," Lee said. "Let's play something else."

Calling his brother crazy, Lee had found, effectively put an end to any argument.

Alan sputtered.

They walked on towards the meadow silently. Then Alan said, grudgingly, "Well, all right. What do you want to play?"

"You name it," Lee said, knowing the younger boy's ideas were always better than his. Lee's mind ran wholly to other things, like taking a gun apart and putting it together again. Once he had worked a week trying to get all the cogs and springs back into an old alarm clock.

"Suppose you and I are early settlers and there are no Indians around to give us corn, and we have nothing to eat except what we can find among the plants and animals. We've named the animals. Now let's name the plants." To be fair, he said, "You go first this time."

"Blackberries," Lee said.

"Dewberries, huckleberries, gooseberries," Alan chanted.

"Raspberries, strawberries, elderberries, muscadines, grapes, and crabapples," Lee said triumphantly.

"Persimmons, plums, redhaws, blackhaws, hickory nuts, walnuts, chestnuts, and poke sallet," Alan said.

"Beechnuts, hazelnuts, pawpaws, black cherries, mushrooms, wild lettuce, speckled dock, and water cress," Lee said.

"Wild mustard, ramps, fiddlehead ferns, dandelions, peppergrass, branch mint, and . . ."

"Honey-locust pods," Lee finished.

"You win," Alan said, unable to think of anything more. He looked about him. "The only trouble with plants is that you'd have only nuts in the winter. Unless we knew more than the Indians. They only dried what food they had. We'd know how to can stuff though," he said, "because we're white men. The early settlers brought such things as cans with them."

"Of course," said Lee. "I can just see Daniel Boone tramping through the mountains with his pockets full of Mason jars."

Alan reddened. Lee wasn't much fun to talk to anymore.

They had reached the foot of the long, slanting meadow which Alan had named By Path Meadow from his reading of *The Pilgrim's Progress.* The air was full of the light hum of insects over the flowers, the sigh of wind shifting through the nearby trees, and the strangely dry sound of water falling over the last low fall that Madden Branch made in its descent from the mountain into the world of hayfield and cornland below. Along the meadow's edge the boys found their first blackberries, great bowed clusters of fruit that glowed with a dark brilliance on their stems. Carefully, they picked the berries, one by one, dropping them with as great care into their buckets. Belle despised crushed berries, even if she were going to make jelly. These, she expected to can, and she wanted each separate berry to be perfect and whole, so that in their jars they looked appealing, almost demanding to be made into luscious pies or eaten with sugar and sweet milk. She wanted no leaves and other trash to be picked out in the washing either. She hardly forgave them the stinkbugs which, in all reason, she knew could not be helped. There seemed to be plenty of them this year, as well as June bugs, whole wads of them clinging to the briars, sucking the juice from the berries.

Lee caught one and tied its hindleg with a string. "Now, june, dang you," he ordered. The bug complied, flying in circles around the boy until it worried its leg off and flew away. "Didn't need it, anyhow," Lee said. "Never walks any place. Got wings to travel by."

Alan spat, making a face. The berry he tasted had been tasted before by a visitor who left his unmistakable odor behind him. "Gad," he said, "that was no perfume pot. I don't blame Mom. I wouldn't want stinkbugs in my berries either."

"You'd better stop eating them," Lee said, "or we'll never get these buckets full. You know Dad. Either we fill up this morning, or back we come this afternoon."

A train blew. "We won't be home before this afternoon," Alan said. "It's eleven-thirty already." He picked a handful of berries strutted with juice and almost translucent, so that the seeds could be darkly seen inside the tiny globes. This was the kind of berry Belle said she dreamed of picking, seeing them hanging everywhere around her, most of them aggravatingly just beyond her reach. Her worst dream of the summer, she said, was dreaming that the blackberries were ripe and going, and she without a single berry in a can, and the winter coming and no food. Talk about being frightened, she said. That was pure horror. Hearing her, Alan thought his mother was a little like the hungry Greek god who was punished for something he had done by being put under a bunch of grapes that jumped back every time he tried to pick one. Tantalus was his name. In her dream, the berries tantalized Belle. That was what dreams were for, he had decided, to tantalize and terrify.

"I know what," he said. "Let's go see the railroad track. The last time we went was the first time I ever saw it in my life."

"Not for my grandmother," Lee said. "It's five miles from here, I bet. I wouldn't walk more than home in this hot sun for a yankee dime. Besides, you'd keep me awake for a week, yelling about it, like you did the last time."

Alan blushed. "That was the first train I ever saw," he said defensively. "It wouldn't scare me now. I'm used to it." To get even with Lee, he said, "I guess it would depend on who gave you the yankee dime, whether you walked or not. I bet if Suzy Overholt offered you one, you'd walk."

"For a sweet kiss from her," Lee said, "I'd shovel my way from here to town through a five-foot deep snow, using a teaspoon for a shovel."

Alan looked at Lee's bucket. "You'll be black dark getting that full," he said. "I've got twice as many as you."

"Stop talking to me," Lee said, "and I'll show you."

He went to work in earnest, silently stripping the ripe fruit and plumping it into his bucket. Alan picked away from him now, up the slant of the field towards the waterfall. He wanted a cold drink from Madden Branch. Gradually, they lost sight of each other. The berries around Alan now were the finest he had ever seen. He finished filling his bucket, and began to eat the biggest berries he could find, staining his lips and tongue black with the rich juice. His hunger satisfied, he sat down by the waterfall and pulled off his shoes, bathing his hot, tired feet in the icy water. The branch was so cold it hurt, pouring its glassy flood from the deep shade. Alan knew that up and up the mountain there was an orchard where the spring began, and a strange abandoned house in the center of the orchard, whose trees each year furnished the McDowells with a wealth of wild apples. He looked forward to going there again this year, though the mystery of the place deepened with each visit. The more he thought about the mountain farm and its former owners, the more complicated the problem of who and what they were became. The clues evident on every hand were more confusing than helpful. And the stories the people in the neighborhod told were mixed and conflicting, as if they were recalled from other times and places and were only fitted loosely and carelessly about another circumstance. The memories of people appeared to be hopelessly mixed up; it seemed at times as though people remembered, not what they themselves had experienced, but only what they had heard, making the things that had happened to others happen to them, by default of a clear reminder and of a certain wishfulness that life be not so terribly dull. Maybe what happened to other people always seemed more dramatic and meaningful than one's own personal experience. Thinking about it, Alan concluded that everything was a sad mix-up. His head ached a little with the thought of it, and with the heat. He bathed his face in the stream and began to watch the flicker of small minnows from stone to stone.

About two o'clock he heard Lee call from the bottom of the meadow. His bucket full, heaped in the center above the rim, Lee was ready to go home. "If you spill yours," he said to Alan, "It's your own bad luck. I wouldn't wait for you to fill up again even if Dad booted me one."

They walked slowly and carefully downhill.

"Some Fourth of July," Lee grumbled. "Climbing up and down hill, scratching the blood out and getting covered with chiggers. When I get home, I'm washing with coal-oil." Already around his belt-line he was beginning to itch and sting.

"Let's play another game," Alan said.

"What kind of game?" Lee asked, not interested, but willing to try anything that would shorten the walk home in the sun.

"Suppose," Alan said, "we're early settlers in this valley."

"That again?" Lee said. "All right. Suppose."

"There isn't any doctor," Alan said, "and you're sick. You've got the bellyache and you go to the woods to find a plant to cure you. What would you get?"

"How the heck would I know?" Lee said. "You're the doctor. What would I get?"

"Calamus root, of course," Alan told him. "You would soak it in whiskey and drink the juice."

"Of course," Lee grinned. "You wouldn't catch me eating the root and throwing the juice away!"

"Suppose you had worms," Alan said.

"Suppose you had worms yourself," Lee said.

"Suppose anyway. What would you take?"

"I know that one," Lee said. "I'd take Jerusalem Oak seeds in molasses."

"But you don't have any molasses," Alan pointed out.

"I'd eat 'em raw," Lee said. "Anyway to get 'em down. After that, they take care of themselves."

The boys were approaching Muddy Bottom. Across the creek they could see the farmstead, with its weathered gray buildings and the livestock dotted here and there under the trees for shade.

"One more," Alan said. "Suppose you had the piles, what would you do?"

"I'd carry a rotten buckeye in my pocket," Lee said. "And I wear a rabbit's foot around my neck, and I hide a horsehair under a rock in the creek. That's what I'd do. And any other slaphappy thing I could think of. Come on!"

"No, you wouldn't," Alan said, walking rapidly along behind him.

"You'd just carry a buckeye. The rabbit's foot is only for luck, and the horsehair would turn into a snake."

"Says you," Lee retorted. "And all the other old witches!"

As they crossed the barnlot, Pretty Boy began to bark. He rushed furiously towards them, wiggling so hard his ends almost met. Whizzer, in his cat's pride and personal independence, merely stood up and arched his back, his mouth opening to show his clean, sharp teeth in what seemed to Alan to be a bored yawn at seeing them return. Belle inspected the berries. "These are beautiful," she said. "Where did you find them?"

"In By-Path Meadow," Alan told her, "where we always pick. There's more there this year than I've ever seen."

"And more bugs and chiggers, too," said Lee. "Some Fourth of July," he added. "Picking blackberries."

"The Fourth of July won't seem so important this winter when I bake a pie," Belle said. "You're like the grasshopper that wanted to dance all summer and have a full stomach when the snow began to fly."

"I've been and had everything else today," Lee said. "And now I'm a grasshopper." He grumbled out of the house.

"I declare," Belle said, "I don't know what's got into that boy. He doesn't want to do anything worthwhile anymore."

"He wanted to go to the picnic," Alan explained. "I think he's afraid Ira Wade's going to take Suzy Overholt away from him."

"If that's what's bothering him," Belle said, "he can ease his mind. Ira Wade went to no picnic. He's home cleaning a fencerow."

"Who told you?" Alan asked.

His mother turned on him sharply. "Don't get sassy with me," she snapped. "You're both getting too big for your britches. He came to borrow our briar scythe, that's how I know if you have to know." She measured her words, bitingly, as only she knew how. Even Oscar quailed before her fierce verbal onslaughts. It was not so much what she said, as how she said it. She was, Alan realized, not feeling well. The closer the time for the baby to be born, the more bitter and acrimonious she seemed to become. It was all a part of something he could not very well understand.

"Do you want me to help you wash the berries?" he asked.

Belle softened. "No, son," she said wearily, "I'll wash them myself. You go play. You boys picked them. I should be able to wash them."

Alan went into the yard. Lee was sitting on the stone wall between the yard and the orchard. "You can stop worrying," Alan said. "Ira Wade stayed home, too. He's cleaning a fencerow. Mom said so."

"What did you tell her, Big Mouth?" Lee scowled. "You're worse than an old granny woman yourself. Always blabbing your brains out." But he looked happier. His voice sounded relieved. The Fourth of July was suddenly not so bad, after all. He stretched out on top of the wall, whistling.

17

BEFORE the dew had dried on the round hard heads of the cabbage, Alan and Lee were in the garden clipping them from their roots with a butcher knife, leaving a nest of bottom leaves where each head had been. Behind the boys each row looked like an array of white-green cups on a shelf. On the beanvines, long since past bearing, the morning-glories were pink and blue and white, with sometimes a flower almost scarlet. In fact, everywhere around them, except in the tobacco field where no vines had been able to grow because of cultivation and the thick shade the plants had made, the running vines had decked out all uprights with a streamer of blossoms. One sure sign of the maturing summer was the morning-glory's race to perpetuate itself plentifully before the first frost. The dew was already autumn cold on Alan's bare feet. The season was building up to a change.

He and Lee piled the clipped heads of cabbage into a washtub and carried them to the back porch, where Belle, sitting in a chair, directed her sons in the washing of the vegetable. "Look carefully for worms," she said, "if you don't want to eat one pickled."

Carefully Alan stripped off all damaged leaves and tossed them aside for the hogs. With a butcherknife, Belle cut the heads into quarters, dropping the sections into a scrubbed wooden box, in which Lee had already begun to chop the cabbage into a fine, juicy mass. As her knife slid through the packed leaves of the heads, there was a dry, crisp sound, sometimes like the rattling of stiff paper. Belle wanted only the heads to pickle which made this sound. The others she put aside, to be kept in the dairy to supply the table's daily need. The stalks from the sliced heads she put into a bucket.

"Stop eating them," she said to Lee, who was chomping one of the thick, white cores. "They'll give you the stomach trouble."

"Aw, one or two won't hurt," Lee said, chopping away at the box.

"Are you going to pickle some?"

"A few on top of the kraut," Belle said. "But only a few." After a moment she continued, "I'm sure glad it didn't rain today. The cabbage would have ruined before the signs are right again."

"Miss Woodson," Alan remarked, "doesn't believe in signs. She says people who do are superstitious."

"I don't care," Belle said flatly, "what Miss Woodson believes in. It's not her kraut I'm making. Her trouble is, she's read too many books. Just because something gets printed in a book doesn't make it so. And don't you forget it," she finished, looking angrily at Alan.

"Mr. Llewellyn believes in signs," Lee said, glad to take sides against his smart-alec brother. "He says that if the moon rules the tides in the sea, there's no reason to think there's nothing in the signs. What works one place can work in another."

"Mr. Llewellyn's got himself some sense," Belle said. "He hasn't let books ruin him. 'Of the making of books, there is no end; and much study is a weariness of the flesh,'" she quoted. It was a beautiful time to give her boys a text.

Alan was silent, afraid there were superior powers, of which he was doubtful; and angry because he felt disloyal to Miss Woodson whom he could not defend against his mother's general indictment of learning from books. Anyway, arguing wasn't going to help matters. Lee probably made it up about Mr. Llewellyn just to take sides against him. He dropped more cabbages into the tub and began to wash them.

By now the big gray crock was over half full of the finely cut vegetable. First, Belle had placed a thick layer of chopped cabbage inside the jar, following this with a light sprinkling of salt, adding layer after layer from the box as Lee worked the cabbage down to the right texture. The jar was rapidly filling up. Alan stopped washing the heads. Slicing one in half, he studied the arrangement of leaves about the central spine, finding the formation curiously like that in a section of sea shell he had seen in a book at school.

From the barn, they could hear Oscar sawing and hammering, making the rub-blocks for the farm wagon, whose old ones had given way last week while he and the boys were hauling fenceposts. If the mules had been on a real hill when the brake failed, the wagon would have pushed them all the way to the bottom. As it was, Alan and Lee had been able to hold back on the tailgate until the load reached the end of the small slope. "If it isn't one thing, it's another," Oscar had said. "A poor man has poor ways."

The jar was now full of chopped and salted cabbage. Belle told Alan to wash the white rock she used year after year for weighting the pickling mess, and Lee to bring her the large cake plate from a shelf in the kitchen.

This, she turned upside down in the mouth of the crock and placed the scrubbed stone on top of it. Then she tied a clean white cloth over the top of the jar.

"It's ready for the dairy now," she said. "If nothing happens, in seven or eight days we ought to have some real good kraut."

About the fresh cabbage was a faint smell of rot which had brought a buzz of green flies to the back porch. "If they got to it," Belle explained, as she explained every year, "there'd be maggots in it. They always come, even when I'm cooking cabbage. It's fresh, but it smells rotten." Her talk was a bit disconnected. "That's why I use the cloth," she said.

She sat for a moment, looking, not outside herself at anything, but in, as if she dreamed in a dull, stupid sort of way. Her face was withdrawn, secretive, too, as if she contemplated some point of interest deep inside her even while her expression was foolishly blank. Alan had noticed that his mother often sat lately in such a trance. He and Lee left her, sitting, on the porch, dreaming her personal dream, and went to help their father at the barn.

Alan tried to imagine Buckeye with his head bloody and shorn. Dehorning the calf would be like trimming a young tree down to its trunk and expecting it still to be green and to grow. Belle herself had said that taking an animal's horns made him less than an animal, a ghost of what he had previously been. It was always man, she said, who bent and shaped the other creatures to his will. Nothing could resist him for long. It had always been so, and it would always be so. She had sounded so final. Alan felt hopeless, not only about Buckeye, but about everything. His father *had* been, he realized, the animal-namer in the world to him, a kind of awkward, red-faced Adam among the clans and tribes of the barnyard and the field, naming them all in their classes and kinds, describing them so that in a sense their being became more real and valid. But while he could trust Oscar to name the animals, he couldn't always rest in the belief that his father knew the right thing to do, or how to do it when it actually needed to be done. He had seen Oscar botch too many ordinary tasks about the farm, fail in too many elementary missions, to trust him in matters of action. Belle had said in explanation of her husband that Oscar was simply ungifted in the ways of a man with tools, but Alan felt that his father's inability to take exact measurements along a plank was not so much a lack of gift as it was the result of carelessness and indifference. Any makeshift seemed to suffice for his father.

Alan had begged his father to spare Buckeye's horns. "I'll take care of him," he promised. "You won't have to come near him. Not ever."

But Oscar was adamant. "Those horns," he declared, "have to come off."

When he entered the barnyard, lagging behind Lee, Alan saw Buckeye, already roped and tied to a fencepost near the gate. The calf's horns had grown like new shoots on a well-nurtured tree. From tender, rubberlike knobs, they had become lengthening half-moons of stone, curved and dangerous, so that if he hooked now, Buckeye would leave not merely a dark bruise but a bloody gash as well. Alan rubbed Buckeye's head. The calf pushed against him with a shoulder.

"Here," Lee said, "hold this."

The saw his brother thrust into his hands dismayed Alan. It was not a regular dehorning saw, but a handsaw, the kind used for cutting an ordinary board. The coarse, wide teeth would mangle Buckeye's head. Alan realized that. "Dad," he said desperately, "let's wait until we get a real saw. Mr. Wade has one. Let me go get it."

"I'm tired of asking John Wade to borrow something every time I turn around," his father said. "This will do. It'll have to."

Catching Buckeye quickly, so that the calf, being off-guard, staggered and almost fell, Oscar threw the animal upon his side and held him down while Lee tied his feet so he could only struggle with a faint muscle movement under his sleek hide. Alan rubbed Buckeye's shoulder and spoke to him, hating his job of putting his knees upon the calf's neck to hold the head stationary for the saw.

At the first run of the saw, Buckeye bawled, rolling his eyes like blue-veined marbles in his head; a thin white foam began to fleck his mouth where the tongue lolled out in the dirt of the barnyard.

The sight almost made Alan sick. His heart beat unpleasantly under his left shoulder.

Oscar must have disliked his part of the job, too, for he grew hurried and cross. He cut into the quick of Buckeye's head and blood rose like a small fountain, spraying him and Alan. Lee, holding Buckeye's hind feet, and leaning forward also had blood on his face. He had begun to look worried. Oscar swore, flinging the severed horn away, and began to cut the other, getting too close to the forehead again. Swearing violently and bemoaning the luck of a poor man who had poor ways, he untied the suffering Buckeye, and the calf got to his feet and staggered, bleeding, around the barnyard, his forelegs wet and shining with blood.

"He'll bleed to death like that!" Alan cried. "I told you, Dad! I told you!"

"Well then, by god, you do something! I've done all I know how!" Oscar yelled, his face working with anger at his own clumsiness and at this son who always knew best. "You're always telling me something."

He hasn't done one thing right, Alan thought, pitying Buckeye more at the moment than he loved his father. Streaking towards the house to get Belle, Alan wished Buckeye had stayed lost on Walden Ridge, that he had never been found. Better to have let him starve than to tie him down and kill him with a saw.

Belle brought bandages torn from one of her old sheets and bound the spouting holes in Buckeye's head. But the bandages did no good. Alan watched his mother work quietly while Oscar stood by in anger and shame, finding between his parents such a contrast of nature he wondered, even in his fear for Buckeye, how they had ever managed to make a life together. Cautiously, with pain on her face, Belle plugged the scarlet holes with cotton. Buckeye was now not so wild. He stood in the stable where he had been corralled and looked at his tormenters with dumb, unquestioning eyes, his forelegs braced against the wet stable straw. The blood ran freely, still in a shining rut from his forehead to his nose, and there was a steady dripping sound in the quiet, summery stall.

Belle said, "Alan, we'll have to have some devil's snuffboxes to stop this blood. Find some as quick as you can."

He ran to the slope behind the house, trying to remember where he had seen the small pin cushions growing. They were not there. He tried the hill behind the hogpen, frantically searching, his eyes close to the earth, knowing that if he lost Buckeye, not only did he lose his pet calf, he lost his books for the next school year as well; but, worst of all, it seemed, he would lose his love for his father, who, despite his harsh clumsiness, still held the world on his shoulders for his son. In the heart of a child, the reasons are not many, but are rooted deeply. Already Alan knew that there are only a few things in life worth the difficult effort one must put forth to keep them.

He found the first snuffboxes behind the hogpen on the hill. Under the plantain and the weeds, themselves almost shaded to death by the thick cedar branches, the small, dusty cups flourished, as though only something gray and seemingly lifeless would grow in the neighborhood of a cedar tree.

Alan gathered as many of the spore-filled cups as he could find, careful not to press them until they smoked and lost the chocolate-colored dust his mother needed. Then he remembered the white-flint knoll under the cedars by the spring, and ran there, his breath almost slipping on him now. There, again, he found the soft, spongy spheres standing in clusters; grabbing a handful, he raced back to the barn.

Belle dusted the rich brown dust into the red cavities on each side of Buckeye's head, and it was wonderful to see how the blood slowed down in its pour and came to a small, diminishing drip under her wise hands. "Cobwebs would have done just as well," she said, "if I had only thought." Buckeye knelt now on the wet, shining straw, too weak to stand; he no longer looked at the people around him; only a glaze, heavy and windowlike, lay like a shutter over the dark bull eyes. There was almost no sound in the stall but Alan's labored breathing.

Oscar helped Belle from her kneeling position on the straw, gruff and relieved now at the outcome of his venture. He and Alan looked at each other with neutral eyes. Lee was still on his knees by the calf, stroking the animal's shoulder. Never again, Alan told himself, would he doubt the goodness of Belle's simple remedies. He would roam the fields, searching for all the herbs she told him, the plants and berries and barks and teas that grew there. He understood now that the earth was filled with more than beautiful names like queen-of-the-meadow or butterfly-weed. Beautiful things were useful, too. And useful things were beautiful. For when his mother, red-faced, breathing hard, and shapeless with her unborn child, walked from the dark stall, in his grateful mind he saw in her the grace and height of angels.

18

IT rained in the night, a sudden downpour that drenched the land and made the cornfield too wet for plowing. After breakfast, Lee said as he and Alan finished the chores, "Let's go fishing. The creek's up just enough to have them biting good." All around them, in the barnlot and in the nearby garden and orchard, there was the smell of wet earth, rich and loamy, an earthworm smell, that made fishing almost imperative. They drew in deep breaths of the wet, earthy air, as they dug for worms behind the barn and then near the hogpen, harvesting in the process a can half-full of the fat red wigglers. Alan found two fat late grubs, beginning to turn brown where the legs of the new bugs would have been. Taking their river canes, already strung with hook, line, and sinker, the boys headed for the bend in Muddy Bottom Creek where the fallen tree made a bridge over the water from the bank to a big limestone jutting out into the stream. Here, in the shallows just below the deep hole in the bend of the creek, in early spring Alan and Lee had seen an amazing congregation of fish schooling over the submerged sandbar. The water was brown with horny heads, the short, earth-colored fish that tasted so well when rolled in meal and fried crisp in the kitchen at home. The fish were spawning, the boys knew.

Above the fishing-place two sycamores towered, their white and gray scaly trunks like ragged, moulting bodies of some half-tree, half-animal creature. Alan loved the smell of the wet, limp sycamore leaves. The trees also furnished him and Lee with the stemmed seed-balls which they covered with colored foil and contributed to the Christmas tree decorations at school and at the church. In summer, however, it was their color that made the trees so extraordinary among all the other trees of the neighborhood. On sunny days, sycamores could be seen everywhere about the valley, their white trunks giving back the light to all eyes.

Lee and Alan settled themselves on the trunk of the tree-bridge and began to angle for the small finny citizens of Muddy Bottom. Only silversides seemed to be biting. These small, minnowlike creatures, whose sides gleamed silver when they altered direction in the water, were bait-stealers. Occasionally, one big enough to keep was pulled in, but mostly the boys unhooked them as carefully as they could and threw them back into the creek. To catch them again, at times. "Better to throw them out on land and let them die," Lee said. But Oscar had forbidden that. "It's not your job to clean the creek of fish," he said. "Take a little, leave a little. It's a good practice." So back into the water went the silversides, to start nibbling again.

By the middle of the morning, the fishermen had used up their bait.

"Let's stick out our poles and go hunt some 'tawba worms," Lee suggested.

They worked the end of the canes into the soft mud of the bank, allowing the middle of the slender rod to rest across the tree trunk at the proper angle for the line to dangle into the water, and left the creek, following a cross-bottom fencerow towards the hill where the catalpa tree fattened a host of thick green worms on its juicy leaves. In their preoccupation with getting their fishing-poles set at the right slant, they forgot the bait-can.

"Dang it," Lee said, when they reached the tree. "Why didn't you remember to bring the can?"

"Why didn't you?" Alan said. "It was your suggestion."

Grumbling, Lee started to ascend the tree. "Jumpin' Jehoshaphat, look at the 'tawba worms!" he said. Before he gathered any, however, he climbed to the top of the tree. "I can see everywhere," he said. "The cliff, the quarry. If the leaves were down, I could see Enoch Wall's house from here. There's the swimminghole!" he shouted, swinging himself in the branches. "And there's the gap in the ridge where the railroad goes through."

Descending to the lower branches where the worms fed on the leaves, Lee picked several and put them carefully into his pocket. On the ground he said, "I can't stand those slimy things in there," and turned his pocket wrongside out. The worms tumbled to the ground. "I know," he said. He took out his handkerchief, spread it flat, and deposited the handful of worms in the middle of the small cloth, and then, like a peddler tying his pack, he gathered up the four corners and tied them crosswise into two center knots, squeezing the worms together as he did so. His handkerchief stained with a rich yellow-green liquid. "I guess I mashed their guts out," he said. The handkerchief was ruined. "I'll catch it when Mom sees this, but she won't see it until dinner," he concluded cheerfully. "No use ripping my pants until the time comes. Let's go back and see if we've got anything."

On their way to the creek, the boys stopped by the small sulphur spring that trickled out of the side of the hill. Around the sluggish flow of water the earth was a dull brownish-yellow where the mineral had solidified out of solution. "Want a drink?" Lee asked. Alan shook his head. "It's good for your blood," Lee insisted. "Make a man out of you." He took a mouthful and gagged. Around them, the stench of rotten eggs mounted. "How Mom can stand this stuff, I don't know," Lee said.

"I don't really think she drinks it," Alan said. "She poured out the last I carried her."

"She drinks some of it," Lee said. "I saw her. All I can say is she's a better man than I am."

"Almost anybody is," Alan said, and began to run, Lee after him. They reached the creek, winded. "Whew," Lee gasped, stretching out on the tree trunk, "I ain't got any more wind than a busted horse."

Alan lay on his back on the rock, his mouth open, gulping the air, like a stranded fish, he thought, feeling the sides of his throat tautly working with each breath. Maybe we do have gills in our throats, he said to himself, like the book says.

Lee tested his cane. "There's something on this," he said, puzzled. "Heavy, but no wiggle." He pulled steadily, the cane bending in a long arc. A brown shadow as large as a washpan showed under the surface of the water. "It's a horn-swoggling turtle," he said, as the stretched, prodigious mouth came into view, hooked barely under the edge of the upper lip. The turtle hung heavily, motionlessly for a moment before the flesh tore, and then sank backward into the creek. "Am I ever glad of that," Lee breathed. "I'd never got him off by myself."

Rebaiting his hook with one of the green worms he had tied up in his handkerchief, Lee fished again. Alan had already caught two small mullets. The greenish-hued fish, covered all over with small horny knots, tasted too earthy to be good, but he kept them anyway. "I'd as soon have a mouthful of mud," Oscar had said, trying to eat one Belle had fried. "Worse-tasting fish than mudcat, and that's saying a whole lot. Next time, son, how about throwing such trash as this back and letting it go. It's not fit for a man to eat."

They did fill up a string, however. So Alan kept them. He was using the catalpa worms now. He caught a horny head, a good six inches long, and was very proud. The flesh of the horny head was clear and fresh and delicious. He showed the fish to Lee. Lee refused to praise it. Alan slipped the horny head onto the catchstring with the mullets and dropped them all into the water. Sticking his pole into the mud, he waded across a shallow stretch of the creek and stood on the sandbar, now high and dry above the water. As he stood there, he saw in the clear run of the creek around the sandbar a watersnake surface and rear high, a small mullet in its mouth.

He struck quickly with the stick in his hand. But the snake disappeared. He waded back to the bank and returned to the tree trunk where Lee, in a glow of excitement, was holding up a large sunfish, round almost as a plate and speckled with bronze against its lighter gold. Still dripping, it was beautiful to see and would taste as good as it looked. Lee swelled with pride. "There's a fish for you," he said. "Beats everything else all hollow. I wouldn't give you one perch for a whole sackful of mullets."

Alan unstrung his two mullets and dropped them back into the water, watching them slowly revive and swim away. He kept the horny head on the string, however. With the sunfish, it would make enough to go around the table at home.

Just as Lee cast a hopeful line back into the water, the horn began to blow, its deep, golden tone questioning and commanding the boys. The sound echoed from the hill, seeming for a moment to haunt the countryside.

"Well, let's go plow corn," Lee said. "This hot sun's played heck with the fishing. It didn't rain quite enough last night."

Wrapping their catch in a wet towsack, the two boys went home through the drying meadow. Already the sun had scorched out the smell of wetness. Even the sense of the earth itself was dispelled, the rich, loamy presence of the soil not being so noticeable as in the morning. Transposed upon it now was the scent of hot weeds and flowers, like drying hay, mounting steadily into the sun.

"Old Ranger," said Oscar at lunch, "has cast a shoe and his foot is getting pretty tender. You'll have to take him to Henry Casteel's this afternoon, Alan, while Lee and I plow the corn. Let him take his time over the gravel road, and he'll make it all right. You're not heavy enough to hurt him."

Alan was glad his father was sending him to have the shoeing done. Visiting the blacksmith shop was a real adventure anytime, and particularly so since he had learned from a book about mythology that Mr. Casteel was really Vulcan, metal-smith to the other gods, and that his sooty shop was an underground cavern in which he worked, not only the metals for the armor of his Olympian patrons, but from which also he occasionally sent up, in the form of smoke and flame belching from his chimney, the wild fire of the volcano itself. To have mentioned this fancy to Lee would have been to call down again his brother's charge of lunacy; so he kept his imaginings to himself. Nevertheless, he was glad to be going to Mr. Casteel's. So glad he hardly heard Oscar saying, "I looked all morning in the pasture for the lost shoe, but there was no sign of it. Henry'll have to match the other three with a new shoe. He'll have one, I think, the right size for Old Ranger. Tell him, I'll hand him the money when I get it."

Belle was looking interested in the conversation for the first time in weeks. All summer, as the days passed, her concern with things about the household had seemed to diminish. "Do you remember," she said to Alan, "the little rhyme I taught you when you were about four years old? The one about the horseshoe?"

Alan nodded. The words were still clear in his mind, etched more deeply in his memory, perhaps, by the horseshoe Belle had wrapped with a blue velvet ribbon and hung inside over the front doorway, with the prongs up. "To keep the luck from running out," she had told him and Lee. She had explained further that the general belief was that a horseshoe found in the road should be immediately carried home and nailed above the doorway, with three nails to hold it, each nail to be driven in with three hammerblows. It had something to do with the trinity, she said; the Father, the Son, and the Holy Ghost. But just what, she didn't know.

Now she creased her forehead, remembering the rhyme, and beginning to recite in a half sing-song voice the story of the loss of a country's independence:

> For want of a nail,
> The shoe was lost;
>
> For want of a shoe,
> The horse was lost;
>
> For want of a horse,
> The rider was lost;
>
> For want of a battle,
> The country was lost;
>
> And all for the want
> Of a two-penny nail.

The ancient rhyme suggested dark battlefields, and a king crying out in the ruin of his chances, "A horse! A horse! My kingdom for a horse!" John Wade had once let him borrow a stained and very ragged copy of *Goodrich's New Sixth Reader,* dated 1857. It was in that book that the king cried. It was also there that Alan had found, on one of the front endpapers, the legend: W.W. Morrison, Lake City, Alabama, 1868; and on the other: Fannie W. Arson, Belleview, Virginia, as nearly as he could make out under the dark brown splotches that looked like the faded purple stars he himself had placed in his schoolbooks with the quartered shell of a muscadine, seeded and turned inside out. There was no date with the last name. Reading the names of the book's owners, long since dead, had made him shiver with a new apprehension of how objects, even frail papers and faded inks, outlasted flesh.

The verse his mother had just spoken was very likely written about the despairing king, he decided; though he had not supposed them connected in any way before. The summer was linking many things for Alan; a mysterious process of mental hide-and-seek was going on in the provinces of his growing knowledge, with the balance tending always toward a greater discovery. He was becoming increasingly able to shout "I Spy" in the matter of many things that before summer began had been an utter bafflement.

As he rode slowly towards the blacksmith's shop, repeating for his own pleasure the verse his mother had recalled, he thought it curious that the prongs of the goodluck horseshoe should have to be turned up. Why not turn them down, and allow the bad luck to pour out, he wondered. After all, the matter was just as broad as it was long. There was no telling about superstitions, though. Some of them contradicted others; sometimes, as in the case of the horseshoe, directly opposite procedures were used to obtain the same results. For instance, turning the horseshoe towards the front door, with the prongs pointing to the outside, so that bad luck would run out of the house, contradicted the idea that the horseshoe held good luck in its cup, in the first place.

It was the same way with the moon. Alan had heard his mother say that the new moon, sitting balanced on its back like a thin golden bowl, held water, and that rain would not fall until the moon tipped either one way or the other and spilled the water over the rim. John Wade had said, though, that the moon tipped was a dry moon, and that no rain could be expected until it rested on its back and filled up again and overflowed onto the earth. There was a twinkle in John Wade's eyes while he talked, and Alan had felt a slight misgiving about the man, who seemed to be half-way teasing him. Oscar sometimes sounded this way when he discoursed about the moon's phases and the proper time of moon to cut stovewood to keep it from "sobbing." Alan knew his father meant molding and turning damp and green, so that the wood would hardly burn in the kitchen stove. It might be, he began to suspect, that grown-ups often talked one way and believed another. The world was a fascinating place all right, but it certainly was peculiar. He wondered how far he could safely go in trusting his elders.

The moon occupied his thoughts now for awhile—the cold, white moon that at times flooded Walden Valley with such a colorless reflected light that the trees, even at midnight, threw dark clumps of shadows. So far as Alan was concerned, the moon was always bad luck, bringing with its light a sense of unreality, of lostness, as though he looked on an illuminated picture of a dead world, once very real and alive in the direct rays of the sun, but now only a hollow reflection of the living sunlight, as a face in a mirror was only a light-produced image of the real flesh and blood. His impressions were confused, as confused as his reactions to the heavenly body that filled him with a sense of utter loneliness and fear. His feelings had not been improved much by his learning that lunacy itself was moon-madness, contracted perhaps by sleeping with the head exposed to moonlight. His mother said, too, that moonlight spoiled meat left lying where the moon shone.

He would always remember the night at the Wades when he went with Ira to draw water from the well. Peering over the stone parapet, he could see, far away at the bottom, an image of the moon reflected in the water, cold, diminished, even lonelier than the real moon which hung directly overhead. The way light was bounced again and again off the surfaces of things amazed him. He remembered the well in daylight, when the upper stones of the casing, overgrown with a strange green moss that appeared more yellow than green, gave off a golden glow that seemed to rise in a soft, whole body of light, bulging his eyes with emerald, sun-glim, and some admixtured gold like lemons in a green pitcher. All his leaning into the damp mouth of the well could not smother the staggering transfusion of golden light pouring from the wellside.

It was from this same well that Ira had drawn the salamander with the exterior gills, short, fringy outgrowths on each side of the creature's head that looked like small coral-colored trees. The fact that the smooth, brown, footed animal came from the dark underground was as baffling as the glowing mouth of the well through which the salamander came into the ordinary daylight. The well was marvelous and mysterious for many reasons. But Alan had found it hard to believe Ira when he said that he had seen a star shining in its depths at mid-day. Light was admittedly incomprehensible, escaping always the boy's attempts to understand it. But a star at noon was too much to believe. Even Ira must know that stars didn't originate at the bottom of wells.

Old Ranger stopped to browse the grass at the roadside, and Alan was brought out of his daydream by the sudden smoothness of his seat in the saddle. In motion, the horse went with a slight, limping pace, setting his unshod hind foot gently against the earth as if the pressure pained him. Waiting for him to get a good mouthful, Alan saw two red-headed woodpeckers fly across the road in front of him; they were followed by a third. Looking for a fourth, which never came, he wondered whether the mate had been killed by a hunter. There was always some trigger-fingered boy or man to shoot at the wild things. In past years, John Wade had told Alan, the ivory-billed woodpecker had been plentiful in the valley, but for some time now, he said, that magnificent bird had been almost extinct from the slaughter exercised upon it by indiscriminate hunters. The red-heads, Alan thought, looked almost like ivory bills, though they were much smaller. The only member of the larger species he had ever seen had flown late one afternoon over the swamp, straight to the pinewoods, turning its head constantly from side to side as if on the lookout for an expected enemy.

Chewing his mouthful of grass, Old Ranger moved on down the road. The sunlight poured warmly on everything, light that was almost yellow among the pale green boughs of the willows that fringed the banks of the brook ahead. From the fencerow a strong, sun-baked smell, that seemed a color also sprang up. The color was brown. What Alan had called "fence-row brown" in a small story he had written for Miss Woodson. Whether she had understood his explanation that certain smells were also colors, he didn't know. She had merely looked curiously at him, and gone on reading. He was not sure that he himself understood how a summer-green fencerow, baked in the sun, could come out smelling brown. But that was how it was.

Henry Casteel was in his shop shaping a plow-point when Alan arrived. The shop itself, a shanty almost, was surrounded by giant oak trees that dwarfed the smoky clangor that went on daily under the rusty tin roof. Above, in the oak branches, the wind blew ceaselessly, sighing or whistling, undisturbed. But inside the shop the noise was ear-splitting, earth-filling. Alan watched the swarm of sparks, like those emitted by a Christmas sparkler, fly off the edge of the red-hot steel being tamped by the smith's hammer. Deftly, Henry Casteel fashioned the scooping edge of the bull-tongue.

"Be with you in a minute, son," he called above the racket he was making.

Naturally dark-skinned, and now smudged with soot and smoke, Henry Casteel looked like a citizen of the underground, where coal veins lie and metals are at home. He was a little man, not much like the mighty smith in the poem Alan had read at school; his hands, of an ordinary size, were short-fingered, the palms themselves not much wider than Alan's own. But they were powerful hands, and swung the hammer truly, certainly, as those of a much larger man might have done.

Giving the point one last ringing blow, Henry Casteel took a look at Old Ranger's bare foot while Alan explained.

"I think I have a shoe already turned of the right size," the smith said going to a row of pegs in the wall, where shoes of several sizes hung. Selecting a shoe, he measured it against Old Ranger's ragged hoof.

"He couldn't have stood much riding shoeless," he said. "This will do if I shorten it slightly and re-caulk it. Pump the bellows for me, will you, son?"

Alan worked the handles of the bellows, opening the leather sack as far as it would open and pressing it flat again. The flow of air made the coals hiss and turn a deep red. Into the glowing mass, the blacksmith thrust the open end of the shoe, pushing it deeply into the fire with long-handled tongs. Then he returned to Old Ranger and began to trim the horse's hoof to receive the shoe. From where he pumped the bellows, even over the smell of the fire and the heating metal, Alan could catch the unmistakable odor of Old Ranger's hoof. Soured, manure-like, the stench struck his nose with a force that even the heat could not cleanse. His Uncle Granville had once told him that chewing gum was made from horses' hoofs, and Alan had not chewed any gum for weeks following the news. It had been Belle who had dislodged the notion.

"It's only some more of Granville's foolishness," she said. "Glue, not chewing gum, is made from horses' hoofs."

The explanation had satisfied Alan, but it took time for him to forget the sickening suggestion his uncle had made.

Finished with the trimming, the blacksmith thrust the tongs into the glowing coals, hissing now with the air Alan pumped, and withdrew the red-hot shoe. With a chisel, he cut the prongs to the proper length, and then over the edge of the huge anvil, caulked the shoe neatly, so that it was as balanced as if it had been measured with a ruler instead of a man's eye. Then holding the still glowing shoe with the tongs, he thrust it into a wooden tub filled with water. A screeching hiss arose, a great bubbling that slowly subsided. When he drew the shoe from its bath, well-tempered and smoking, the blacksmith tested it with his finger.

Alan stood close by while Henry Casteel lifted Old Ranger's great foot and placed it between his knees. The hoof needed only a bit more paring before it was ready for the shoe. Turning his head, the horse looked mildly at the man handling his hindfoot, and tried to nuzzle Henry Casteel's back with his nose.

As he nailed the shoe carefully on, the blacksmith explained some points of his trade. Following Alan's questioning, he spoke of his father, who had been a smith before him, and of how horseshoes in his father's day had had to be made from a piece of unturned steel, heated, shaped, cut, caulked, and holed for the nails, all in one continuous operation, while the animal and its owner waited. Things were more modern now, he said. Shoes might be bought at the hardware in town. These nails, for instance, were especially machined for the shoeing. "But then, a man started from scratch," he said.

The shoe set, the blacksmith tested it with his hammer. Old Ranger did not flinch. Apparently no nail had reached the quick. Dropping the shod foot to the ground, he slapped Old Ranger on the hip, and the horse pushed at him with his great swinging head.

Deftly, Henry Casteel wrapped a horseshoe nail around the handle of a small chisel, and made a ring. Alan gazed in wonder at the perfect circle constructed by the man's single unbroken motion. The tip of the nail arced smoothly against the side of the head, barely touching it.

"Here," said the blacksmith, "you can give this to your girl."

Alan grinned, slipping the ring onto his own fnger.

"Boy, I'd hate to be a girl and have to wait until you gave that ring to me." Henry Casteel's teeth shone suddenly in his sooty face. "Up with you now," he said. "I've got other work to do."

Alan mounted from the anvil. "Dad said for me to tell you that he'd hand you the money when he got it."

"That's all right," the blacksmith said. "Anytime between now and Christmas suits me. The closer to Christmas, the more of Old Santa Claus I'll be able to afford."

As Alan left the yard, the clangor of beaten steel rose again. But above the measured blows of the hammer, he could hear, ringing clear on another highway of sound, the blacksmith's lilting whistle, sounding for all the world like a red-wing blackbird tuning up down in the swamp.

The whistle of the blacksmith and the noise of his hammer grew faint in the hot afternoon, and soon died out altogether, as the boy and the horse moved briskly along the road towards home. Old Ranger seemed to be in a hurry to reach the farm, stepping evenly now in his new shoe and showing no interest in the lush roadside grasses. From among their green fronds, interspersed with a small blue flower shaped like a star, came the smell of branchmint, strong, pungent, as if freshly trod upon. Alan breathed it deeply, finding it as cleansing and refreshing to his throat as a drink of cold water. He could see the shadows of the trees almost visibly lengthening, checkering the gravel in the roadway with patterns of brown nd gold, of sun and shade, where the sun filtered through between the sparser branches or hung, half-sun, half-shadow, on the edges of the moving leaves. The wind was light, but beginning to bring a coolness from the depth of the woods and fields that told him nightfall was near. Sphinx moths came and went across the roadway, and once a huge yellow wasp striped with a brilliant reddish-orange flickered by.

Alan noted these things idly almost, his mind still on Henry Casteel and the grimy shed in which the man wielded his expert hammer. Blacksmiths, he knew, had been among the earliest of Europeans to come to America, being, because of their trade, more important to the colonies than lawyers or preachers or teachers. He knew, from his reading at school, just how important they had been. For it had been they who had shod the horses upon which men made their necessary, and sometimes fabulous, passages about the unknown landscape. They were behind the great migrations, the movements northward, southward, westward from the Atlantic seaboard. They were the mainsprings of the clockwork of exploration and expansion. In their hands had sprung the tools with cutting edges to fell the forests, clear the land, and break the soil for crops. They had, in a very real sense, tempered the American steel, put an edge even on the courage of men themselves, so that their confidence never flagged in the face of mammoth tasks. Having the proper tools in hand had been half the battle.

It was true that each man on the edge of the settlements had his own equipment. On every outlying farm could be found the hammer, the sledge, the chisel, and the grindstone, each man being, insofar as possible, his own blacksmith. But the true smith had possessed the utensils of fire and the flame itself, perhaps the greatest tool man had ever turned to his own use; and to him his neighbors looked in their final needs. For without the blessing of the forge, with its fiery coals and its bellows for the heats no man could produce from a mere kindled fire alone, they were doomed to failure. The grindstone sufficed for a day or two in helping the settler hold his own against the wilderness, but was a makeshift at best, a stop-gap, until more expert service could be secured.

Alan thought of the blades sharpened, the points shaped, on the great gray stone in the yard at home—the stone that sang at all seasons as, with its harsh caress, it returned the cutting edges of the farmstead to a temporary but usable keenness. Remembering Whizzer's fondness for the stone, he smiled. In winter especially, the cat liked to lie upon the broad rim of the stone wheel at mid-day, after the chill had departed and the sun had warmed the rim to a summer comfort. Then, Whizzer liked to stretch along the upper circle of the grindstone and receive what warmth there was from both below and above. Whizzer was a smart cat; no doubt about that.

The roadway became almost dusky as the sun dropped behind Walden Ridge. The scented coolness of early night spread like a rising wind. Gold flared to the zenith, rayed behind the peaks of the ridge; cloudless, clear gold, unbroken except for the paths of blue flung upward and the dark forms of the crows flying north to the rookery in the pine wood.

As Old Ranger stopped at the barnyard gate, Lee and Oscar were entering the barn lot from the other side, leading the plow mules. Alan dismounted and let himself in. Old Ranger, with the rein across his neck, moved directly to his stable, without waiting for his rider. Over everything was the sudden closure of night.

The darkness seemed to grow up from the ground and spread like a soft, branching smoke tree against his face as Alan climbed over the inner gate on his way to the house. Beside the path a shameweed was barely visible, its round lavender-pink blooms strung like a pair of his mother's beads along the narrow green fronds. He kicked at the plant, but the darkness was too heavy for him to see whether the sensitive leaves began to fold along the spines. Doubtless, the shameweed was already shut up for the night. Its faint, elegant odor, however, like the perfume of women in church, was still on the air—an odor which at mid-day expanded to a full, rich, almost nauseating attack on the nostrils. Alan had breathed that perfume many times as he knelt, calling out to the plant, "Shamey, shamey, shamey!" crooking his index finger, palm upward, in the familiar gesture of ridicule and belittlement. Sometimes, if the force of his breath struck the leaves, they really did begin to close, as if in shame before his taunting sing-song; but he was well aware of the plant's refusal to cooperate unless it was actually touched. Sometimes, too, he willfully deluded himself by stirring the thorny fronds with his foot before beginning his chant. The nervousness of the plant always delighted him. He kicked at the weed again before going on up the path.

By the time he reached the backsteps, darkness was full in the valley; only westward, beyond the trees, light made a final assault against the rolling shadow. Near the horizon was a feathered band of russet and orange, deeper in hue towards the underside where the colors ran together and mingled, reminding him of the brilliant rust spots and border trimmings on the wings of the cecropia moth that had hatched, rolled and crumpled, on his bedroom windowsill in the early spring. As the low sunlight flamed, the horizontal band of color broadened, seeming to gain on the forces that strove to put it out, as the moth color had increased while the leaf-like wings shook out of their wrinkles and began to wave back and forth in the air to dry. But the sunset, engulfed, went suddenly dead, becoming light gray like the dry silken pouch from which the moth had emerged; then it became sullen as lead. Gradually, black trees merged with a black sky. The noise of Alan's feet on the backporch seemed to light the lamps inside the house, with sound.

Later, under the lamp, going to bed, he stared again in his old near-disbelief at the patchwork quilt turned down for him by his mother. The whole amazing scale of summer—morning, noon, and night—seemed caught in the squares of daisy-dotted green and yellow cloths, grape, purple vetch, multi-hued plaids, brown, black, and savage red—an insanity of tones commingled and clashing that stretched from his chin to his toes as if he were an earth-giant buried to the eyes under the patternless rough dyes of the whole valley assembled in one bouquet, the coverlet on his bed. It was the quilt's utter disregard for harmony that made it harmonious in a way no careful selection of color and pattern could have done. Looking down, he saw the knolls his knees made, one a sheeny violet, like silk the color of a shameweed flower, or more like a passion flower, the field apricot, with its lavender bordering on the purpleness of blood; the other knee was a rich but subdued plum color, sober for all its interfused fruity tinges. Both colors, and particularly the violet, seemed to run in the moonlight when he shifted the position of his knees. He thought of the scraps of watered silk his mother kept in a cloth Red Cross bag his youngest uncle had brought home from the World War. Some of these scraps, imprinted with peacock feathers in a maze of changing hues, Belle had sewn into a cushion for the rockingchair.

His body itself he saw as a landscape, looking down, with a green field and a yellow bird in the flat of his stomach. Only the bird had lost its tail, involved as it was in the stitching of the next square. There it sat, in the hollow of his body, looking head-heavy and about to pitch forward off its perch. Alan laughed for pure pleasure. Hearing him, Lee muttered in his sleep, turning on his side away from his brother. Thinking of his Aunt Tennie, who had made the quilt, the strange, thwarted woman who had gone quietly crazy after her lover had deserted her, and who had thrown her engagement ring into the garden where it had been plowed under and found again many years afterwards—thinking of this odd aunt, he began to drift in the first soft distances of sleep, feeling sleep settle down, coming like a colorless wave through fields of haunting color, fading them as it came, until they were perfectly bleached, of one color that was no color at all. The lamp, he thought, diving deeply under the gigantic, spreading wave of sleep. I forgot to blow out the lamp.

19

BUCKEYE'S head healed slowly. Daily, Belle swabbed his running wounds with a solution of Epson salts in warm water, following this bath with an application of clean white cloths that resembled a turban when wound around the calf's head. In the process of treatment, he grew so gentle that he came to her whenever she entered the barnyard, offering his head for her touch and inspection, pushing and bleating for attention. Buckeye was gentle with Alan and Lee, too. But with Oscar he seemed shy and fearful, as if he remembered the ordeal of the saw.

One morning about a week after Buckeye had been turned from his small lot into the pasture with the other cattle, Alan heard Oscar yell from the barn: "Alan, you'd better see about that animal of yours. The heifers are trying to kill him."

Alan raced to the pasture to find Buckeye surrounded by four young heifers that were butting him mercilessly, their heads lowered, their forefeet braced far apart, so that when they struck him with an upward motion, he was lifted from the ground. His head bandages, still renewed each day, had angered them. Banged about by their attack, the calf seemed to be doing some kind of light-footed dance.

Forgetting everything but his beloved calf, Alan charged the heifers, his fists and feet flying. Surprised, suddenly afraid, they retreated, all but one young cow that showed fight. She came at Alan, bawling loudly, eyes rolling, her tail standing out behind her as straight and stiff as a poker.

"Come on, old fool bossy!" Alan shouted. "It's time you got some of your own!"

He doubled up his fists to throttle her, forgetting for the moment that she was literally an engine of war, swept forward by angers and energies that put his to shame. Before she reached him, he began to understand that he had more on his hands than he had bargained for. Sidestepping, he grabbed the enraged animal about the neck as she pranced past him, bucking and snorting, the whites of her eyes shining in her yellow head. Furiously, she carried him along in spite of all his braking efforts, bruising his heels, which he had dug into the pasture earth, on the hummocks of grass and loose stones. He did not succeed in halting her, let alone in throwing her, as he had seen Ira Wade do to the calves in the Wade pasture. Finally, he lost his footing over a protruding rock; but he did not let go. The heifer was dragging him now.

A persimmon bush whipped him stiffly as he went by; sawbriars caught at his bare feet with their hooked, tormenting thorns. But, oddly enough, he felt a sense of elation in the swift ride he was taking; even more curious was the fact that he noticed the breath of his abductor smelled strongly of wild onions. That was how he knew it was Old Emily, Belle's favorite heifer among the several on the farm. His mother was always threatening to sell Old Emily because of her one great failing. Her milk in summer would never be fit to drink, she declared. But so far Belle had been unable to part with the handsome young cow that had Alan in tow and was now entering the blackberry patch, towards which, the boy realized later, she had been headed all the while.

The tall, thorny canes were her allies, and among them she literally scratched Alan off her neck. Bruised and stung with briars, he lay among the brown canes of last year's blackberry crop. But Old Emily did not pause in her flight until she reached the creek at the foot of the hill, where she whirled and, hoisting her head, looked back up the slope. She bawled a challenge.

"Well," said Oscar as Alan crawled out of the briars, "that was a smart thing to do. Catching her by the neck, I mean. You must have thought you were steer-throwing in a rodeo. She could have killed you."

"Made me think of a Junebug going after a duck," Lee said. "Wow, was that ever a ride!" He looked at Alan almost enviously.

"The next time you can take it," Alan said. "She almost killed Buckeye. Her and the others. I don't know what's got into them."

"That rag," Oscar said. "They don't like that rag on your calf's head. Better take him back to the barnlot for a while. He'll be out of that bandage in a few days."

Alan looked around for Buckeye and found the calf standing close behind him, his swathed head bloody again from the butting he had taken. Buckeye bawled plaintively. Angry tears filled Alan's eyes as he led the calf away to the barn, vowing vengeance against the heifers. He would fix them. Just let the world wait and see.

At lunch, he silently planned how he would get even. There was a maple tree by the creek, under which the cows sometimes took shelter from the sun. He would hide among the branches with his flip, a crude slingshot he had made from a forked shoot, two rubber bands cut from an old inner tube, and a basket for the stone, shaped from the tongue of one of his last year's shoes. He would hide there, and when they came in out of the sun, he would give them something to scratch for!

When he had finished eating, he borrowed one of his father's shotgun shells without permission, opened it carefully and extracted the shot, which he slid into his pocket. Then he slipped away to the creek. Ensconcing himself on a lower limb of the maple tree, he waited for the enemy, who, this afternoon, were slow in coming. He climbed to the top of the tree and looked out over the pasture. The heifers were grazing in a small knot in the corner of the grassy field. They showed no sign of interest in the shade tree. Alan climbed back down to his fighting position and tried to wait patiently. Once he dozed and almost fell off the limb.

About two o'clock the cattle came in, switching their tails at the biting flies, bellies roundly filled, ready to ruminate the morning's pick of grasses. Their anger forgotten, the heifers looked mindless and silly as they chewed their cuds.

Emily, his nemesis of the briarpatch, lay directly beneath the limb which Alan straddled. He loaded his flip and took careful aim at what he considered to be Emily's most vulnerable spot on the end of her body away from her eyes. Whing! The lead pellet struck her rump. Her skin flinched in one broad, rippling movement like a wave on a pond, except no successive waves followed it. A little nodule of skin bunched under the impact of the pellet. Nothing else. Apparently, Belle's Emily was not a very sensitive cow.

He tried another. Another flinch, another small knot of skin. Emily chewed placidly on, occasionally switching her tail as though she imagined some big-mouthed fly had appeared in the pasture and chosen her for a meal. Alan felt insulted. Her very indifference was a commentary on his prowess as a hunter. No longer did he feel deadly and primitive among the leaves. He blazed away at the other cows, but with no better luck. He wasn't pulling back hard enough on the levers of his machine, he decided. So he pulled harder. But in getting leverage, he leaned too far backward and lost his thigh-grip on the limb. Down he started among the cows, exposed to his enemies by his own thirst for revenge.

Dropping the slingshot, he clutched the limb with both hands and broke his fall by swinging, with a thrashing of leaves and twigs, directly over the resting animals. They did not bolt. They simply gazed up at this addition to the tree. Getting to her feet, Old Emily smelled the soles of Alan's bare feet with her cold, wet nose; and, satisfied, lay down again, finding them harmless. Half a cow's length they lay below him, like a brown hummocky floor. He tried to draw himself back up among the leaves to the security of the limb, but his arms had cramped in the waiting and were not able to lift his weight. "Shoo!" he yelled. "Get! Hi!"

The cows did not move. His arms began to ache alarmingly. In desperation, he began to rock himself back and forth, so that if he were lucky when he did fall, he would land outside the now immense and slowly broadening continent of cow. Looking out to the edge of the gently breathing ring was like looking over a continental shelf for a place to dive in the real depth of an ocean. In a growing mild astonishment, they had begun to stand up now, one by one. His feet grazed their backs.

It was either drop onto a brown back for another wild ride, or jump now. Giving one last heave, he let go of the limb and flew, obliquely, almost as slantingly as the hypotenuse of a right triangle, toward the outer rim of cows. He landed just outside the fringe, on his back, breathless, and lay gasping. An awful stench began to fill his nostrils. He had landed in cow dirt. Crawling away on his hands and knees, he headed for the creek, where he stripped off his trousers and cleaned them with water and sand. The scrubbing left only a black-green stain in the worn cloth, which he hoped his mother would not notice.

An hour later his trousers were still damp and man-shaped on the willow tree where he had hung them to dry. Another hour would do it. But Oscar began calling him from the barn. He would have to go. Pulling on the uncomfortable breeches, and smelling sour and acid, he made his way home.

Lee noticed the unusual odor first. "Somebody," he said, "has cowflop on him."

Oscar looked at Alan. "Been fooling with them cows again," he said. "You never give up, do you." He was not asking questions, only making statements. The stubbornness in this seemingly soft son of his caused Oscar no little wonder.

20

IN late April the apple slick, pink as a sunrise cloud on a spur of Walden Ridge, could be seen from the McDowell farm. "The Old Lillard Place" Oscar called the abandoned high farm, where the orchard grew wild and fruitful each year and the strange, old-fashioned house stood with its central hallway open to the wind. When the trees were still bare, both cultivated and forest tree, a small stream could be seen flashing away from the edge of the applebloom, to be covered later by the greenness of mid-summer, and later still by the seal of autumn color, so violent in years of moisture as to pulverize the imagination. But regardless of the Joseph's coat that the farm wore in late summer and early autumn, the apple trees and the water were still there.

Since the orchard had long since been abandoned and the house long unused, the farmers of the neighborhood helped themselves to the wild apples that began to ripen there in early August, the first man on the premises after the fruit was in season being the owner of as many apples as he could carry away before his neighbors discovered the harvest was ready. Each year the McDowells went to the orchard and brought home hard, bright apples for marmalade and apple butter. Because of Belle's condition, Lee and Alan were going alone this year, Oscar remaining at home to be near his wife in case he should be needed.

Alan loved the yearly journey up Walden Ridge. Always it was like a holiday, a final outing at the edge of summer, before school opened and his life was patterned for another session in the classroom. Something about the place, perhaps the half-stirring ghosts of people who had once owned the trees and lived in the rooms of the curious house, intrigued him. He had once read a poem about a man who bought a farm and heard strange feet walking in his fields; the feet he heard belonged to all the previous owners of the farm. Perhaps the dim, unexplained sounds at the Lillard

Place were once living sounds, made by people, like him and his family, going about their daily tasks in the rooms and under the trees. The idea gave him a pleasantly cold feeling, as if he really believed in ghosts. He thought he didn't. He hoped he didn't. But he wasn't quite sure. A man's hackles didn't rise for nothing. He was, after all, perhaps, like John Wade, who said he didn't believe in ghosts, but he'd certainly hate to meet one. In any event, old houses had been lived in. Alan knew that, for he felt about him in the rooms the presences of beings whose earthly parts, he knew from reason, were long since melted to dust.

For the apples, Lee and Alan carried two buckets and a towsack, the bright tin vessels being for collecting the apples from the grass under the trees. "Be careful of those buckets," Belle said, "and don't dint them. We'll need them again when the syrup is made."

Making syrup from the sweet green juice of the sorghum was another of the end-of-summer delights the McDowell boys revelled in before the school bell sounded.

"We'll be careless," Lee said, teasing her. "We'll bring home a sackful of crabapples sour enough to lock your jaw." Belle had been asking for all kinds of sour foods lately.

She smiled at him. "You'll get your jaw locked," she said, striking her fist into her open palm. "Ka-pow!" She stuck out her chin. "Look, my jaw's locked. I can't talk."

"I'd hate to hear you when it was unlocked," Oscar said. "I bet you'd be real wordy."

The boys went on their way, down the road to the rickety bridge where Muddy Bottom Creek crossed from the McDowell farm into John Wade's land. Here, they followed the creek along the edge of their neighbor's corn-field to where a smaller stream, known as Madden Branch, entered the creek; turning right, they began to ascend the long, slow rise down which the smaller stream fell from the side of Walden Ridge, at whose foot they could see, far away, the glimmer of the first low fall by which Madden Branch rose up to the mountain meadow in which it sprang.

Already the water was so cold it hurt to tread. Lee, who considered himself too big to go barefooted, wore heavy shoes. As for Alan, he would not don footgear until frost forced him to. He loved the feel of soil and water under his free feet. Wading now, he felt his feet go slightly numb under the impact of the mountain water, unbelievably cold in the hot sun-shine striking his shoulders. Periwinkles, like straight, stiff horns, covered the rocks along the stream's bottom, and now and then a mussel, ridged and black, could be spied among the rocks and mosses. Minnows, small and shadowy as brown smoke, streaked here and there. And once, in the crystal clearness of a protected pool, wavering alongside a submerged log for an instant before it dashed off, was a sizable fish, whose sides were dotted with vermilion. A trout, maybe, Lee said. The fish had gone like a thought. The boys half doubted they had seen it.

Maidenhair fern grew low beside the stream, and other taller, stiffer ferns, dark with spores on their undersides. Christmas ferns, Belle called them. And there were horsetail ferns, and ferns whose names nobody knew, at least in the McDowell family. A stand of scarlet bloom would be Miss Woodson's cardinal flower, Alan thought. His teacher had brought a bouquet of the dark red flowers to school last year.

"Come on," Lee said, when Alan stopped to examine a clump of blue gentians. "We'll never get there, if you stop to stick your nose into every posy you find."

Lee thought flowers were for girls. His only botany was the botany of love: dodder, kiss-me-and-I'll-tell-you, forget-me-not, heart's-abusting, love-everlasting. Outside these few plants he had learned from his mother's romantic stories concerning them, he neither knew nor cared about vegetation: the only other plants were either weeds or vegetables, to be rooted out or eaten. It was as simple as that. He couldn't understand his brother's interest in a flower's color or perfume.

A kingfisher flew up out of the water ahead of Lee, grating deep in its throat as it flew, sounding a bit like a rusty gate opening. The bird was too fast for him to waste his arm throwing. He skittered the stone along the surface of a pond. Another kingfisher mounted. The blue and white bird with the oversized, uncombed head perched on a mountain willow a few feet from the water. "Leave him alone," Alan ordered. "I want to see."

Lee responded by heaving a heavy stone into the stream. The cold splash struck Alan between the shoulders. The kingfisher flew, grating harshly. Angry with Lee, Alan climbed swiftly on ahead up the murmuring slope where the water rushed downhill, glinting like silver. Something was wrong with Lee this summer. He wasn't at all like the boy he had been last year. Come to think of it, he didn't even sound like Lee. His voice was deeper, and he had those curious long white hairs sprouting on the sides of his face, like spiderlegs. In the words of Oscar, Lee seemed to have been jacked up and a new boy run under him. Oscar was always saying that, about any old thing that needed replacing.

Near the edge of the main ridge was a honeylocust tree, heavy with pods, whose clacking in the wind sounded like a wooden sword war going on in the mountain. Lee broke one of the pods and sucked the sour-sweet greenish jelly secreted along the rim. He claimed it was good, just as he pretended sorghum juice was good. "Nobody but a pig would eat that," Alan declared. To him it tasted like glue smelled. Anyway, if he hadn't already known how it tasted, he wouldn't have eaten it. Lee had played too many tricks on him lately, and he was fast developing a hearty dislike for his brother, as well as a deep suspicion of Lee's every move and suggestion. It never occurred to him that the jokes Lee made at his expense had been made to Lee's embarrassment by Ira Wade, who, no doubt, suffered from someone higher up in an unbroken chain of passing the laugh onward. In the henyard, who pecked whom was definitely established. Alan knew that. That it was the same in the world of men, and particularly in the world of boys becoming men, he didn't know yet.

Entering the wood at the base of the mountain spur, along whose upper side lay the farm with its apples, the boys proceeded through heavy trees, still following the broken rise of the stream from black rock ledge to black rock ledge. The water was even colder in the shade, and clearer against the dark, almost black sediment, that had collected in the bottoms of pools. Where the water ran straightaway, there were gravel stretches, with patches of fine pebbles, pearly blue, gray, tinted with rust, and ribbed sand where water eddies had sifted powdered sandstone into formations like the delicate ribs of a bird. The low gray rocks beside the stream were starred with silver-blue rosettes of lichen, like curious scabs on the scarred hide of a dead elephant, Alan thought. This was always the best part of the visit to the farm: this fantastic world of rock and tree and stream that changed visibly, momently, all the way.

Entering the small pasture at the lower edge of the orchard, the boys approached a wide pool, over which small birds, flying in close communion, looked like a ray of light bounced from the cold surface. The flock dipped and swayed, wheeled and came again, touching the water before flying off, scattering drops in a light shower. Around the pool mints and cresses were a bright, brilliant green, almost blue in shadow where the scarlet heads of bergamot attracted a hummingbird that poised in inspection above a blossom, then moved backward on invisible wings as if to get a better view. The reversal fascinated Lee, who saw in the bird's easy retraction of itself something wonderfully mechanical, like a smoothly-moving car that backed as effortlessly and with as much precision as it moved forward. The bird's thready, coral feet, looking wholly inadequate even for its minute body, were folded against its gray underside. A drop of ruby suddenly spilled on its throat where the feathers, ruffled for the display, brought the bird's identification mark into view.

A scent of sourness was on the air, of leaves drying, of apples down in the orchard, spoiling in the grass; reminding of milk gone sour in the crocks in the spring at home. A mixture of odors, vegetable and animal, not pronounced, but suggestive: a year-end odor, an autumn tone mixed with a summer suggestion. About it, unmistakably, was the sweetish musk of deer. Around them, in the grass, the boys could see where the animals had bedded, where they had stamped for apples in the grass. But no deer were visible on the orchard. They would come later in the day, past mid-afternoon, to browse and feast on apples.

Leaving the buckets and the sack under a tree, Lee and Alan followed an apple-strewn path across the orchard to the house. Built on an old-fashioned mountain pattern, yet more lavish than the house the McDowells lived in, the house consisted of two large rooms separated by a hall, wide as a room itself, that began with the front porch and ran through to the back and became the porch again, though narrower, alongside of an ell which housed the kitchen, another room which Alan supposed to be the dining room, and a large pantry.

But it was not only the unusual make that characterized the house for Alan, but the wide painted design in the middle of the hall just back of what would have been the front door had the hall been enclosed. At that spot, between the two forward rooms, was the odd design of a jack-of-spades, neatly and mathematically done, curiously real and out of place in that back country region. Faded but elegant, as though borrowed from a more sophisticated world, it dominated the entrance.

Alan thought of the stories told about the house and those who had lived there. Two brothers, one story went, had lived here once on a time; twins, they had each one blue eye and one brown in his face; and both had been found shot to death one afternoon many years ago, before anyone now living in the community could remember. They had come there from the outland, bringing books and a phonograph with them. To corroborate the phonograph bit, Alan had one of the small cylinder records used by the early Edison players, which he had found in a corner of one of the front rooms. But the phonograph record did not explain the painting. Perhaps one of the brothers had been an artist.

Another story was more likely true: that of the crippled boy whose parents had sacrificed to send him out to the county high school, where he had studied, of all unlikely things, art and Spanish. This account more closely dovetailed with the house itself, for, Alan already knew, a motto in Spanish had been painted on one of the inside doors.

He looked out to where the russet sedge blew under the old trees, into the calm, dun world, and felt something of what the crippled boy must have felt, the urge for color, for more than the sleepy natural design. His eyes ran over the sway-backed barn and the stack of rotting hay inside the broken railing, which assumed, in his mind, a look of insult, as if cows had gotten through and found the hay not to their liking and gone away again.

Then his eyes returned to the jack-of-spades. Even the crippled boy did not explain that. The two men had, certainly, more claim to that, for the way their lives ended spoke graphically of gambling.

He pushed open the door to the right-hand room and went in. On the floor there was the rug of unbelievable roses he remembered, painted onto the bare boards. Three-fourths of the floor was matted with outlandish roses, as large as saucers; and around the fancy, impromptu garden, paint of another color made a wide, startling border.

Lee had followed him in. Alan turned nervously at his brother's voice. "He was a nut for roses, wasn't he?" Lee said. He scraped with his knife at a festoon of lilac-colored wisteria and yellow roses that began over the mantel and ran each way down the jambs to the floor. Over the center flowers, painted in watery white letters, were the words:

HOME IS WHERE THE HEART IS

"Sounds like something Mom would say," Lee said. His voice sounded small and repetitive in the room, as if uncertain of beginning and more uncertain of coming to a close. Echoes were beginning to build up in the place.

In the other room, there was nothing but a heap of junk; though, in the fireplace there, someone recently seemed to have built a fire. Oscar said foxhunters often camped there. Belle said bootleggers lighted the light that often from great distances could be seen moving among the trees. There was, for a fact, Lee said, a still lower down, nearer the meadow. He and Ira Wade had found it; had, in fact ("in fact" was a favorite expression with him), drunk some of the stillbeer from the two huge wooden vats in which the mash was working. The still was a lulu, he said; capable of running off a hundred gallons at a time.

"You stay away from there," Oscar had told him. "A man mean enough to make whiskey is mean enough to do anything. He'd as soon shoot you as look at you, if he caught you snooping around."

Whoever lighted the fire had done no other damage, if the fire had to be counted damage. As far as the boys were concerned, the old house seemed a perfect camping place, though neither one of them would have been willingly left alone in it during the day, let alone at night. Should they have been there at night, a fire would have been the first thing thought of: that magic red circle to drive back the dark and all that inhabited it. Being boys, they never thought of what comes and sits with big, watching eyes just outside the dancing firelight, itself not illuminated but testing its dread vision on its flame-lit kin. Such a thought as this would have sent them appleless home, even at mid-day and, as Oscar would have added, in the mildest weather.

Next, the boys went to explore the kitchen, as they did every year, seeing on the first door leading off the narrow porch along the ell more bunches of the ballooning roses, twined this time around the little verse:

The kettle's on,
The hearth is wide,
So lift the latch
And come inside!

The invitation had an ominous ring, faded as the paint was on the sun-warmed board. Alan tried to imagine what it would read like on another door, under dark trees, with two frightened children creeping up to it after a night of being lost in the forest. But this was no Hansel and Gretel house. He was rather glad Lee could not read his mind. This was rather a house where good-for-nothing foxhunters and unscrupulously dangerous moonshiners consorted. Not that that was any comfort; he suspected he had rather meet the old witch herself.

The kitchen was the most amazing room of all. The stove had been placed so that the pipe entered the chimney low down. Above the flue, painted in a long bow of words, was the information:

THE WAY TO A MAN'S HEART IS THROUGH HIS STOMACH

Weaving out and in among the words were the fabulous roses.

The house was beginning to read like a library full of familiar, memorized books, with flowery, decorated pages.

"That's Mom, for sure," Lee said. "She said it just the other day."

A side wall bore, of all things in that still warm country of sedge and trees, where squirrels came down to the front porch to hide nuts and even then a flicker was frilling on the oak boards of the roof, with the sound of small rifles popping in the distance—a side wall bore a ballet dancer. Poised on the rough planking, she seemed about to dance out into the kitchen and present somebody with a bow. In her hand, she held a gigantic rose.

The door on the opposite side of the room, leading out into the garden, was decorated with the rose-entwined assurance:

MI CASA EST SU CASA

My house is your house, Miss Woodson had long since translated for Alan. The epitome of hospitality, and the pathos of country loneliness. My house is your house. All the other walls were covered with Mexican drawings. Gourds and sombreros and a fat man sleeping in the shade of a palm tree made sleepy resistance to the intruders. And everywhere on the rough boards, unplaned and twisted with age, among the objects, Mexican and otherwise, the inescapable huge roses.

"He had roses on the brain," Lee said again, as the boys left the house and headed for the orchard. "Funny thing, though, there isn't a rose in sight here, and never has been. Not even a wild one.''

Somehow for his brother, Lee's statement of the apparent fact included all things that were most mysterious about the house. Of course, there were no roses. Is there ever in the world the world we want to create? The thought struck Alan like a match being scratched suddenly in a dark room.

The boys drank from the spring at the top of the orchard, a great gush of water as thick as a man's thigh that came gushing out of a cleft in the rocks there. Here, Madden Branch began as big as a small creek to begin with; gathering increase from small springs along its course, it arrived rough and cold and tumbling to enter Muddy Bottom, making at its entrance a fine fishing place where Lee and Alan often caught perch, small trout, horny heads, and the like. Its clear water, shooting far out into the slower, greener stream made a color like old winter snow. The boys liked the creeks more than the big green river, the Hiwassee, near whose banks they had been brought up in constant admonition and fear of its treacherous depths. Broad and swift in its decline from the mountain gap where it entered Walden Valley, the river had so frightened Alan when he was small that even now he hardly dared to cross alone the immense iron bridge that connected the Valley with the townside of the stream. He knew the Hiwassee, gathering tributaries like Madden Branch and Muddy Bottom along its short way, finally reached the Tennessee, which itself entered into the Ohio. The Ohio emptied into the Mississippi, and that great river, carrying half a continent of waters, finally disgorged into the Atlantic Ocean by way of the Gulf of Mexico. It was an interesting journey the river took, interesting to contemplate, but too far in space and time to be traversable except in a young boy's imagination.

On home grounds, Madden Branch itself offered more possibilities of exploration and discovery than did Muddy Bottom; moreover, it was pure enough in all its course to the top of the meadow to be drunk without fear of sickness. Even if deer and other smaller animals dabbled in its water along the way, a stream such as Madden cleansed itself in a few yards over the sand and gravel. Like the great St. Lawrence Alan had read about at school, the one North American river still free of impurities despite the people who had begun to clutter up its banks, Madden Branch was, in the smaller confines of Walden Valley, the one pure stream. He loved the lively, sparkling leap of the water from the spring deep in the earth behind the gray wall of limestone.

The minnows here, he noted, were mere slivers of brown, half an inch long, fleeing in the glassy pool. At the lower edge of the spring, a small brown crayfish backed hastily under a stone. Unlike the large gray and red crayfish of the sallow meadowland, this one, when folding his tail under him, looked like a picture of a shrimp Alan had once seen. Periwinkles dotted the submerged stones with their still spirals; a water strider hurried over the surface, his thready feet skating on the mysterious tension of the water's face. A late dragon fly, a "snake-feeder" Alan called him, paused like a strange aircraft, half helicopter, over the water, his blue icy wings veined with black and his darker body thin almost as a needle.

"Hey, let's rooster-fight," Lee called.

Thinking he meant the game in which two boys hunched up their shoulders and ran together, trying to knock each other down, Alan was about to say no, when he saw Lee picking late violets from a few clumps below the spring. Alan was surprised to see, among the unseasonal flowers, one blossom with two darker petals that looked velvety blue in contrast with the other lilac-colored rays that made up the rest of the flower. A bird's-foot, he thought. I'll have to remember to tell Mom. He gathered a handful of the long-stemmed violets, and he and Lee began the fight.

Hooking the head of his flower around the crooked neck of Alan's violet, Lee yanked without warning, and the purple bloom was decapitated. "I wasn't ready," Alan complained.

"Well, get ready," Lee said.

They played again. Again Alan lost. Lee's violet had a neck of iron, it seemed. At the fifth try, Alan managed to yank viciously first, and the head of Lee's violet plummeted into the dust. Now Alan had the champion, but Lee had tired of playing. "Oh, well," Lee said, tossing the headless stem away, "every dog has his day. I couldn't go on winning forever."

Alan wondered what would be so wrong with his winning awhile, now that he held a winner. But Lee's mind was made up. When a fighter retired, he retired for good. No use to talk about it. He was finished. "F-i-n-i-s-h-e-d spells *done*," he said.

Below them, hunting under the trees, a great brown hawk, displaying a white tail, swept by. "Rabbit-hawk," Lee said. "Wish I'd brought my rifle." High in the blue air above the orchard, another hawk screamed, shrilly, as though in anger. Or was it an announcement to the world to grow aware, to be on the alert, for the death that would come dropping out of the sky. Big cats screamed, Alan knew, to signal the beginning of a prowl; maybe hawks did the same.

The two o'clock train blew, its wild notes trembling suddenly in the quiet air. All summer the train had summoned the valley to a relevance with time, a rendezvous, as it were, with the knowledge of the passing hours, the increase and decrease of the warm middle of the days, the slowly lowering south of the sun. Not only had the train dominated the days; time and time again it had crept into the valley dreams, bringing with it, especially to the young, visions of the great journeys youth dreams of taking. To some, it was a reminder of a journey taken and gladly done with, a going in earlier years that had been bitterly disappointing and a return, secretly glad and determined, to the valley to resume old ties, old ways. To Alan, somehow, the train became commingled with all the events of his life, as a herald announcing and as a goad to remembrance. The lonely sound of the train gave him an indefinable heartache.

Lee was saying, "It's two o'clock. No wonder I'm empty." He rubbed his stomach. "Been hours since breakfast. Let's get the apples and get going."

Only the red-streaked apples were ready. Lee and Alan filled the towsack three-quarters full and heaped the two buckets. They would take time about carrying the sack, resting each other with the lighter load. Before they left the farm, they inspected the crabapple tree on the knoll. The apples, small and hard as stones, were still appallingly green, stinging the tongue with a bitter sourness that was more chemical than fruit. No use to bother with them. Later on, when they came again, perhaps with Oscar, the apples would be slightly yellow and ready to be made into a surprisingly tasty jelly, not bitter at all but filled with the essence of good apples.

"Let's take a short-cut home," Lee said. "By Enoch's. Going that way, we'll knock off a mile."

"You know what Dad said," Alan reminded him.

"He won't know if we don't tell," Lee said. "Besides, I'm hungrier than a she wolf. I can't wait all day for some grub."

They left the creek at the lower edge of the apple trees and struck off in a southerly direction, following a trail that would take them down the cliff and into the McDowell meadow at the foot of the ridge. On their way they would pass Enoch Wall's sled-house and, if he happened not to be at home, perhaps have time to inspect the curious premises.

As luck would have it, the little clearing in which Enoch's house stood was deserted except for a gray tabbycat that glared down at them from the low roof, without bothering to come down in welcome or to flee in fear. The animal seemed to have the confidence of all things left strictly alone, unmolested because of a fear they seemed to generate in themselves, and which other animals respected, not altogether for physical reasons so far as Alan was concerned. There was something eerie in that cat, something aloof, unconcerned, private, crouching there at the roof's edge and surveying the yard.

Lee was not afraid of Enoch. "Hey, Enoch," he called. "You've got visitors!"

But nobody answered. Alan looked apprehensively about the clearing; then he crept up to the small window and looked through. What he saw was, somehow, what he had suspected. The room was tiny but surprisingly clean. A table, a cot, a stove; these he saw at first glance. Then, as his eyes became accustomed to the change of light, he saw a farm calendar tacked to the wall, some neatly folded clothes on a chair, the familiar red shirt hanging on a nail, and on a shelf above the table, the fantastic plates Enoch had purchased at the hardware in town. The one room which was Enoch's house and home was an orderly sanctuary from the world, a place of mountain retreat. Suddenly Alan almost envied the man with the crooked brains. Perhaps he was saner than any of the people who mocked him, and better off simply because he knew what he wanted and was not ashamed or afraid in the possession of it.

Lee was inspecting one of the runners under the house. "I bet this used to be a cotton house," he said. "I remember one just like it that could be pulled from field to field. Only this one is bigger. I bet he made this house special for living."

The cat stood up and rubbed itself against the small tin flue that came through the roof. "Me-o-o-ow!" it yowled, as if to say, "That's enough."

The boys were startled.

"Let's go," Lee said. And Alan was willing.

As they reached the edge of the clearing, Alan imagined he heard a human sound, something between a laugh and a shout, perhaps a curse, down the trail before them. Nothing seemed to register with Lee, however. And they went on. A quarter of a mile below the clearing, rounding a bend in the trail, they came upon Enoch, kneeling in the woods, searching, his hands tossing sticks and leaves aside, his eyes intent on the ground, his mind completely absorbed in the task of finding something precious which had been lost.

They shrank back into the undergrowth. Enoch had not seen them. But they could neither go forward nor backward without discovery. Ordinarily unafraid of the queer man, Lee now recognized something doubly strange in Enoch's manner. His lips burbled a constant song of half-sobbing, eager and furious; his hands clawed and thrust at the hiding leaves. Suddenly, he stood up and kicked great bunches of leaves together; then a match sang. When he stooped again a flame began to climb from the dead heap. He kicked other leaves onto the fire, all the while straining his eyes at the ground, burbling his small song of fury and loss.

Just as suddenly he stooped again, and when he stood up this time a long-bladed knife was in his hand. Wiping the smoke-tinged blade on his sleeve, he laughed a laugh that froze the boys' blood, a high, warbling, almost screeching sound that went lilting among the trees like a wail of a banshee. Then Enoch passed them running, headed up the trail to his house. Before he was out of sight, Lee and Alan were running in the other direction, down the trail towards the safety of the meadow, Alan scattering apples from the buckets as he went.

21

ALAN and Lee helped themselves from the bowl of new honey on the kitchen table, eating the clear yellow fluid with chunks of bread, saving the comb until the last to chew into a white, waxy mess that would last for hours. It was almost as good as chewing gum. A dish of the new kraut and a platterful of baked sweet potatoes were on the table. But the boys only ate the honey and drank glasses of cold sweet milk Alan had brought in a crock from the spring.

The honey was sourwood, bright and sweet and brimming in the hexagonal waxy cells. The product of sourwood flowers, the bloom of a slight green tree that trailed lengths of small white flowerets in mid-summer, the honey was the prize substance from the hives kept by John Wade in a meadow near the ridgeline. Every year when he removed the supers containing the sourwood honey, he sent the McDowells a quart jar full of the mixed comb and syrup, knowing the boys delighted in the sweetness. With Alan, particularly, John Wade wanted to share his honey. He had a particular fondness, a love almost, for the light-haired boy with the big brown eyes. The darker Lee was darker in many ways for John Wade, as dark almost as his own son Ira, who had become a stranger to him. He never forgot to send the jar of honey, and the boys, for their part, always grew expectant in early August for the gift to arrive.

"When did Mr. Wade bring it?" Alan asked.

"This morning," Belle said, "about nine o'clock. Just after you boys left. Were these all the apples that were ripe?"

"Only the streaked ones were turned," Lee said. "The crabapples were as green as gourds."

"We had a late spring," his mother said. "The fruit was late in being set."

She called to them as the boys started to the barn. "Alan, John Wade

136

said you might help him finish robbing the bees this afternoon if your daddy doesn't have something else for you to do."

But Oscar was moving the tobacco into the shed and needed the boys to help. The bright sheaves of the plant had been hanging upside down on ricks in the field for two days, and were now ready for storage in the barn. Alan was sorry to miss the excitement of helping take the honey from the hives. The anxiety of the bees themselves, his own anxiety lest one decide to defend his winter stores, the smell of the burning rags in the smoker, John Wade himself in long gloves and the netted helmet—all these things filled his mind as he went toward the tobacco patch. It seemed odd, though, when he remembered the summer days that had flowed past him like a swift dream. In his mind were only the great high spots of the season; he recalled hardly at all the sowing, plowing, and reaping of garden and field, so far as the labor and sweat were concerned. The fruits came, and were there, round and colorful and perfect as big apples, hard and smooth and lacquered as wheat grains, nodular as corn, lengthy and green and vegetable as cucumbers. He rememberd only the excellent, almost breath-taking awareness of being alive. He did not mind work. It too became a part of his summer experience, but only as a minor tune played under a major melody.

"Did you boys build a fire on the mountain?" Oscar asked on one of the trips to the barn. "If I'm not mistaken, I saw smoke in that direction about two o'clock."

"No," Lee said truthfully enough, "we didn't. I didn't have any matches." Then, not being willing to let well enough alone, he added, "I thought I smelled fire myself."

Alan caught Lee's eye. Lee was a big-mouth, always telling him to watch his tongue and then blabbing himself. But Lee had no intention of embroidering further than this.

"Probably moonshiners," Oscar decided. "The Bradleys, I suppose. It's about time to start buying winter shoes."

"Not many apples were ripe," Alan remarked, hoping to change the subject. "Only the red-streaked ones."

"If I had a cider mill," his father said, "I'd turn those mountain apples into cider. I'd like nothing better than a glass of hard cider right now."

Alan wondered whether cider acted any differently from peach brandy. Without telling her family, Belle had filled a half-gallon jar with sliced raw peaches and hidden it in the soft earth of the garden, following a recipe she had found in *Comfort Magazine, The Key to Happiness in a Million Farm Homes*. About a week later, the McDowells had been awakened by a dull thud in the night, a muffled sound that might have been made by dropping wrapped bricks on loose planking. Oscar got the lattern and went outside. "Belle," he had yelled from the garden, "what in tarnation is this?''

Alan and Lee followed their mother into the yard. In the garden, just beyond the fence, Oscar was down on his knees examining something in the soil. "If I'm not crazy," he said, "this is a can of peaches."

Belle had laughed. "That's my peach brandy," she said. "I took a craving for some fruit juice. Looks like it blew up."

"Fruit juice," Oscar said, smelling his fingers. "One sup of that and I could jump this fence. That stuff's going somewhere."

Everybody had laughed at Belle's moonshining and had gone back to bed. Perhaps, Alan decided, cider was less excitable than brandy. He wished, too, that they had a cider machine. Suddenly, after the delicious honey, it seemed to him that he wanted to taste all the different tastes in the world.

"We used to make it," Oscar was saying, "by the gallon. By Christmas time, it was real sporty. After a glass or two of that, we really enjoyed busting the hog bladders."

Alan knew his father and his brothers had had marvelous Christmases from hearing his father and his Uncle Lance talk about them. No firecrackers, of course. They had been far too poor for that. But the boys had saved all the hog bladders at slaughtering time. Blown up with a river cane and dried, by Christmas the leathery bags made a loud popping noise when struck with the head of a pole-axe. Alan imagined those Christmases to have been the picture Christmases he had seen on some old-fashioned cards his mother kept for sentimental reasons. At school, Miss Woodson had shown him a Currier and Ives print of a country Christmas. In comparison, his own holidays seemed somewhat dull; for instance, there was not always snow. Sometimes in December Walden Valley was quite warm, and the green pines looked almost summery. But there had been at least one white Christmas in his memory, when the snow fell on Christmas Eve and remained on the earth for days. The pines had looked like pictures then, and the red holly berries his mother had brought in from the giant tree in the yard had glowed like waxy fire. A holiday like that, with cider and hog bladders, he thought, would be a real holiday. The snow, at least, was something to remember. Often, in the depth of summer, he had this fine, snowy dream that mingled itself with black, frozen streams, blue-green pines on the slope behind the house, trains, and, surprisingly, strange people whose names he had never even heard of. How these people got into his dreams, he didn't know. But he did know that they seemed to be assembled from various dismembered faces and limbs of people he was familiar with. All the people he knew fell apart just before he went to sleep. Like words, they became fragments floating free, joining haphazardly into new features and personalities. But, unlike words, they were bodily, and because of their physical dimensions they could disappear. Words just swam around in fractions of themselves like motes in a jar of dreggy water. They did unite in strange combinations, to form words he had never heard of; but they broke up again and seemed to go whirling on in search of meaning. The nearer he came to sleep, the more deformed the words grew, the odds and ends becoming more senseless than ever. As he dropped to sleep, and this was the wonderful thing about his confused impressions, the words righted themselves and became, at times, beautifully patterned and meaningful in dreams, as though he read from some book words with an infinitely deeper meaning than day words possessed. Where did words go at death, he wondered. Bodies dissolved, rotted away in the earth; but where did sounds go? Perhaps the fragments he experienced near sleep merely settled down to the bottom of the foggy jar of water and lay still, not to be stirred up again. He would like to ask Miss Woodson. His mother would ordinarily have answered in some fashion, but these days she was sick and cross, and Alan dared not trouble her with his questions. He knew his new brother when he arrived would begin to learn his language from him and Oscar and Belle and Lee. That was understandable. But where had language come from before he learned it from his family, and his parents learned it from theirs. Backward, backward into time, he supposed, to the first man and the first woman who taught a kind of speech to their children. But where language went when man finished with it, he couldn't understand.

"Come on, slow poke," Oscar said, "and stop catching gnats. We've got to get this tobacco in the dry. It's been out too long as it is."

In the barn, arranging the bundles of strong-smelling leaves turning a bright brownish gold on their stems, Lee asked, "Dad what makes a man like Enoch Wall?"

"He was made like all the rest of us, I reckon," Oscar said. "Why?"

"I don't mean that," Lee said. "I mean his brains. What happened to him? To make him queer and all?"

"He was thrown from a merry-go-round at school, and bashed his head on a tree," Oscar said. "At least, that's how the story goes. The boys turning the wheel went too fast, and Enoch, a little fellow then, lost his hold and was slung off. He hasn't been right since."

Lee was silent. A dozen times, perhaps more, the same thing could have happened to him. Diving into the swimminghole once, for example, and splitting his head on a rock at the bottom. Or falling out of the tree when he was gathering hickory nuts. Monk Carter had been killed that very way, falling on his head and never regaining consciousness. It seemed funny that things happened to some people but never happened to others. Really serious things. Like Enoch, for example, who would never be normal in his head, and who would always be unwelcome around people who had average intelligence. Lee himself would hate to have to live in such a lonely spot as Enoch chose. He wondered what Enoch did with the long knife, feeling cold again as he remembered the strange, wild look on the man's face as he straightened up with the knife in his hand. Lee was suddenly glad that he had been born an ordinary boy into an ordinary family. But maybe Enoch had been born all right, too. It was what happened that made the difference.

For the first time in his life, Lee stood consciously in the shadow of events over which he had no control. No longer, not ever again, would he feel wholly secure and in the right place; the beautiful sense of belonging was beginning to disappear, being replaced by the knowledge that his position in the world was largely allotted him through chance. His own efforts, he realized, were themselves finally conditioned by chance. Like his father, who was always complaining that things were against him, he was held in a delicate balance of plus and minus, positive and negative, Mr. Llewellyn would say, that could change at any moment. Enoch had not been responsible either for what had happened to him. Just being alive was a responsibility, he supposed. Being there on the merry-go-round had been Enoch's fault, in a way. But Enoch hadn't asked to be born in the first place. That surely wasn't his fault. Was the wheel, then, itself responsible? It turned, and turning, exerted the natural centrifugal forces of a wheel. But it hadn't turned by itself. The boys furnished the power that made it go. Lee was confused. He had arrived at the centrality of action in life, without fully realizing the pattern of his thought. He wished Mr. Llewellyn were there to argue the question. They had had some fine debates on Fridays at the school, and this seemed a good subject for a regular knockdown-and-drag-out argument. In a way, he'd be glad to get back to Mr. Llewellyn's classes. There were certainly many things he'd like to know. This summer had been a lulu, he thought, for posing questions nobody seemed able to answer.

22

THE sun was trying to burn away the mist when Alan awoke in a house
so quiet the ticking of the clock sounded like small hammer strokes inside
his head. Lee was still sleeping beside him, fists clenched, mouth open
as usual, the sound of a trapped bumblebee in his nose. With each deeper
breath Lee drew the singing rose to a slight snarl, like the sound made
by the big black bee Alan had entrapped in a jimson weed blossom by
squeezing the tips of the petals shut. The flower had been strong enough
to hold against the bee's struggles, the fat clumsy body not being able to
maneuver itself handily enough to break the flower's tissue. But Alan had
forgotten that the bee was headfirst in the blossom, and had squeezed
perhaps too enthusiastically; for suddenly through a petal came pricking
a tiny blade that stabbed him in the ball of his thumb. The wound had
ached and itched for days, Belle explaining that the stinger had undoubtedly
carried a grain of pollen. Fertilized or not, the thumb swelled and bloomed.

Lee, sleeping, sounded just like the bee, trapped and angry. From the
other room, Oscar's snoring was a deep sawing sound like that made by
a dull ripsaw worrying its way through a board. Occasionally, Belle made
a small beeping sound that built up from a slight nasal flutter to a little
whistle. Alan wondered what he sounded like, listening to the symphony
of sleepers, which reminded him of the frog story Oscar told about Father
Frog, who said in a big deep bass: "Come over! Come over! Come over!"
And Mother Frog, who said in her fine, soprano tone: "Knee-deep! Knee-
deep! Knee-deep!" And Baby Frog, perverse little imp that he was, who
said, on trying the depth of the water and finding it too much for him:
"You're a liar! You're a liar! You're a liar!"

Belle didn't like the story because she said the young ones were mean
enough without having stories of disrespectful children told to them. They
should not be encouraged, she said, in any way whatsoever. She really

couldn't see what the younger generation was coming to anyway, going on until Oscar had said, "For heaven's sake, woman! Can't a man even tell a harmless little story without having a sermon preached to him?"

"It wasn't harmless," Belle said. "It *was* a sermon, a bad one. A story like that can do more damage than a dozen sermons preached by Preacher Musgrove can do good. And he's a good man, too."

"I suppose I'm not a good man," Oscar said, throwing up his hands. He knew Belle was sick and cross-tempered, and humored her. "Well, I'll tell another story another time," he promised.

"It won't be any better," Belle said.

Sometimes it seemed to Alan that his mother was unduly sharp and narrow-minded about things. Particularly, these days, she seemed to have a grudge against his father, a feeling of violence almost at times, that increased as the summer grew older. Occasionally, Alan found her staring at his father with a look of loathing on her face, the while she complained of the hard lot of womenfolks in this world. At least once, recently, she had refused to cook supper for her family, telling the men to go into the kitchen and cook it themselves, if they were so hungry. This wasn't like his mother, not at all. He supposed it had something to do with the new baby, but what he could not comprehend, since about the baby itself his mother was as enthusiastic as he.

He lay now listening to the sounds of his sleeping family. Around him, the newspaper texts on the walls were light or dark, according to their date of issue. The mother with her child, and the other boy at her knee, leaned forward comfortingly, resting her cheek on the baby's head. Through the window, where the sun was trying to burn off the early morning mist, he saw a bird flying with wings so sharply tilted it looked like a flying heart. Other birds wheeled by, faint and faded as half-erased pencil marks on brown wrapping paper. Sunday was his favorite day.

The McDowells never rose early on Sunday, giving themselves an extra hour or two of sleep to compensate for the early risings during the weekdays. But some kind of internal clock always triggered Alan's mind. Whether he got up or not, he always waked up and lay listening to the morning sounds, his mind running over with a collection of ideas and memories. Sometimes he felt exhausted by breakfast time, as if he burned up more energies simply lying there than he consumed all day doing ordinary things. But a breakfast of the best the house afforded always returned him to himself. Seeing him coming in listless to table, Belle, always the daughter of a doctor—she never let anyone forget that—usually said, "It's only something sweet you need. Your bloodsugar is low. It always is after a night's sleep." Bloodsugar or not, Alan knew it was his mind, raging at things, that had sapped him, half-dreaming its wonder and frustrations. Once he was up, out of bed, away from any suggestion of the night, his mind slowed down, made some arrangement among the odds and ends of daily living. Belle called it being "hag-ridden." A witch, she said, rode your back when you were asleep. That was why you waked up tireder than when you went to bed. A witch had used you for her horse and had ridden you miles around the countryside.

Clockwork bugled suddenly outside the window. Alan could see him on the fence, his colors washed to a solid brown by the mist. Pretty Boy barked twice from his sleeping place under the porch floor; cows mooed; Buckeye, whose bleat was unlike any other animal sound on the farm, *maa-aaa-ad* hungrily from his pen at the barn. An early rising hen, anxious to get her day's work over with, cackled loudly at the egg she had just deposited in the nest. Clockwork whortled again. His world was a going concern, under his complete control, and, Alan thought, going like clockwork. The boy turned over luxuriously in the bed. Although his mind was active, his body felt superbly rested, easy, almost without sensation. He was completely relaxed, not the growing, jointy body he would become the moment he climbed out of bed and put himself in action.

Sunday was wonderful. Rain or shine, he loved the slow, moveless day whose only irritation, he had to confess, to himself but not to Belle, was his enforced attendance at Sunday school. He disliked going to Friend-ship Church and sitting through the routine of a performance that never varied from weekend to weekend. Always the same dull monotone of Miss Pearman as she explained the text for the day, the same childish pictures, badly colored, of the great Christian events, the same inattentive children, who grew, from such sessions as this, to equate goodness with a deadly dullness that would make them fear Sunday associations for half their lives, and do without them for the other half. That was what, he believed, had happened to Oscar, who never went to church at all, Sunday or otherwise.

Once, though, Sunday school had not been dull. That was the day he and Jesse Jarnigan had put a dead shrew under Miss Pearman's reading stand. He could see her now, prim, pallid woman (who, Oscar said, needed to get married more than anything else) standing before her class, her brown hair done up in a bun at the base of her skull like some kind of chestnut-colored fungus, reading from the lesson sheet, her nose twitching as the shrew announced its presence from the depth of her lectern. Then, look-ing as if her text had caught fire, her lectern were burning, she announced no more lesson for that day and passed swiftly from the room. Above the lectern, on the wall, the picture of the red-haired, very brown-eyed man with the red lips and cheeks and the fantastic chestnut beard looked mild-ly out over the sinners, at least two of them. The children had finished the hour playing among the headstones in the cemetery.

That had been a memorable Sunday school class, thanks to the little animal boiling away under Miss Pearman's nose. An odd thing about a shrew, Miss Woodson had told him, was that it ate several times its weight in food each day. The energy it burned must have been enormous, for the shrew, when he had lifted it by the tiny tail, just simply wasn't there. He couldn't feel its weight. The food it ate must have been turned into pure energy, for none of it had been stored in muscle and fat.

No hope for anything like that today, though, he thought. Just another one of those desolate get-togethers, where nobody thought or said anything. If only Miss Pearman were like Preacher Musgrove or John Wade. These men said things worth listening to, though often he did not understand exactly what was meant. Of Reuben's death, Preacher Musgrove had said: "After a death, a darkness, and the full spring again." Alan felt that the preacher had said, under his words, that death leaves us in a mournful darkness, which, after awhile, turns into the full light of morning, like winter turning into spring. It was Belle's way of saying that time heals all grief.

But what John Wade had meant was another matter. They had been talking that day of education, of what living in Walden Valley gave them, and of what that same living denied them of knowledge about the greater world lying beyond the blue ridges. Repeating Miss Woodson, Alan had said that knowledge was the key to progress and happiness, and John Wade had answered slowly, as if what he said was a great pain to be saying. "No, the learning is always too late, and the world always too sad to be happy." Only faintly could the boy surmise what the man was talking about. But because he couldn't quite understand, he could think about it. And that was better than sitting listening to Miss Pearman read in her lifeless, precise voice something he himself could have read with more feeling and expression, and perhaps without the sheet to guide him.

"When you've gone once," he told his mother, "you've gone all year."

"That may be," his mother had answered, "but you're going just the same. Myrtle Pearman is a good woman. And anything she says is worth listening to."

There it was again. Goodness. Lying there in bed and thinking wicked thoughts about abolishing Sunday school forever was good. It was good to slip off to the swimminghole without permission, though Belle often warned that disobedient boys were drowned in punishment for such breaches of parental law. It was good to say a bad word now and then, well out of earshot of the family. And it was good to smoke rabbit tobacco behind the barn. Apparently, he and his mother were not talking about the same kind of goodness.

The house began to wake up. Oscar stirred in his bed. Little fringe noises of wood, half pop, half creak, edged about the house like a mouse edging around a room, there but almost refusing to come in. Once a sharp tear, as of paper snapping under pressure, disturbed the morning quietness.

A text on some wall had given way to an outside pressure of wind or a wall's expansion. The quiet hour was over; day had begun.

Breakfast was slower than usual in being prepared. And in the eating of it, the McDowells lingered over the wheatbread, bacon, yellow butter, honey, milk, and coffee. There were never any eggs for the Sunday morning meal. Belle saved them to bake the egg custards which were her midday Sunday specialty, the deep, rich pies which made the weekend only slightly less enjoyable than a regular holiday. Added to them for the dinner would again be wheatbread, fried chicken, white gravy, potatoes, cucumber pickles, and sliced tomatoes, in season, with coffee for her and Oscar and milk for Alan and Lee. The meal was a ritual, much more important to Belle than breakfast.

But the breakfast itself left nothing to be desired.

By the time the meal was over, the sun was up a quarter in the sky, and the mist was gone, leaving an utterly blue day for the Sabbath celebration.

Alan fed Buckeye while his father forked hay into all the mangers and Lee milked Old Cherry. The calf, now that his head had healed, was becoming fat and handsome, though the horns seemed to be growing raggedly again. It was possible Oscar had cut the buds too early. Alan shelled corn into Buckeye's pan and left the gate to the pen open, so that the calf might water himself after he had finished eating. Then he returned to the house and slopped the hogs, throwing the bucket of soured milk and food quickly into the trough before the fattening animals could rush from the other end of their enclosure and heave themselves against the fence.

Bathing for Sunday school, Alan decided he would ride in the buggy with John Wade, not walk with Lee as he usually did. The Wades had been using the McDowells' buggy for going to church since the surrey had come apart in the quicksand. And since the journey always began and ended in his own barnyard, Alan felt he might as well avail himself of the convenience the arrangement offered. Besides, he liked John Wade, liked being in his company and hearing him talk. As for Lee, he would walk the distance to the church, with or without Ira Wade, depending on whether that young man had a valid reason, other than that usually assigned to Sunday school, for going to church at all.

The drive through the valley was always pleasant, and on Sundays doubly so; for the hustle and hurry of the week had ceased, and there was almost a squirrel quietness on the fields and fencerows, along the creeks and in the woodlands—a quiet so deep that the sound of a woodpecker drilling could be heard half a mile away, or the screech of a bluejay exploded immensely in the blue air.

John and Hannah Wade sang on the way to church, her soprano ringing against the baritone he tried to deepen into base. "I'm like the boy,"

he said to Alan between songs, "whose voice was changing. I sing bass,"
letting his deep man tone go wild on the word "bass," and ending oc-
taves higher than his wife's voice. "Your voice will soon be doing that,"
he told Alan. "Starting off in one direction and ending up in another. Mine
never really changed much though, not as much as I wanted. I always
wanted a voice like a country bullfrog."

He grinned at Alan. "We don't get what we want," he said. "We
learn to want what we get. That is, if we learn anything." He stroked
his chin. "Funny thing though. I've seen men not over five feet tall and
skinny as a plucked chicken with voices as deep as a bass organ. Hearing
them coming, before you saw them, you'd think a giant was on the loose.
Then you'd see them, no bigger than you, boy, booming away like a
foghorn. Life's funny, that way." Then he began to sing:

> There's a church in the valley by the wildwood,
> No lovelier spot in the dale;
> No spot is so dear to my childhood,
> As the little brown church in the vale . . .

Hannah Wade joined in, and finally Alan sang.

The Sunday school class itself was enlivened by a woodpecker that,
apparently, had addled brains, for he perched himself on a solid windowsill
of the classroom and drilled furiously away at the painted surface.

"Pretend he isn't there," Miss Pearman said. "If you get interested
in the lesson you won't hear him at all. 'Let him who has ears hear,'"
she began; but seeing that the text did not fit the occasion, stopped mid-
sentence and considered in which direction she should go.

"Miss Pearman," asked Jesse Jarnigan, "is it true that if a tree falls
in the forest and there is nobody there to hear it, it makes no sound?"

Miss Pearman looked flustered. "Jesse," she said, "what, in heaven's
name, brought that up?"

"I just wondered," Jesse said, "whether it took an ear to make a sound
or a sound to make an ear." He laughed. "We argued about that for an
hour last year in school."

"I say there is a sound," Alan said, hoping to distract Miss Pearman's
attention from the sheet she held in her hand, the same one, he decided,
she had been holding for three Sundays in a row. "If there's no ear in
the forest to hear the sound, that doesn't mean it isn't there. There's music
in this room now all around us. Only we can't hear it. Without a radio,"
he added.

"Boys," said Miss Pearman, "that's not in the lesson at all. We do
not study in Sunday school what we study in day school. They're separate
things altogether." She sounded stern and determined. "Listen," she said.

Her voice droned on and on in the sunny room, reading. Leaf shadows played on the polished wood of the lectern in changing patterns, turning the aged brown pine into a dark, glassy surface like a woodland pool. The stare of the man in the picture above the lectern became, in the green light, almost hypnotic. The children, listening, noted the leaf-shadows; half-listening, they began to imagine the tree; oblivious altogether now to Miss Pearman, dreaming half-asleep, they climbed among the cool, green branches. Still the man in the picture looked steadily into the room. Miss Pearman read on. The woodpecker drilled again, this time farther away in the wood.

Finally, however, the reading ceased, the class was over; and the pupils drained out into the bright yard, where their elders talked and shook hands. There would be no sermon this morning, they learned, because their minister had been called to preach a special sermon in a neighboring church. Alan rather missed hearing Preacher Musgrove's booming voice and shaking his enormous hand.

Before starting home, John Wade, his wife, and Alan walked through the graveyard, quiet and warm now with sun at mid-day in its enclosure of trees, above whose tops great steamy clouds built upward to the middle of the sky, towering and many-shaped like huge squashed cones of cream. In places the clouds seemed to rise suddenly like leavened dough and then sink like a shaken cake in an oven. The sky was not at rest; something seasonal was almost afoot.

"September's in the air," John Wade said. "Almost time for the big winds." He referred, Alan knew, to the equinoctial storms, one of Belle's favorite subjects, since a great September storm had struck the peninsula of Florida and blown great ships upon dry land. There had even been a song made about that one. Uncle Granville had sung it, Alan recalled, when he last came visiting in the valley.

Reuben's grave was still red and raw among the flatter, grassy plots in a nook of the churchyard; but already thin wispy grass was showing in the clay, indicating that by another summer there would be little difference visible in the ages of the mounds. Someone, Reuben's mother perhaps, had that morning left a handful of garden flowers on the grave.

"He was younger than you, wasn't he?" Hannah Wade said to Alan, adding something about those who are taken in the flower of their youth. Hannah Wade was like his mother, always speaking words from old authorities that chilled the sunlight out of the day. He mumbled something in answer.

John Wade strode on, far ahead, the walk continuing until a circuit had been made of both sections of the cemetery. Coming back to the church and the impatient mule tied to a low limb at the edge of the grave, they climbed into the sun-warmed interior of the buggy and turned in the direction of the valley and home. The smell of old leather rose heavily in the sun, an odor compounded of saddlesoap, animal grease, sweat, and the earth itself. There was something in the smell that reminded Alan of horse collars, sharp and ammoniac, hanging on the wooden pegs in the harness room back home. Alan sneezed and felt his head go suddenly clear, as if he had just breathed a lump of his mother's favorite remedy for colds, Vick's Salve.

"I'm making molasses next week," John Wade said. "I've made arrangements for Oscar to help me. You boys about ready with your cane?"

"Everything but cutting the heads off and hauling it to the mill," Alan said. His back was still sore from following Oscar up and down the rows, catching the handfuls of top-heavy canestalks which his father severed from the roots by one sweep of the heavy cutter, and which he and Lee had laid straight in the field in readiness for having the tassels removed. They had finished only the day before at noon. Alan remembered gratefully the feel of the cool creek water on his body when he and Lee had gone swimming. It had been a job, washing the white cane powder and the seed chaff out of his hair. Syrup making time was always busy, laborious even, but the taste of the new molasses took away the sting of the hard work, which itself, occasionally, was fun, when the men and boys of the neighborhood, joined in the cooperative enterprise, found time for tricks and jokes. Even being stung by a bee was a joke to everyone but the man who had been stung. And since the bees, of every sort and description, moved in by the hundreds to make holiday over the sweet mess, by the time the making was over, everybody had been stung and laughed at, at least once if not several times. The trouble was you never knew from what direction the attack might be coming, nor for what reason. An angry bee entangled itself in your hair without warning, and you could stand quite still, hoping it would go away, or beat and slap in the slim chance of doing it in before it got through to you. You usually lost, of course. To paraphrase his mother, the bees were the flies in the sweet ointment. However, they did lend the proper sense of awareness about the mill that alerted the workers to other dangers: that of getting a hand in the presser, for instance, or of falling into a hole filled with hot skimmings. Alan looked forward to watching John Wade, reputed to be the best molasses maker in the country, boil off the syrup just right, not too thick, not too thin, but of the proper consistency and dark amber color that signalled a sweetness in the liquid just short of the saturation that would send it into heavy granulation long before it was consumed. John Wade was a master at cooking the syrup to perfection. As a result, farmers from throughout the valley hauled their sorghum harvest into the Wade meadow where the mill was set up. At one time, John had moved the mill from location to location in the valley; but now the people came to him. For two weeks in his meadow each year, he was king of the skimmer and ladle, the workers about him merely his subjects and, occasionally, it seemed to them, his slaves. For the man brooked no interference in his task. The juice must be fed in right proportions, no more, no less, into the end of the pan where the great fire was built; the fire itself must be kept at even glowing temperatures throughout the day and half the night; no one must, even in fun, handle the giant utensils he himself used in the skimming and clearing away of impurities from the bubbling flow oozing in the sections from end to end of the copper pan. In Alan's mind, the process of transforming by heat, the greenish, sickening juice of the sorghum into amber-clear sweet syrup was something like a miracle; not like turning water into wine, perhaps, but something very nearly like. The man with the big brown hands deftly flipping foam into the skimming hole was, for a week at least in the year, the boy's hero.

He looked at John Wade now, at the big hands gripping the reins and the light willow switch the man used to touch the mule into greater speed. "If I didn't switch Old Shad once in a while," the man said, "I declare I believe he'd go to sleep right in the middle of the road. If that ever happens, we'll have to build a fire under him to get him up again."

He stopped in front of the McDowells' yard gate. "Tell your dad I'll bring the buggy home in the afternoon," he said. "Enjoyed the ride a right smart. I don't see much of my boy these days."

Alan remembered that Ira had not been with Lee in the churchyard. Gone somewhere else, he imagined. To town, maybe.

He waved good-bye to John Wade and his wife and went into the house. John Wade watched him go. "I wonder if he'll turn out like all the rest of them," he said, half to himself.

Hannah Wade looked at her husband. "John," she said, "he's young, too." She was silent, as if in her statement she had expressed the almost inexpressible, come as close to a confusing truth as people her age and John's would ever come.

* * *

Having walked Suzy Overholt home from Sunday school, Lee was late for dinner; and Oscar was angry. "That boy," he declared, "is going to be taken down a notch or two if he isn't careful. Who does he think he is anyhow, sparking at his age."

"He's getting big enough," Belle said, "to know his family aren't all the people in the world. He's going on fifteen. At his age you didn't know where home was."

"I didn't have a home," Oscar said bitterly. "My father died when I was thirteen, and after that home was anywhere I could hang my hat."

Listening to his parents bicker, Alan decided that he wasn't hungry.

It seemed lately almost impossible for any subject to be discussed without tempers flaring, especially his mother's. And Lee had begun to be between Oscar and Belle an increasingly sore topic. Oscar seemed somehow to resent his son's growing up.

The family ate in silence without Lee. As soon as he was able to do so without comment from his mother, whom he helped in clearing away the dinner dishes, Alan slipped from the house and made his way to the top of the high knoll in the west corner of the big pasture, taking his battered copy of *The Pilgrim's Progress* with him. Here, he could see much of the nearer valley spread out around him: the meadows, crop fields, creek-runs, fencerows, and beyond the gaunt sycamores, standing like strange white vegetables, stalky and scabbed against the summer green, he could see the white walls of Friendship Church.

All summer he had been trying to understand *Pilgrim's Progress*. But after having read it twice, he was still baffled by the book, which, he knew, had been penned while its author was in prison. He surmised vaguely that the story had some connection with the author's own experiences, but he knew too little about the life of John Bunyan to draw satisfactory parallels. Nevertheless, the book not only challenged, it attracted him, with its description of Vanity Fair, the Slough of Despond, the Interpreter's House, the Celestial City. In a way, it was a sober-sided fairy tale, similar to the stories in Grimm, not too different in its air of unreality from "The King of the Golden River," which he had re-read several times during his vacation from school. Any tale that differed radically from the atmospheres and climates of Walden Valley was fairy-taleish to Alan. Now "A Dog of Flanders" was another matter. Despite its strange countryside, with windmills and the big stone houses, the story of Nello and Patrasche had to do with things he could understand; he could easily imagine himself superintending the milk cart, drawn by his beloved dog; the miller's pretty little daughter would not be too unlike any of the girls he knew at school, except perhaps for the pointed white cap she wore; even the cathedral with the beautiful painting Nello so wanted to see, was only a church bigger than Friendship Church, with a picture actually no more beautiful than the one of the woman and child on his bedroom wall at home.

But *Pilgrim's Progress* he saw through a glass darkly, as Preacher Musgrove would say, the whole book being as fantastic, in its fashion, and as beautifully expressed as many of the half-original, half-Biblically imitated statements the preacher himself made. Sometimes Preacher Musgrove talked like a book. The Sunday, for instance, he preached on truth, ending with the story of the warriors from a book in the Bible, which one Alan had forgotten.

"Their shields shone like mirrors," the Preacher said, "and the enemy was blinded to their destruction. How wise it was of the warriors to face the sun, their shields held edgewise until the moment of truth arrived. The truth was symbolized by the sun, neighbors,'' he explained, "and was to be used against the defenders. But the enemy had forgotten a smaller truth: that the reflection of the truth itself can be blinding. And so they were all killed that day.''

John Bunyan's book was like that. You knew and yet you didn't know what was meant. The Slough of Despond could very well be a swamp, the swamp, in fact, into which Alan had fallen the day he had chased the young pig for hours before cornering the escapee and returning it to its pen. He had fallen into a cress-bogged canal up to his waist and been almost paralyzed at the thought of a water moccasin. The pig could be the things of this world that sometimes brought a man into such a slough, which, his father had told him, was an arm of a creek or river left stagnant and to itself when the stream moved from its original bed and cut a new channel. That parallel seemed likely enough. Vanity Fair, whose description he found the most exciting chapter in the book, could very well be the county fair, to which each year the carnival came, with its load of cheap bright goods, its games and tricks, its rides and thrills, and, perhaps most fascinating of all, the handsome dark-skinned people, whose babble made him think of the story of the Tower of Babel. There were boys, with gold earrings, no bigger than he, tending the games, shouting their wares, their faces sometimes peering out from the backs of gaily-colored wagons. And men with colored kerchiefs around their heads, and women in clanking jewelry and dressed in silk dresses that swept to the ground. The carnival drew all of his attention, despite Belle's flat declaration that the carnival was a cheap, flashy mess, and the people who ran it pure trash.

The Interpreter's House, in which, the book said, were to be found all manner of excellent things, seemed to him to be nothing other than Miss Woodson's small house at the edge of the valley, with its book-lined, picture-laden walls, its collection of potted cactus plants, and sea-shells, and the player piano which jangled out a tune all by itself, while the music was somehow being picked out of the holes in a winding roll of paper. Miss Woodson's house had all manner of excellent things. He never tired of looking at them on his infrequent visits to the house of his beloved teacher.

As for the Celestial City, he knew that was heaven, but the town of Tellico, as diligently as he sought to find them, offered no likenesses. Nor could that town, with its beautiful name and surrounding mountains, furnish any parallels to the City of Destruction. No one he knew resembled Mr. Civility and Mr. Legality. Doubting Castle, whose lord, Giant Despair, threw Christian and Hopeful into a dismal dungeon, was straight out of some book of fairy tales. As for the Enchanted Land and the sweet and pleasant country of Beulah, why, Walden Valley, he thought, as he fell asleep on the soft grass, was both of them. It had always been.

How long he slept, he could not say. Except that when he awoke, feeling an unusual weight across his chest, the sun no longer beamed into his eyes. Startled, he tried to sit up and found himself pinned to the ground by Buckeye, who had found him on the knoll and had gone to sleep with him, his head thrust across the boy's body. Relieved, Alan sank back and stroked the calf's ears. "You scared me out of a year's growth, you old booger," he said.

Buckeye batted his eyes contentedly, the long red lashes like stiff reeds around ponds of blue, oily water. But he did not move.

The addition to their pasture of a young heifer was always a cause for rejoicing with the McDowells. But not so with a young bull. Him, they might caress; but already his fate was sealed. Troublesome to raise, and selling for only a few dollars when the time came for him to be disposed of, a bull calf often caused a loss of a few precious dollars to his owners, who, in Walden Valley, could ill afford to lose. On the other hand, a young heifer might be as troublesome to raise. But in her glossy skin, stroked by devoted hands, there was already a dream of the good milk to be given. No sale or slaughterhouse for her. Rimmed in by the green mountains, the people in the valley were, in a sense, a clan of transplanted cow-worshippers beside Muddy Bottom Creek, the narrow, shallow Ganges of their backcountry world.

Alan loved Buckeye, but between him and the calf always was this knowledge of the calf's destiny. He had wisely chosen to heed his mother's advice not to love too much, for the calf, now becoming a yearling, she said would have to be sold at the end of summer; and all summers were short. Nevertheless, he felt a pang at the thought of letting Buckeye go, new books notwithstanding. He could get along as he had in years before, borrowing a book here and there, and using Miss Woodson's texts at night.

But he had grown into the knowledge that in the life of his family there were certain patterns, certain aims and intentions, necessities even, that would willy-nilly, if life remained, be fulfilled. Buckeye's fate was one of these goals; was, rather, a way of achieving one of these goals: books for him to learn from when the time came for school to begin. In a few weeks, he knew, the calf would be sold at the stockbarn in town and a handful of new books would begin to play their part in a new kind of winter existence that would itself turn into spring . . .

He fell asleep again, to be awakened this time by the sound of a short blast from the conch shell, which his mother blew mutedly as if reluctant to disturb the Sunday calm.

"Let's go, boy," he said to the calf. "I'll race you to the foot of the hill." Picking up his book, Alan started to run.

Whether he understood or not, Buckeye rocked and bucked on his thin legs, and then with a surge of speed that carried him far ahead of the running boy, reached the foot of the hill fully a minute in front of Alan and stood waiting for him to arrive.

As he raced, Alan noticed the crows flying high, in twos and threes, going north to the rookery, looking like periods and commas drawn on a sheet of gold paper near the woodline to the west, but more birdlike near the zenith, where the sky turned from pale yellow to a willow green. They flew nearer to him there, it seemed, and were like the plus signs in his arithmetic book. Crows fascinated him. The coarse rough birds, smelling like the chlorophyll of ditch weeds, were given to robbery and carrion-eating, he knew, and were much unloved by farmers because of their disregard for boundaries. Nevertheless, they were, because of their difference from the other birds, of great interest to him. He knew from observation that crows were used to small ranges—a few familiar acres which they knew more intimately than any geographer knows his coastline. He knew about their perfect knowledge of all nests and fledgling in the vicinity, having seen them flying with eggs in their beaks, or the bodies of young birds. This enraged him at the crows, though he recognized hunger as one of the predominating forces in the world, among men as well as the other animals.

But watching the crows pour north, he forgot their crimes, and raced along beneath them, shouting, to where Buckeye waited for him. The crows were coming more thickly now, banding together, so that a long, almost unbroken string of the birds linked south and north. He wondered where such a ceaseless stream might be coming from. It was useless to try to count them. It would take all night, he thought. They were still arriving over the farm from some seemingly inexhaustible source south in the valley when darkness fell, and Alan was sitting on the front porch watching the fireflies speckle the frontyard dusk. He had an idea that the fireflies might be all the flames from all the blown-out lamps in the world, congregated and dancing together. People only thought they blew out the flame from a candle's tip; it really didn't go out, though. Blowing into the air and out of sight of eyes, it merely went to another place and became a firefly, to come back on nights like this and mock the people by playing a hide-and-seek game among the hollyhocks. "Now you see me, now you don't," each firefly seemed to be saying as it flew.

"You know," Alan said to Lee who was stretched out on the floor, sulking because Oscar had scolded him for not coming home to dinner, "a lightningbug is not really a bug at all."

"What is it, then?" Lee asked sullenly. "A horse?"

"No," Alan said, "it's a piece of fire that got blown off its anchor and hasn't any place to go to. It just drifts around the world, trying to find where it came from. Looking for home-base, maybe."

"Like you got blown off your rocker," Lee grunted. "Only you're never going to find home-base. Holy catfish, man, you *are* crazy. Enoch Wall couldn't hold you a light."

He got up and went into the house, grumbling.

"What ails you, son?" Belle asked, trying to read under the lamp, but finding it difficult because of the moths that had slipped in through the window. Inside the lampglobe, a large brown moth whirled for an instant around, and then sank scorched and shriveled to the burner.

"Oh, it's Alan," Lee said. "If he gets any crazier, we're going to have to tie him to a bedpost."

"There's all kinds of craziness," Belle said sharply. "Where one's tall, the other is short. When you're talking about your brother, you're only robbing Peter to pay Paul." She looked worriedly at Lee. The boy was becoming unmanageable, as proud and boastful as a bone on a blue plate. You worry, she said to herself, until they are born; and then you find out where worry really begins.

Putting aside her book, she carried the lamp into the boys' bedroom. She herself climbed into bed in the darkness, beside Oscar, who was already snoring.

When Alan blew the lamp out, Lee was asleep, or pretending to be. He might be crazy, all right, but he could have sworn he saw the tip of fire blow loose from the wick and float off in the dark room. The image gradually faded from his vision. Actually, he told himself, he knew what an after-image was. A person wasn't nuts simply because he preferred explanations of his own.

23

THE McDowells were awakened by the scream of the peacock on John Wade's farm, a high, fretful sound that shattered sleep. Strange to the valley, the splendid bird with his great purple and gold-eyed feathers was one of John Wade's most treasured possessions. The farmer had bought the cock along with his hen at an auction outside the valley, when all the effects of a farm owned by the town attorney had been put on the block. But despite his most careful efforts, no more birds could be hatched from the pea hen's eggs, which, for some reason, spoiled instead. Nevertheless, he was very proud of his birds, and especially so of the great cock, whose tailspread looked like some magnificent, gigantic fan. On his mantel, he kept a jarful of the fine feathers that the peafowl lost. And once he had given Belle a feather that had dropped from the peacock's tail, which she kept in a vase on the dresser, the feather no more colorful than the vase of carnival glass, itself purple and gold and red, and spotted with great whorled eyes. The vase had belonged to her grandmother.

Now the bird's cry jostled the morning.

"I dread this week," Oscar said, sitting on the side of the bed, yawning and scratching. "First thing, I guess, we'd better get our cane over to Wade's. No telling when he'll get to it. But when he does, I want it to be there, waiting."

"I hope," Belle said anxiously, "he makes our syrup first. The cane's been cut two days now."

"It needs to be made soon, all right," Oscar said. "But I'd as soon he waited about mine till the second batch. Give him time to get in practice."

After breakfast, Lee and Alan handed up armloads of cane to Oscar, who placed them lengthwise in the wagonbed until the bed was level, and then crosswise between standards until the load was enough for the mules to pull. When they arrived in the meadow where the big pan had already been set up, other farmers from the valley were hauling in their sorghum and stacking it in designated places between poles driven into the ground. The McDowells unloaded their wagon near the mill, in a place John Wade pointed out to them. Apparently, he was going to make Oscar's syrup first. Five loads later, and near noon, Oscar's cane was all in place, green and shining at the tips and golden-brown towards the bottom of the stalks. Already, Alan noticed, a swarm of yellow-jacks hovered over the butt-ends of the cane, where the juice seeped out. When the grinding started, he knew the air would be almost brown with the insects.

All morning the fire had been replenished under the pan, with the pole-lengths of wood Oscar had hauled to the meadow last week. Each man furnished the fuel for his own batch of molasses. John Wade wanted, first of all, a bed of steadily glowing coals, and fired quickly to get them. Near the pan was the huge bellows he used to fan the fire into roaring flame. Once the pan was thoroughly heated, the coals deep and glowing, the firing could be relaxed and the steady heat maintained necessary for the slow even cooking of the molasses. In his job of master, John Wade was easy and at home. Since his boyhood, he had boiled off the molasses of the neighborhood, beginning by assisting his father, and ending by being assisted by his own son, who managed the pressing-mill itself. Ira was now busy sluicing the mill with water from the creek to wash out the dust that had accumulated on the rollers. This job was one of the few things in which he took real pride. It made him a man among men. It also gave him a chance to order Alan, Lee, and the other boys around a bit. Nothing like authority to give a man confidence, he felt. All a man needed was a chance to throw his weight around. It was Ira's notion that a man was as big in his community as the space it took him to turn in, and he aimed to occupy a right smart space in turning.

"Hold this," he said to Alan, who was standing near him.

He dropped the reins of the draft mule into Alan's hand, and went to adjust the lead-strap on the end of the beam that would lead the animal around and around the mill as the cane was being crushed. He swore and spat tobacco juice when he gouged his hand on a piece of baling wire. Taking some tobacco from his mouth, he placed it on the scratch.

Alan knew this would be the remedy for the numerous bee-stings that had already begun to happen. Tom Lawson, a man from the other side of the valley, wore a brown poultice on his forearm; and William Adams sported one in the jaw just below his right cheek. Things were warming up, all right.

Ira had now begun to pass the stalks between the giant rollers of the mill, and a slow trickle of greenish-yellow juice had begun to fall into the wooden tub, from which the pipe, bending from the tub to the ground and covered with straw where the mule walked, carried the juice to the end of the great pan, near the open mouth of the furnace. Already from the pan, the sweet, unmistakable odor of molasses was beginning to rise.

"Heave her in here," Ira said to Lee, who was carrying armloads of the stalks and placing them near Ira, between the circling mule and the mill itself. "Get 'em closer," he ordered, seeing the mule stepping on the ends of the stalks. "And watch your head. That beam'll knock your brains out."

Alan wandered down to the pan, where John Wade had begun to move the long-handled skimmer up and down, keeping the green juice in the first sections until was ready to move up nearer the crude chimney and the boiling-off place, where, in an hour or so, the first thick run of the molasses would be ready. Oscar was near him, keeping the fire steady and attending the syrup-maker in whatever fashion he was able. Now he was mostly listening to the story John Wade was telling.

"Yes, sir," he said, "the bull had Simpson backed up in those trees in the corner of the pasture and wouldn't let him come out. He just stood there and paced and bellowed every time Mark tried to escape. He even went into the trees once to get him, but Mark climbed a young hickory out of his way. I saw the hickory later. There wasn't a scale of bark left on it where that bull had gored. Mark would have stayed there all day, if Enoch Wall hadn't come along. Yes, sir. That lame-brain just went right up to that bull and thumped his rump with a stout cudgel he had, and that bull acted as gentle as a baby. Mark said Enoch thumped him all the way across the pasture, singing something or other. Said it sounded like 'Old man Bull! Old man bull!' Or something like that. Said he thumped once for each word. Mark said if he hadn't been so surprised at seeing the bull so gentle, it would have been funny. It's a strange thing," John Wade finished, "that an animal recognizes a natural. Always does, and acts accordingly, like a fierce dog being gentle with a child."

This was the part of syrup-making that Alan really loved. Sometimes, it seemed to him that he lived in a kind of storybook world, hearing all the fabulous accounts of things that happened in the valley. Only what he heard wasn't fables, unless a fable was the truth grown out of the ordinary, become somehow different from the nature of daily fact. He smiled, seeing in his mind the slight figure of Enoch advancing behind the retreating animal, thwacking the stupendous rump and singing his song. Bulls were immense creatures, not only in size but in the way they dominated the memory of Alan's first experience with animals. He had, when he was about three years old, followed Oscar to the barn, where, peeping through the slats of a stall-door, he had looked directly into the great blue eye of the bull Oscar had owned then. He never forgot the lowered head, the steady, unblinking eye of the awesome animal. Out of that had grown his immense respect for bulls, and a deep fear of them as well. That Enoch had handled Mark Simpson's bull, he had no doubt, unbelievable as the story sounded. And somehow he was glad as if this ability in the man inexplicably balanced his deficits, and made him the equal of those who, at times, mocked him. There certainly had been respect in John Wade's voice, a new feeling for Enoch Wall, as if the master stirring the amber-colored juice along the pan realized that there were other qualities in a man than the ability to make good molasses.

Oscar raked the coals even in the furnace and shoved in another small log. The smell of molasses was rich and heavy in the air. Into the boiling syrup, John Wade dropped apples from the tree in the meadow, adding ears of late sweet corn. "It won't hurt the syrup," he told Alan. "All impurities come off in the skimmings. The little water from the apples and the corn won't last long in that batter. It takes gallons of juice," he added as an afterthought, "to make one gallon of molasses. Juice is mostly water, you know."

"How many gallons of juice?" Alan wanted to know.

Oscar frowned at him. The boy was too forward with his elders. "Stop asking questions," he said. "You're bothering John."

John Wade carefully skimmed a ladle of foam from the pan and tossed it into the skimminghole. "From ten to fifteen gallons, most likely," he said. "I've never really measured it." He smiled at Alan. "It wouldn't be an easy thing to do. Some men make thicker syrup than others, which means more juice going into the gallon."

Lee was carrying the limp crushed stalks away from the presser with a pitchfork. Already a ridge of the pomace was beginning to form, and the bees had begun to fly in swarms over it. By the time the making was done in the meadow, there would be loads and loads of the crushed stalks to be scattered over the thin places on John Wade's farm, or to be hauled away by the owners for the same purpose. Oscar always used his on bare spots in the cow pasture.

"Get a move on, Lee," Ira yelled. "You're slower than Christmas. This stuff is piling up."

Lee reddened. He was beginning to be tired of Ira's bossy manner. "Keep your britches on," he said. "I'm working as hard as I can."

"Go help him, Alan," Oscar said. "Make yourself handy."

As Alan reached the tramped circle surrounding the mill, Ira Wade rose from his crouching position under the swinging beam, slapping and beating at his right thigh. "There's a bee up my leg," he yelled, ducking under the beam as it made the slow swing around. Backing away from the mill, his fist gripping a fold of his breeches, he squeezed until he was satisfied the insect was dead. "Pesky little devil," he said. Loosening his belt he dropped his trousers to his knees. From his mouth he took a wad of tobacco and smeared it on the two welts that showed on the inside of his thigh. His face was red. Alan felt sorry for him. But the men laughed, even John Wade, who said, "Out of his mouth came forth sweetness." Lee was delighted at Ira's embarrassment.

"That'll teach the big-mouth to be so bossy," he said to Alan. "I wouldn't have cared if it'd stung his hindend off."

Alan and Lee cleared away the massed pomace from under the mill, and carried a supply of unground stalks to the other side for Ira to begin pressing. Ira said nothing, keeping his eyes on his work. Alan noticed however that he had tied the cuffs of his breeches tightly around his ankles with pieces of binder's twine.

John Wade had begun to fill the shiny tin buckets Oscar had brought for his syrup. From the spout near the chimney, the golden liquid spilled in a ropy stream as big as a man's thumb. In another hour or two, the McDowell cane would all be ground, the juice all on the pan, making its way slowly, under great heat, to the head of the pan, to be drained off in the rapidly filling containers.

"Looks like you're going to have to borrow some buckets, Oscar," John Wade said. "Either that or I'm miscalculating."

"Maybe not," Oscar said, bringing a lard can from the wagon. "I've got twenty gallons worth of these. Three more in the wagon."

By now the men were eating the syrupy apples and corn. "Come on, boys," called John Wade. "Dinner's ready."

Lee and Ira came from the mill. Nobody had thought of the noon-day meal, except, perhaps, the three boys. Alan felt starved. He tasted the amber-colored corn, once white but now dripping with molasses, and found it delicious. The apples were candied to a turn. In reaching for one, Lee slipped and stepped one foot into the skimminghole. Ira laughed loudly, glad to be even with the company, even Lee's small part of it. The men chuckled. "You're in for it now," John Wade said; "either you go to the creek and wash both shoe and foot, or you'll have more visitors up your leg than Ira ever dreamed of."

Lee hopped off to the creek.

"I don't think it was hot enough to burn," Oscar said. "I slipped and sat down in one of those things once, and got me a hot seat."

"You must have got awfully tired of standing up, Mr. McDowell," Ira said. "How did you eat?"

"Off the mantel, for two weeks," Oscar said. "I was sorer than if I'd been riding bareback."

Lee came back from the creek, squishing the water in his shoe. He and Ira returned to the presser. Alan dipped some of the new syrup from a cup, using the chewed end of a joint of cane as a sopper. Everything about the making of molasses intrigued him: the thickness, sweetness, and amber color of the syrup itself; the great copper pan divided into its sections, along which the thin green juice, almost yellow in the sunlight, crept, changing color as it went, until it became honeylike in its pour from the spout. The whole process seemed a little magical, and the maker like a master chemist in an open-air laboratory.

"Have you changed the strainer yet?" John Wade called to Ira. "The juice is coming too slow. See about it."

Ira shook the heavy white cloth that covered the head of the wooden tub at the side of the mill. It was massed with fragments of crushed stalk and sugar already granulating in the dry heat. With a quick flip, Ira tossed the sediment onto the earth, and went back to his grinding.

John Wade had begun to talk about one of his favorite subjects, the history of Walden Valley. "Yes," he said, "this valley was a stop-over place for those moving west. Like Tennessee herself, this land was not the west, only in that direction. Our whole state, after all, was a road leading across and beyond the mountains, a wild path between the Alleghenies and the River, lying as long as three states put together and narrower than one. It was more like a ski, a thin snowshoe," he tried for a more familiar and exact comparison, "a sled-runner," he said, "signifying travel. Boone came through here, and other Kentuckians and North Carolinians, with their long rifles. But many of them stopped and stayed. Walden Valley must have been a paradise then, good enough for even the dreamer of the best dream. And even those who went on looked back and called our area 'the garden spot of the world.'"

When John Wade talked of the history of the valley and of the state, whose history was only the sum total of the histories of a thousand small valleys like Walden, his voice soared, became almost prophet-like, though he prophesied nothing. It pleased him only to contemplate the beginnings, the different days and ways of those by-gone times.

"Dad's raving again," Ira said to Lee. "Off to the woods with Daniel Boone and Davy Crockett. Sometimes I wish he could take my American History class. He'd eat it up. And Mr. Parker would love him, too."

Ira and his history teacher were, to say the least, neutral toward each other. When a positive relationship was established, as it sometimes was, it came as the consequence of a failure on Ira's part and a session in study hall in the afternoon following school hours. Ira purely hated to walk home after his punishment, the bus having long since gone without him.

Lee didn't answer. He rather liked hearing Ira's father talk. Oscar spoke very little in the presence of his sons, preferring to converse with neighbors or strangers, joking and laughing in public, but talking, if at all, privately with Belle at home. A father who said such things as John Wade said was a novelty to the McDowell boys. Lee knew that John Wade read everything in print he could lay his hands on: books, magazines, pamphlets, auctioneers' bulletins, sales catalogues. He also knew that it was one of Oscar's proud boasts that he had never read a book in his whole life. Still the difference between the two men was deeper than a book read or unread. The larger blond man, with the freckles lightly salted across his face, had about him a quality of gentleness completely foreign to the smaller, stormier man, with his coxscomb face and raven hair. The one was rather like a father, the other more like his son, still rebellious and unconquered. Trying to figure his thoughts out about the two men who were closer to him than any other men he knew, left Lee with a small, nagging sense of disloyalty, as if he had let Oscar down. Betrayed him somehow. Ira was something of a fool, he concluded. There were worse things than having a father like John Wade. Or Oscar either, for that matter.

He brought an armload of cane to the presser. The heap was growing smaller. Another hour or two, and the juice from the McDowell crop would all be on the pan. That meant they would finish by nine o'clock. Lee was glad his part of the syrup-making was about over. Tomorrow, he and Alan would stay at home with Belle, relieving Hannah Wade who had visited with her today. His mother was not feeling well. She was hardly able to move about the tasks of her household. Lee surmised the new baby would soon be born.

"Age," John Wade was saying to the men around him, "means nothing except the older you get, the longer it's been. Age is history, or the other way around, just an accumulation of years and the things that made each one of them different from any other."

Not quite sure he understood the man, Alan felt nevertheless as if he sat in a church, listening, perhaps, to Preacher Musgrove examine his thoughts, not particularly for the congregation's benefit, but more for his own. It was as if men like John Wade and Preacher Musgrove read their minds like books, or scrolls slowly unrolling before them, finding out for themselves, for the first time, some of the things written there. However it was, hearing them was a kind of revelation that elated the boy, making him feel as if he were several sizes bigger than he knew himself actually to be. That was the way Miss Woodson, too, made him feel. He was glad the revival meeting had begun at Friendship Church on Sunday night. Though he was often appalled at the graphic descriptions of hell which Preacher Musgrove, with the touch of a poet and something of the appreciation of that artist for his work, laid down in such glowing terms, some of the more impressionable members of the congregation groaned and cried aloud; though he often trembled, too, as it were, on the brink of the fire, he remembered most vividly the quieter statements of the preacher, remarks that might have been made by John Wade over this boiling pan, or Miss Woodson in the brown study of her classroom. Alan had already encountered several kinds and sources of education. At the syrup-making, he added yet another, this one, too, with its distinctive smell, not too dissimilar from the odor at the church, with its smell of old heart pine and worn hymnals; the syrup was a kind of distilled honey and resin. But the odor at the school mingled as it was of stale floor oil, books, sawdust, chalk, and the faint, ammoniac smell of urine, coming from nobody knew where, since the toilets were well away from the school building—that was an odor distinct unto itself, brash, penetrating, insidious; a warring odor, at conflict always with the smell of any other building he knew.

At times, the boy's senses were quite confused, blurred, so that no one of them seemed quite distinct or operative on its own.

John Wade's talk stimulated this impression of mixed senses, volatile and changing as a peacock's wing.

Oscar was telling a story about the man who heard the devil in the churchyard counting out, with God, the souls to be harvested there. ''There was this man passing by the church,'' he said, ''and he heard this voice saying inside the churchyard fence, 'You take that one and I'll take this one. You take that one and I'll take this one.' On and on. Nearly scared him to death. He ran a mile to the crossroads store and told the men there about what he had heard. A one-legged man on a peg said Pshaw, he didn't believe it. 'Go with me, then,' said the scared man, 'and I'll show you.' And so they went together back to the churchyard. Here, again, the voices were to be heard, counting out: 'You take that one and I'll take this one. You take that one and I'll take this one.' There was a silence, and then a voice said, 'Let's go outside now and get the two we dropped.' You know, that one-legged man beat the man with two good legs back to the store. They found out later it was two boys sitting in there counting out their walnuts.''

''Reminds me,'' said Tom Lawson, ''of the story about the two devils. The man in this story had to pass a certain church-house each night as he went home from his work. And every time he went past that church, he saw, sitting on the ridgepole, a big white ghost that scared him so mightily he ran himself breathless getting home. By and by, he couldn't stand it any longer, and so he told his friends about what he saw, and one of them decided he was making it all up. He'd give him something, his friend decided, to run off at the mouth about. So along about dark, just before the man usually passed, wrapped in a bedsheet, he climbed up on the ridgepole and sat waiting. Finally, the man came along, took one look, and said, 'Hm, there's two of 'em tonight.'' The man in the sheet looked around, and there sitting behind him on the ridgepole was another somebody or other in a sheet. He jumped down from that ridgepole and started to run, the other ghost right after him. The last thing he heard was the man shouting: 'Run, big devil, little devil'll catch you!'''

These stories always made Alan shiver a little, even in daylight, despite their graveyard humor. He loved to hear them though, particularly at night, with no light about except that given off by the fireplace. After an evening of such excitement, he would not venture outside the house except in the company of Lee.

"I've always had a theory about ghosts," John Wade said. "They always follow people into the settlements; they're never there first. That is, real native ghosts. Of course, people bring ghost stories with them when they arrive in a new place, but you can almost always tell them from the real product. People have to live and die in a place before their own ghosts can live in it." He chuckled. "To hear me tell it," he said, "you'd think ghosts were realer than people."

"Tell me, John," Oscar said, "do you believe in ghosts?"

"It's like I always said," John Wade answered; "I don't believe in 'em, but I'd sure hate to meet one."

His listeners laughed. "Alan believes in them," Tom Lawson said. "I can tell by the look on his face."

"The boy just has an open mind," John Wade said. To Alan, he remarked, "Keep it that way, son. When you close it, you shut more out than you shut in."

At sundown, Lee and Alan went home to do the chores and to bring back to the mill a basket filled with supper for Oscar and John. On a piece of roofing tin near the mouth of the furnace, a pot of coffee was simmering. Ira had brought from the Wade barn several ears of corn for the mule tethered to the end of the long beam.

"Here, Alan," Ira said, unhitching the mule, "you can water him while I shell this corn." Alan led the tired mule to the creek at the center of the meadow, noticing on the way that the animal seemed unsure of his feet, appearing to stagger slightly now and then. Like playing spinner, he thought. The game was one in which the player spun round and round, his arms outstretched until he was quite breathless and, coming to a stop, tried to stand perfectly still with his eyes closed. The earth went right on rocking and spinning, of course, until the senses righted themselves. The mule, going in a circle all day, had a right to be dizzy. Alan was reminded of an argument he had heard in the afternoon between Oscar and Tom Lawson about whether the animal pulling the grinder always traveled clockwise or counterclockwise, Oscar saying clockwise, Tom Lawson arguing for the opposite. John Wade's mule moved in a counterclockwise direction; but Oscar contended that he had seen a clockwise movement, too. The syrup-maker settled the argument by saying that if there was a right hand, there had to be a left, which Alan understood to mean that there were pressers capable of going either way. He didn't know, however, because John Wade was smiling to himself when he said it as if he had played a joke on the two men.

163

If Alan had learned one thing in the course of the summer, it was that most questions asked in this world never receive a direct answer. He was beginning to suspect that people were indirect in their replies because they themselves were not sure of the truth they had been asked to define. Perhaps they didn't even understand the question. Miss Woodson had told her class that their duty, as young people, was to ask the right questions. If so, she said, there will be right answers. But the questions must come first. Without the questions, there are no answers. There can't be.

Were, then, Alan wondered, the questions that received doubtful answers really the wrong questions, in the first place. He hated to doubt the wisdom of Miss Woodson's statement, which sounded fine from the outside. That was another thing bothering him: Words, even splendid words, could be fooling and false. If a man thought with words, he also felt with them. And Reuben's death had taught him that a wide gap existed between reason and emotion. Because death, as Belle had explained to him, was necessary, it didn't mean that he altogether accepted the fact of death. Confusion had grown momently during the summer, as he tried to link his small valley world with the larger world outside, the country beyond the ridges to which the train in its wild lonely passage through the valley summoned him; his confusion as he tried to link his mind with the minds around him was even greater.

From the mule's mouth, touching the water to drink, small concentric circles spread towards the center of the pond; or half-circles, they were, since the animal leaned from the bank to drink, and the near halves of the circles were stopped almost at Alan's feet. The boy flipped a pebble into the center of the small pond formed by the creek, and watched the perfect circles flow towards him, each centering in the other in a widening ripple until the outermost ring reached the bank and broke, and the second and the third followed. The slight motion would continue long after he and the mule had retraced their way to the mill. It seemed to Alan that his own thoughts, trying to reach the outside world, of which the train so sadly but so triumphantly spoke, were stopped half-way by the ridges, rimming the valley as the water-circles around the mule's nose. The impediment between his mind and the minds of those around him could not be explained by a single stone dropped into a pond; it was rather exemplified by the patterns, no two of which coincided or had any appreciable effect on each other.

Elementary, only half-formed in his mind, such ideas were, nonetheless, tormenting, creating in him a sense of loneliness and of separation even from those he loved most. The talk of the men at the mill, casual, unconcerned as it was, was for him an added riddle in a mental landscape that already seemed the work of a master puzzle-maker.

He led the mule back to the mill and hitched him near the small tub

164

in which Ira had shelled the corn. "Gad," Ira said, "what did you do? Take a swim?"

"Tend to your own business, Ira," John Wade said.

"I just asked him," Ira said sullenly. "I could have gone to town and back myself in the same amount of time."

"Are you fast on foot?" Lee said, beginning an old joke to tantalize Ira. "If so, catch that sneeze going yonder." The joke would have been rowdier in freer company. Lee toned it considerably in the presence of the older men.

"Who pulled your chain, small fry?" Ira said, scornfully. "The littler they are, looks like, the louder they sound."

Lee grinned. Ira was hopping mad.

"Take these supper things home, boys," Oscar said to his sons, "and stay with your mother so John's wife can get her chickens fed before midnight. We're about through here."

'Yes, no more for tonight, boys," John Wade said. "This is what the shoemaker hit his wife with, the last." Everybody knew the old saw about the iron shoestand and how the cobbler beat his wife with it.

Tom Lawson, who had waited all day to see whether his cane would come to the grinder before quitting time, laughed. "Guess I'll be getting along," he said. "Come tomorrow, the last shall be first." Enjoying his little Biblical sally, he strode off into the darkness of the meadow.

"Early, Tom," John Wade called after him. "About six o'clock."

Alan and Lee took the basket and started home. Oscar would follow them in the loaded wagon. For them, the syrup-making was finished, and with it, another summer, as John Wade had remarked, was rolling up its little ball of yarn. Around the tired boys as they went through the small wood on their side of Muddy Bottom Creek, fireflies gleamed fitfully, seeming few; now and then, in the dampness of a rotted log, an icy bit of foxfire, greenish blue, almost like the glimmer of frost in moonlight, flashed for an instant and then, the angle shifting, was gone. Once an early cricket peeped, a small sound, cold and still foreign to the summer landscape. Then, suddenly, among the other sounds of dry leaves walking down from the tops of the trees, spinning end over tip, and the brawling sound of the creek in its shoals below the barn, there was added another sound, a thin scuffing in the leaves.

"Be still," Lee said. Both boys froze in their tracks. The scuffing came nearer, and what seemed to be three parallel white bars scurried between them. Only a deeper darkness underlay the stripes, jet, ebony, in the browner dusk of the night. The skunk disappeared in the underbrush. "Holy cow," Lee whispered. "If we'd moved, we would have got it. Good thing about them, though," he added in a louder tone, "if you don't bother one, he won't bother you."

"They make nice pets if they're worked on," Alan said. "Jesse Jarnigan brought one to school that way. Miss Woodson told us town kids like them."

"Well, I'd rather have a coon any day," Lee said. "They're about the best pets there are."

"And the meanest, Mom says," Alan added, remembering his mother's tales about his Uncle Sheridan's pet coon, McKinley. Her younger brother had raised the baby raccoon on a bottle and by so doing had contributed a major nuisance to the Abernathy household.

"We couldn't have jelly or anything," Belle said. "We'd hear him at night, stacking the empty jars, looking for a full one. When he found something to suit his fancy, he'd rip off the paper Mother had tied around the top of the jar and help himself. The funniest thing, though, was watching him catch frogs down by the spring. He'd sniff around until he smelled a frog under the mud, and then he'd squat over the place and work his hind feet down until he touched him, and then he'd flip him right out and eat him but not before he took him to the creek and washed the mud off him. He always dug with his hind feet and legs, using his front paws to wash whatever he found before tasting it. I've seen him wash and wash my father's old pipe, trying to get the scent out of it."

His mother had laughed heartily. "I do remember the time he found a cold wasp on the front porch. The wasp was too frozen to sting, but McKinley kept pushing the thing around and breathing on it until it warmed up sufficiently to get him right on the nose. I'll never forget how that coon leaped straight up in the air and wet all over himself. I had to scrub the porch."

"Coons are prettier than skunks," Alan said, "with their black faces and ringed tails. But skunks are different."

"You'd have to be different," Lee said, "come heck or high water."

That finished the conversation, as something similar always did, and the brothers continued their way across the barn lot in silence.

24

JOHN Wade was telling another tale. The second afternoon of the syrup-making was coming to a close, and Tom Lawson's batch of cane was wearing down, under Ira's relentless grinding, to a handful of stalks. The pan bubbled and bounced along its surface as the juice thickened and changed colors; there was little work to do except lift an occasional ladle of skimmings and toss it into the skimminghole. So the syrup-maker, master of all he could see, looked otherwhere for employment, and began to tell another tale.

Alan, who had been allowed to visit the mill for two hours while Lee stayed home with Belle, sat and listened.

"That was the driest summer I ever saw, so dry the only water we had left was the little in the bottom of the spring and some in the stock pond. Not much there, for the cattle had been drinking steadily through the hot days, and the pond had dwindled. We didn't live then near a creek, with the blessing of water always near us. Those mountains," John Wade said, pointing to Walden Ridge and the faint purple peaks just visible beyond, "are the greatest blessing the people in Walden Valley ever had."

"I was a little shaver then, and didn't understand too much about what was happening. I knew my father had stopped working in the corn, which had turned a sick gray—a fact that, even to me, was a bad sign. Corn was what we lived on then, as now; and the sight of it dying in the fields was sobering enough even for a youngster who still believed in Santa Claus. My father talked very little, except perhaps to my mother. I never knew because I never heard him. But I could tell by his face that he had about given up hope. I watered the hogs from the spring, and drove the cattle to the pond twice a day. We didn't allow them in the pasture anymore, for they wanted to go lie down in the little water they had left for drinking. I rode the gentle mule down to the pond, leading the young one, for their water. Sitting up there, high on the mule's shoulders, I got dizzy watching the water run in little muddy waves under the mules' noses like it was feet deep instead of inches. One day I slid off the mule's shoulders into the mud, and was surprised to find the water as thin as my hand. Still I didn't worry too much. I think I believed with my mother even then that the Lord would provide. My father, though, was less of a believer, and went about looking glum and despairful. 'John,' my mother would say 'a body has to take what comes and be thankful for it.' Believing that, I could see, put quite a strain on my father.

"There was one funny thing that summer, though. It concerned a neighbor of ours who gave up doing anything whatsoever and took to the cliff to watch for rain. Day after day, he sat on the hot rock jumping up into the sky and watching for a cloud; and day after day, he couldn't find one, not even the size of a man's hand. His wife sent their little boy with his dinner at noon every day, because he wouldn't come down till darkness drove him home. He sat up there for weeks alone, just watching. Not a cloud the size of a bird's nest even. His wife grew impatient with him, claiming he was crazy. And by that time perhaps he was, a little. Either that or he had begun to make a game of what he was doing. For he would just smile and go back to his watching.

"One day though it did rain, a regular toad-strangler. Me and the boy, a friend of mine, he was, about my age, had just started up the trail to the cliff to where his father was watching. It was my second time to go to the cliff, and I remember even now how white the world looked and cracked with heat; and how so much plant death all around made me, for the first time, really afraid. We climbed and climbed up the hot limestone, as the thunder began to roll behind the mountain. Lightning forked suddenly upward like the tunefork the singing-master used at the church. The whole earth seemed to be waiting, soundless except for the noise of the storm. Suddenly, the rain came, in a small cloudburst, almost washing us back down the trail. But what took our attention was the man. Up above us, he was dancing on the edge of the cliff, like a lank doll, flinging his arms wide to the rush of the wind and rain, and laughing like he'd heard the best joke in the world. And maybe he had, in a way none of the rest of us ever understood. For he very nearly got washed right off the face of the cliff into the valley. He was the local water-finder, a dowser, the books call him, and he could find water anywhere under the ground by using a willow twig. I know, because I saw him locate water in places dry as the back of my hand at least a dozen times. He won fifty dollars once on a bet that he couldn't put his switch on water on the property of the postmaster in town. He found it all right. My father was there, and saw him cover every inch of the knoll almost before the twig came alive in his hands and pointed downward over where, later, the diggers found a stream as big as a man's wrist.

"Anyway, after the big storm people weren't so sure the name, 'water-witch,' was just a word in the book. They appreciated the rain, but they grew a little afraid of the rain-maker." John Wade laughed. "Wasn't it always that way?" he asked.

"Rainmaker or not, the downpour saved us. We managed to scrape by that year, as the Irishman said, by a 'dom tight squeeze.'" Being Irish himself, John Wade had a stock of Irish jokes which he sometimes told to very select company. But the syrup-mill was too public for these choice items. In the presence of boys, or of grown-up strangers, John Wade minded his tongue with a care very few of the other men in Walden Valley could understand or appreciate. He was to them a mixture of gentleman-preacher-country scholar, and so was regarded with humor, contempt, and a slight fear, as so many sons might regard a strong, capable father who demanded and received a grudging respect. They liked his stories and admitted among themselves that he could talk the bark off a tree.

"He's a better tale-teller than Preacher Musgrove," Tom Lawson admitted privately. "If he'd just tack a little more point to his stories, I'd rather hear him."

But Alan loved the stories as they were. Morals might or might not be part of a tale. The tale came first. Miss Woodson had pointed out to him last year that Aesop's Fables would still be Aesop's Fables to anyone with half a mind, even if the lines containing the "moral" were chopped off. The moral was added, she said, for those people who might otherwise miss the point. And many of them would. For the ability to read and write was the rarest ability in the world. Real readers and writers were (she had used a community expression) as scarce as hen's teeth. And, listening to John Wade spin his myths of past times and bygone memories, Alan had concluded that being a real story-teller was a gift not often encountered. Listening was like looking through an old picture album of photographs that had lost their names, and having them revived by a pointing finger, a remembering tongue. He recalled with a thrill of pleasure the thick brass-clasped, blue-velvet bound album on the front-room table in Miss Woodson's house. On the plain polished circle of wood, under a blue kerosene lamp with a tall clear globe, the album lay, its gold-colored tiny key beside it. The table and what it held was like a picture from a faraway place and an unimaginable time. It took the words of a man like John Wade, or of a woman like Miss Woodson, to breathe life into the still objects. Even the pictures in his teacher's house, with their frames of wood that seemed illuminated from within, that glowed with the distant gold of an old woodland on a summer day, fused with the winey air of an orchard reddening towards fall, caught him in an unresolved mesh of conjecture. These pictures had no connection with anything outside themselves. They hung there and glowed, some of them, with light all sunk below the surface, like a bottle in which a golden liquid moves unreached beneath the hand. Others, not the ones with the rich, fantastic frames, seemed to progress outside the thin bands of wood stripping that bound them. Of these, one print, especially, of children having a funeral for a dead bird, which Miss Woodson said was a Currier and Ives, was the most memorable. Its homemade frame of pine slats, crossed at the corners, and crossed again diagonally with a shorter strip of the same material, so that each corner had four tips, was something he himself might have made. But it was the children in the picture who mattered, and the simple thing they were doing. As it moved along, the procession, with its old-fashioned boys and girls in their strange dress, and the canopied hearse, flower-decked and carrying the dead sparrow with its tiny feet thrust upward into the air, seemed to rehearse another world, something, perhaps, out of a child's book from another century, when the now very old had been very young.

For the moment, dreaming, Alan had forgotten the syrup-making, another landscape having invaded his mind. He came to with a start. Half of his confusion resulted, he had begun to realize, from the associations begun in his mind by a word, a gesture, a color. The more he read, heard, felt, or saw, the more richly puzzling the sphere of experience became, and the embarrassment that sometimes as richly attended it. He had stood in disgrace with Oscar for half the summer because, in plowing with the cultivator, he had forgotten to lower the plows into the earth after having made a turn at the end of the field, and had plowed all morning without really plowing at all. It got to be a community joke, the way Oscar told it. He had aroused Alan by throwing a clod at him and telling him to go to the house and help Belle if he couldn't do a man's work. "Had his mind on some blamed book he was reading, I suspect," Oscar told John Wade, laughing. "If I'd let him, he wouldn't do another thing but read."

"Let him read, Oscar," John Wade had said. "There are more things in this world than you and I ever dreamed of."

"He eats," Oscar said tartly, "like one long gut open at both ends. I can't feed him on fairy tales."

"He's growing in several ways," John said. "You can't make him like Lee or Ira. No use trying. It would be like putting a square peg in a round hole. The shape's different, that's all. Some of us are fit for one thing, and some for another. I think he'd make a fine teacher. That's what I always wanted to do." John Wade sounded wistful and sad.

Oscar looked surprised. "I declare," he said to himself, staring at his neighbor with a strange thought in his head, "my boy would have come off better being his son." Often, in fact, Oscar felt as if John Wade were his own father, a feeling not so incomprehensible in a man who had been an orphan for most of his life.

Now he called to Alan. "Come on, son. Help us load this syrup."

Alan climbed into the wagon and placed the gallon buckets of warm molasses carefully side by side in the bottom of the bed.

"Watch this one," cautioned Tom Lawson, handing up a bucket. "It's hotter than blazes." Bucket after bucket and finally two lard cans were stored in the wagon.

"That ought to keep you sweet for the winter," John Wade said. "Temper and all. Nothing like molasses to sugar up a man."

Tom Lawson grinned. "When a man's as sweet as I naturally am, he don't need no outside influences," he said, "to help him along."

He drove off, whistling.

"Too late to begin another run," the syrup-maker said, looking at the sun, now topping the trees to the west and beginning to color the heavens there. "We'll bank the fire, move this syrup to the house, and call it a day."

The molasses he referred to was the toll he took for the making. The Wades never grew any sorghum of their own.

"You're going to have more syrup than you know what to do with, John," Oscar said, loading the wagon.

"I doubt it," John Wade said. "Last year by January, I was completely sold out. People came begging to buy even a half gallon, and I ended up by not keeping enough for my own family. People like it better than honey, in the long run. I do myself. I get tired of honey faster."

"Honey's mighty fine," Oscar said. "Along in the winter I may be trying to swap you gallon for gallon."

"By that time I suspect you won't have any trouble making the trade," John Wade said, smiling. "By January, I'll be so beeswaxed my stinger will be showing."

25

REVIVAL meeting was the year's greatest event for both the young and the old of Walden Valley, though for somewhat different reasons. Coming in late summer as it did, when there was a lull between the laying-by of the crops and the general harvest, the meeting offered a chance for socializing on all levels, a yearly visit between neighbors who had not seen each other for twelve months, an opportunity even for the furtherance of trade carried on stealthily under cover of the churchyard trees, by the men who described their merchandise, named prices, arranged visits among the farms. The women talked of everything from pickling to the new mail-order catalogue with its outlandish styles and ridiculous prices. As for the younger tribe, revival meeting simply gave them somewhere to go. Hair bright with bows, or slicked with water until it showed the outlines of the skull, the boys and girls trooped churchward, laughing and making eyes along the country roads, holding hands in the dark, the boys walking the girls home after the service. This was the season when the girls of Walden Valley made their debut, or re-made it, year after year, until they managed a match, if they were lucky, or settled back in resignation, as Miss Pearman had done, to teach a Sunday school class or become church secretary. For them, the luckless ones, the church became even more a center for their devotions.

After each service, the still hopeful girls flocked to the high front steps and stood talking and giggling, like show animals in a ring, to be looked over by the boys in the yard, edging the darkness, not eager to be seen for the simple reason that they might have changed their minds from the night before. Many a young lady, refusing a bid to be walked home, looked in vain for her escort of the previous evening, only to see him, at last, disappearing into the night with someone else. She had been, she realized, too hasty in biting off the thread. She would know better the next time.

The very young found the series of meetings either fearsomely dull or, if they were imaginative, horrifyingly bright with the pictured landscapes of hell. Spurred on by the preacher's words, they were left with only two avenues of reaction: either they went to sleep or sat, big-eyed and feverish, on the numbing benches in the making of a nightmare, the more nervous ones feeling the flames already lapping around their ankles.

It was an odd thing to consider that the gentle readings of the Book disappeared in autumn; there were no green pastures then. Love seemed to have been forgotten in the whirlpools of wrath the preachers sent swirling out over the heads of the congregation, to the accompaniment of clapping hands from the anciently old and their shrill amens. God's mercy had suddenly and irrevocably turned to God's anger, and nothing could be done about it except grovel in repentance at the foot of the altar. And grovel, many of the people in the valley did, year after year, seeming to find in autumnal penitence a release from all the spiritual bruises and frustrations that hounded their lives in the months between.

Oscar, whose affiliation with the church was intermittent and shy, as if emotional outbursts of any but an angry kind embarrassed and shamed him, called the agony and joy of these annual backsliders "roasting-ear religion," because, he said, the late corn was in milk and more rows in the valley fields were ruined in that single season than in all the summer months combined. He sometimes called it "fried chicken grace," telling the story of a Mr. McBrier, who kept killing his chickens for traveling preachers and their wives and families, until only one old rooster and one guinea were left on the farm. The rooster would, Oscar said, come out morning and rear back and crow, "Mr. McBrier! Mr. McBrier!" as if in challenge to his owner, but the more cautious guinea would hide under the house and call out to his bold friend, "You'd better come back! You'd better come back!" This always tickled Alan uproariously, because his father could make the conversation between the birds sound immensely like a crow and a guinea's quacking stutter. Belle always scolded her husband for his irreverence. Oscar grinned. It seemed to him a man was one thing or another, and not one thing one day and another thing the next. Belle, however, believed strongly in the theory of redemption, no matter how many times a man had to be redeemed before redemption stuck. Between them, Alan was confused, as usual, tending, however, to believe with his father that permanence was desirable. Oscar's views were somewhat similar to those of Miss Woodson, who was a Presbyterian and who happened to remark one day in his presence that she believed in predestination. A word which, when he looked it up in the school's encyclopedia, frightened him with its inescapability, particularly when he made the cross-reference indicated and read further under the heading of "Calvinism." He was horrified by the rigidities of that stern religion. Nevertheless, even with its theory of limited atonement, Calvinism appealed more to him than did a belief in which a man was in heaven one minute and out the next. Even with the Baptists it was not so easy to get out of hell; though, as the preacher so carefully outlined, it could be done. At least the Calvinists had the problem of children solved; something the Baptists seemed puzzled about. *They* went to the easiest room in hell if they died unbaptized—a state the Baptists referred to, if at all, with considerable confusion, preferring to have their young ones wait for salvation until they reached an age popularly known as "the age of accountability." At twelve, Alan had begun to worry about the conditions of his salvation, though, like his father, it seemed to him that a man's salvation was a private matter, something one did not talk about too much; and a matter more involved with a wider knowledge of the world, not a less, as the preachers advised, even Preacher Musgrove, who seldom preached at revivals in his church, leaving that to the visiting brothers, but who, nevertheless, regarded study as a weariness of the spirit and argued against the reading of many books. The Bible was sufficient, he stated. Not so with Miss Woodson, however, who was careful to point out in her reading to them from the wisdom books of the Old Testament, that a man who knew only his Bible, didn't know his Bible.

This clear separation of idea and feeling among the older people who helped to shape his thinking was something of a comfort to Alan. Where there was such a division of approaches, there must be a multiplicity of ways. It still seemed to him, however, that the more a man knew, the closer he would come to being right in his decisions, even if Belle had told him to "go wonder and perish."

26

AS Lee and Alan approached the church in the darkness, the lamps were all lit and the congregation was singing. From the windows the yellow light streamed out from the lamps in their brackets along the wall, like fingers spearing into the dusk of the trees, highlighting here and there a man squatting in the darkness, whittling, talking to another man squatted near him. Horses and mules, tied individually to branches or left hitched to the wagons, moved in the dissolving light. A car or two, rickety and old, were parked to one side of the church, and there was one sleek beautiful machine near the front door, which belonged to the town singers, The Ever-Faithful Quartet, who came to the revival to help with the singing.

"Boy," Lee said, seeing it. "If I had that, I'd not be walking." He reminded Alan again that he might be taking Suzy Overholt home, and if so Alan could expect to walk home in the darkness alone.

"So what?" Alan said. "I've walked home by myself before. Besides, Jesse Jarnigan more than likely will be here. We'll walk home together."

Inside the church, the crowd began at the altar and flowed backward to the last row of benches in the house without a break. Lee and Alan stood leaning against the wall, listening. The room was hot and odorous from the crowding people, and dim despite the lamps; for around each yellow glow a swarm of insects danced thickly, weaving in and out like a globe of river midges on an autumn day. A small bird, trapped in the half-light, bumped the ceiling as it flew, seeking the outside dark. Above the window in the choir, a dirt dauber had built his house, like the pipes of a diminutive organ, against the brown planking of the wall.

The preacher, a thin, wispy little man whose suspenders were so tight they yanked his trousers high above his shoetops, so that his body seemed to be swinging from the shoulders, had already begun his sermon. His voice, surprisingly deep and full for so small a person, filled the big room;

175

soon it would wash through the windows and echo among the trees, as his fervor mounted, and the audience warmed to him. Already his eyes had the strange, burning look of passion the eyes of Preacher Musgrove sometimes got when he was earnestly preaching his Sunday morning sermon, a look Alan could not in any way associate with the look of the very brown-eyed man mildly staring out of the picture on the Sunday schoolroom wall. This preacher looked like the picture of John Brown in a history book at school, his eyes full of futures, prophesying, predicting, his arms outflung, his hair shaken wild. Only his smooth brown face, like the face of a boy suddenly old, seemed out of place in the general impression he made. He preached loudly of death and the resurrection.

"Neighbors," he shouted, "on that great and awful day what will your answers be? What will you say then to the questions of salvation and eternity? Nothing, my friends. For it will be too late. The old account will have long been settled, and you will be divided, to the left, to the right, some into eternal morning, some into the blackness of hell and utter despair. Will you be on the right hand of the King coming in glory? Decide my friends. The Judgment Day is coming. The time is at hand. Make ye straight the pathway of the Lord. Be ready! O be ready!" he repeated, his voice rising until it filled the room with a terrifying roar. "Be ready for the day when the trumpet shall sound and the dead, every one, shall arise. When all the mouldering forms will quiver in the earth, and get up from the grave and stand forth and stand, ready or not, for the Judgment! O you sinners, how will it be with you on that day?"

He paused, his arms outstretched as if pointing to some awful event even then bearing down on his congregation. Waiting for some sign, some encouragement from his listeners, he did not go on with his sermon, but gazed down upon them, sternly, raptly, as if caught for a moment himself in the fearfulness of the picture he had created.

Someone in the congregation moaned, a low, strangling sound; and then a piercing shriek echoed in the room. Mrs. Alloway had begun to shout.

"Bless you, sister!" the preacher cried. "You're not ashamed! O brothers," he shouted, as if he preached only to the men, "if you are ashamed of Him now, he'll be ashamed of you then!"

"Amen!" Mrs. Alloway shouted, clapping her hands. "Amen! Amen!"

"On that day," the preacher continued, wiping his face with his hands, "men will cry for the rocks and mountains to hide them from the face of God. There will be wailing and gnashing of teeth, my friends. But only the righteous will stand. I tell you the truth. Only the righteous will stand!"

Alan felt someone touch his shoulder. John Wade was standing near him. "I'm tired," John Wade said. "Too much syrup-making, I guess. I'm going home now. Want to double with me?"

The service had hardly begun. But the walk home alone, for all his assurance to Lee, did not appeal to Alan. Besides, he was himself a great deal tireder than he had thought when he left home. His legs would hardly support him; but for the wall behind him now he would be sitting on the floor. He nodded his willingness to be away from the terrible intimacy of God and man so published and advised in the sultry churchhouse, whose sides seem to split and dissolve in the fiery glow of the preacher's words. His head swimming, the preacher's harangue, wild and disordered and wonderful, ringing in his ears, Alan began to pick his way towards the door. The ending of the world would not have much surprised him at that very moment.

As they left the church, the congregation began to sing "Softly and Tenderly Jesus Is Calling," the town quartet sounding high above the rest of the singers. People were walking toward the altar, weeping and wringing their hands. The mourner's bench was not empty.

"This way," John Wade said in the yard. "I tied my horse near the graveyard."

The earth felt surprisingly solid and unmoved under Alan's feet, as if it contemplated no change; not immediately, anyway.

The rift between day things and night things was deep and broad for him, but the gap that widened between the outside world and the events the preacher so graphically portrayed inside the church was unbridgable. He simply could not make the leap from the kindly man who now helped him mount the horse, and the warm, smelly animal himself, to the inflamed fear and wonder of the crowd now so enchanted by the traveling prophet, who himself seemed to be crucified by his own suspenders. The difference was the difference between the bright, lively light of the sun and the cold reflection of the graveyard moon that struck the slanted gravestones with an icy overtone. From his position behind the man, his arms halfway around the thin, tall body, Alan could see indistinctly Reuben's grave in the moonlight, small, crowded, almost lost among the larger mounds. Vaguely he wondered how his cousin would look on Resurrection Day. The dimes would not be on Reuben's eyes, Alan knew, for his Aunt Kate now carried them, wrapped up in a silk handkerchief, in her pocketbook.

They rode in silence for awhile. John Wade sighed, tiredly. "Big crowd for the middle of the week," he said. "Too big for me," he added a moment later. "Sometimes I'd like to preach. Mine would be funny sermons though, and I guess no church would have me. Instead of preaching about the Judgment Day coming, I'd tell the people that every day is judgment day, so far as we are concerned. Every sundown is the ending of the world and every morning is a new creation, with a new chance for us to make seven new and better worlds in a week, with the best perhaps on Sunday when we could just sit and think about the worlds we had made, and pick the best from all of them to make the last world in the week. And then, when we got to heaven, the last world of all, we could just sit and make it from our memory of the best of all the worlds we had made on earth. ''

Alan listened. "Sounds crazy, doesn't it?" John Wade asked.

"No sir," Alan said. "No, sir."

The kind of world the syrup-maker described was the world wisdom made, fashioned from a greater, not a lesser, knowledge of all things. It was the ever-changing, ever-developing world that built upon all histories and races the more nearly-perfect earth that Miss Woodson had named Utopia, a Greek word, she had said, which meant "no such land," and which Preacher Musgrove seemed to condemn out of hand when he preached against evolution. Alan would never forget the consternation on Miss Pearman's face when he announced in Sunday school class that all dead bodies made good fertilizer. After all, Miss Pearman had herself brought up the subject in her talk on Thanksgiving. Somehow or other, though, she couldn't see the similarity between the fish the Indians put under a hill of corn and a human body put into the ground. Belle had been informed of his statement, and had lectured him stringently. Gradually, he was learning to keep his thoughts to himself.

A calf bawled in a fencerow. Both Alan and the horse jumped. John Wade laughed. "The devil's in the fencerow tonight. Got your goat, didn't it? Brandy's a bit edgy, too."

"Scared me a little," Alan admitted.

His arms tightened slightly about the man's waist. Being grown-up would be wonderful, he thought. Grown-ups didn't jump and flounce around at every unexpected sight and sound. Nothing seemed to startle them. It took such a long time to be a man. Tomorrow and tomorrow and tomorrow passed, and he was still a boy. At times he believed he was a midget, a dwarf, and that he would never grow. He wanted to ask the syrup-maker why growing was so slow. Instead, he asked another question that he had been intending to ask John Wade for a long while, a question he could not remember in the rare times when they were alone together. "Mr. Wade," he said, "why did you call Brandy, Brandy?"

"When I bought him as a colt," the syrup-maker answered, "he was the color of a bottle of apple brandy held up to the sunlight. A rich reddish-yellow color. He's begun to fade now. Old age is getting him."

"How old is he?" Alan asked.

"Nearly eighteen," John Wade said. "A good age, for a horse. He was a beaut, though, when he was young. Just the color of apple squeezings." He laughed, sensing Alan's thought. "That was a long time ago, boy," he said. "A long time ago."

John Wade swung the second rider down without himself dismounting. "Sleep tight," he called, waiting until Alan reached the front porch.

"Tell Oscar I'll be expecting him tomorrow."

Alan went back to the gate. "I forgot," he said. "Thank you for bringing me home."

John Wade was pleased. "You are welcome, boy," he said. "Entirely welcome."

27

NO sooner had he gone to bed, it seemed to Alan later, trying to remember more clearly the details of his dream, than he was involved in Judgment Day. Around him bloodred willows, spotted with peacock wings, were blowing on the bank of a small river, in the center of which gleamed a shoal as white as a clean sheet. Why the shoal was there, he could not say, except that its snowiness seemed impossibly far and clean, new-washed and ready. Where he was, though, the trees flamed, and the sky above the ridge was itself flamboyant, radiant, like the staves of an umbrella whose scarlet color was braced with gold. At first, a heavy silence reigned. But a sound grew, slowly increasing, until it became recognizable as the sound of footsteps going slowly past him on the ground, footsteps uneager, reluctant, as the people came from the willowy places, no exultation on them. He stood back in the willow branches to see. The people all fell to their knees and touched their foreheads to the ground. A horn-sound broke the world in two. The river and the willow grove disappeared; a cold, white plain spread all around. Now he heard the sound of marching men, and knew that it was time for him to go. He ran and knelt in line with the others. Oddly enough, he found himself next to his mother. Like her, he bowed his forehead to the ground. Along the line of kneeling forms came the man with the spear, menacing each in turn with a short, quick jab of the blade. Some of the forms twitched, some were still. Without being told, Alan knew that the twitching forms were damned, and steeled himself into motionlessness. The spear approached. It menaced his mother, who seemed not to know that the spear had passed. It came to him. He held himself rigid. A burning light struck him between the shoulder blades, and in reaction he leaped almost out of bed.

Hearing him, his mother said, "Is that you, Lee? Is that you, Alan?"

Shaken and sweating, he said, "It's me. I almost fell out of bed."

"That boy's overdoing himself," Belle said to Oscar, who had waked up. "I'm worried about him."

"He'll be all right," Oscar said, going to sleep again. "He's just not built to take it, that's all."

When he slept again, Alan did not re-awaken, not even when Lee climbed into bed beside him and began to snore. Dreamlessly, the night merged with morning, till Clockwork beat his dusty wings in the front yard and sounded a new day.

28

TO the east, towards the zenith above the sycamore trees, two very short clouds, one blue, one pink, moved like fish or ponies in droll companionable color, munching the distance. But near the horizon, the great cloudbanks of September were already forming in August along the treetops, in great steamy stacks and layers and heads; distant and bulky towers were crossed by the nearer strata of whites and grays; and behind all these, glowed the deep and empty blue, from which the moon at early morning spread only a glow through the magnificent masses, until it rolled free on the highest crest and seemed to rest there for hours, paling, as both moon and cloud-bank rose up towards the meridian. There was a hint of moisture everywhere, as if late in the night the showers had come. But there was no wetness on the ground. Only the air seemed saturated; and both moon and sun, above the September water belt already deepening in late August, suffered a circular diffraction into prismatic auras of rainbows. Gradual-ly, the warming sun put the moon and its cover of cloud into abeyance for the day. A sense of waiting grew in the morning. The big autumnal winds were on their way.

Going out into the yard, Alan felt the presence of another season grow-ing around him, a great, natural change in the earth that mocked the sud-den irruption of his resurrection dream. In the morning light, he could almost smile at his midnight terror, as the world swung, boldly and sure-ly, through the turn of the year. He remembered the flame-tongued man in the pulpit at Friendship Church as he might have remembered a place he had one time visited, perhaps not bodily, but through a combination of senses and feelings that made him believe he had sometime or other made the same journey, stood in the same place, experienced the same reaction. The night was already taking its place in the limbo of sensations to which all dead feelings go. The dream itself was the fruit of the night, the summing up, the bringing together of the patterns invoked in his memory of the man and the room and the waiting throng that heaved his words back to him by the strength of their deep, absorbed attention and belief.

But the morning belied it all. The whole landscape of his mind had suffered a day-change. Around him, in the yard, with Pretty Boy bumping his hand with the hard round surface of his head, and Whizzer, Belle's big yellow cat, stalking through and through his legs, leaning stiffly, purring for attention, the light itself had patently fallen from summer, as his mind had fallen from the dream. In the thready, passing mist blowing from the creek, the air was a pale, thick, strawy reflection like weak coffee spilled on an old brown table; or like honey mixed with water. Tan light, dry and dusty for all its comparison with liquids; a light that opened from the ground in wide conduits for the dust to rise in and fly out over the landscape, itself not mellow yet, not ripe, but already holding in its breath a scent of ripeness and rot. The blue pines stood solidly above the house, beyond the orchard and between the house and the wheatfield. They had suddenly grown immense in bulk and concentrated in color as if metamorphosed, looming twice their summer size in the changed air.

By the creek the song of a late cicada was like the sound of a runaway mower, loud in the yellowing willows, themselves coming back across the barrier of gold into brown sleep. Alan remembered them in the spring coming from their brown-stemmed dormancy across the threshold of gold into green. Now they retraced their way, as the year retraced its way, in a ceaseless pattern of change that was not change but ordered succession, any phase of which was no newer or older than any other phase. He remembered suddenly that the willows had been in his dream; differently colored, but nonetheless there. In their strange scarlet, meaningless, perhaps; perhaps the result of the preacher's words: "Though your sins be as scarlet, they shall be made whiter than snow." Which might also explain the white heart of the dreamed river. He could only imagine the why of the dream. But the willows were real, in a real landscape, one he had been born to and which offered him no great problem in understanding. They stood there, waving their sedge-yellow branches in the light wind, returning to winter sleep. He had for a moment a strange feeling of having lost his way, of having missed a truth too apparent for any but a numbskull to overlook. As though a face, half-seen, had peered across a windowsill a moment and then was gone, a faint thrill at a lost understanding passed over him; a dreamy half-recollection that the cycle of the willows and the process of his dream were somehow one and the same. For some time, the vague sensation of having entertained perfumed angels lingered on the remoter plateau of his confused comprehensions. Still under the influence of the words hurled like thunderbolts from the pulpit, he reached for another kind of confirmation in the familiar aspects and tides of the seasonal year. Failing both ways, he gathered from the assault of his night memory and his morning senses the impression a bird must have gone to sleep in a cloud.

Still the cloudbank rose and steamed, incredibly white at its rim, boiling inwardly, breaking in snowy pustules as his own flesh might break when afflicted with the hard, hurting mounds Belle called his "risings." The willows heaved and sighed, and from the ridge behind the house a dry, treading sound began in the leaves, where a few early dead twigs delivered their burden to the earth. A sharp feeling of indeterminate loss grieved him for a moment, sharper for its being undefinable. Feeling only partially himself, wondering what segment of his being he had mislaid and where, Alan went towards the barn and his chores.

Pretty Boy ran along the path in front of him, Whizzer choosing to walk the garden fence, stopping now and then to arch and purr in a superior way above the babbling pup. Buckeye bawled from his pen. He had a distinct bull look about him now, Alan noticed; dark and lowering in his thickening neck and chestnut color that had turned almost black with age and sun. Alan stopped to pet him through the bars. Tuesday, his Uncle Lance and Oscar would take Buckeye to the stockbarn in town, where he would be sold to the highest bidder at the weekly cattle sale. He hated to see his calf go. But he knew by now the turn of the wheel of necessity, as his mother had known when she warned him against becoming too fond of the animal given into his keeping.

Turned from the pen into the barn lot, Buckeye followed Alan to the corn crib, where the boy shelled several ears of corn into a pan. Impatiently, the calf thrust his nose into the pan while Alan was still shelling. The calf's tongue was like a rasp against the boy's hand. Pretty Boy sat back on his haunches, well out of the way, and barked at Buckeye. Whizzer eyed them all from the fence, a fat, striped house-tiger, his eyes mere slits of observation in his barred face.

Whizzer was the most disdainful of all the animals on the farm, stepping delicately, lightly, around them all, uninvolved and uninvolving, accepting what came his way as unquestionably his due. Unlike Pretty Boy, who was tiresomely grateful for any favor, Whizzer merely bestowed a veiled glance, whenever he chose, upon his benefactors, and stalked off to the interior of the jungleland of his own cat-mind.

Alan found the cat more interesting than he found Pretty Boy. But do what he could, he still found himself totally excluded by the strict privateness of the yellow tom. Even the day Alan held Whizzer up to a hole in the oak tree by the smokehouse where a mouse had momentarily taken refuge, the cat merely hooked a paw into the hole, lifted the mouse out, slithered from Alan's grasp, and stalked off without any sign of the team-spirit Pretty Boy would have displayed. Whizzer's very aloofness fascinated the boy; the way the cat saved himself from being transgressed against, even by Alan who liked to pull his tail, but pulled it at a price, was a matter for laughter even when the blood was drawn. But no intimacy ever grew between them. Whizzer's one great friend on the farm was Belle, whom he attended in her walks about the yard and garden as faithfully as Pretty Boy attended Alan and Lee. But the cat allowed nobody else any liberties with him at all.

Lee came from the barn with a pail of milk in his hand. Whizzer eyed the foamy liquid narrowly, carefully concealing his interest. To coax him, Lee poured milk into Buckeye's pan, which the calf had licked clean and abandoned for a bundle of fodder which Oscar had broken by the fence. Whizzer did not move from his place. Only when the boys started towards the house did he come down, moving slowly, rippling along the corner brace of the fence, to lap the milk, eyeing Pretty Boy fiercely as the dog trailed along behind his masters.

"How did you get home last night?" Lee asked. "I looked for you after meeting broke up, but nobody had seen you."

"I left early," Alan answered, "with John Wade. I rode home with him, double-back, on old Brandy. Mr. Wade was tired." Alan had begun to refer to John Wade sometimes by his first name, as the older boys in the community referred to all their elders, behind their elders' backs and in the safety of their own company.

"If Dad wasn't such an old gripe, he'd let me ride Old Ranger," Lee said. "Always fussing about running the horse and giving him a cold. Likes him better than he likes me, out there walking my legs off up to my straddle."

"I suppose you'd let Suzy ride behind you?" Alan said slyly. "Or maybe you'd walk and let her ride sidesaddle?"

"That's my problem, not yours," Lee said. "I'd solve it in my own way. I wish," he said irritably, "Dad had let me go to meeting night before last. I always miss what's going on."

"What happened?" Alan asked.

"The Ku Klux came," Lee said, "to pay the preacher. Suzy said they just marched in, hoods and all, before the preaching started, and gave the preacher some money, and marched out again. She said you could have heard a pin fall in the church. Said in the sheets, they looked like ghosts or something."

Alan could imagine the effect on the crowded church. The first time he had ever seen a lone Klansman riding along the road by the McDowell house, hooded and sheeted, he had squatted apprehensively in the fencerow until the rider had passed, and then run quickly to the house. Something about a man who kept his face hidden was wrong; he felt this, without being told. Though Oscar's admonition to him and Lee about acting so they could face themselves in the mirror while shaving, without being ashamed, undoubtedly had something to do with Alan's belief that a man carried a record of his good intentions in his face for all to see. The Klansman had frightened him more than had the first Negro he had ever seen, though this had been an occasion, there being no colored people living in the valley. Only at infrequent intervals did a Negro pass through. The one Indian in the neighborhood was too familiar to the boy to bother him with his dark skin and long, plaited black hair. Esi Maloni High Sky was the way he pronounced his name, and he sometimes led singing at the church during revival meeting, or sang alone in the Cherokee tongue some unrecognizable hymn such as "Rock of Ages," raising his voice to a singsong chant that filled the church with a sad mournful sound, dry as dead leaves, heathenish, a little savage, as if the Indian bemoaned in the Christian song all the past glories of his vanished people. Charlie, as the people in the valley called him, had a respectable knowledge of the use of herbs in medicine, and long ago he had cured a young woman in Walden Valley of a mysterious ailment, after the local doctor had given her up. Returning to health, she had married her benefactor. Their one child, a dark-faced boy, was in Alan's room at school, no different from anyone else, no darker really than Lee. There was an interesting tale, however, of the hominy the father made of corn and birds'-feet mixed, a food which, Belle remarked, had its own built-in seasoning. Alan felt slightly sick. But the lunch Little Charlie brought was like Alan's own, simple and good and from the land, and always wrapped in a clean white cloth in the bottom of the tin bucket. The Indian boy sat quietly through his days in the classroom, his eyes glowing only when Miss Woodson explained some fact of Cherokee history to the class, or mentioned the Cherokee word "Tsali," which the class knew meant Charlie in English.

The only other foreigner Alan had ever seen was the peddler. Short, stocky, Jewish, Mr. Goodefriend came each spring and autumn with his white pack on his shoulder, going from house to house throughout the countryside. On the front porch or in the middle of the floor of the room, Mr. Goodefriend untied the sheet in which he carried his goods; carefully, he laid back each corner to expose the wonders of his walking store. Aside from the knickknacks he displayed, and sometimes sold—handkerchiefs to the young girls, a comb or sachet to the women—he brought with him news of the world of fashion, the very latest fripperies and furbelows, mind you, of the big towns, Chicago, New York, Philadelphia—these names rolled off his tongue with the ease of some neighborhood landmark. Alan marvelled at a man so knowledgeable and so widely traveled. The visits of Mr. Goodefriend always fired him with a new ambition to grow up and to go see the world from which the old man came tramping, stooped and bowed under the heaviness of his pack. Often, the boy had sat while the peddler ate the meal Belle had prepared for him, listening open-mouthed to the stories the old man told. Mr. Goodefriend always left Belle a small present in return for her kindness.

In addition to the peddler, and among those who came from far outside the valley, were the medicine men, who came each year to hawk their wares from the acre beside George Hamilton's crossroads store, and to put up a night or two with the owner, paying him small board and lodging, but leaving him a generous supply of stuffs in bottles. They brought with them such anatomical charts as to amaze their audience; the human body, well and diseased, was displayed in all its colored, usually red, complexities and intensities. The people stared, finding such revelations of their own inner structure, both flesh and skeletal, hard to digest; some were not even able to imagine that their smooth surfaces covered such intricate designs and collaborations. But these difficult thoughts were as nothing to the thinking of the fetal twins, joined at the side and carried in a large jar of alcohol, which one of the yearly visitors displayed as his feature attraction. The Siamese twins disturbed sleep in the valley.

Arranged in rows, like containers in some kind of field laboratory, the elixirs were mysteries in their bottles. Rush's Rejuvenator for men, snake oil—renderd by a secret process no one else knew but the man who happened at the moment to be selling it, and used for all kinds and descriptions of rheumatic pains; a beauty bath for women, guaranteed to remove freckles, warts, age spots, and all other blemishes—and maybe the face itself, John Wade had remarked, laughing; a hair restorer for both men and women, sold with before and after photographs of actual users, who had gone from glistening baldness to heads of astonishingly luxuriant hair—all these were sold by the dozens to hopeful customers.

Though these traveling gentlemen, who came in their canvas-covered, light-springed wagons with their names and profession embossed on the sides, were often not individually the same from year to year, collectively they were of a recognizably similar stamp, so that they seemed to be the various members of an occult guild, outside the association of such men as Dr. McClary, who grumbled that they should be horsewhipped with their own harness straps and run out of the country. Into which country they should be run, he did not specify; he only wanted them beyond the limitations of his own domain. It was a cinch that they were supplied from the same central source with the goods they pushed from the backgates of their wagons, even down to the platform palaver they used as salesmanship. Alan was not so much intrigued by the potions in the bottles, which he suspected to be variously colored water from what he had heard Dr. McClary say, as he was by the travelers themselves. Invariably dark-skinned, often wild-haired and unshaven, they were, one and all, of an outlandish breed, seeming to arrive in the valley from a place beyond the ridges where life naturally placed a greater emphasis on the organ of smell than Walden Valley afforded; for each man's face sported, like a Fujiyama surrounded by thirteen provinces, an enormous nose, which, to people unacquainted with foreign mountains but knowledgeable about ships, suggested a ship's prow riding high above the dark waves of mustache and chin whiskers. Those who did not know ships found a likely comparison in the homely corncob, which simile was as good as any and certain not to be misconstrued by any comer.

"It wouldn't do to have a smeller like that and be short-sighted at the same time," Oscar said. "A man would have a problem getting his book close enough to read."

"One good thing," Lee said, "he'd never have to worry about getting water in his mouth in a hard rain."

Fascinating as these individuals were in their baffling likeness and different names, they were sometimes momentarily overshadowed by their assistants, who came in various shapes and colors each year. The black ones were usually animated and danced and sang for the crowd's entertainment. But the white helpers, though they were usually quite young, were subdued and silent, robot-like in their mute handing back and forth of the objects the master required. They seemed, in truth, to be runaway boys gone to see the world, and half-fearful of being caught and returned to unpleasant households. Perhaps this accounted for the furtive, fugitive look they usually had about them. Alan's imagination played vividly with the reasons they might have had for escaping from bondage, inventing adventures he himself would like to have happen if he were, by some impossible chance, flung into their luckless positions. He didn't envy them; he was too young to pity them. They were merely a part of the night's landscape, pallid under the yellow lamps swung at the tailgate, slightly mysterious, but passing and replaced at next sunrise by the reasonable, stay-at-home valley that was like a large house to him, with very familiar rooms; a house in which he was, for most of his time, quite bearably happy.

Sometimes, however, he was jarred by the annual return of the medicine man. Last year, in May, he had come bringing with him an unpleasant reminder of what might be going on, secretly, in a man's insides. Alan knew people had worms. He had taken enough Jerusalem Oak seed in molasses to kill a dragon; and at least once, Dr. McClary had had to give both him and Lee a vermifuge that left them listless for a day. But the monster displayed in the quart glass jar, wound round and round in what seemed endless coils, almost stupefied him. The tapeworm, the traveler said, had been removed from the host's body by one dose of his famous Dead-Shot worm oil. Alan was horrified by the flat, segmented creature, gray and tubular in its jar. The thought of being an unsuspecting victim of such an animal outrage seemed an insult to human dignity. But people did have them, he knew. Someone in the valley, it was reported in good faith, had been relieved of one that, when stretched out, reached half-way around the courthouse in town. Perhaps it was the very worm in the jar. Alan didn't know. What he did know was that the idea of the voracious coils of such a monstrosity embedded in his own body made him queasy and sick, so that he turned his eyes away. But his eyes would return, reluctantly, again and again to the platform at the rear of the wagon where the bottles were arrayed. The men, interesting as they were, representing as they did a world he was more and more curious about, had to play second fiddle to what they displayed.

Lee was interested in the medicine shows for a variety of reasons. He and Ira went each year in hope of seeing either a mermaid or what they called a "morphadite," a creature, Alan gathered from what they said, whispering and giggling together, that was neither male nor female, but a combination of the two, like certain worms and flowers he had read about in the encyclopedia at school. Needless to say, no such half-fish-half-woman or half-man-half-woman ever appeared on the tailgate of the traveler's wagon. The boys had mixed the medicine show with the sideshows of the carnivals that sometimes came to the town and occasioned much marveling talk, which, transported to the valley and exaggerated in passage, reached them in some rather wonderful forms. They were, however, yearly hopeful of seeing a sight, and so appeared as regularly as the medicine man on the grassed plot beside George Hamilton's store, despite John Wade's assurance that the man was a fake, a dead-beat, making his living off ignorant, superstitious country bumpkins like them. Ira grinned at his father's dismissal of the medicine man. "Anyway, it's some place to go," he said, conferring with Lee. "Not so good as the Fourth of July and a little better than revival meeting." Oscar himself went, liking the chance to be out of the house, and enjoying the jokes, sometimes bawdy, which the traveler told. If John Wade went at all, he stood up front, by the edge of the platform, and stared the medicine man straight in the eye, challenging him to a true statement. But the seller was practiced and glib. An amazing spate of words poured off his tongue, until even John Wade shook with laughter.

Other than these people who, by their various and distinct differences, had helped acquaint Alan with the diversity among mankind, only his books and Miss Woodson had further enabled him to understand how wide and different from Walden Valley the other world really was. The Ku Klux, however, were his own people. Oscar claimed to know some of them. Their difference lay, as far as he could see, in their fear of showing their faces. Belle had explained that the Klan, in its beginning, had played a useful part in the life of the South immediately following the Civil War. But so far as she could see, she said, the organization had outlived its usefulness. No group of men had the right to take the law into their own hands, she added darkly. She could remember a lynching, knots of hickory withes tied to doorknobs, and at least one cross burned on a hilltop in the days of her youth. No one knew where these things originated; even those involved in the warning of the hickory withes often did not know of what wrongdoing they stood convicted of in the eyes of the Klan. This was what Belle despised.

Washing his face and hands on the back porch, Alan wished he too had been in church the night the Klansmen came. But he knew that making molasses was more important than hooded men to his general welfare. He was bothered, though, by the thought that while life in one place was so busy and seeming-real, life in another place was no less so. He was self-centered enough still to think that life except where he was, was only partially in motion, waiting in a half-sleep for him to appear and signal it fully awake. That people in a million other places, whom he had never seen and would never see, were living and dying without any hint of his existence, was a thought too monstrous to be entertained.

"You'll have to set the table," Belle told him, as he entered the kitchen. "I can't make it any longer." She was sitting, on a chair by the door, her face much redder than usual and her breathing hard. Occasionally, she opened her mouth wide and drew in a gulp of the fresh morning air. "Fry the eggs," she told Lee. "The bacon is ready."

Lee broke four eggs evenly, cleanly into the large skillet. Alan set the table with plates, cups, and glasses, and added knives, forks, and spoons. Coming in from slopping the hogs, Oscar washed on the back porch and helped the boys with breakfast, pouring the coffee from the pot simmering on the back of the stove. He looked anxiously at Belle, who averted her eyes and gazed out the doorway. Alan brought the warm biscuits from the oven, and breakfast was ready.

There was little talk. Belle drank the hot coffee, still staring out the door. When she had finished, she got up heavily and went into the bedroom. The creak of the bedsprings told that she had lain down. Alan drank his milk hurriedly and went to the door. His mother was lying on her back, sweating and staring at the ceiling, a faraway, closed look in her eyes.

While Lee and Alan washed the dishes and swept the kitchen, Oscar churned the turn of milk he emptied from the big brown and white crockery jar into the clean cypress churn, which was Belle's most prized possession. The churn, with its golden grained wood and wide brass bands, had belonged to her grandmother.

"Wash your hands clean, Alan," Oscar said, "and take up this butter."

Alan scrubbed his hands at the water bench and lifted the lid from the churn. Inside, the thick yellow butter, centered with a hole where the dash went through, looked like some kind of circular cake still in its batter. It felt oily but pure in his hands as he patted it into a bowl. Salting it lightly, he worked the buttery mass until the salt was evenly spread throughout; then he packed it into the pound mould, turning out on a plate a thick rectangle of butter imprinted with beech leaves on top where the paddle had pressed. There were two pounds and over from the churn. The butter remaining after the second mould, Alan scraped into a shallow bowl and left for table use. At least one of the pounds, if not both, would be sold to the rolling store on its weekly round through the valley, coffee and sugar being accepted in return. He washed and scalded the churn and left it on the cook-table, upside down, to dry.

"Both of you boys stay close today," Oscar ordered. "If I'm needed, run to the mill, one of you; the other stay here. I'll bring Hannah Wade when I come."

Alan knew that the arrival of his baby brother was imminent. He peeked in at his mother, who still lay staring at the ceiling, now and then mopping her face with a large cloth. Oscar came in. "I've told the boys," he said, "what to do in case I'm needed." He patted his wife awkwardly on the shoulder and left the room. Belle's stare never wavered. Alan felt uncomfortable, as if in the presence of some hostility he could not understand.

At noon, she did not get up from the bed. Alan brought her a glass of milk which she drank thirstily, and a cup of cold water from the spring. She would eat nothing. He and Lee ate left-overs from the night before.

In the afternoon, he tried to read while Lee lay in the shade of the back porch and snored. For a boy so young, Lee had a man-sized whistle in his sleeping nose. From little cricket sounds, peeps and cheeps, the sound rose to a roar at the full intake of breath and subsided to a long wheeee as the air was expelled. Alan laid the book aside and looked across a corner of the orchard into the pasture. Something seemed to be bothering Old Emily. She switched her tail, stamped her feet, and suddenly began to run. A bee, he supposed. Ranger drifted slowly uphill, cropping as he went, lifting little by little to the summit, where he finally stood like a statue of a horse contemplating the countryside. Buckeye followed him. Between the horse and the calf a constant companionship had developed, as though each preferred not to associate with others of his own kind in the pasture. Buckeye had reason, Alan knew, to shun Old Emily and her crowd. How long a calf remembered, he didn't know; but if Buckeye had half the memory of an elephant, it would be a cold day in August when he made overtures to his tormentors. As for Old Ranger, he seemed to scorn mules as being his deep inferiors, and turned away from them as naturally as an aristocrat might have shunned a roadworker in his neighborhood.

Pretty Boy slept with his nose against Lee's hand. Whizzer dozed on the water-shelf, between the washpan and the bucket. Occasionally, an eye opened to inspect the nearer world, then closed. From his vantage point, he felt relatively secure. Like all cats, he preferred to be looking down on the life about him, rather than up. Alan dozed. It seemed he was in Miss Woodson's classroom. He could see the sun striking the blackboard and smell the old, much-used wood of the desks, which had absorbed the sweat of generations of students. Hearing Belle muttering to herself, he came wide awake. Tip-toeing to the bedroom door, he found his mother, half-asleep, repeating something he could not understand, something like an old rhyme. He caught the word "window" and that was all. Going back to the porch, he stared into the afternoon, which now was beginning to seem endless. Lee snored gustily in the warm silence. Soon, although the afternoon seemed like forever, Alan knew it would be winter, with the faded valley beseiged with sharp winds and occasionally made beautiful with a fall of snow. He would miss summer, for it was in summer that the real things in life happened; a boy grew in the summer. Books and school were all right. He even looked forward to them. But they were another kind of living, a dormancy in which, when he thought about it, he seemed actually half-asleep. But like a tree, he supposed, he was in the winter only getting ready to grow, preparing for the sudden shoots his mind and body seemed to put out each spring for summer increase and renewal. Miss Woodson had told him that reading a good book, a true book, was like doing homework or listening to the explanations of how a problem was to be worked. You always understood better after the preparatory lesson. Though she *had* confused him slightly by explaining that a true book was not necessarily a factual book; that the things in it need not ever have happened to any specific person. I mean true to life, she said. Vaguely, he suspected her meaning; though he was still far too young to apply generalities to his individual existence. Everything that happened to him, happened for the first time, in all its freshness and originality. It could not have happened to anyone else before him. It certainly could not be happening to anyone else at the same time. He was unique in his relation to the interesting world about him. Or so he believed. Yet this summer a faint suspicion had begun to dawn on him that, in addition to being individual in his own mind and body, he was also a part of a larger mind and body that started, first, with his own immediate family and grew to include his uncles and aunts and cousins, John Wade, Jesse Jarnigan, Enoch Wall, the Jewish peddler, anyone at all. The notion irritated him, seeming to detract from his own sense of personal importance. Strangely enough, he resented, in a half-ashamed way, the coming of the new baby, whose arrival he awaited with such impatience, knowing he would not ever again be the youngest member of his family group, coddled and respected because of his position, but the middleman in a series, superseded by another boy who, in turn, would become the one to be loved and protected by all concerned, and most especially loved and protected, perhaps, by himself, whom the new brother had displaced. He felt bewildered and uncomfortable.

Early crickets began to sing in the long shadows falling across the yard. Behind the orchard hill, the sun flung its usual golden segments divided by blue into the evening sky. Where each radiant path was, Alan knew, there was, low on the horizon and hidden by the nearer hill, a gap or a peak in the ridge, through or around which the sun cast its low yellow light. The cows congregated at the bars that let in to the barnyard from the pasture. Old Ranger stood with his head thrust over the fence, wagging his great jaw. Buckeye looked through the railing beside him. Waking Lee, Alan told him to listen for a call from Belle, while he did his chores at the barn. Afterwards, he would listen while Lee milked.

Lee was just coming up the path with the full milk pail in his hand when Alan, shouting to his brother, ran swiftly through the yard in the direction of John Wade's meadow. In the house, Belle was moaning softly, her hands clinched. Lee wet a towel and wiped the beads of moisture from her face. Feeling helpless and afraid, he waited at the door until Oscar and Hannah Wade arrived.

"Saddle Old Ranger, son," Oscar said, "and ride to Dr. McClary's house. Hurry. Tell him we need him now."

Lee scurried to the barn.

29

AN hour later, he joined Alan at John Wade's house, where, on the front porch, John Wade was talking to Alan and Ira about the winter he had spent in Indiana long ago. "Supper's on the table," he said to Lee. "Help yourself. Bring your plate out here if you want to."

Lee heaped a plate with the cold food from Hannah Wade's table and came to sit on the edge of the porch, to be within hearing distance of the man's conversation, or rather the tale he was telling, for no one but the teller spoke for some time there in the darkness. The boys were content to listen.

"I remember the cold in winter most of all," John Wade said. "Beginning in November, when the ducks and geese started south along the Mississippi flyway, snow began to fall and continued falling until about May. Where we have one or two snows a season here, they have only one or two weeks during the winter when the ground is entirely free of snow. And the wind! Boys, that level wind literally chilled to the bone. One night on White River, we stayed out late, duck-hunting. About dark a storm sprang up. Even in the willow brake the wind was so strong a man couldn't walk straight. Pellets of ice stung like needles when they struck. Out in the river, over the sound of the dry, rattling barrage of ice, we could hear the squalling of ducks grounded on a small island, their wings coating with the sudden icefall. We felt our way through the clashing trees, along the banks of the river, towards the island where the ducks had foundered. But we made no headway. The wind drove us back. Finally, we gave up and started across the open fields home. Such cold I have never experienced since. By the time we reached the farmhouse, I noticed the ends of my fingers, down to the first joints, had turned a frosty white." He chuckled. "I cried like a baby when those fingers began to thaw. Never had anything to hurt so bad.

"But the hunting and trapping were fine," John Wade said. "We'd get up before dawn in zero weather, take our rifles, and set out on the ponies to run the traplines. In that flat country, drainage ditches crisscrossed the fields, and along the sides of these ditches we set our traps, catching rabbits mostly, but now and then a coon, a fox, or a weasel. But not often. Once we caught a mink, a clean-looking little fellow so small I was surprised. I had never seen one before. Once, too," John Wade chuckled again, "we caught a skunk. I didn't know much about skunks either in those days. We shot him and left him in the trap for a day or two. One afternoon late we decided to clear the trap. I noticed the other boys stayed well back from the edge of the ditch. But I couldn't smell anything, so I made my way down into the cut and approached the trap. I still didn't smell anything. Deciding he'd run out of odor, I stooped down and took the dead skunk by the leg. Something that felt like a baseball bat hit me across the head. I ran for half a mile, it seemed, before I could even straighten up. How long it was before I drew a breath, I don't know. That was the worst thing I ever smelled. I called to the other boys, but they wouldn't let me come near them. At the house I had to strip to the skin and throw my clothes out into the yard, where they lay until washday. As long as I wore that outfit, I smelled like a woods-kitty."

His listeners laughed. John Wade looked closely at Alan. The boy's eyes were shining, the worried frown having disappeared in his absorption in the account of winter-trapping. Lee had almost forgotten to eat. "Boy," he said, "I wish Walden Valley had animals like that. I'd hunt all the time."

"One morning," John Wade said, "before I had become accustomed to the western ponies' response to the rein, and before I learned they could stop on a dime, I headed my mount across a stubble field on a long lope. I wanted to reach the trapline before the other boys did. Suddenly, my pony stopped for a cross-ditch I didn't know was there; but I didn't stop. Gun and all, I flew out across the pony's head and landed in the frozen clods on my hind-end. Nearly broke my tail-bone, though I never let go of my rifle. Those ponies were quick souls. A man had to watch if he kept his seat."

After a moment, he continued. "It was, in my thinking, a little like early America; maybe like Walden Valley was in the beginning before too many people crowded in and crowded the bulk of the animals out. Only the very crafty beast or the very small seems to get along where man is. But they too become scarcer as the space between the houses decreases, until in towns they disapear. All but the rats, and cockroaches. That's why I'm against towns and all they stand for. I love open land, boy; the kind of land the first settlers found in this valley. But you can't shoot people," he said, "no matter how much they multiply."

His voice heated a little. "The more there are of us, the less any of us have, in food, clothing, fresh air to breathe, even standing room. Democracy is a fairy tale after the land fills up. Freedom is like a circle drawn around a man. The circle grows smaller as other circles crowd in, until after awhile man's freedom is not broader than the circumference of his own shoulders. It becomes harder then for individual rights to be guaranteed, for man naturally is not going to be scrouged too closely by his neighbors. He's going to enlarge his circle at the expense of others. Somebody's going to get hurt."

He stopped short. His anger, he knew, was partially directed at Oscar McDowell and the addition being made to the McDowell family. He hoped Alan and Lee had not established any connection between his words and the birth of the new baby. But, by all the laws of common sense, two children were enough for a dirt farmer. Some people didn't know when they were well off. Ira had been enough, sometimes he thought too much, for him and Hannah. To have doubled the boy would have been to double the worry and disappointment. Yet he loved him, deeply, abidingly. His hurt told him that. And it was his hurt at the scorn of his own son that made him love Oscar McDowell's boy with such a silent devotion. In Alan, he saw a chance for a real man to grow. John Wade's trouble, as his wife pointed out and he himself sometimes dimly realized, was that he expected too much of people. "He who expects little shall not be disappointed with less," Hannah said. But John Wade was irritated. Somewhere, he believed, there was a way for man to become better than his ordinary self. He had no patience with those who threw up their hands and quit trying to climb whatever ladder was theirs to climb. All men on earth were caught somewhere between the bottom rung and the top rung, and there were only two ways to go. As for any boy, if he wasn't a better man than his father had been, no one had gone anywhere. But even if he wanted to go somewhere, a man had to have a chance.

His anger at Oscar McDowell hinged here. The more mouths there were to be fed, the less food there was for everybody. The more children to be sent to school, the fewer books there were for them to study in. A good life, it seemed to John Wade, was a simple matter of keeping things in balance. Lee and Alan, now, would naturally have only half each of what Ira might have. In the McDowell household, the family goods would now be divided, so far as the children were concerned, by three instead of two. In raising the general opportunity, the particular opportunity had been lowered. Not because a man was opposed to the general good, but because the good itself was limited. He would like to point out a thing or two to Oscar McDowell.

A screech owl whimpered in an oak in the yard, an oafish sound that broke the man's thought. The boys, stretched out now on the porch, seemed to be sleeping. "Time for bed, boys," he said. "You'll find soap and water on the bench there."

Lee and Ira washed face and hands. Alan, barefooted, added his feet. Even when school started, he would not put on his shoes, not until the first frost came. With him, being shoeless was a freedom he gave up with reluctance.

"Lee and Ira can sleep together," John Wade said. "Alan, you can bunk with me."

Lying awake in the dark, Alan wondered what his parents would name the new boy. The night was a little like Christmas night, when one got up the next morning to see what gift had been brought. He was tremendously excited. Lee and Ira kicked each other in bed, laughing loudly, and then subsided into secret whispers. As Alan drifted towards sleep, he heard John Wade muttering a prayer.

When he awoke, the sun was pouring through the window onto the bed and the bright braided rug in the center of the floor. A rooster was crowing. He felt a weight across his chest, and was surprised to find it was John Wade's arm. The man was awake, too. "Well, son," he said, "I bet you're anxious to get home and see what the doctor brought. What do you want anyway, a boy or a girl?"

"It's just got to be a boy, Mr. Wade," Alan said. "What would we do with a girl?"

"Feed her and raise her, like you would a boy," John Wade said. "Girls are necessary to the human race, too. Come on," he added, swinging his feet over the side of the bed, "let's get those yahoos up and go see."

Hannah Wade was preparing breakfast when her husband and the boys entered the McDowell kitchen. "My, you're early," she said smiling. "Somebody must have been downright curious to know something." She pursed her lips mysteriously, as if to say she knew more than she was willing to tell.

"Not too early for this boy," her husband said, his hand on Alan's shoulders. "He's been switching around like a worm in hot ashes for a couple of hours. Ever since he woke up, in fact. Says he wants a look at his new brother. Doctor been here yet?"

"You know the doctor's been here," she answered, peering into the coffee pot to see whether the water had struck the boil. "If he hadn't, you wouldn't be here. I didn't say it was a boy," she added teasingly, glancing at Lee and Alan. "I haven't said anything yet."

"That's the truth," said John Wade. "You haven't said anything, but you've talked a whole lot."

Alan grew angry and impatient. Tears welled up in his eyes.

"Hush," Hannah Wade said to John, as if he had been babbling. To Alan, she said, "Your mother's awake, son. Go in if you want to."

Alan tiptoed into the room where his mother lay cradling the new baby in her arms. Lee followed closely behind. Smiling at her sons, Belle pulled the covers back for them to see. A red, twisted little face, cheeks puffed out and in motion like tiny balloons, met their gaze.

His lips dry, Alan whispered, "What is it?"

"A baby, son," Belle said, "a boy baby." She reached up and stroked her second son's bright hair. Lee edged closer, looking embarrassed when his mother patted his hand. Both boys were smiling broadly. Alan felt like letting go with a big whoop, but remembered Hannah Wade's finger on her lips. As he watched, the tiny puckered face scowled mightily and the baby's eyes opened. Like two wet blue buttons, the eyes looked without focus at the faces bending above the bed.

"He has eyes like you, son, and hair like Lee," Belle said. "He's about equally divided between you."

"What's going to be his name?" Lee asked.

"He's already named," Belle replied. "David Nathan. David Nathan McDowell. I named him last night so the doctor could fill out the birth certificate. His given name means 'beloved gift.' They're both from the Bible." She looked at her new son. "He came at midnight. We don't properly know whether he was born yesterday or today."

It doesn't matter, Alan thought. He's here. The long wait is over. All his mother's anger and resentment of the past summer seemed to have dissolved in the presence of her newest son, and Alan was deeply thankful.

Oscar came in from the barn, his face scarlet with pleasure and pride. "Sorry I don't have a cigar," he said to John Wade. "I'll roll you one though, if you want."

His neighbor laughed. "No, thanks. I believe I'll wait until this slowpoke of a woman gets some grub on the table." He moved in Hannah's direction to help her. Alan washed his hands and set the table.

"All right, men," Hannah Wade said, "I cooked it. If you can't eat it, don't blame me."

The men seated themselves. Before they could begin the meal, John Wade said, "Hold on. If nobody has any objections, I think I'll say a blessing for the new boy." In the silence above the bowed heads, he prayed simply, "Let him be, Lord, the best you can afford. Among your men, let him be a man. That's all we can ask. We thank you for him and all your other goodness. Amen."

His voice rang in the house. From her room, Belle said quietly, "Thank you, John Wade. Amen."

To Alan, no breakfast had ever tasted quite so good.

30

THE new baby in the house meant only a pause, however, in the activity of the summer, which was almost suddenly, it seemed, coming to a close. Even on the first day after Nathan's arrival, Oscar returned to the syrup-making on John Wade's farm, and Lee and Alan, under the supervision of Hannah Wade, who remained at the McDowells' to keep house, went out to gather the fall crop of muscadines. Along the edge of the swamp, the wild vines grew abundantly, but the boys always went to the pine tree on the top of a dry knoll just east of the swiminghole. Here wound intricately among all branches from bottom to top, a giant muscadine vine covered its host pine tree with odorous thin white blossoms in spring, a darker mantle of green than the pine needles in summer, and, in autumn, a thick spattering of purple small globes, succulent and tasty, which Belle used to make the preserves so delicious with warm bread and butter in winter. This year Hannah Wade would perform the almost worshipful rite of transforming the muscadines into their delectable jelly. It was Lee and Alan's task to gather enough of the wild fruit for both the McDowell and the Wade families.

They skirted now the springy edges of the marsh, smelling the tangy goodness of the wood where the leaves were, though summery still, beginning to acquire the winy essence of fall. There was the faint smell of sweet maple leaves, the stringent scent of pines, the almost scarlet odor of the red haws just beginning to ripen on their thorny bushes—all mingled together and heightened by the deep aromatic greenness of the moss and ferns, still cold and loamy, as they always were, both winter and summer. The sharp, medicinal taste of the pine needles, when chewed, reminded Alan of his mother's favorite remedy for all cuts and bruises: turpentine. The smell of that liquid in the house meant that forces had been arranged against the evil of mishap and lucklessness.

Over all the other odors in the wood, either separate or mingled, however, was the tangy, inviting breath of the muscadines themselves. As the boys approached the tree, up a mossy cut in the knoll, the wind was heavy with their fruity perfume. Not far from the tree, Alan stopped to examine a bottle lying in the ditch. Pointing upward, so that its mouth had received a small portion of washing earth, the greenish-clear glass had become a miniature garden. Inside it Alan could see a small expanse of moss, with its scarlet-headed beards, a tiny fern, perfectly formed, beautiful as its adult kind, a white fragment of pebble, and most interesting of all, a young snail, whose white limy casing gleamed against the darker background. It was a perfect world, he thought, for the snail; a small, comfortable world, like the walls of a beloved room close around and protecting. The fern, he decided, was most likely a young Christmas fern. His sensibilities stirred at the suggestion of his favorite holiday. How the bottle got there, he could only surmise. Perhaps a woodcutter bringing kerosene to ease the run of his saw in resiny wood, had thrown it down empty, leaving it in the ditch to fill with soil and become this tiny universe. He called to Lee to come see the world in the bottle, but Lee refused, being ahead, almost now at the muscadine tree. Alan trudged on up the small ravine and came out on a grassy spot which formed a wide circle around the tree. How well he remembered the spot, and not for muscadines alone. Nearby was the low-hanging limb of a young pine which Old Ranger had used to wipe Alan off his back on a day when the horse had decided, during a hunt for the cows, that being ridden had ceased to be profitable. Old Ranger had stopped and gazed back at him, sitting rather stunned on the ground, but had refused to be caught again, walking just fast enough to keep ahead of Alan all the way back to the barn.

Lee tried to encircle the great vine with his hands, and found himself unable to bring the tips of his fingers together. "Grows more every year," he said. "It'll soon be as big as my thigh."

The boys began to gather the ripe fruit from the ground, careful not to kneel on the choice spheres. Working in a circle around themselves, they cleaned the earth of the usable berries, until the supply on the ground was exhausted and it became necessary for someone to climb the tree. Alan was elected, being the lighter; and up the vine he scrambled. It was a rough climb, but by gripping with arms and legs, he managed to reach the lowest limb of the tree. From there, the going was easier. Lee, in the meantime, had set the full buckets out of the way of careless feet, and had begun to drop scattered findings into a large basket.

Alan began to shake, quartering the tree. The muscadines rained down in a purple shower, like buckshot, thumping and bumping on the earth and Lee and the basket. Just over the spot where Lee had set the basket there was a heavy unshaken part of the tree, the last laden limb to be relieved of its burden. Alan began to shake. The berries seemed stubborn. He shook harder. Something heavy, like a part of the vine itself, came loose and warped the ground. "Godfrey's cordial!" Lee screamed, falling backward away from the basket where the snake had landed, half inside, half out, dangling over the side like so much animated black rope. The racer was also frightened. Hastily removing himself from the basket's rim he scuttled away through the grass, headed for the deeper wood. Lee ran after the snake, angry now, beating the ground, but always just behind the tip of its tail, with a stick he had been using to knock muscadines from the lower coils of the vine. "Old son-of-a-gun!" he said, whacking the ground. "I'll learn you to go hanging around in a tree and come flopping down on a man's head! Scaring the daylights out of him!"

The snake disappeared with a rattle of twigs and leaves. Lee came back to the tree, puffing and blowing. "Stopped the breath right in my mouth," he said. "Dadburned snakes. They always knock the wind out of me."

Alan grinned. "It's all right for you to laugh," Lee growled. "I bet if you'd seen him up there, the shoe'd be on the other foot. You wouldn't have stopped running yet."

By the time the 11:30 train blew, deep and rumbling in the noontime air, the boys had filled all their containers and were on their way back to the house.

Alan was curious about the different sound of the train. "Why," he asked Lee, "does the train-whistle sound so much nearer now than it did in the summer?" He knew that as winter approached, and came, and reached its depths, the whistle would go on changing, until in the sharpest cold the sound would seem to be coming from no farther away than the barn. Lee didn't know the answer, but supposed it had something to do with the summer temperature, the thickness of the air, he said. His brother wondered how air could be thicker or thinner, being only air. He had heard his mother say that a bird seemed to be sitting on thin air, but he knew this to mean only that she couldn't see the twig or wire on which the bird rested. He'd have to ask Miss Woodson. Suddenly, he wished school would start. It seemed forever since he had had anybody to answer his questions. He would, he determined, learn more this year than ever before, for it would be his duty now to answer the questions Nathan would begin to ask once he learned to talk. He didn't intend to fail Nathan.

At the house, Hannah Wade said, "Alan, one of you will have to go to the store for sugar. Together, your mother and I don't have enough to start these preserves. The other can go to my house and bring back a boxful of jars."

Alan chose to go to the store, finding a visit to George Hamilton's country emporium one of the highlights of any season. Somewhere in the welter of goods, anything from fishhooks to horse-collars to a bolt of frosty blue velvet could be found. You asked for it, and George Hamilton ducked under the heaps and mounds, scrambled and dug and shifted, and emerged with the desired item, triumphantly proud to please, though a wit worse himself for the wear.

Before he left the house, however, Alan tiptoed in to look at Nathan. His brother was sleeping, his tiny pink fists clenched and thrown above his head. Propped on pillows, Belle was slowly combing her hair. "How were the muscadines, son?" she asked.

"A lot of them," he answered, touching his brother's fist carefully with the end of his finger. "Enough that Mrs. Wade says I'll have to go to the store for some extra sugar."

"Don't poke him," Belle warned. "I believe he's going to be a good baby." Then she said, "Bring my pocketbook from the dresser drawer."

Alan brought the worn pocketbook to his mother. "Get ten pounds," she directed. "And hurry back. But don't run. It'll be too warm for anything but walking, especially with ten pounds to carry." She handed him the money.

Alan smiled at his mother. She was being herself again. Somehow Nathan had worked a miracle in her disposition. He looked down at the sleeping baby, wondering how long it would take him to grow. The long dark lashes on the tiny lids seemed like doll's lashes. As he watched, the red cheeks began to puff and churn.

"He's hungry by now, I suspect," Belle said.

"I am, too," Alan said. "The muscadines just made me hungrier."

"Eat before you go, then," Belle told him. "Dinner's ready. I've already eaten, about an hour ago. First time I've felt like eating in days."

Lee had taken a basket of food to the men at the syrup mill. The remains of the meal were on the table. Alan ate hurriedly, gulping down two glasses of cold sweet milk. Feeling better, he started to the store.

Anxious to spend as much time as possible at the store itself, he did not loiter to look at things along the way. When he reached the crossroads, George Hamilton was having a late meal of crackers and cheese and a glass of milk on the store-counter. He smiled at Alan. "Help yourself," he said.

"No, thank you. I'll just look around." Alan was glad the storekeeper was eating. He had an excuse now for being late in returning home.

George Hamilton ate leisurely. Alan wandered about, staring. The great glass cases with their pink and white candies, needles and balls of thread, pencils, writing tablets, rolls of colored ribbon, and dozens of other small articles, formed an aisle from the front door to the middle depth of the long, narrow room, ending where the pot-bellied woodstove blocked the aisle with its sandbox and circle of upended boxes and nailkegs, on which customers and loafers sat and passed the time of day. Behind the stove, the room was all stacks and heaps and full shelves of merchandise.

Back of each glass case was another aisle, where the storekeeper stood or stooped among his treasures, searching and finding some almost forgotten item for a needy customer. Against the wall, from floor to ceiling, a tier of shelves rose, holding in its lower divisions heavy black, white, and gray crocks, and graduating upward through lighter goods, to end with glass lamp bases and globes in the safety of the highest shelf. There were lanterns there, too, and a few tin sorghum buckets. One red school lunch box with double handles rested between two lamps. After he sold Buckeye, if there was any money left over from buying the books, Alan told himself, he meant to have that lunchbox. And one of the book satchels, too, hanging on a nail by the front door.

Towards the back of the store, horse collars hung from pegs on the wall. Farther on were bridles, two saddles straddling a sawhorse, and a stack of saddle blankets on a wooden box. Hoes and pitchforks leaned in a corner. Alan could see, to one side, bolts of cloth, blue and tan workshirts, piles of blue denim overalls. One giant pair, with legs spraddled, hung from a crossbeam. Heavy shoes and denim jumpers completed the work department. His eyes, traveling now along the shelves toward the front of the room, could see the Sunday shoes, both men's and women's, displayed in their boxes; dress trousers and gingham dresses, with here and there a more elegant flowered print, followed. On top of the glass case to the left was a stack of straw hats. But what interested Alan most was inside the case—a boxful of barlow knives, their handles and blades shining. The knife in his pocket was hardly a reasonable imitation of what he saw there. Along the center aisle, against the bottoms of the glass cases, were kegs of staples and nails.

Alan's head swam with looking. His nose tried to accommodate itself to the mingled odors of plug tobacco, marked with a red tin apple, inside the glass jars that kept it fresh but did not prevent its scenting the whole store; the reek of kerosene; the faint, sweet smell of candy; the stench of oiled leather; the pale, cold odor of soda crackers; the warm, sweaty presence of a room long used and lived in. Visiting George Hamilton's store was like having an out-of-season Christmas.

When the storekeeper finished eating, he reached into a case and took out a stick of peppermint candy. "A boy never gets too big for candy," he said. "Even I still have a sweet-tooth when I don't actually have a tooth to call my own." He displayed two perfect sets of white teeth in appreciation of his own joke. "These are store-bought," he said.

Alan thanked him for the candy. "I have to go now," he said. "Mom wants ten pounds of sugar."

"Right-o," the storekeeper said, going to a washtub sitting on a table at the rear of the store, looking for an extra empty sack. Alan had forgotten to bring one from home. George Hamilton found a white cloth bag and brought it forward.

"Ill return it," Alan said, while from a large sack leaning against a wall, adding a little, subtracting a little until the weight was right, the storekeeper scooped ten pounds of sugar.

"If you will," the storekeeper said. "I've been out of paper pokes all week."

On his way home, Alan tried to rename all the merchandise he had seen. In a way, going to George Hamilton's was better than a visit to town, for the country store had everything in one place. You didn't have to run up and down the streets, looking. One thing was missing though. George Hamilton did not carry the books he had to have at school. Only the drugstore in town did that. On Tuesday he would go with his father and Uncle Lance to sell Buckeye at the stockyard; then he would buy his books. Again he felt a surge of excitement at the prospect of returning to school. The summer had been brief; yet, in a way, it seemed forever since he had gone with Lee to see the railroad tracks and the train the day after school was out in the spring. He certainly did not feel like the same person any more. It was a curious sensation of being bigger than himself that he felt, as though his arms and legs stuck out of his clothing. Yet he knew it wasn't that. His clothes fitted perfectly. Some undefinable something had happened to him between April and September. Something that he could only feel, not know.

Reaching the house, he found his mother asleep. Tiptoeing through the room, he left the peppermint stick by her pillow and carried the sugar to the kitchen, where Hannah Wade was already measuring the muscadine juice into a large dishpan.

31

ON Saturday, Oscar announced that he would not be working at the syrup mill the following week, John Wade having agreed to find another man in his stead. "There's too much to do," Oscar said, "in the week left before school opens. For one thing, we must take Buckeye to town next Tuesday and sell him at the cattle-barn. We'll get the boys' schoolbooks while we're there if we command price enough for the calf. The market is slow, John Wade says. So we'll have to keep our minds open. No use counting the chickens before the eggs hatch."

Alan hoped fervently that Buckeye would bring enough to buy his and Lee's books, with a little left over for the red lunchbox and the satchel he had seen in George Hamilton's store. But as Oscar said, there was no telling, the bottom being out of the market. He found it hard to wait, going about his tasks through the warm autumn hours, the smell of new books already in his nostrils. Nothing was more of a thrill than to breathe deeply between the pages of a new book. Miss Woodson had warned him. "Don't make a fetish of books, Alan," she had said, when she found him turning the pages of the one new book he had owned last year with the clean handkerchief he carried folded in his pocket. "They're only to be used for what is in them. Physically they are only paper and ink and very subject to decay." Nevertheless, he liked his pages clean and unbroken, and became violently angry if someone borrowed his book and left a pencil between the pages to mark a place.

On Sunday, in the afternoon, he and Lee went to the baptizing. The meeting, like the syrup-making, held for two weeks; but also like the syrup-making, the product had to be worked off in batches. All ready to be baptized, or rebaptized, were forty candidates. Alan watched them in their white clothes gather in a long line at the edge of the river, where the bank shelved gently to the water and the shallow current just beyond was bottomed with round river stones. Just above the baptizing place was a low mill-dam remaining from past years, over which the green water of Hiwassee River poured with the look of spun glass, to plunge deeply into the eddies at the foot of the dam and come up frothing white, whirling and racing toward the edge of the circling pool, finally to break over the rim and be carried away by the main current of the river. Once a great overshot water-wheel had worked just below the sycamore under which the worshippers had gathered. Behind them, in the meadow, were the ruins of a flume line. A great millstone lay just inside the edge of a willow growth, its center now accommodating a young willow tree that had pushed up out of the soil beneath. Little by little the slow growth of the willow-stem was cracking the great stone. Round about were other willow patches, their feathery fronds whispering thinly under and over the throttling sound of the water's pour.

The congregation had begun to sing "Shall We Gather at the River," a beautiful hymn which dealt with things Alan could understand. Only the part about "with its crystal tide forever flowing from the throne of God" was a bit inaccurate in its description. The river was a willow green, dotted here and there with clumps of white foam and speckled with clear eye-like bubbles that kept popping in the sun even while he looked. If crystal rivers flowed from crystal thrones, like being derived from like, Alan thought, then the throne of God here, on this Sunday, must be rich in color as emerald.

The preacher prayed when the song was finished, and began his sermon. "Brothers and sisters," he said, "we have gathered here to perform for these, our new-born in Christ, what we were commanded to do: to go forth and baptize all nations and kindred in the fashion of Jesus being baptized in the River Jordan by his cousin, John. It is altogether fitting and good that we do this. But we should remember that we baptize only with water, useless in itself, unless accompanied with the baptism of the Holy Ghost." His voice sought other texts.

A kingfisher flew from sycamore to willow, then from willow to the center of the milldam where he perched on an exposed stone, looking over-balanced and ridiculous in his large head and crest. But his color was a soft, powdery blue in the afternoon sunlight; his breast shone like clean white linen below the dark collar he wore. Alan could see the touches of cinnamon on the underbody just below the edges of the wings. The bird stood there, eyeing the river, not concerned with the crowd. Looking at him, Alan felt a sudden, swift elation at the beauty they all made, bird, river, the men and women themselves listening to the preacher's voice under the sycamore tree. In the afternoon sun, framed by the willows, the scene appeared to be momentarily frozen into a picture. There was a mystery about it, a meaning, that the boy could not fathom.

Now the congregation began to sing "Wash Me and I Shall Be Whiter Than Snow," in low, yearning tones, as though in the whiteness of snow new-fallen and unsmutched there was an impeccable cleanliness, an unsullied grace. The long line of white-clad people began to move towards the water, where the preacher, having gone before and tested the depth and footing, awaited them. The first one in line, a young boy, gave the preacher his hand. The others swung out from him in a long semi-circle, like a white pennant flowing from a staff, or, Alan thought, like a very white and glistening chain of players in Snap-the-Whip. The crowd was silent. Only the noise of the rushing green water over the dam and of the current at the center of the river was heard, and one harsh cry as the kingfisher lifted and flew over the heads of the assembly towards the farther meadow.

The Preacher's voice now rose from the river. "In obedience to the command of our Lord and Master, I baptize thee, my brother, in the name of the Father, the Son, and the Holy Ghost." There was a light murmur of water nearer shore as the young boy disappeared into the green flood. "Amen!" shouted the preacher, bringing him up and wiping the boy's face clean with his hand. "Amen!" responded the crowd, beginning to sing again. The song became a chant, accompanied by the clapping of hands, sinking to a hum at the preacher's words and rising to full song after each Amen. Alan noticed that the preacher himself never moved in the water, but remained standing in the same place while the line moved past him. In his full black suit, he became after a time a dark center to two white wings equally wide on each side of him, like some kind of strange, parti-colored bird. The moving line somehow reminded Alan of his dream of resurrection, at the same time suggesting one large angel, with snowy wings, trying to get his black body clean in the river. Or her body clean, he amended. He didn't know. Reading about them, you imagined angels to be all men; but when you saw them in pictures, they had women's faces and women's hair, and wore long dresses. That, he imagined, might be only the style of angels.

The preacher had come to the last candidate in line, a woman who came up out of the water sputtering and grasping at the preacher's hand wiping the water from her face. The baptism was finished. A chorus of Amens rose from the bank. As the line edged its way from the river, Alan was gripped by a feeling of awe as the low afternoon sun, through a hole in the clouds, plunged a strong shaft of light earthward. His skin stirred with prickles. There was in the Bible at home a picture of such a scene as this. He could almost hear the words of ineffable grace being spoken above the river.

On his way home, he kept in his mind the strong impression of the afternoon. Describing the baptism to Belle, he tried to make her see what he himself had seen in the people, the river, the trees, the bird, the strange light that flooded suddenly over the landscape. Belle's eyes glowed. There was a power in her son that she could not account for. But Alan, holding the tiny Nathan in his arms for the first time, was unaware of powers except for the power of feeling. His baby brother quite overshadowed all other events of a very eventful day.

32

ON Tuesday morning, Alan's Uncle Lance was at his brother's house in time for breakfast. He brought with him the pick-up truck he had borrowed to transport Buckeye to town. "Let's get an early start, Oscar," he said, "before the buyers spend all their money. By eleven o'clock they'll be spent out and we'll be left with a calf on our hands. Or have to give him away," he added.

Lance backed the truck up to the low wall behind the house, and Buckeye followed Alan tamely into the high-framed bed, nuzzling the boy gently as he came. Alan felt a pang at this betrayal of his pet. If Buckeye knew what was being done to him, Alan thought, he would run to the farthest corner of the pasture and refuse to be caught at all.

On the way to town, seated between his father and his Uncle Lance on the front seat of the truck, Alan's mind was on the calf. Occasionally, he turned his head, to find Buckeye staring at him through the glass. The rough, knotty growths where the calf's horns had been cut showed plainly. He hoped they would not affect Buckeye's sale. As traitorous as he felt, if he must let Buckeye go, he wanted something substantial in return. His books would, he felt, compensate somewhat for the loss of his pet; but to have to sell him for almost nothing because of his ragged head, would be too much to bear. Alan glanced sideways at his father, who was talking over his head to Lance. It was still hard for him to forgive Oscar's careless dehorning of the calf, though Belle had helped him to see that it was Oscar's desire to do things well, and his utter inability to do many things at all, even passably, that resulted in his frustration and anger. In his own inabilities, Alan was already beginning to find a reinforcement for Belle's compassionate explanation of his father's sudden tempers and furies.

They drove through the town without stopping, crossing the public square where the courthouse stood and continuing up the hill street that led past the depot, over the viaduct, and out to the farther edge of town to the open field where the stock pens were. It was Alan's first trip to the market, and he was amazed at the number of animals that neighed, lowed, and bleated around him in the stalls. To one side, were the hogs; beyond them the chickens squawked and sang, the hens voicing as happily as if they had been at home. The roosters were kept in separate coops. One, a large Rhode Island Red, gleaming as though he had been polished, kept ducking his head, giving all passers-by the challenge. Beyond the coops, the pen where the sheep and half-grown lambs were crowding in a small knot to one side, was only half-full. There were not many farmers in the vicinity who kept sheep, Alan knew, for reasons of pasturage. It was the saying in Walden Valley that three sheep were better than a mowing machine.

The mules and horses were in stalls inside the barn, as were the bulls. The cows and calves, dozens of them, were outside in the field, in open pens, since they comprised the largest sales item of the day. A few goats were mixed among them, here and there.

Among these pens, inside and outside the main building, the buyers and sellers crowded, many of them carrying walking sticks, with which they jabbed likely animals to make them move around. The auctioneer himself, his voice booming in a singsong of what seemed to Alan pure wordlessness, went from pen to pen, sometimes mounting a block momentarily to dispose of some smaller item before resuming his major task of selling the animals. Once, during one of these short sales, Alan saw an old picture frame change hands; again, he saw a wash kettle and a large gray crockery jar transferred from one owner to another. Of greater interest to him were the individual sales and trades that went on all about him, particularly among the men who had parked their vehicles just off the sales grounds. By so doing, they escaped the payment of a trade fee and had all the advantages of having their animals and gear on display in the central arena. Lance had done this, leaving Buckeye in the back of the pick-up.

Returning from his stroll about the grounds, Alan arrived just in time to see Buckeye being led down a plank ramp onto the roadway. The buyer was an old man with a handful of money, from which he was counting out to Oscar, one by one, a respectable handful of bills. "Sixteen, seventeen, eighteen," the old man said. Oscar was jubilant. "You just bought yourself a mighty fine animal, mister, " he said. "Half Guernsey, half Durham. Wouldn't be surprised if he didn't make you a fine bull. If I could afford to, I'd keep him myself for breeding."

"That's what I had in mind, " the buyer said. Noticing Alan, he asked, "Is this the young man who raised him?"

"Yes, " Oscar said. "This is him. He's going to buy his schoolbooks with this money. He's worked all summer for those books."

"Well, good luck with the schooling, sonny," the old man called, beginning to lead Buckeye away. "Get as much of it as you can and you won't have to work so hard for a living. I never went to school myself, and I can tell you it's hard going for a man who don't know how to read."

Alan's eyes stung with tears as he watched Buckeye go reluctantly at the end of the rope. "Don't worry. I'll take good care of him," the old man shouted. Buckeye turned once and bawled plaintively.

Climbing into the truck, Alan sat silently between Oscar and his Uncle Lance, neither of whom said anything now. Once Lance patted him awkwardly on the shoulder. A tear slid down his cheek and landed on his hand, as the truck backed out of its crowded parking place and began to bump along the dirt road to the street that would lead them back into town.

On the courthouse square, several pigeons picked about among the pebbles and sparse grass. The maple trees around the structure were beginning to tinge slightly with a duller green than the summer leaf. Within a month they would flame with autumn yellows and reds. Now even at midday, their branches stirred with dozens of the starlings that came, in the evening, blackly by the hundreds to roost. Rising three stories high and surmounted by a huge white dome with four clock faces, the building itself was gray with age, the weathered bricks going back to their original earth color. The paint on the great window sills flaked and fell into the grass. Yet, despite its disrepair, the courthouse had the second most picturesque design the town afforded; the other, by far the more interesting to Alan, being the quaint old architecture of the railroad depot at the top of Viaduct Hill. The decorated eaves with their carved wood, the intricate doorway, and the solid lead blue color of the building gave to the depot, not only a strangeness of line and hue, but heightened also the sense of excitement inherent in the knowledge that here was the point of departure for all places unknown. Of all buildings in the town of Tellico, the depot, to Alan, was the most intriguing, having about it a sense of adventure that amounted almost to enchantment.

The courthouse was a more prosaic affair. Yet as Lance parked the truck at one corner of the square, Alan felt the gathering tension of the town, with its crowded streets and busy stores. Tuesday, like Saturday, was always a boom day in Tellico. On the other days of the week the countrymen and their wives and children were rarely seen. Today, Alan noticed, there were many boys and girls his own age in town, being outfitted with books and clothing for the opening of school. His grief at the loss of Buckeye receded slowly. Getting out of the truck, he followed his father and Uncle Lance into a restaurant. Oddly enough, he was not very hungry. He picked at his food while the men ate.

Outside again, Oscar said, "Well, before we squander all this money on books, I've got a little change of my own to spend." He walked ahead until he reached a store in whose front windows dresses were displayed. Alan saw his father select a soft gray dress spotted with tiny red and blue flowers; the cuffs of the slender sleeves, ending some distance above the wrist, were threaded with blue ribbons that formed, where they met, into small bows. The collar, too, was interwoven with the blue bands. "It's beautiful," Alan thought. "It's for Mom."

Oscar carried the package from the store. "It's a present for Belle," he told Lance, again walking ahead. His father seemed now a bit unfamiliar to Alan, younger, and with a gayer look in his eyes.

They came to the drugstore, in front of which even the sidewalk was crowded. People passed in and out of the door, with bundles in their hands. Many of those leaving the store carried bright red and blue and brown books, new and unwrapped, among their other possessions. Oscar and Alan pushed their way into the long, clean room where the counters were topped with marble, and the glass cases and the shelves carried a wealth of boxes, jars, and bottles of many sizes and colors, each of which was scrubbed and shining in its utter cleanliness. The smell, despite the crowding people, was sharp and medicinal.

To the rear of the room, a series of shelves were filled with the new textbooks for the county schools. When it came his time to buy, Oscar pushed Alan in front of him. "It's your money," he said. "You do the buying."

To the clerk, a red-haired man Oscar referred to as Mr. Wilson, Alan said, "I want a full set of sixth grade books."

Mr. Wilson placed, one by one on the counter in front of Alan, a reader, a speller, an arithmetic, a geography, a dictionary, and a writing booklet. "They're using this, too, this year," he said, adding a large blue book to the stack. "It goes along with the geography."

Alan noticed the title was *People of Other Lands*. A sense of excitement gripped him, and a desire to take the books and escape from the store before he lost them. The brightly colored heap was too good to be true. "Is there anything else?" he asked.

"Yes, there is," said the druggist, "as a matter of fact." He took down a yellow music book. "There is this."

Alan looked longingly at the music book. "I don't know," he said. "It all depends on what these others come to." To Oscar, he whispered, "Lee's got to have books. What are we going to do about him?"

"I intended to get Lee's myself," Oscar said. "Let him add up and see."

Mr. Wilson wrote and figured. "Eight-fifty," he said, "music book and all."

Alan grinned with relief. "Give me a whole set of eighth grade books, he said happily. The druggist looked surprised.

"Hold on," Oscar said. He explained. "It's his money. Now he wants to buy books for his brother. He just sold his calf," he added. "He's rich and running wild."

Mr. Wilson laughed. "Well, shall I?" he asked.

"Only half for him," said Oscar. "I'll pay the other half."

After the transaction, Alan had six dollars left. Enough, he told himself, for the lunchbox and the satchel, as well as a good supply of pencils and paper. He almost forgot the ache in his heart which Oscar's mention of Buckeye had reawakened. Only a nagging thought of how one good, even beautiful, thing could be traded for another equally good and beautiful, and yet leave an undefinable regret, a slow-dying sense of treason and disloyalty, came over him at times. There was, as yet, very little connection between Buckeye and the new books he carried; only a remote association hinged them together. It was in his mind, rather, that the haunting rebellious thread was strung, a line of feeling, stubborn and irresistible, no change could bring down.

As the truck topped the rise, however, that lipped the eastern edge of Walden Valley, and Alan could see, spread out before him, the old loved terrain of farms and homes, marked by the creek runs, fencerows, and the tall ghostly forms of the sycamores, he felt like jumping from the truck seat and beginning to run down the earth road home, speeding along between the overhanging bushes as only a young boy could speed, lightly, effortlessly, filled with an enduring sense of the earth and of the adventure the earth contained. He knew now something more about time and memory, something that the ending summer had taught him. He would always remember Buckeye, but it would be a memory, like so many memories of the past summer and of all the summers of his life before, on which he would build a foundation for the new experiences and dreams and other loves that new summers would bring. That being alive in any season would bring. For he understood now, too, that summer is mostly a season of the heart. Buckeye, like the new books he held so carefully in his hands, was only a link in a wondrous chain that stretched from dawn to dark, from spring to summer to winter, and beyond to all the days, nights, seasons, and years of a whole lifetime. A good memory was like that: a starting-point found again in what had seemed, from the short view, to be only a destination, a stopping-place, a dead-end.

Before the truck had quite come to a stop at the yard gate, Alan was out of the front seat and running up the path to the house. Around him, in the cosmos and hollyhocks, the sunflowers and the four o'clocks, summer burned to a hot close. Pretty Boy, roused from sleep, charged up and down the porch, yelping. Whizzer arched and stared narrowly into the sun-struck world.

"Mom!" he shouted, bursting into the frontroom. "Mom! I got all my books and Lee got all his books and you got a new dress with blue ribbons in it! Where are you, Mom?"

He found Belle on the back porch, combing her hair. Lee was with her, rocking Nathan in the big rockingchair and humming loudly through his nose.

"Be quiet, son," Belle said, catching him by the shoulder to calm him down. She indicated Nathan.

Lee scowled at him. "Hush, big-mouth," he said, "before you wake the baby."

PS 3537 .C18 S78 1986

86-36597

Scarbrough, George, 1915-

A summer ago

WITHDRAWN

State Library OF Ohio

SEO Library Center
40780 SR 821 * Caldwell, OH 43724